SKOKIE PUBLIC LIBRARY
C0-BOR-521

THE GHOSTWING'S LIE

ALSO BY REBECCA MIX

The Mossheart's Promise

THE GHOSTWING'S LIE

REBECCA MIX

HARPER
An Imprint of HarperCollins*Publishers*

The Ghostwing's Lie

Map illustration by Molly Fehr

 For information, address HarperCollins Children's Books, a division of HarperCollins Publishers, 195 Broadway, New York, NY 10007.

www.harpercollinschildrens.com

Library of Congress Control Number: 2023944822

ISBN 978-0-06-325410-7

Typography by Molly Fehr

24 25 26 27 28 LBC 5 4 3 2 1

First Edition

In memory of my grandmother Carol Wilson.
And for anyone missing someone they love.
They are in every sunset.

Keep the balance,

Mind the wood,

And bid the green light grow.

Folk to summon

Flyers to anchor

And Divers to help it flow.

Beware the lies of Ghostwings freed

In them the rot remains

Seek the heart within the reeds

For the Blight shall rise again!

The Wood
N
Grazers' Domain
Northern Meadows
Divers' Domain
Western Cedar Grove
Weavers' Domain
Eastern Swamp
Flyers' Domain
Pebble's House
Siltshore
Southern Wood
The Gardener's Cottage

We all have the power—and it grows when it is shared.

—*Ferngully*

PART 1
SUMMONER

ONE

Sunlight

Ary's wings ached something terrible.

Sunlight painted the world gold. Ary Mossheart stood on the lip of a massive windowsill, heart fit to pound out of her chest. The world before her was so bright that she couldn't look directly at it. After a lifetime of darkness, she didn't know how to face so much light.

"Well?" someone prompted. "Lead the way, little hero."

Ary tensed. After living in the shadow of her gran—her world's last, true hero—it felt like a curse to hear that title applied to her here and now.

Mama's fingers tightened around hers. *I've got you,* her grip seemed to say. *I'm here. We'll do this together.*

But Ary's legs wouldn't move.

Only a few weeks ago, Ary had made a terrifying discovery: her entire world had been trapped inside a giant, rotting terrarium for two hundred years. Now, the impossible was accomplished—they were *free.* Instead of a rotting, mold-filled world, the former inhabitants of the terrarium found themselves in a massive, giant-sized cottage, the shards of their former home gleaming behind them.

"Ary," someone else whispered behind her. *Owl.* His voice was like an anchor, steadying her, and it held everything he could not say: *I'm scared, too.* Ary turned to look at him. Beside Owl, a beautiful fairy girl with stunning wings stood with her arms folded next to a nervous-looking pill bug and a particularly grumpy-looking newt.

Owl offered Ary his hand. "Together?"

She wasn't alone this time. She had them. It would be okay.

"Okay," Ary whispered. "Together."

She blinked against the endless sunlight. Its warmth was unfamiliar, but not unwelcome. Behind her, fairies and bugs alike waited.

Hiding behind a child already, Gran's familiar voice snarked somewhere in Ary's head. *Well, little Mossheart. After you.*

Ary took a breath and stepped into the world beyond.

There was so much *green.*

A vast sea of plants sprawled before her, a thousand times larger than the mushrooms Ary had once scaled. They swept upward toward an impossible blue sky, canopies rustling like old shroom-paper. And the air *moved,* curling around her, bringing with it the scent of grass, sunlight, and something sour. Heat beat down on her, accompanied by a bone-shaking hum of insects and rustling grasses.

Gran, thought Ary. *I wish you could see this.*

The citizens of Terra had not moved. Some held

themselves tightly, wing stubs twitching uneasily as they looked longingly at the pile of glass.

Ary peered down. Far below, soft-petaled plants swayed lazily in the breeze.

"Um," said Owl. "How are we going to get down?"

Ary inched closer. If only she could fly.

She pushed the thought away. "Sootflank, Shrimp—do you think you can climb the walls?"

The newt and the pill bug slipped over the edge, testing their grip.

"We can each safely take one of you," Sootflank said, one wary eye on the ground below. "One of you will have to stay behind—"

Behind him, Briar snorted. Before Ary could stop her, the fairy girl strolled to the edge of the windowsill and flung herself into the open air.

For a terrible, heart-stopping moment, Ary could only watch as Briar hurtled toward the ground, her dark hair snapping behind her. And then, suddenly, Briar straightened. Her wings flared, her body twisted, and she was *flying*.

"The air!" Briar cried, her voice ringing through the air in clear, delighted peals. "It *moves*!"

After a lifetime in a windless, dark terrarium, it must have felt like a miracle to fly.

Ary's hands drifted to her own shoulder blades.

Unlike all the adults in Terra, her wings had not been sliced from her back and ground into fairy dust—but she was flightless all the same. Where Ary's wings ought to have been, only a ghostly skeleton remained. They caught no breeze, stirred no air, yet in them Ary felt a phantom ache. Gran had not been the only thing she'd lost when she shattered the terrarium.

"Show-off," Owl muttered.

Ary hid her grimace and cupped her hands over her mouth. *"Briar! What do you see?"*

Briar twirled in the air, gave Ary a thumbs-up, and in a brilliant arc shot out and up, until she was only a tiny dot against the endless blue sky. She hovered there for a moment, and then she dropped again, barreling toward them at an impossible speed. At the last second, she slowed and dropped to her feet beside Ary, her wings snapping shut against her back. Her eyes were wild, her cheeks flushed pink and windblown, her smile so wide it threatened to split her face in half.

"Ary," Briar gasped. She clutched Ary's wrist, sending a nervous spark through her. "It's so beautiful."

"Are we going to stand here all day?" Sootflank interrupted. "We have no idea what's out there, watching us, and I'd like to find some shelter considering the one we had is now a pile of dust."

Briar looked at him crossly, but Sootflank simply glared right back.

"You can do your acrobatics later." The newt approached the edge of the windowsill. "Little Mossheart—it's time."

Ary nodded. Beside her, Owl clambered on top of Shrimp, clutching the pill bug's shell tightly as he eased them over the edge of the windowsill. Briar flipped back into the air and made it a point to float upside down with her tongue poking out at Sootflank before she vanished. Then it was only Sootflank, Ary, and Mama.

Mama put a hand on Ary's shoulder and squeezed. "I'll get the others ready to climb down."

Ary's stomach did a nervous flip. She'd see Mama again in only a few minutes. This wasn't like last time. She didn't trust herself to speak, so Ary hugged her mother tightly and climbed onto Sootflank's back.

"Ary!" Mama called. "I'm proud of you."

Ary waved, her eyes on Mama's face until they disappeared over the lip of the sill, the new world sprawling below her in brilliant green.

The world was so much bigger than Ary ever could have imagined.

As they descended, it loomed before her: plants she had no name for, a breeze she'd known only in her dreams. As they drew closer to the strange, slender green plants swaying below, everyone grew quiet. Ary had lived twelve years in the terrarium, knowing only darkness, the scent of mold ever-lingering in the air, the flicker of the glow-shroom lamps ever-dimming. But Sootflank had been alive for Gran's journey sixty years ago, and who knew how old Shrimp was?

What was it like, to spend so many decades in the dark and finally step into the light?

Sootflank and Shrimp slowed their crawls, clinging to the rough exterior wall of the Gardener's cottage. The ground was only a fairy-length below them now. Briar hovered above the strange plants. No one said a word. No one moved.

They all stared at Ary.

They had offered to do this with her—but that did not mean they were capable of taking that first step.

That was for Terra's hero, and Terra's hero alone.

It wasn't fair. *Gran* had been the chosen one. *Gran* was the reason they were free. But it was not Gran who'd emerged from the wreckage of their world, coated in fairy dust and carrying the skeleton of what she'd lost fluttering on her back. It was not Gran who'd led them to the sun.

Ary slipped from Sootflank's back and dropped into the new world.

Everything transformed into shifting, shining green, and for a moment, she was entirely alone, wrapped in a cocoon of sun-warmed, damp soil. Tentatively, Ary ran her hand along the edge of one of the plants. It bent, softer than she'd expected. Prickly, instead of cutting.

Ary laughed, pleasantly startled.

"You can come down," she called.

Her friends dropped to the ground alongside her, Briar alighting primly as though she, too, had not been waiting nervously for Ary to touch the new world first. Briar ran her hands across the plants as Sootflank and Shrimp shifted on the new earth, their bodies relaxing.

Sootflank looked beyond the grass with a kind of yearning on his face.

"I smell water. *Clean* water." He paused, his long, dark throat flexing. "How is any of this real?"

Beside him, Owl knelt. He dug both hands into the rich, black soil, a look of wonder on his round face. "We're not alone."

Everyone froze.

Owl was wingless. He'd been scorned in Terra, but on their journey through the terrarium, he'd made the stunning discovery that he, too, carried magic—a type that connected him not to the air, but to the earth and to memories long buried in the soil. Ary had thought when she shattered the spell sealing the terrarium that any magic the fairies carried would be lost, too. The distant look on Owl's face said otherwise.

Ary crouched in front of her friend. "What do you mean?"

Owl licked his lips, his brow furrowed. "I—I don't know. It's just a . . ." His voice trailed away helplessly.

"A feeling?" Ary finished.

Owl nodded.

"Is it telling you anything else? Like who else is out here?"

"Or if they want to eat us?" Sootflank added dryly.

"I just know there were others here before. It could have been yesterday or a hundred years ago." Owl looked at his feet. "I'm sorry."

"Oh, no need to apologize. A little existential dread is good for the soul." Sootflank sighed. "I'm getting too old for this. I should have died in the terrarium. Would have saved me the trouble. Ah, well. Let's scope out the area ahead, and then we'll return to fetch all those cowards huddling in the cottage."

Ary craned her head, peering up at the dozens of faces peeking over the sill far above. She cupped her hands around her mouth. "Come on down!"

Though she was too far to hear their response, she could practically feel the displeasure rippling off the fairies. They'd likely hoped that the ground would swallow Ary and her friends whole, proving the outside world uninhabitable, and that through some miracle their terrarium would be magically restored. Well, they were out of luck. Ary wasn't exactly thrilled about this, either, but they weren't going to fix things by standing around. When the last of the fairies were on the ground, Mayor Nightingale looked around with a huff.

"This world is unnatural," she complained. "And accepting the help of pill bugs and a newt is even more unnatural."

Sootflank gave her a bored look. "I completely agree."

Mayor Nightingale scowled at him and hiked ahead.

Ary's heart sank. Her people were a pitiful sight. Sootflank looked terribly out of place among them, but if it bothered him that the other newts had left without a backward glance, he didn't say a word.

"I can find us water," Sootflank said. "Where there's water, there's likely to be food—and we can find a place to hide, once we know we have the other two secured."

Ary took a deep breath. "Okay. We move together then. Everyone stay close."

Word rumbled back down the line. One by one, the fairies clambered onto the backs of pill bugs. When a few went to climb atop the rope-bound glow-moths, Ary's heart seized.

"Wait," she blurted. "We all get to start over in this new world—*all* of us. Even the moths. Untie them. If they want to come, they get that choice."

No one spoke. The fairies looked away, clearly intending to ignore her unless Nightingale gave the orders. Ary's face turned hot.

Mama stepped forward.

For most of Ary's life, Mama had been ill. Ary had grown accustomed to the shadows beneath Mama's eyes, the weariness of her voice, the slump of her shoulders. She'd gotten used to stepping up, not back. But *this* Mama, who leveled a steely gaze at the fairies and stood tall even as she still trembled from the aftereffects of mold sickness, was like a distant memory made flesh.

This Mama reminded Ary, painfully, of Gran.

"You heard my daughter," Mama said firmly. "If you're coming with us, it won't be with enchanted creatures in tow."

The fairies exchanged uneasy looks. No one had ever questioned the enchantment of glow-moths back in Terra. The gentle, light-generating creatures had been used for everything from transporting supplies to guard patrols. So much of their world had already been lost; now Ary was asking them to give up this comfort, too.

"Robin—" Nightingale started.

"Are you coming with us," Mama interrupted, "or staying?"

Ary had never loved her more.

All but two of the fairies dropped the ropes binding their glow-moths. Mama strode past them with a steady gaze and undid the final ropes herself. They fell to the dirt with a sad thump. The moths lifted their wings a little higher.

"Ary," Owl whispered, his eyes wide. "Your mom is *so cool.*"

Love bubbled up through every part of Ary. "Yeah, she is."

Mama looked at Sootflank with a level gaze and lifted her chin. "Take us to the water, newt. Let's see exactly what this world has to offer."

TWO

Not Alone

Ary couldn't shake the feeling that they were being watched.

The bladed sea of green faded, giving way to damp earth and carpets of moss. Massive, towering plants stood like silent watchers overhead. The legends Ary had grown up with rushed through her. She knew these behemoth plants—they were *trees*. They were magnificent, all towering bark and reaching branches. If she listened closely, Ary thought she could hear voices murmuring among the rustle of their leaves. It was like a song she'd spent her lifetime searching for.

But the farther they went, the more the back of her neck prickled.

The light they'd encountered when they had first left the terrarium dimmed. Out here, in this wide, impossible world, the effect was more dramatic, slipping them from warm gold into dusky shadow. They moved faster. Back in Terra they'd known the worst of what the night could bring. Fire-wielding newts, hungry beetles, even the odd centipede. But out here?

Fatigue lined the faces of the older fairies. When they

stumbled, Mama looped an arm through theirs and helped them up. Shrimp moved among the remaining pill bugs as they walked, clicking and trilling softly. Several times they would click back, and always, Shrimp would swivel his antennae toward Ary.

Ary clambered over the massive root of one of the trees, muscles straining. She scaled a root and it hit her—the intense, creeping feeling that she was being watched.

"Ghostwing," someone whispered.

Ary jerked to a halt.

The line behind her crashed to a stop. The fairies muttered among themselves; a few of the pill bugs let out uncertain squeaks. The forest stared back, silent save for the rustle of leaves. But Ary had heard a voice. She was certain.

Sootflank looked at her with concern. Ary went cold. He hadn't heard anything, either.

Maybe she really was losing it.

As the light dimmed, they pressed deeper into the forest. Sootflank took over leading, his nose to the air as he sought fresh water. Briar flew ahead, her pretty face scrunched as she scouted for potential danger.

Mama eyed Briar appraisingly. "You found that one in the Underground?"

Ary nodded.

"She's quite pretty."

Heat flushed Ary's cheeks. "So?"

"Just making an observation." Mama brushed an affectionate hand over Ary's hair and turned to help one of the fairies struggling to scale a root.

Ary was still trying to come up with something to say when a shout came from ahead.

Sootflank had found water.

It stretched before them in beautiful, weed-dotted pools. Spindly plants reached up from the depths, and white-petaled flowers bloomed on the surface, filling the air with soft fragrance. The Terrans hurried past her. They *knew* this flower; it was the very one that bloomed in the outstretched hand of the Gardener's statue, the same plant that had been carved into their pillars, that appeared in all their sacred texts. Surely this was a sign. Surely they were saved!

The fairies beelined for the water, scooping it into their palms, marveling at how *clear* it was. Others rushed to the thickets of thorn-lined bushes that grew along the banks, their boughs weighed down by an abundance of vibrant pink berries. Strange, silvery ropes draped the bushes. When Ary touched one, her fingers came away sticky. She frowned.

Ary lifted her hand. "Does anyone know what this is?"

The fairies of Terra ignored her. They brushed past the silvery ropes and reached for the berries. Before Ary could stop them, they ripped chunks free and shoved them in their mouths.

"Wait!" Ary blurted. "Those could be poisonous, it's not safe—"

If they heard her, they didn't care. Ary watched helplessly as other fairies began to drink the water, eat berries, and dig in the squelching mud for hidden tubers or other food.

You're a hero until they don't need you, Ary imagined Gran snarking, one eyebrow raised. *See how they listen to you? What did I tell you, little one? We're always disposable.*

Ary dug the heels of her hands into her eyes. She turned and found Briar and Owl, their arms full of berries, lips stained pink. Silver threads clung to their clothes.

Ary glared at them. "Really? You too?"

Briar held out a chunk of berry flesh to Ary. "Come on. It's good! And there's so much food here."

"There is," Sootflank agreed. "So why has it been left alone?"

The other fairies carried on around them, oblivious. There was talk of making this site their new village, of putting up fences and building homes. Why explore further, when so much could be found here? Ary felt cold.

Something was not right. She could not forget the voice in the woods, the sense of eyes on her. And those silver ropes . . .

"Sootflank," Ary said quietly. "How do we know it's safe?"

"We don't." He looked at her, and then back at the water, clearly deliberating over something. For the first time, Ary noticed how tired he looked.

"I'm going to scout ahead," said Sootflank. "Quickspark is out there, as are the rest of the earwigs my daughter controls—I wouldn't put it past them to try something. You stay here, little Mossheart. Keep an eye on your friends. And try to keep the villagers from killing themselves."

The newt loped away, his black-mottled flanks vanishing into the water with the softest ripple. Again, a strange envy burned in her. Briar could fly, Sootflank could swim. Owl could—well, she still wasn't entirely certain what was going on with Owl. But he could do *something*.

So where did that leave her?

An elbow nudged her side.

"Hey," Owl said quietly. "We'll still be friends now that we're no longer in mortal danger, right?"

Ary rolled her eyes.

"I'm serious. What if terror was the glue holding our friendship together?"

"Where does that leave me?" asked Briar.

"Who said we were friends?" said Owl. "I barely know you. And you're mean."

Briar threw a chunk of berry at Owl. He threw a glob of mud back at her. Ary scooted away as her friends lobbed things at each other, trying to ignore the way love and fear shared equal space in her chest. Her world had changed so quickly. But she could not shake the foreboding rippling through her, or the terrible sense that everything they'd found was like the glow-moths that had flitted over

Terra—beautiful, but too fragile to touch.

"Does anyone know," Ary asked again, "what these ropes are?"

No one answered her. No one cared. Ary drifted back to the bush. The ropes clung to her skin, her clothes, and her hair with a frightening stickiness.

Briar managed to put Owl in a headlock. "Caught you!"

The feeling drained from Ary.

"We have to leave," Ary whispered. She whirled, heart thudding, noticing for the first time the way the silvery ropes wrapped around the entire clearing. The water. The food. *Of course.*

It was a trap, and they'd walked right into it.

"We have to leave!" Ary cried.

A scuttle came from behind her. Ary turned.

Rising up on all eight legs as its pincers flashed was a massive, hairy spider.

THREE

Echoes

Ary had only ever heard stories about the few spiders that lived in the terrarium. To her knowledge, even Gran hadn't encountered any in the Underground. If any of them survived into Ary's lifetime, they'd made themselves scarce.

Ary wished this one had done the same.

The spider loomed behind her. It was bigger than Sootflank, and unlike the delicate, spindly-legged beasts she'd seen drawings of, this monster was stocky, with eight thick legs covered in bristling brown hairs. Four black, bulbous eyes spaced equally across its face stared down at her; four smaller ones in a neat line below them rolled, taking in the surroundings.

"Um," Ary squeaked. "Hi?"

The spider hummed. Its eyes were strangely blank.

Ary took one cautious step back and held up her hands. "We're not here to hurt anyone. I can see this is your clearing. Thank you for the berries, but we'll be going now."

Gasps sounded behind her as the fairies of Terra took note of their new guest. Ary forced herself to breathe. She'd faced down centipedes and ants. What was one spider?

Besides, she didn't even know if this one was her enemy yet.

Something wasn't right about the spider's eyes or the way it moved. It was familiar, but Ary couldn't place why.

"My name is Ary." She took one cautious step backward. Another. "We just got here. We're from a terrarium—"

The spider lunged.

Ary hurled herself sideways, gasping as the spider barreled through the space where she'd been only a moment before, mandibles snapping.

"Run!" she cried. "Everyone, *run*!"

The fairies of Terra needed no further encouragement.

They scattered, fleeing to every possible hiding spot. Ary caught sight of Mama, white-faced, helping the older fairies duck beneath curling green leaves. Owl tugged Ary to her feet and then they were running, breaking for the cover of the trees.

"I changed my mind!" cried Owl. "I don't want mortal danger to be the reason we're friends!"

"Great timing!" Ary shouted back. "Too late! *Run!*"

Wind rushed past—and the spider slammed to the ground in front of them, cocking its head at a terrifying angle. It had leaped right over them. Owl and Ary scrambled back on all fours, bumping up against a long, solid root. Behind the spider, the scared faces of the fairies poked out from the leaves, but none broke forward to help.

Owl and Ary were trapped. And they were on their own.

The spider crawled closer.

It loomed over them, mandibles quivering. Someone shouted her name. Owl trembled beside her, his eyes rounder than a glow-moth's. His shaking fingers found Ary's and squeezed tight.

"Please," Ary gasped. "Please, we mean you no harm." She twisted, grasping for something, anything. Her fingers brushed her pitiful, battered Seedling shovel.

This was it. The spider drew one hairy leg across Ary's throat. She braced herself—and swung.

Time slowed down. From deep in Ary came a tug, a twinge, a faint burning like an echo of the spell she'd cast back in the terrarium. Maybe it was her terror, maybe it was nothing at all, but for a second, Ary could have sworn she felt fear that wasn't her own. She saw herself through someone else's eyes—just a tiny, underfed, ghostly-winged girl, pinned beneath a massive spider. The shovel clanged uselessly against the spider's mandible.

And though it could have been her fear-addled mind, Ary could have sworn she saw the faintest flash of pale pink light.

Time resumed. The shovel clattered away. The spider hissed—and like fog chased from water, the blankness left its eyes.

It shuddered violently. Ary did not know much about spiders. She found creatures without expressive faces hard to read, but she could have sworn this one was suddenly very scared.

The spider hummed—and then a voice billowed through Ary, vibrating through her teeth, her head, her very bones.

Let us go, demanded the spider, voice tight with equal parts hatred and fear. *Let them go!*

"I don't know what that means," Ary wheezed. "We just got here."

The spider hesitated.

You smell, the spider said slowly, each word burning with loathing, *like the thief. And he smells like the liar.*

The spider flared its mandibles—and then Ary heard it.

A whine in the air, a rustle of wings, the hum of something small zooming toward them—and fast.

Ary braced herself.

Someone—many someones, actually—slammed into the spider's head, whirring around the spider at an impossible speed, weaving up and down, back and forth. They carried a rope woven from vines between them, binding the beast until its many legs were pinned against its body, zipping in impossible spirals around its fearsome mandibles, which had been bound closed. It was over in a blink, and the beast toppled to the earth, squawking indignantly as it struggled against root-vine ropes.

Ary looked up.

Five fairies she had never seen before flexed their wings and landed in front of her.

They were different from the fairies of Terra, their hair wild, their clothes made from bark and moss. All of them had beautiful, shining wings. There was a strength to them Ary had never seen in the fairies of Terra—the ease of those who grew up wanting for nothing. Dozens more fairies hovered high above.

One of them landed directly in front of Ary and pointed a spear at her.

"Now," said the fairy, one dark eyebrow cocked. "Who in the name of the Gardener are *you*?"

FOUR

Alder

The fairy man looked to be around Mama's age. Like the others, he dressed in strange clothes made from bark and moss, his tanned, muscled arms lightly scarred. Four more fairies landed behind him, their eyes darting from Ary to the other Terrans clustered in the trees.

On the ground, the spider that had attacked them gave a miserable twitch.

"Who," the fairy repeated, jabbing the end of his spear closer to the end of Ary's nose. *"Are you?"*

"*We* are newcomers." Mama stepped between Ary and the spear. With a scowl, she pressed her palm against the blade and knocked it away. "And while we are grateful for the rescue, we are just as confused as you are. Now, if you'd get that spear out of my face, maybe we can speak like adults instead of children waving pointy toys at each other?"

A long, uncomfortable silence stretched in the air. Ary half expected him to stab Mama—and then the strangest thing happened.

He *blushed*.

The man dropped his spear, cleared his throat, and held out his hand.

"My apologies, miss," he said. "Name's Alder—and the folk behind me go by Ivy, Bramble, Thrush, and Squirrel. We heard shrieking and came to investigate, and—well, you'll forgive us for being confused about the appearance of a whole flock of fairies in our woods."

"Maybe we live in these woods, same as you?" Mama ignored his hand. Her fingers shook at her sides, but her voice was strong. Ary had not heard Mama talk like this since before she got sick—proud, even a touch arrogant. She sounded like Gran.

Alder blushed deeper, hand still dangling in the air. "I don't think so, miss. I've lived in these woods my whole life, and I've never met you before. I think I'd remember."

Now Mama's cheeks turned pink.

Adults were so weird.

Mama reluctantly shook Alder's hand. "I'm Robin. If I'm being honest, we have no idea where we are. We just, ah . . ." Her voice trailed away, and she looked helplessly at Ary.

Ary jumped up, grateful to be of use. She held out her hand to Alder, who looked distinctly less excited to shake her hand than he was Mama's. "We were trapped in a terrarium for two hundred years."

The fairies looked at each other quickly.

Ary plunged ahead. "We just got here. We have no idea where we are, or why that spider is so mad at us—"

"Ah." Alder cast a quick, uneasy glance at the spider, and said, a little too quickly, "We're no friends of the weavers, and it seems you found the nastiest of the lot. That one's a wolf spider." His lip curled. "Pure killers, those ones are. They don't even bother spinning proper webs. They just ambush. Don't worry, it'll be dealt with quickly enough."

The fairies stalked toward the bound spider with grim resolve on their faces. It shuddered violently, eyes bright with fear, that strange, earlier blankness gone entirely. Ary couldn't shake the strange words it had whispered.

The fairies raised their spears.

"Wait!" cried Ary.

Before she could think twice, Ary flung herself between the fairies and the spider.

Silence descended on the clearing. Ary stood with her back only inches from the spider, her arms splayed wide, chest heaving.

The nearest fairy, Squirrel, scowled. "*Move*, girl."

"Don't hurt it," Ary begged. "Please just—just let it go."

"It's a *spider*."

Ary could feel the attention of the gathered fairies, Terrans and newcomers alike. Disgust darkened far too many gazes for her liking. A murmur went up in the clearing. Ary couldn't hear anything, but she caught words like *traitor* and *newt lover.*

They'd been more than happy to follow Ary's lead when she was the first to venture into the dangerous new world. More than content to let Ary risk her life and her loved ones for their freedom.

And now that Ary was doing something the folk of Terra didn't like, they looked at her as though she were as detestable as the newts they loathed.

Footsteps sounded to her left.

Briar stepped up beside her, dark eyes blazing, and took Ary's hand.

"You better know what you're doing," Briar muttered out of the corner of her mouth.

Footsteps to her right. Owl took Ary's other hand.

Ary's heart soared.

Behind her, the spider went still.

What a strange picture they must have made—three fairy children, hands linked, forming a living wall before a creature that had tried to kill them only moments before. Squirrel glared at Ary, and she glared back.

Finally, a voice broke the standoff.

"Squirrel," Alder said reluctantly. "Stand down."

Alder approached the spider with narrowed eyes. The weaver remained deathly still. Alder pointed his spear at it. "I'm going to let you go, but if you make one wrong move, we've got enough fairy dust among the four of us to take down an entire web of your lot. Got it?"

Faintly, the spider hummed.

Alder swung his spear. He cut through the ropes in one arc, and the spider leaped up with a hiss and scrabbled backward away from them. Ary turned, hoping to catch its eye, those strange words still floating through her. But if the spider knew of Ary's hopes, it didn't answer. Without a single backward glance, it scuttled across the ground and shot into the woods, leaving only remnants of web behind. Ary watched the gap in the trees where it had disappeared.

She turned and found the new fairies staring at her. Her cheeks heated.

Alder lifted a brow. "Now, what was that about a terrarium?"

"None of us knew we were stuck in one until—well, I found out on accident. It's a—"

"Big glass bubble? A miniature world within a world? Probably started rotting a long time ago?" asked Alder.

Ary's mouth hung open. She managed a nod.

Alder looked from Ary to Mama again, jaw flexing as if he wanted to say more. He glanced at the other fairies of Terra, who were still hiding in the bushes. "This is all of you?" For the first time he seemed to notice Ary's ghostly wings. The color drained from his face. He cleared his throat and spoke again, this time a little too quickly. "Thrush—head back to Siltshore and tell the others what we found.

Tell them the Gardener's Promise has come true at last." He looked at Ary and crouched down so that he was no longer towering over her. "Now then, little hero—we've got a long walk ahead of us. I think you and I should probably have a chat about how you finally broke free."

FIVE

Welcome to Siltshore

Alder led them up through the trees.

They had been walking for nearly an hour now, the fairies of Siltshore leading them across a dizzying path of roots and vines. As they walked, the world shifted, and Ary realized they were not just going forward, but *up*. Vine bridges wound through the bristling, magnificent trees, covered in dust but well worn, as though they'd been used frequently many, many years ago. Alder and the other Siltshore fairies flew near the Terrans as they walked, zipping this way and that. They all kept their spears at the ready.

"What are the chances they want to eat us?" Owl whispered to Ary.

She elbowed him. "They're not going to *eat us*."

"They might want to eat Ary," Briar said darkly. "They sure are looking at her weird."

Ary had been trying to ignore it. Some of the fairies seemed kind—they offered to walk with the elderly Terrans, to carry the youngest in their arms, and had even brought bandages for those who had sliced their palms trying to scale the cottage walls. But Ary couldn't help but notice the way they all *stared* at her.

Like she wasn't a girl, but some strange creature of legends.

It was the way people always looked at Gran.

Owl looped his arm through Ary's. "If they eat you, they'll have to eat me, too."

"Thanks, Owl."

"I'm not being nice," Owl said with a frown. "It's supposed to be a threat."

Ary and Briar stared at him.

"Come on," pressed Owl. "Seedling with weird magic? My menacing aura? All the poisonous mushrooms I've taken tiny bites out of over the years?"

"You *what*?"

"Okay, I haven't done the last thing," admitted Owl. "But if they start talking about what vegetables would go best with an Ary-flavored soup, I *will*."

"All three of you be quiet," Sootflank snapped.

Sootflank had returned from the water after Mama had smoothed things over with Alder, and he'd been unusually silent—even for Sootflank. The newt's tail lashed.

"Whether they want to eat Ary, put her on a pedestal, or they just think her wings are weird, it doesn't matter," said Sootflank. "The point is, we don't know them, they *are* looking at her weird—and they're looking at me weird, too."

Ary's skin prickled. If the fairies of Siltshore looked at

Ary like she was a legend, they looked at Sootflank like he was a nightmare.

They weren't being subtle about it, either. They constantly cast him dark looks, cut in front of him, and ignored the newt when he asked questions. They made the Terrans' uneasy frowns look like warm smiles by comparison. But it wasn't just Sootflank. Shrimp, too, had pressed close to Ary with an uneasy whine after the fairies leveled glares at him. Ary walked with her hand protectively braced on Shrimp's shell. She'd already lost one family member. She would not lose anyone else.

The sky took on a bruised, hazy quality. In the dark, the vine bridges, stunning in their ancient strength, grew menacing. Though the wood was quiet, dread swirled in her. She couldn't forget the despair in the spider's voice or the name it had called her. Ary let her friends wander ahead, hanging back so that it was only her and Sootflank.

"Sootflank," Ary said in a low voice. "When that spider attacked us earlier—this is going to sound ridiculous, but I think it *spoke* to me."

Sootflank cut her a quick look.

"It said I smelled like a thief," Ary said. "And that Owl smelled like a liar. It asked me to let someone go."

The newt looked troubled. His attention darted from Ary to the wood beyond. Before he could answer, though, Briar's voice cut through the air.

"Shouldn't we be stopping soon? I'm exhausted."

"No," Alder answered behind them.

They all jumped.

"Sorry—I forget, you folk aren't used to listening for wingbeats." Alder gestured up ahead. "We've only about an hour to go. Better to walk in dusk than be stuck out here overnight."

"Why?" Ary frowned. "Are the woods not safe? Who else would—"

"Just best we get there sooner than later," Alder said quickly, and then, in a lower voice, "Let it go, little hero."

Before she could argue further, Alder flew ahead. After a beat, Mama nodded and squeezed Ary's shoulder with a tired smile. "Let's worry about one thing at a time."

Ary nodded back and tried to ignore the creeping sense that the folk of Terra had traded one problem for another.

Terra had been built from dirt, carved into the damp that made their world—but Siltshore was of the sky.

It was a living city, cradled in the branches of an ancient oak tree. Hundreds of homes clustered along the trunk, stretching as high as Ary's eyes could see, their worm-silk windows glowing with gentle yellow light. Vine bridges connected the branches in a dizzying web; fairies walked, ran, and skipped along, only to dive over the side, soaring effortlessly through the many levels of the village. High above, fairies worked in teams, tending to newly sprouted leaves, inspecting for pests or signs of illness. Others manned a bucket-and-pulley system, hauling up pointy nuts with strange little crowns from the forest floor. Glow-shroom lamps bobbed along the vines, their pale blue and pink glows at once familiar and strange in this new, abundant world. Ary stretched forward on her toes—far below, the faint outlines of fairies carefully tended patches of mushrooms. There was no mold marring the stems, no black patches of rot disgracing their crowns.

Ary could hardly breathe.

Was this what Terra had been like, all those years ago? Before the mold and the rot and the dying magic of the terrarium took its toll? Was this what Gran had known, before she was sent on a journey that cost her everything?

Wide-eyed faces turned toward them; fairies smaller than Ary, wings still wrapped in papery, itchy cocoons, sprinted up the vine bridges with no heed for the dizzying drop below as they shouted for their parents. Adults paused in their work, gaping openly.

The Terrans didn't breathe a word, stricken into silence. Maybe it was the abundance before them, or maybe it was because, after all these decades, and all the sacrifices they had made, they were not alone.

A few fairies drew close, narrow-eyed and frowning.

"Alder," an older fairy with faded lavender wings said finally, "is this what I think it is?"

"It is." Alder gestured back at the fairies of Terra. "They come from the other terrarium. The Gardener's Promise has come true—we are reunited at last."

A crushing silence followed. Ary's heart thudded a rapid-fire song of panic and confusion in her chest. The fairies of Siltshore had been expecting them? They had known all along?

Most of the Siltshore fairies looked as bewildered as Ary felt. They stared at the newcomers and muttered among each other, doing nothing to conceal their frowns. But a few pairs of kind eyes found the folk of Terra and gave them a timid smile. One fairy, an older woman who wore a strange contraption on her face made up of two little clear discs held in place by a frame, drew closer to Ary. Wing stubs shivered from her back.

"You're a Ghostwing," she said.

Ary stiffened. "I'm sorry?"

The old woman frowned, looking as though there was something she wanted to say, and then shook her head, as if thinking better of it.

A hand settled on Ary's shoulder.

"I'll take it from here," Mayor Nightingale whispered. Terra's former mayor took several steps forward, her chin high despite the stains and tears in her once-pristine white robes. "My people are tired, and we are hungry. And though we have many questions, right now I am only concerned with one. Tell me, Alder—are we welcome here? Are we safe?"

Alder jerked, eyebrows shooting up in surprise, and

nodded a little too quickly. "Of course! Please, come inside. You must be starving. Let's get you all settled in your new home."

"This is not our home," Nightingale said pointedly. "But we will accept help, if you'll give it."

Alder smiled at her as though she'd said something funny. Without another glance, he gestured to the village behind him. "Welcome to Siltshore."

SIX

Just Be Ary

The next hour passed in a blur; the fairies of Siltshore guided Ary and her people up more vine bridges and beyond, until they filed into a large, empty room carved within one of the branches. Siltshore fairies carrying bandages and healing poultices hurried in, binding sprained wrists and giving mold-sick fairies a strange, bitter draught that made them cough violently but had the color returning to their cheeks within minutes. Others carried in cots, bundles of clothing, and food.

Ary had never seen so much food.

It was everywhere—bowls of a sweet, rooty broth; plates of rich boiled tubers; and thick, nutty breads that smelled of grass and earth. The folk of Terra ate hesitantly at first—and then their eyes widened, and they began to eat with ravenous speed. A bowl crafted from the shell of one of the pointy nuts was passed to Ary. She sipped the sweet broth and found she could not stop.

Ary had never tasted food that was free of mold.

The only ones who didn't receive a warm welcome were the pill bugs and Sootflank; the fairies of Siltshore seemed unsure what to do with them. At some point, Sootflank slipped away, murmuring something about scouting out the village. Shrimp remained with Ary, clicking softly, his antennae twitching with longing as Mama, Briar, and Owl were all passed bowls of broth. When a fairy boy hurried past the pill bugs without offering them any of the nut bread, Ary caught his arm.

"They're hungry, too," she said.

The boy recoiled. "You want us to feed *bugs*?"

"They are not just *bugs*," Ary said fiercely. "They are our companions and allies, and without them we would be dead."

"But we don't—"

"Sumac," warned a new voice. "Do as they ask."

An old fairy stood only a few feet away. Unlike the others, with their fine, moss-spun clothes and tree bark jewelry, this man wore patchwork trousers and a shabby old coat. He looked to be about Gran's age, with thin white hair combed neatly away from a wrinkled forehead.

The boy's fingers tightened on the basket of bread as he looked from Ary to the pill bugs again.

"Sumac," the older fairy prompted.

Sumac scowled, shoved the basket of nut bread into Ary's arms, and scurried away.

The older fairy wearily watched him go. He looked back at Ary with an apologetic smile. "Forgive us. Some of us have more trouble with change than others. If there is anything you need, just say the word, Ary. We're happy to have you here."

It wasn't until he'd gone that Ary wondered how, exactly, he'd known her name.

"Sumac seems nice," Owl said dryly. He plucked a loaf of nut bread from the basket and handed it to Shrimp. "Here, Shrimp. Remember I'm your favorite."

Shrimp whirred appreciatively, nibbling as Ary and Owl distributed the loaves to the other pill bugs and unfolded the stacks of blankets the fairies of Siltshore had brought. They were old and scratchy, but clean, and still finer than anything Ary had back in Terra. Her head spun. Only a day ago, they'd been inside the terrarium. Now they were here, in the outside world—and everything had changed.

She wished Gran were here.

Ary clutched the bowl of broth against her chest, every part of her aching. Around her, the fairies of Terra began to settle, curling up on old blankets as though it was a typical day; others sat against the far wall, backs flush against the wood, talking quietly to each over steaming bowls of broth. The sky outside was pitch-black now; only the soft light of the glow-shrooms broke the dark. With a yawn, Mama stretched out on a makeshift cot Alder had brought for them. "You need to sleep."

"I'm not tired," Ary said quietly. She still had some broth, but suddenly, she was no longer hungry.

Mama looked at her a long moment. Gently, she pried

Ary's fingers free of the bowl and set it aside.

"Ary," Mama said gently. "I know you're tired. I know you're scared. You have done and seen terrible things—and I feel like I failed you, that it came to that. But it's my turn to take up that mantle now, okay? Not yours. Your only job is to just be Ary. Just my girl." She cradled Ary's cheek in her hand. "Now, I'm going to sleep, because I am old, tired, and my feet hurt. I think it'd be a good idea for you to sleep, too."

"Yes, Mama," Ary whispered. She let Mama pull her onto the cot, curling up flush with her mother's front. Mama stroked her hair the way she used to when Ary was small, her touch a gentle comfort in the strange dark.

But long after Mama slipped into sleep, Ary remained awake.

For a while, she stared at the ceiling, listened to the breathing of those she'd saved. To her left, Briar and Owl dozed against Shrimp's side. The pill bug let out a quiet snore. They looked frail, wrapped in their patchy blankets, Owl's fingers still clutching his empty bowl, Briar's curled into fists. Behind Ary, Mama's breathing slowed.

Something moved in the dark.

Ary's pulse raced. Where was her shovel? Were they under attack? What if—

"Rest easy, little Mossheart," Sootflank whispered. "It's only me."

Ary nearly went limp.

The old newt picked his way silently through the sleeping piles of fairies. No one woke. With a sigh, he settled against the wall. The long stretch of his tail curled around them.

Ary reached a hand upward so her fingers brushed the cool skin of Sootflank's side. What a strange world she lived in, that the creature she now felt the safest around was a newt that had once hunted and hated fairies exactly like her.

"Sootflank," Ary whispered. "Are we safe here?"

There was a long silence. Outside, insects Ary had never met before hummed on the warm breeze. Fairy folk stirred and murmured around her, twitching at the noises of this strange, too-wide world.

"Get some rest," the newt said.

Ary was too tired to argue. As she slipped into sleep, the last thing she saw was Sootflank, wide awake, watching the endless dark for a danger that had not yet arrived.

SEVEN

The First Dream

Ary dreamed of trees.

In her dream, she stood in a strange, cool hollow where no sunlight reached. The wind was dead; the air was cool. Were it not for the trees, she would have thought she was back in Terra. Something tugged at her attention, pulling her forward, begging: *look*.

A person ducked behind a tree ahead of her.

"Hello?" Ary called. "Is someone there?"

Laughter trickled toward her. Ary hurried after it.

The hollow grew darker the farther she went. The ground was spongy; water bubbled between her toes. The air grew damp. The leaves thinned, black flecks of rot stretching across their veiny green surfaces.

Ahead of her, Ary caught a flash of pale hair.

Gran?

Ary began to run.

"Gran!" shouted Ary, her heart threatening to burst. "Slow down! It's me, Ary! Wait for me!"

It was impossible, but she was *here*. Gran had survived the terrarium. Ary didn't have to say goodbye. She needed only to reach her. But no matter how fast she ran, Gran was always ahead of her, just out of reach, dry laughter crackling through the trees.

Ghostwing, someone whispered.

"Gran!" cried Ary.

A screen of leaves blocked her path. She burst through.

She was back in the hollow again. It was as though she'd traveled no distance at all. A strange, silvery cocoon hung between the trunks of the trees ahead of her. Ary turned in a circle.

Ghostwing, someone whispered. *Find me.*

"I don't know what that means," Ary said helplessly. "I don't—Gran! *Gran, where are you?*"

A hand touched her back and *shoved.*

She fell, her knees squelching against the wet ground of the hollow. A strange, skittering scratch sounded before her.

Ary rolled onto her back—and froze.

Eight eyes glittered over her.

A pair of fangs flashed in the dark and bit down.

"Ary, wake up."

Ary lay on her back in the storeroom. Mama knelt over her, face tight with concern. Briar and Owl hovered behind her, Shrimp peering over their shoulders. Ary's cheeks heated.

"Sorry," she whispered. "Nightmare."

The threads of the dream floated around her. That had

been Gran in her dream. But why? And why lead her to a spider? She had never seen that hollow before—of that, she was certain. Maybe it meant something?

No, Ary thought forcefully. *We are not doing this. Not again.*

She had only just left the terrarium. She was not getting involved in some magical hero shenanigans again, only a day after her family had finally found safety. Her dreams back in Terra had been because Atlas was using magic to call out to her. But there was no Atlas in Siltshore. There was no great danger calling from beyond.

Ary was just exhausted and missing Gran. That was it.

"I'm fine," Ary lied. She slid her hand in Mama's, trying to ignore the way Mama squeezed her fingers a little too tightly. "Do you know where Sootflank is?"

Owl shook his head. "He was gone when we woke up."

Around them, the folk of Terra clustered together in nervous little knots, peering toward the storeroom door. A uneasy energy buzzed through the air. Yesterday had carried a dreamlike quality; they'd emerged from the terrarium and stumbled into the wood only to be attacked, rescued, and whisked away to an impossible treetop village. But now they'd slept and eaten, and with clearer minds were seeming to reach the same conclusion: they needed somewhere to live, and so far Siltshore seemed like the only option.

"I'm not going back out in those woods," one man to Ary's left was saying, "not with those spiders out there."

"Can you believe that child? Throwing herself in front of it, right after it tried to attack us?" snorted another fairy.

"Are you surprised?" another muttered. "She brought a *newt* in with us."

Shame burned through every part of Ary. But instead of telling them off or reminding them exactly what she'd done to get them here, Ary pretended she hadn't heard.

If this was the thanks she was going to get, it was no wonder Gran had spent her entire life in hiding.

Ary's head was still spinning when Mayor Nightingale appeared in the doorway of the storeroom, flanked by Tulip and Basil's parents, Yarrow and Clover Frostline. Ary didn't trust the mayor; she couldn't forget the food Nightingale had hoarded, nor the cruelty she'd shown Ary after they had fled Atlas' cavern. But at least she was a familiar enemy. Nightingale looked dully at her people, closed her eyes for a moment, and then forced a smile. "Come. It seems the leader of Siltshore has decided what to do with us."

An audience had assembled outside. The fairies of Siltshore clustered above, peeking over branches and from behind leaves, peering at the newcomers who had arrived in the night.

An elbow jabbed into Ary's side. She winced, whirling. The boy from earlier, Sumac, whistled innocently and disappeared into the crowd.

So much for their warm welcome.

One by one, the folk of Terra gathered. Owl and Briar

fidgeted alongside Ary, but Mama stood still as stone. She rested a hand on Ary's shoulder, and there was something protective in her touch. Something fierce.

I feel like I failed you, Mama had said.

Ary hated that a part of her agreed.

Movement came from ahead. It seemed a little ridiculous to have such a big production for someone they'd already met. But instead of launching into a speech or telling the folk of Terra his plans, Alder gave them all a tentative smile.

"People of Terra," he said. "Folk of Siltshore. I present Oleander, worldbreaker of our own terrarium, and founder of our home."

Ary blinked. She had assumed Alder was their leader—otherwise, why hadn't the leader come to see them sooner? The assembled Siltshore fairies rippled, and from their ranks stepped a small, unassuming old man.

Ary froze.

It was him. The old man from before, who'd known Ary's name and had forced Sumac to share with Shrimp. His clothes were the same—unassuming and dull, the garment clearly worn hundreds of times over the years. He wore the same calm expression, but his shabby old coat was gone.

Behind him, stretching wide and shimmering with eerie iridescence, was a set of ghostly wings, identical to the pair Ary now carried on her back.

EIGHT

A New Normal

The world snapped into narrow focus. All Ary could see were Oleander's wings, which so perfectly mirrored her own. She recalled the other shattered terrarium back in the cottage, glass pieces long coated in dust and bleached by time. She had not stopped to wonder about the fairy who had set *them* free.

She was certainly wondering now.

Murmurs rippled through the folk of Terra. Eyes flew to Ary, but she didn't dare look away from the sight before her.

"Ary," Owl whispered beside her.

"I know."

On her shoulder, Mama's fingers tightened.

Oleander spread his hands wide. His eye caught Ary's for the briefest moment, and he winked.

"People of Terra," he called. "You have done an incredible thing, surviving a terrarium for a hundred years longer than the Gardener planned. I'm sure you're exhausted. Scared. But know this: every year, the fairies of Siltshore have prayed to the Gardener for your escape. You were always meant to find your way here."

A few rumbles passed through both crowds—folk of Terra who seemed unconvinced of this, and fairies of Siltshore who looked less than thrilled to have a hundred hungry mouths arrive on their doorstep. But others smiled gently or gave welcoming nods.

So they weren't getting kicked out. That was a start, right?

"We are a small village," Oleander continued, "and yet we have space for you—homes that have sat empty, families with extra rooms. What we need, more than anything, is help. There's much to be done here. Acorns to shell, bridges to repair, and crops to tend. As we've discussed how to welcome you in while also ensuring we can all thrive, we've come to a decision."

"Why do I have a feeling *we* just means *he*," Briar muttered under her breath.

"Any fairy of Terra who wishes to stay in Siltshore is welcome. You'll be assigned to families to help you adjust, people will be split into chore groups based on your specialty, age, and skill. Your children will be welcome at our schools; your sick will be cared for. All we ask, in turn, is that you give back what you'll take. With fall fast approaching, it's vital we all pitch in and prepare Siltshore for winter."

"What's *winter*?" Owl whispered to Ary.

She shook her head wordlessly, trying to keep the worry from her face.

"And why should we have to work?" an older Terran

called, visibly bristling. A few others rumbled in dissent.

Oleander regarded him calmly. "Everyone in Siltshore does their part. So if you are going to live here, you must contribute—"

"Who said anything about living here?" another fairy cried. "This isn't our home! Our home *exploded*!"

"We don't belong up here!" another cried.

"What happens if the newts come back?" someone demanded. "That girl already brought one in with us!"

Ary whipped around to see who had spoken ill of Sootflank, but their voice was lost in the crowd.

Oleander kept trying to answer, but the folk of Terra kept cutting him off. Their voices climbed higher, and the expressions of the Siltshore fairies grew stony.

Finally, Mayor Nightingale stepped forward, her tired face more haggard than usual. She held her hands for silence until the folk of Terra quieted to a discontented grumble.

"We have nowhere else to go," Mayor Nightingale said flatly.

Silence filled the trees as reality sank in. It didn't matter if they didn't love Siltshore immediately. They were unprepared for this world, and they were lucky anyone was welcoming them at all.

"It will be good for us to work," Mayor Nightingale continued, her voice level, "until we learn enough about this world to survive on our own. I know this is a big change. I know you're scared. I'm scared, too. Our homes are gone.

No one is pretending this will be easy. But we must rebuild. For our children, and their children. And for everyone who never made it to this world at all."

Ary shrank into herself, and behind her, Mama stood taller.

Oleander stepped forward.

"Change is difficult," he said, seizing the lull with an expert smile. "I know it will take time for us to adjust—*all* of us. But the people of Terra have arrived at a fortuitous time. We are only a few months away from the Festival of the Gardener. And it is my hope we will celebrate it together as *one* people."

At the mention of the festival, fairies from both villages perked up. It didn't matter how odd their situation was; everyone loved a party.

Oleander clapped his hands.

"Your host families will reach out to you by the end of the day. Until then, our work leaders are going to split you into groups—and our head teacher, Mrs. Grumthrush, will sort the children into classes." He paused. "Your people are free to do as they wish here, so long as you complete your chores and do your part. But there are two rules I must make clear. One: in Siltshore, only those who work for me may practice magic. I understand a few of you were competent fairy dust manipulators back home. I ask that, for now, until you have been evaluated, you refrain from upsetting the delicate balance we have cultivated here."

Behind him, Mayor Nightingale struggled to hide her frown.

"Two: you must remain within Siltshore." Oleander's face grew grave. "The wood beyond our gates is dangerous. No fairy may leave Siltshore without permission from me. No exceptions."

Was Ary imagining it—or did Oleander look at her when he said that?

Oleander's smile returned, warm and welcoming as ever. "Welcome, people of Terra. I know you have sacrificed a terrible amount to get here. We've been waiting for you."

At that, Oleander stepped back. Exhaustion swept over his face, and he looked like a tired old man once more.

Terrans began to organize themselves into different groups—children, teenagers, adults, and the very old. Her people were a ragtag bunch, and it was almost embarrassing, looking at them compared to the fairies of Siltshore, whose cheeks were full and healthy, and whose clothes, though plain, were not full of holes and stained with time. Siltshore fairies split the groups up by chores, assigning Terrans to tasks like tending mushrooms, shelling acorns, weaving cloth, and repairing bridges. They didn't seem particularly thrilled, either, but what were they going to say? Strangers had showed up on their doorstep, half-starved, and Oleander clearly wanted them to stay.

Mayor Nightingale had been right. The Terrans were

not ready for this world; it was a miracle Siltshore was here to help at all.

Guilt weighed heavy on Ary. She had not thought about what lay in wait for them when she fought to escape the terrarium. Only that they needed to find a way out.

Ary took a breath. What was it Mama had said? She'd done her job. She had freed her people. Let the adults take care of the rest. Let Mayor Nightingale and Oleander sort through the problems of finding space and work and food for them.

They were safe. Ary had her loved ones. The mold was gone, and all the problems of the terrarium with it.

Maybe—just maybe—everything would finally be okay.

NINE

Oakview

In those first few weeks, everywhere Ary looked was something strange and new. Some things were easier to understand—she could feel rain, hear the whistle of the wind, and smell the fragrance of pine needles, even if she didn't understand how anything worked. But other miracles were murkier. Like the strange, pale disc that hung in the sky at night, a cold sister to the sun, or the lights that twinkled around it at night. Ary couldn't help but stare.

"What are you gawking at?" Sumac demanded.

Ary's shoulders tensed.

It was just her luck that Alder was Sumac's dad and that he'd invited Ary and her mama to take the empty room in his treetop cottage. The room was clean and warm, and Alder was kind enough, but every conversation with Sumac felt like a fight.

"Those glow-shrooms," Ary said reluctantly, pointing at the sky. "How far away are they, to be that small?"

He frowned. "What?"

"They're tiny." Ary squinted. "They must be very high up."

"They're not mushrooms," Sumac said. "They're *stars*. Do you people not know anything?"

Stars, Ary noted, were likely not glow-shrooms. But that didn't tell her much else.

In a matter of days, many Terrans moved out of the storeroom and into temporary accommodations with Siltshore families, with promises of their own homes to come. Ary's odd little family was another question; it was one thing to take in two stray fairies, but Ary, Briar, Owl, Mama, Shrimp, and Sootflank were a large group to suddenly make space for. In the end, they were split up. The old lady with the spectacles that had called Ary a Ghostwing took in Owl, Briar, and Shrimp. Sootflank announced he'd stay in the storeroom, and everyone seemed too scared of him to argue.

It was fine. It was.

But it didn't *feel* fine.

Now Ary walked along one of the many vine bridges, her skin uncomfortably warm under the morning sun. Fairy children chattered all around her. Nerves buzzed through Ary from head to toe, but not because she was facing off giant ants or leaping into the darkness.

She was going back to school.

Siltshore children rushed by her, their paper-wrapped wings crackling as they jostled each other. Many of them were a few years younger than Ary—most of the older Siltshore kids zipped overhead, laughing and calling to each other, showing off with backflips and daring twists. The exception were the children of Terra. They walked together, severed wing stubs twitching, looking at their new classmates flying past with ill-concealed longing.

Ary tore her gaze away.

The nervous flutter she felt was excitement. That was it. This was what she had wanted, wasn't it? All those years of skipping school to work the mushroom fields, feeling bitter and embarrassed as Tulip and Basil reported on what they'd learned, daydreaming of spending her days scratching out letters on moss paper instead of scraping away mold.

So why did it feel like this was a waste of her time?

"I can't believe we saved the world and we have to go to *school*," Owl whined. He and Briar had shown up early to Alder's house, dressed in clean, neatly pressed clothes. Ary, on the other hand, wore an old uniform Sumac had grown too tall for. It was stretched out in the arms, and there were holes in the knees, but at least it was clean.

"Technically, we didn't save the world," Ary pointed out. "We ended it."

"So we *are* being punished."

"Is it really that bad?" Briar asked nervously, twisting and untwisting a lock of hair around her finger.

"Bad?" Owl exclaimed. "School is *torture*! They make you sit all day and *read*, and you're not even allowed to eat snacks if you didn't bring enough for everyone else, which really doesn't make sense, because how am I supposed to supply snacks for everyone around me? I'm twelve!"

"Owl," Ary said sharply, casting a pointed look at Briar.

The other girl was deathly pale. Her chest rose and fell rapidly, and she was staring ahead with the grim resolve of a fairy who'd been sentenced to permanent exile in the Gloom.

Owl cleared his throat. "I'm just kidding, Briar. Except about the snack thing. You'll be fine."

Briar didn't look convinced.

The school reared before them, a multilevel building carved into one of Siltshore's many branches. Vine bridges wound from level to level, and large, flat platforms with netting to catch stray fairy kids whose wings were still furled stretched below. The Siltshore children rushed forward, automatically knowing which bridge to take, which building to head toward, but the Terran children slowed and stopped. Soon it was only them, standing on the platform with uncertain expressions. They were a pitiful group—only sixteen Terran children in all, most of them missing wings, underfed and weak.

Adults weren't the only ones who had caught the mold sickness.

Ary spied Tulip and Basil standing off to the side. Basil's eyes were red and puffy, as though she'd been crying. Maybe she was just nervous? Ary was tempted to check on them when a small, severe-looking woman approached. It was the woman Oleander had referred to as Mrs. Grumthrush.

"Oh," she said, her hand flying to her mouth. "Oh my. Look at the lot of you—well, welcome. I'm Mrs. Grumthrush." She hesitated, her eyes darting uncomfortably to Tulip. "Typically we sort children by their wings, but . . ."

Tulip stiffened. Back in Terra, it wouldn't have been unusual to see a child whose wings had been freshly severed—but Tulip stood out like a sore thumb amid the flying, flipping students of Oakview Academy.

"We all received the same education back in Terra, regardless of whether our wings had been harvested or not," Ary blurted. Mrs. Grumthrush flinched at the word *harvested,* but Ary wasn't sorry. It was the truth. "And most of us haven't been in school for a year or two, anyway."

Mrs. Grumthrush blinked at them. "At *all*? Why not?"

"It closed," said Ary. "Because so many kids dropped out to work and earn ration tokens."

The words hung in the air between them. Back in Terra, it hadn't seemed so strange—Ary's family had been hungry, and though she'd longed to be in school, she'd longed to have a full belly more. But here, standing in the sunshine and the breeze, she couldn't help but wonder at the cruelty of it all. They had been told back in Terra their sacrifices were essential because their world was all they had. That was clearly a lie.

So what, then, had it all been for?

Now you're getting it, Gran's voice snarked. *Now you know how it feels to be used and tossed away.*

Ary shook herself. Mrs. Grumthrush was still gaping at her, clearly grappling with the knowledge that she not only had a bunch of traumatized children on her hands, but children who were years behind in their studies. She cast her eyes to the sky, mumbled something about the Gardener, and then forced a smile. "Very well, then. We'll fold you into the middle classes and go from there. Welcome to Oakview."

TEN

Not Special

At first, the Siltshore kids mostly avoided the children of Terra. They didn't seem to know quite what to do with the strange, underfed, wingless fairies who had joined their classroom. Ary was just fine with that. After so many years of being the subject of whispers and stares, being left alone was a welcome change.

And this time, she had Briar and Owl. Being the odd one was one thing when you were by yourself; but when you had friends, it was kind of like having your own weird club. Owl and Briar were strange even for Terrans. Ary felt like they were her responsibility.

If she was being honest, she felt like *all* the Terra kids were her responsibility. There were so few of them.

"So seasons are when the weather changes," Briar was saying, her brow wrinkled. "And apparently it can be really hot or cold. Right now it's hot, and that's summer. And somehow that's all going to go away and become winter?"

"First it's got to be fall," Owl said. "Or spring. I'm not sure what the difference is."

They walked along the vine bridge, lagging behind the

other kids. It took Owl and Briar longer to get to school because they had to collect Ary from Alder's house, but the three of them agreed it'd be better to walk together. It had quickly become the highlight of Ary's day.

"What is snow?" Owl said. "Does anyone remember?"

"No clue," said Ary. "Some of the kids seem to love it, and others act like it's a personal attack."

Briar groaned. "I can't believe I'm saying this, but I almost miss the terrarium. The weather was always just *dark* or *even darker*."

Ary didn't think that counted as weather, but she wasn't going to tell Briar that. She was just glad her friends were as confused as she was.

Every day was a waterfall of new information—from creatures lurking in the wood to whatever weather was to Siltshore's history. There was so much to learn, so much to take in, and most days Ary was so exhausted after class her brain felt like mud. But at least Briar and Owl felt like mud, too. Ary didn't know what she'd do if they weren't in this together.

In the second week of school, as they slipped down the hall, a voice said, "Hey, you three."

Ary, Briar, and Owl froze.

A small, fierce fairy girl named Violet stood behind them, flanked by a few of her friends. Ary didn't know Violet well—all she knew was that the girl usually had all the answers in class, and that, like the other Siltshore children, she mostly ignored Ary and the other Terrans.

Violet peered at Briar and said, not unkindly, "I heard you were, like, held prisoner by a bunch of carpenter ants or something?"

Ary stiffened and stepped protectively in front of Briar. "Briar doesn't—"

"Mind talking about that," Briar finished quickly. She nudged Ary out of her way and crossed her arms. "The ants held me prisoner for years."

"Neat." Violet cocked her head to the side. "If someone wanted to take me prisoner, I simply wouldn't let them."

Ary had the strangest feeling Violet was entirely right. Something told her she didn't want to be on Violet's bad side.

Briar nudged Ary and whispered, "I don't need you to protect me, okay? You're not my mom."

Ary's cheeks heated. "I was just trying to—"

Violet raised an eyebrow at Owl. "And you're a . . . a wingless, right? My brother said you guys have weird magic."

Again, Ary opened her mouth to say Owl didn't need to explain his magic.

"I do, but I don't really understand it," Owl said quickly, before Ary could come to his defense. "I made the earth explode on accident, though. I think."

"Oooh," said Violet. "Can you explode our school?"

Owl frowned. "I . . . don't think Mrs. Grumthrush would like that very much."

Violet gave him a sweet smile. “I know.”

The other fairy kids edged closer, asking Briar and Owl more questions. Ary kept waiting for one of them to say something unkind, but it seemed that the indifference of the winglings of Siltshore had given way to genuine curiosity. Even weirder, Owl and Briar seemed to like the attention. They took turns, Briar telling them stories about the Underground, Owl telling them stories about his magic and how it had felt to make the earth explode. The kids crowded around them, their faces alight. It was like Ary wasn’t even there.

Finally, a gangly, freckle-faced fairy boy looked at Ary, his eyes bright with interest. “And you?”

Ary started. “I’m sorry?”

“What’s your special thing? What can you do?”

Ary reddened. “I . . . I don’t—I don’t really—”

“Ary’s the reason we escaped our terrarium,” Owl cut in. “She broke the spell with her grandma and set us all free. That’s why her wings are like that. Like Oleander’s.”

The kids went quiet. They looked at her wings, and fear flashed briefly on their faces. Ary’s shoulders hunched up.

The freckled boy gave Ary an uneasy smile. “That’s, um, nice, I guess. Our grandparents always used to talk about that terrarium stuff.” He shifted his weight from foot to foot and then turned back to Briar. “Was the Underground scary?”

The conversation swept on, Briar and Owl safely back

in the center. No one asked Ary any further questions. No one even looked at her.

Ary told herself she didn't mind. After a lifetime of being special, this was what she wanted, wasn't it? To be uninteresting.

But Owl and Briar weren't.

Ary wasn't sure where that left her.

For two weeks, Ary tried to keep her head from spinning off her shoulders with how much there was to learn about this strange new world. Sunlight washed through the window in golden beams as Mrs. Grumthrush paced before them, a tiny spider-silk bag balanced precariously in her palm. Ary's skin itched as power crackled in the air. Children began to whisper in excitement; even the surliest among them sat up straight, eyes sparkling.

"Every year, we celebrate the Festival of the Gardener to thank Her for protecting us by building the terrariums until we could re-emerge in the world," Mrs. Grumthrush began. "Given that you're all in the upper grades, you'll be evaluated and assigned a role in the showcase, where you'll be expected to demonstrate mastery over our most precious resource of all." Mrs. Grumthrush snapped her fingers. Pale blue light danced around them; the silver-sweet scent of fairy magic wafted through the air. *"Magic."*

The Siltshore children shivered in anticipation.

"Now," Mrs. Grumthrush, "it's very important you all

remain calm. Even fairy dust is not all-powerful. To work a spell, the caster must be calm and clear-headed. A burst of emotion could disrupt or even break the magic—so do me a favor, and don't scream, please? The last thing I need is one of you startling me." Mrs. Grumthrush raised a brow and flicked sparkling fingers toward her students. *"Float."*

Everyone lifted into the air, their desk chairs rising like dandelion puffs caught on a breeze. Tulip and Basil were the first to rise. They gasped, laughing, and waved their hands through the air between them in the seats. Then Briar showed up, then Owl, and the rest of the class. Everyone giggled, squealed, and whooped.

Everyone except Ary.

Fairy dust rippled over her in a sparkling halo, but Ary didn't budge. Unlike the other students, who were already beginning to sink back to the ground as the dust faded, Ary continued to shimmer. It was as if the magic was repelled by her. As if it was . . . rejecting her.

Ary blinked several times and fought to keep her face carefully blank.

She would not cry. She would not panic. This was fine. It was *fine*.

Mrs. Grumthrush stared at her for a painful beat before plastering on a smile, plunging ahead as if nothing had happened.

"I will spend the next month observing your progress, and then you will each be assigned a role in the showcase."

She gave them a strange, tight smile. "It's vital that you learn Siltshore's history if you hope to honor this world. Remember—the Gardener is always watching. And we must do Her proud."

Mrs. Grumthrush kept talking, but Ary couldn't listen. Why hadn't the magic worked on her?

Ary's fingers curled into fists. This is what she'd wanted, right? To be normal. To be unremarkable.

So why did it feel like she was being left behind?

ELEVEN

Scared

Ary dreamed of the hollow again.

In this dream, like the one before, Ary was alone. Cool darkness enveloped her as she walked carefully across spongy wet ground. There was a tension to the air, as if a hundred fairies were watching, hidden behind the crackly branches of the dead trees. It made Ary's skin crawl.

"Hello?" she called.

Whispers came from ahead. Ary picked up her pace.

What was this place? And more importantly—why had she returned?

The hollow was strangely colorless, as if the very life of it had been long ago leached away. Unlike Atlas' cavern, though, there was a sense of life moving beyond—as if the place where Ary stood had frozen in time. A rustle sounded behind her.

"Gran?" Ary whispered.

Ghostwing, someone whispered. *Find me in the wood.*

The hair on Ary's arms stood on end.

A pair of eyes flashed in the dark. Ary turned.

A spider loomed over her.

Unlike the wolf spider that had attacked her before, this one's body was smooth. Eyes glittered down at her, full of life and anger. Again, something tugged at her mind.

Let us go, the wolf spider had said.

"Who are you?" Ary begged. "What do you want?"

The spider lunged.

Ary woke with a gasp.

Sweat drenched her where she lay. Early-morning light colored the outside world watery blue, outlining leaves in pale gold as the sun woke up. A breeze floated through the open window. Ary's mind whirled. Twice now she'd had the dream of the spider. It couldn't be a coincidence.

But unlike before, when Atlas had been calling out to her, Ary was no longer alone.

Ary shot to her feet and slipped into the kitchen.

"Mama, I need to talk to y—"

Ary froze.

Mama looked like a painting, brown hair tied away from her face, the sleeves of her milkweed-yarn shirt rolled up past her elbows as she worked a lump of dough on the counter. Goldenrod flour dusted her cheeks. Beside her, Alder stood with his head bent toward Mama's, his eyes soft, his face unguarded. Ary had the strangest sense she was interrupting something.

"It's not like Mugwort to just up and disappear, especially with another crop failing—" Alder saw Ary and straightened. "Oh, good morning. Robin, Ary's up."

Ary stiffened. Since when had he started calling Mama Robin instead of *Mrs. Mossheart*? And what did he mean by another crop failing?

Mama turned, dough cupped in her hands. She smiled, too quickly, in that way she did when she was hiding something. Ary shrank.

She needed to talk to her mom—but not with some strange man here. Feet padded behind them—Sumac, wandering into the kitchen. He watched Ary with narrowed eyes as he sat down with a raspberry nut pastry.

Mama smiled at Ary, gesturing at the pastries. "I made extra for Owl and Briar. They like raspberries, right? Or was it blueberries?"

"They like both," Ary said, distracted. She wasn't sure if that was true. She'd hardly talked to Owl or Briar the last few weeks—they were so preoccupied with what they were going to do for the festival showcase that it was all they talked about on the walk to school. "Mama? Could I stay home from school today?"

Mama eyed her shrewdly. "Why?"

"Just for the morning," Ary bargained.

Please, she willed. *I just need to talk to you.*

Mama set down the dough. "What's going on? Are there kids picking on you?"

"No! It's not that—"

"Are you struggling? Because there's no shame in asking

for help. Your dad, he had this thing where words blended together or got lost entirely—"

"I can read *fine,*" Ary protested. "I just don't want to go—"

"It's probably the showcase," Sumac mumbled around a mouthful of berry.

Ary shot him a furious glare. "It's *not* that."

"Is this about your gran?" asked Mama.

Ary went cold. "What?"

"You haven't said anything about her," continued Mama. "It's been weeks—and, I don't know. I keep trying to find a way to talk to you, and . . ."

Mama kept talking, but Ary didn't hear a word. Memory attacked her from all angles—of Gran, in all her lovely bitterness. Gran, scolding her, shaming her, pushing her fear onto Ary.

Gran, clutching Ary's hands at the end of the world.

I love you, she had said. *I'm sorry, and I love you.*

As if that made up for anything. As if it made any difference at all, when Gran had gone and died and left Ary all alone.

Of course this wasn't about Gran. Ary was fine. She *was.* Gran was dead. She had chosen to leave Ary behind and be a hero at last. Ary didn't want to think about her.

The problem was this house. It was school, and the dreams, and the sunlight that wasn't getting easier to deal with. It was Alder and Sumac, staring at her when Ary just wanted to talk to her mom, strange and overfamiliar and unwelcome. It was Briar and Owl, fitting in so seamlessly, either not noticing or not caring that they were leaving Ary behind. It was everything in this new, awful city.

They were supposed to be happy here. *Ary* was supposed to be happy.

Why was she so unhappy?

"Ary," Mama said with a frown, "what's going on?"

Ary had thought Mama would understand. But what if she didn't listen? She was fitting in here, too, moving on like the rest of them, but Ary was still back in the terrarium. She'd never really left.

"Nothing," lied Ary.

And before she could think, before Mama or Alder or—Gardener forbid—*Sumac* could say one more terrible thing, Ary turned and fled out the door.

She needed to get away. All of Siltshore glowed around her, and it only made her feel worse. Everything was so bright, so new, so *alive*. Everywhere Ary looked there were preparations for the Festival of the Gardener and something the folk of Siltshore called *fall*, which apparently was when leaves turned the color of fire before dying and fluttering away, and the world became cold and buried under blankets of frozen water. It sounded ridiculous.

Workers spent their days in the trees, harvesting acorns and tending to the mushroom farms. On the main platform in the village's heart, a massive stage was being constructed, and fairy workers set out dozens of tiny wooden chairs.

"I thought Rosemary was going to put these out," one of the fairies complained.

His companion frowned. "She didn't show up to work yesterday. I went to her house, but she wasn't there."

Ary's stomach did an uneasy flip. She kept walking, the conversation with Mama replaying on a terrible loop.

If Gran were here, she would have made fun of how silly the showcase was. She would have quipped about Owl and Briar and all the rest of them being ungrateful brats, getting so swept up in their new lives. And maybe that wasn't very nice or fair, but Ary didn't care. She didn't want to be nice or fair right now. Why did it seem like she was the only one struggling? Mama was happy, Briar and Owl were fitting in at school. Shrimp was apparently so content with Mrs. Dragonsnap that Ary never even saw him anymore.

Which just left her. Alone.

How was everyone else slipping into their new lives so easily?

Why did it seem like only Ary was still checking for monsters around every corner?

Ary didn't realize where her feet were taking her until she was already there, and she wasn't sure what she wanted more: to be alone—or to talk to the one soul who might understand.

Ary pushed open the storeroom and stepped into the dark.

She saw the flash of his eyes before the door even closed.

"Little Mossheart?" Sootflank whispered.

It was dark and cool in the storeroom, but even here sunlight streamed through, casting golden rays across the floor. Ary let the door fall closed behind her, fingers trembling on the knob. When she looked at Sootflank, she saw Briar and Owl leaving her behind in the school hallway. She saw Mama smiling at Alder, forgetting she was there.

And she saw the hollow. That voice, so familiar but not, and the spider, biting down.

"Ary," Sootflank said gently. "What's wrong?"

Ary took one step toward him. She tried to find the right words. To explain her fear, the way everything was changing too fast but also not fast enough. To ask if he was happy here and planning to leave her alone in this terror, too.

"I'm scared," Ary whispered.

And then she burst into tears.

TWELVE

What Do You Want?

It took a while for Sootflank to coax everything out of her—the way she was struggling with school, Sumac's constant nitpicking, and Mama's questions about Gran. When Ary finally finished, her eyes ached from crying, and her voice had a strange, hoarse squeak in it.

"I'm sorry," Ary said finally. "I know I sound dramatic. But I just feel this constant fear. I'm worried something is wrong with this place, and I'm worried something *isn't*. It seems like in both situations, I lose. If something is wrong, then we're not safe. If something *isn't* wrong, then it means I don't fit in here, and I'm carrying around all this worry for nothing."

When Sootflank finally spoke, he kept his eyes on the storeroom door.

"I don't think you can begin to understand how incredible what you did in the terrarium was. I don't think *I* can begin to comprehend it, and I was there," Sootflank said gently. "You left your home behind, with no training, no weapons, and no plans. You faced down the Ant Court. You somehow got *me* on your side. And when it came down to it, Ary—you set us free."

"Gran did that," Ary whispered.

"No," said Sootflank. "You opened the cavern. You found Atlas. And *you* figured out the spell. Wren certainly helped. But you are the one who saved us. You were too young, but you picked up the sword, anyway."

"I never even got a sword," sniffled Ary. "I just had a shovel."

"You're ruining my metaphor."

"Sorry, continue."

Sootflank seemed to be weighing his next words carefully. "I want to tell you this is the part where you heal. That your goal, now, should be to move on, learn to set down the sword, unlearn all the worry and instincts that saved us. You owe yourself the peace Wren never found."

Ary braced herself. Here it came. Sootflank would tell her she just needed to move on. To try harder in school, to keep her head down, and pretend things were fine. And then she truly *would* be alone.

"But back in Terra," Sootflank said slowly, "you were right."

Ary looked at him.

"I can't stop thinking about the spider," Sootflank said quietly. "There is something . . . strange about this place. It feels hollow; as if there's something missing. I don't want to add to your worry. But you should know, Ary—that feeling you have, that all isn't quite well here? I have it, too."

Every part of Ary unwound.

She wasn't losing her mind. Something *was* wrong here. Ary hadn't realized how much the burden of that worry alone had been crushing her until now.

"Is this the part where you tell me I should stay out of it because I'm just a kid?" Ary asked.

"No," said Sootflank. "This is the part where I tell you I care about you, and I worry for you—but that you should always trust your instincts. If you want to ignore what you feel here, no one could blame you." He paused. "There will always be more monsters to fight. So the question becomes this: Do you want to take up a new fight? Or do you want to let someone else step in? There is no wrong answer. But you owe it to yourself to ask: What is it you want?"

Ary blinked rapidly.

"I can't ignore what I feel," Ary said softly. "But I don't know if I'm ready for another fight, either."

"You have always been a questioner. Now you find yourself with a new puzzle. If you don't have the answers you seek—what should you do?"

"Get more information, until I have enough to make a decision." She wasn't hurting anyone or anything by looking into things, right? If it turned out Siltshore had some terrible problem, it didn't mean she had to fix it. She could bring it to someone else—to Sootflank, to Mayor Nightingale, maybe even Oleander himself.

"Sootflank," Ary said quietly. "How long have you suspected something was wrong here?"

"From the moment we entered this world," Sootflank said honestly. "And every second since."

Maybe that was the difference between him and so many other adults. Sootflank would not stand in her way—but he wouldn't push her into a fight, either. Had Ary not come to him with her fears, she was certain he'd have never mentioned anything at all.

A terrible idea stirred.

Find me in the wood.

It couldn't be an accident. In the terrarium, Atlas had been calling her.

What if something else was now?

"Sootflank," Ary said. "Thank you."

Sootflank's tail twitched. He looked from her to the door, clearly fighting with something. Finally, he grumbled, "Be careful, won't you? I've only just gotten used to you. It'll be very inconvenient to me if you die."

Ary fought a smile. She pressed a kiss to the side of his head, and Sootflank made a half-hearted grumbly noise, as though he was trying to pretend he wasn't touched by the gesture.

"I promise," she said.

Ary slipped out the door and did not look back.

As Ary crept down through Siltshore, past the school, past Alder's home and where Mrs. Dragonsnap lived, she repeated her plan to herself.

Investigate the wood. See if she could find answers. Be back before school ended. Tell Sootflank about whatever she found.

The problem with her plan became evident when Ary finally reached Siltshore's gates.

She peered out from behind a branch. Just beyond the gate, the fairies of Siltshore had built a series of platforms out of flattened tree bark that could be raised or lowered with triple-woven vines. Two guards stood watch, faces bored and their eyes lidded. There was no way to sneak past them—and she didn't know the vine bridges well enough to follow them out of Siltshore on her own. She needed to get the guards to move, somehow.

Unlike the guards when she escaped from Terra, these ones were unfortunately awake.

Briar would just force her way through. Owl would do something ridiculous and dramatic that could either get them in huge trouble or work perfectly. And Sootflank—well, he'd probably just threaten to set them on fire.

What had Gran said, once? You could get into a lot of places you weren't supposed to be by acting like you belonged there. She didn't need the guards to be gone for long—just long enough that she could slip out.

Quickly, Ary messed up her hair and her clothes. She took two deep breaths, dredging up all the feelings she'd had earlier, until her eyes burned and her nose began to run. Once Ary started crying, it was hard to stop.

That was about to come in handy.

Ary braced herself. And then she ran straight toward the guards, crying, "Help! Help!"

The guards snapped to attention. They caught Ary as she crashed into them.

"It's one of the Terrans," the first guard said to the other. He gripped Ary's shoulders. "What's wrong, girl?"

Ary looked at the guard, dredged up all the feelings she'd had earlier, and burst into tears.

"There's a big fight several branches up," she bawled. "A bunch of Siltshore and Terra fairies—they won't stop! The guards told me to run for help! You have to come, please!"

She'd heard the grumblings of the Terrans and Siltshore fairies alike. It was hardly a stretch to believe someone had finally started a fight. Usually, it was annoying when adults looked at Ary, saw how small and young she was, and assumed she was weak. But sometimes it was helpful. The guards didn't even blink. They looked at each other, trying to conceal how excited they were by the prospect of finally having something to do.

Ary cried harder.

"Okay, okay," the second guard said. "Stay *right* here, all right?"

"Of course," Ary sniffed.

The guard put his shoulders back, puffed up his chest, and set off with his companion. Ary kept crying until they turned the corner, and then she wiped her cheeks.

Adults were so gullible.

Ary climbed onto the platform, hit the lever, and descended to the ground below.

THIRTEEN

What Rots in the Wood

As the platform descended, the world grew cool and quiet. There it was again—that uneasy sense of emptiness. Of loss.

Where were all the insects? Why had she not encountered many of the creatures and critters meant to fill this world? As massive and abundant as the forest was, it felt empty. Like the Underground back in Terra, but worse. At least in the terrarium, everything had been rotting and covered in mold. There was so much potential for life here—plants, water, and brilliant sunlight.

So where was everything?

The Gardener had seemed awfully certain that the world would be safe when they returned to it. Ary was starting to worry she'd been wrong.

The platform hit the forest floor with a gentle thud. Ary hesitated, dread gnawing at the edges of her mind. If someone pulled it up before she returned, she would have a whole new host of problems.

"You've come this far," Ary whispered. "No turning back now."

Ary clambered off and into the wood. The trees looked back, blank and impassive. What had Owl said about his magic? That it felt like things were asking him to reach, and that he needed to lean into a feeling?

Ary wasn't a Seedling, but she wasn't a normal fairy anymore, either. Maybe there was something to that. Maybe whatever worked for Owl could work for her, too.

Ary closed her eyes. She pictured the hollow from her nightmares, and the soft, scratchy voice that had reached out to her.

Ghostwing, it had begged. *Find me in the wood.*

Maybe the dream meant nothing. Maybe it was something similar to Atlas, another group of fairies, or even the Gardener Herself. Ary didn't know. But there was one way to find out.

Her mind drifted from the hollow to, of all things, Owl and Briar. They had power of their own—Owl with his strange Seedling magic, and Briar with her wings. Ary had . . . well, nothing. She didn't know why that rankled her so much.

Hadn't she wanted a normal life? To be left alone? Back in the terrarium she'd been so resentful of the role of hero.

Right?

Or maybe that wasn't true. Maybe she'd been righteously angry that a child was expected to save everyone and die—but if she was being honest with herself, a part of her had woken up on that adventure. For the first time in her life, Ary had felt truly alive. It had felt *good* to solve a problem no one else could. And it had brought her Sootflank, Shrimp, Owl, and Briar. There had been terrible parts—but there had been wonderful parts, too.

A breeze plucked at her hair; a prickle swept over her skin. She forced all of her feeling and thought and will into the image of the dream and the voice that haunted her.

"I'm trying to help you," Ary whispered. "I'm *here*. But I need to know where to go."

A rustle came from ahead.

Ary snapped her eyes open.

A spider loomed before her.

Ary flinched backward, but the spider didn't move. It was smaller than the others, with long, spindly legs and pale yellow and white streaks across its abdomen. The spider watched her expectantly.

"Hello," Ary said cautiously.

The spider said nothing. It watched her a moment longer, then turned and crawled away.

Ary cast one last glance at the platform and followed.

The spider led her deep into the wood.

For the better part of an hour, Ary scrambled to keep up. The farther they went, the more the emptiness of the wood sent foreboding spiraling through her. Occasionally, trees creaked overhead, or something snapped a twig in the underbrush—but Ary never saw anything.

"Where are you taking me?" Ary called after the spider. "Where are we going?"

The spider ignored her and kept crawling. It disappeared around a bend. Ary scrambled after it—and collided with a squeak into something furry.

"Oh goodness!" a voice whispered. "Excuse me, I didn't see you there—oh dear."

Ary sprawled on her back. Hunched in front of her, round ears twitching and scaly tail bouncing on the forest floor, was a furry, portly creature that reminded her of Chives, the star-nosed mole that had been a keeper of stories back in the terrarium. Mrs. Grumthrush's lessons came back in a flood.

"You're a mouse," said Ary.

"And you're a fairy," said the mouse, looking at Ary with concern. It carried a little bundle bulging with square objects. "What *are* you doing out here? Did Willow send you?"

The spider stopped crawling. It looked back at Ary and bounced impatiently.

"I, um, I'm looking for something," Ary lied weakly.

The mouse shuddered. "Well, whatever you're looking for, you don't want to go that way. Not unless you're looking to end your little life before it begins."

Ary picked herself up. "How do you mean?"

"Nothing good comes from that way." It peered at her.

"You're clearly not one of Willow's. If you're lost, I can help you find your way home—"

The mouse's words fell away. It shrank into itself, ears flattening, eyes trained on Ary.

Not, not just Ary.

Her wings.

The mouse looked terrified—and something else, too. A touch angry?

Ary's heart pounded. If she died, her mom would be so mad at her.

Cautiously, Ary held up her hands. "I'm Ary. What was that about danger ahead? And who's Willow?"

"No time!" The mouse backed away so quickly it tripped and fell, sending the contents of its little rucksack sprawling. Books flew all over the forest floor, their pages flapping sadly.

"Wait," cried Ary.

The mouse didn't even bother to pick up its books. It scrambled away, muttering something about thieves and liars, and disappeared into the underbrush. Ary stared after it. That was exactly how the spider had referred to her and Owl. She didn't know much about spider-mice relations, but she had a feeling they weren't exactly close.

The spider gave an annoyed hum.

"Sorry," Ary said. "Hold on."

She couldn't just leave the mouse's books scattered everywhere. What if it came back? Quickly, Ary picked the books and dusted them off. She peered at one of the titles.

Seedling Songs.

"What is a mouse doing reading about fairy Seedlings?" Ary muttered. It was odd, but Chives had known a great deal about fairies. Maybe a thirst for knowledge came along with all their fur.

Ary packed the books back into the mouse's rucksack as nicely as she could and propped it up on a nearby branch. If it didn't come back, maybe another creature that needed it would find it.

The spider gave an aggressive bounce.

"I'm coming, I'm coming!"

Ary turned and followed the creature into the wood.

It didn't take long to understand why the mouse hadn't wanted to go this way.

At first, Ary thought it was her imagination. The forest grew colder, the trees scraggly and dry. There was a scent in the air—something rotten, almost chemical. The spider crawled faster; Ary had to run to keep up.

She rounded a bend—and stopped.

A single dead flower curled up from the earth, blackened and shriveled. Every hair on Ary's body stood on end. A terrible, burnt stench rolled off the plant. It was the same scent she'd caught when they'd left the terrarium, the very one that followed her in her dreams.

The spider was gone.

A chill swept over Ary. There was no sound coming

from the wood; there was no life here at all. She looked closer. A ring of death spread out from around the sick plant. The nearby plants grew *away* from it, as if they were afraid whatever had sickened this plant would get them, too.

Ary's heart pounded.

Where terror should have been, exhaustion crept in instead.

Exhaustion—and a little bit of vindication.

She wasn't losing it after all. This whole time, a part of her had been terrified that Siltshore actually was perfect, and the problem was just her. But this changed things. All her problems—her inability to fit in, the way Owl and Briar were leaving her behind—suddenly paled in comparison.

The spider, the mouse, this plant, her nightmare. They all had to be connected. It was a new puzzle. A new mission.

And this time, Ary wasn't alone.

First, she'd go to Sootflank. He was the most likely to believe her and be on her side. Once he had her back, then they could tell Owl, Briar, and Mama. It wouldn't be like before. She wouldn't be scrambling in the dark. She had a team this time, a family. They'd do this together.

That's what I thought, too, Gran's voice whispered. *And I lost them, instead.*

Ary shook herself. She wasn't Gran. This would be different.

The plant loomed in front of her.

Ary drew closer.

She reached out to touch the plant—and a hand clamped around her wrist, yanking her back so hard her elbow cracked. The world tilted out from under her, and Ary sprawled on her back. A familiar figure loomed overhead, chest heaving, sweat rolling down his temples.

"Touch that," panted Oleander, "and you die."

FOURTEEN

The Blight

Time slowed down. For a beat, Ary struggled to understand what she was seeing. She was in the wood, the sick plant only a few fairy-lengths away. The leader of Siltshore stood over her, his face red and covered in sweat. He was—to put it shortly—furious.

"What," Oleander demanded, "were you thinking?"

Ary gaped up at him.

She was in so much trouble.

"Imagine my surprise when the guards came to me and claimed the little Terran Ghostwing made up a ridiculous lie to get them away from the gate—and that when they returned, the platform to the wood had been lowered." Oleander passed a hand over his face. "Do you have a death wish, child? Or did you think you were an exception to the *one* rule we have?"

Ary shrank inward. A dozen excuses rose to her lips. That she'd had a terrible feeling, that she'd done her best to be normal.

Instead, she whispered, "What is that thing?"

Oleander looked up at the trees, as if scanning for any

foes, or hiding fairies. A dozen emotions flitted over his face—fury, anger, fear. Ary wondered how old he had been when he'd freed his people. It seemed like the Siltshore fairies had been settled for a long time, and that very few of them remembered their terrarium at all.

"Please don't lie to me." The words slipped out before Ary could stop herself. "Don't do that thing adults do, where they say I'm too young to understand because they don't want to explain. You freed your people from your terrarium. You already know what I've seen. What I've done."

Oleander gave her a long look. He watched her a moment longer, as if weighing two very different decisions, and shook his head. "Gardener help us. Fine."

Oleander stomped away from her. He snapped a twig from the nearby thicket, tromped back, and paused to show Ary the bright green center. No birds sang overhead; there was only the silence of the wood, as though it, too, held its breath.

"You want to know the real reason I forbid my people from entering the wood? It's not spiders. It's not beasts or creatures that hunt in the night. It's *this*."

Oleander touched the blackened plant with the end of the twig and leaped back.

The twig rotted in midair.

By the time it hit the ground, it had suffered the same fate as the plant. The twig curled on the blackened earth, reduced to a twisted, ruined thing. The earth beneath it turned black, spreading out in a great wound. It might have been a trick of the light—but Ary could have sworn the nearby plants leaned *away* from the blighted spot in response.

Panic wrapped icy claws around her heart.

"I'm sorry, little hero," Oleander said, and it was clear he meant it. "But this wood is no safe haven. Your people escaped one sick world for another."

"What," Ary began hoarsely. "What is this?"

"I don't know," Oleander admitted. "I call it the Blight. It began a few years ago—random black spots in the woods. It consumes any and everything it touches, and even when we tie plants away from it, eventually the circle of ruined earth spreads."

Terror spread through Ary in bright, icy waves. It was so much worse than she'd imagined.

"The festival has become . . . a temporary solution," Oleander continued. "The magic we perform seems to hold back some of the Blight. But the power gets weaker every year."

Ary stared. The mold was one thing; they had understood how to fight it, how to survive, and though it was inevitable, at least it was *slow,* taking days or weeks to creep over homes and fields and into the lungs of fairies huddling in the dark. But this Blight had been instant, as if fueled by magic.

And this time, there was no new world to escape to.

Ary swayed where she stood, caught between the sweetness of fresh air and the horror of what curled in front of her. This world was not safe. Her people were not safe.

And Gran, it seemed, had died for nothing.

"Okay," Ary croaked. "Tell me what to do."

Oleander looked at her, horrified. "What?"

"That's why you're telling me, right?" Ary's head spun. "So I can fix this. I thought I was done sacrificing and saving, but we left one problem behind for another. It's okay. I'm ready. Tell me what to do."

"You're not going to do anything," sputtered Oleander. "You're twelve."

"But I'm a—"

"Child," Oleander finished firmly. "A traumatized child, whose people have asked far, far too much of her. I am being honest with you because I know you're just going to hunt for answers otherwise. That doesn't mean I'm about to let you get yourself killed on some harebrained quest that even I wouldn't succeed at."

"What?" She couldn't look at him, her eyes glued to that twisted, ruined plant. She wasn't safe. She'd never be safe.

Oleander braced his hands on her shoulders to draw her gaze back to him, his touch gentle, but firm. Ary reluctantly met his eyes. She hadn't noticed them before—his eyes were the same hue Gran's had been. They carried the same tiredness, too.

"I have spent my entire life trying to guide Sumac and

ensure my people will have a leader when I pass," Oleander said. "I realize, now, it was never Sumac we were waiting for. Tell me, Ary. What do you know about the wings on your back?"

Ary hesitated. She so wanted to say something that didn't make her sound like the underprepared, naïve kid. But all Ary had were more questions.

"Nothing," Ary admitted hoarsely. "I know nothing."

Oleander gave her a weary smile.

"I think," he said slowly, "I ought to start at the beginning."

FIFTEEN

A Ghostwing's Promise

As the light grew dim, and the forest cold, Oleander told Ary the truth of their world.

It was the truth that had brought them all here. And if they were lucky—it was the key to saving them all.

"Long before the first Blight, before the Gardener built the terrariums and you and I were forced to find a way to break free," Oleander said, "the wood was unbalanced—the divers, weavers, flyers, and grazers each had their own leader, a Keeper who carried incredible power. But the folk were not given a Keeper. As the world beyond the wood changed, so too did the need to protect it.

One day, a weaver came to the folk with a proposal: send one fairy to become a Keeper and help protect the wood, and in return, we'd all be connected to the forest's power as the other creatures were. We'd finally have a powerful leader of our own, capable of working incredible feats instead of mere party tricks. So we did. We sent a fairy deep into the weavers' domain, to be woven into their web of magic. But when the fairy emerged, they were changed.

Their wings were gone—and they could no longer work small acts of magic using fairy dust."

A chill crept over Ary.

"They had become a Ghostwing," Oleander said.

The spell in Atlas' cavern. The magic that had rushed through her. Ary had thought her wings a punishment left over from the terrarium.

What was Oleander saying? That she was something more?

"We kept the balance for a while," Oleander continued. "Folk, weaver, diver, flyer, grazer, minding the wood, bidding the magic grow. But then a Keeper died, with no heir to take their place. Outside forces crept in, poisoning the land and killing the creatures that lived here. The Blight emerged. And another creature—a giant from beyond the wood who had made it her home anyway—came up with a wild plan."

"The Gardener," breathed Ary.

"Yes," said Oleander. "The Gardener. No one remembers who She was, or where She came from. It's been lost to history, same as the other Keepers. But as the wood died—She came up with a plan to save it."

As the wood leaned in, Oleander told Ary the rest in pieces. Because the folk were the only creatures who *all* carried magic, they were chosen to be sealed away with other tiny, small animals that could also someday become Keepers.

"We were a backup plan," Ary breathed. "In case everyone who stayed behind failed and died."

Her whole life, Ary had thought the fairies of Terra exceptional. The last survivors of a dying world. But it hadn't been the case at all. They were just . . . fail-safes. Who knew how long it would take the wood to recover? A hundred years? Five hundred? Magic could only live for so long. So the Gardener made three terrariums and gambled with the lives of the ones she sealed away.

Surely one would be successful. The spell to shatter it was such a feat, surely one would create the Ghostwing they needed.

"But the wood is sick again," Ary said. "Or . . . it never got better?"

"That's the part we don't know," Oleander admitted. "When I escaped the terrarium, the woods were empty. There were no Keepers for the grazers; the flyers and divers had their own, but they were old and weak. The weavers refused to interact with us." His eyes drifted to the Blight. "And then, after only a few years—the Blight returned."

Her head spun. It was too much, too fast. Her entire identity had been about not being chosen. Now she was—and she wasn't.

Anyone could have become a Ghostwing. It could have been Owl, or Briar, or Mama.

But Ary had cast that spell.

She had made herself a hero for real this time.

And now, it seemed, fate was coming to collect.

Ary looked at Oleander. At his wings that matched her own, the tiredness on his face, and the rotting wood beyond. She had the sense of walls closing in around her, and when Oleander spoke, it was like his words were coming from far, far away.

"So what now?" Ary asked, her voice small. "The wood is sick and these . . . Keepers, whatever they are, they won't help?"

Oleander looked troubled. "No one has heard from them in years. Every season, I hold the Festival of the Gardener in hopes of gaining their attention. If we can reawaken their web of power, the wood might just heal. But it's never been enough." His attention slid to her. "You asked how you could help. And while I can't just throw you into danger—there might yet be a way."

Ary hesitated. She hadn't asked; she'd volunteered. But if Oleander saw her unease, he didn't acknowledge it.

"It is a lonely thing, to be a Ghostwing." Oleander's gaze drifted beyond her, back to the plant. "I will not pretend you have a choice. Fate has chosen you to be remarkable. But I can try to delay it, as long as I can. And I would be honored to help train *this* world's next great hero. If I'm never enough for the Keepers—well, Ary Mossheart, maybe you will be."

Ary's head spun.

This was meant to be Wren Mossheart's fate. A world-breaker turned Keeper, a chosen hero raised to sacrifice and lead. Gran had thought she was sparing Ary, but she had sentenced her to a martyr's fate all the same.

Ary had so many questions, so many fears, she didn't know what to say. Finally, all that came out was: "I don't know if my mom would like that."

Oleander laughed. "We don't have to tell her just yet. And don't worry about school. Mrs. Grumthrush answers to me. It can be our little secret until the festival."

Ary hesitated. It felt weird to keep secrets from her mom. But what Oleander was saying kind of made sense. And Mama would understand, right? When she realized how important this all was?

Still. This was no adventure into the Underground. This wasn't a mission she could succeed at and set aside.

This would be forever.

Like Gran. But—no. Gran had done one brave thing when she was a kid. She'd been a puppet as an adult, something for the folk of Terra to trot out when they wanted to remind themselves there was a savior ready to jump in and die for them.

Ary wouldn't just play the *role* of her world's great hero. She'd be expected to keep doing it, probably forever, and then—then what?

Someone else would have to take her place.

She shivered.

Would it be her own child, then? Or their children? Cursed to carry the burden of the wood on their shoulders until they died, knowing the ones they loved were fated for the same misery?

Dread spiraled through Ary.

No. She'd either fix this problem—or never give this world another hero to inherit it at all.

"Who knows about this?" Ary asked, her attention slipping back to the blighted, ruined wood.

"Our people know the myth," Oleander admitted, "but only a select few know about the Blight. You must promise me that you will tell no one."

"And if I do?"

"I'll have to kill you." At her alarmed expression Oleander raised his hands. "That was a joke! But this must be our secret. Until the festival, no one else can know."

Ary hesitated.

Oleander added, "If not for me, for your friends. For your mother. Haven't they suffered, too? Don't they deserve a normal life? Your people deserve stability. And you deserve a chance to live. You have been incredibly brave, Ary Mossheart, but you are just a girl. One day, you will need to be more. But not yet. So learn from me. Train with me. So that one day, when I pass the sword, you will be ready to bear its weight."

She had wanted to be normal—but was that even true? She had been miserable at school and out of place at home.

Maybe this was the solution. She could be special, but not yet. Not a child hero like Gran had been, but an apprentice granted years to grow into the task before her.

She hadn't escaped her role of hero after all. But at least now she would have *time.* She could live her life, learn from Oleander, and let him handle the Blight until she was ready.

And then, Ary supposed, she would do what heroes did—she would step up. Not because she wanted to, but because Oleander was right.

There was no one else.

The presence of the Blight loomed behind her, lurking like a centipede in the dark, but all she could picture was the exhaustion lining Owl, Mama, and Briar's faces. All she saw was everything Shrimp and Sootflank had done for her.

They deserved this. Peace. A normal life.

Ary wouldn't take it away from them.

"Okay," Ary said. She placed her hand over her heart. "I'll do it. I'll learn from you, and help you prepare for the festival. Your secret is safe with me. On my grandmother's memory, on the Mossheart name, I promise I'll tell no one of the Blight in the wood."

PART 2
SEEDLING

SIXTEEN

Reach

Owl Diggs had spent most of his life trying to get people to pay attention.

Even before his parents died, Owl had been plagued by a sense of wrongness everyone else wanted to ignore. It started with whispers in the earth, voices in his dreams. It only got worse once Owl was alone. In that first, awful year, when the mold crept in and never left, Owl had felt like a ghost, desperate for someone, anyone, to listen to him. But he had been the orphan, the wingless boy, the doomsday-obsessed oddball. It was too easy for people to look away.

Then Ary Mossheart pulled him into the Underground, and suddenly Owl was no longer alone. And the feeling went away—not the sense that something was wrong, but the lonely feeling that something was terribly wrong and *no one would ever pay enough attention to fix it.* Ary had done that—she had paid attention. (A little late, if you asked him, but better late than never).

But now the feeling was back. And Ary hadn't shown up to school for three days.

"Owl," a sharp voice said. "Are you listening?"

The entire class stared at him. Owl's face turned bright red. "No. Um, I was just distracted. Sorry."

With a huff, Mrs. Grumthrush returned to her lesson. "As I was *saying*, Siltshore did not exist before our escape," she said, looking pointedly at Owl. "With a massive display of magic, Oleander bent the trees and crafted our home. The festival, in part, is to thank *him* for what he did for the people of Siltshore, and to ensure the oak tree we are nestled in can continue to thrive. For the showcase this year, you will re-create one of the Seedling myths about the different evil monsters Oleander vanquished. One from each kingdom—a weaver, a grazer, a crawler, a diver, a flyer . . ."

Owl's mind drifted again. There was so much to adapt to in this bright, strange world. It would have been easier if he'd been allowed to stay with Ary, but after Oleander addressed the fairies of Terra and sorted them into their new lives, she and her mom had been taken in by that Alder guy, and before Owl could even ask if they had room for him and Briar, too, a tiny old lady with weird glass circles on her face had stepped up to peer at Owl and Briar.

"I have room for these two." Her gaze had drifted to Shrimp and softened. "And that one, too, if you'd like."

Shrimp had sat up.

"I'm Willow. Willow Dragonsnap." Mrs. Dragonsnap had fished around in her pocket, retrieved a tiny loaf of bread studded with little chunks of nuts, and offered it to Shrimp. "It's been years since I've seen a pill bug, but there were whole pods of you back in my terrarium. I know you must be uneasy up in these trees—but if you wish to stay with your friends, something tells me you'd like my home."

Shrimp had gobbled down the bread, looked appealingly to Owl, and that settled it.

Owl liked living with Mrs. Dragonsnap, even if the walk to school took forever. And even if Briar was a pretty prickly roommate. But the distance meant he hadn't seen much of Ary or Sootflank lately, and Owl was starting to feel adrift.

He looked around the classroom again. This wasn't like her. Missing school was supposed to be *his* job.

"Briar," Owl whispered.

Briar jerked to look at him. She'd been staring down at her jar with a grim expression, as if her very life depended on mastering the spell. "What's up?"

"Where's Ary?"

Briar scowled. "Beats me. She better not be off doing something weird."

Owl winced. It seemed like the more Briar fit into her new life, the more critical of Ary she became. Owl had been meaning to talk to her about it, but he didn't know how. Also, he really didn't want to. Talking about feelings stuff was stressful.

But he couldn't blame Briar for being bothered by Ary's absence, either.

Where was she?

She couldn't be sick. They had left the mold behind in the terrarium—they were safe now. Memory flashed behind his eyes, of how empty his home had been after the mold had taken his parents. How quiet. Owl shook the thought away. Siltshore was safe; the mold was gone. For all he knew, Ary was off doing weird, secret hero things with Sootflank. The thought should have been comforting, but instead it made his stomach lurch.

If Ary really was off doing something more important than school, what did it say about their friendship that she hadn't bothered to include him?

"Owl?" Mrs. Grumthrush's voice cut in. "Sometime today?"

Owl started. Everyone was staring again. They'd all uncapped their jars, fingers lifted as they prepared to cast a spell. Shame burned through Owl's cheeks.

He could worry about Ary later. He needed to fit in here; to prove that he belonged.

Owl reached for his jar, fingers hesitating before the glass. When he looked up, Mrs. Grumthrush's bright eyes were zeroed in on him.

Focus, Owl told himself. *Just make something happen. Anything.*

Owl's fingers met the fairy dust—and the world changed.

He was still in Siltshore, still in the classroom, but everything was different. And he *felt* it—that pull he'd had back in Terra, the buzz in his bones and the itch in his skin, that desperation of power hidden in the earth, long ignored by winged folk until a wingless boy came along and was willing to reach for it.

And suddenly, in a wave, the whispers returned.

Reach.

Owl froze. He looked around carefully, but no one else had heard anything. Briar was glaring at her jar.

Owl glanced up. Everyone around him, even Briar, was focused on their task. Mrs. Grumthrush was kneeling beside Tulip, patiently explaining how to handle the fairy dust.

He needed to talk to Ary—but he needed to figure out why the feeling was back, too.

Owl slid out of his seat and, without a backward glance, he slipped out the door and left the school behind.

SEVENTEEN

Mrs. Dragonsnap's Bookcase

Owl followed the feeling down.

In Terra, most days, the whispers had been barely there. Now, as he slipped through Siltshore's sunlit world, they were returning to the rumble that had followed him through the Underground.

Reach, reach, reach.

Could this be why Ary hadn't come to school? Did it have something to do with the Gardener's magic that had sealed them away? Or was it something older, tied to the Seedlings themselves?

What he wouldn't have given for his parents to be here.

His mom had always said wingless were the keepers of history. She had loved puzzles and myths, had memorized them so effortlessly. Owl knew if she were here, she'd help him figure out what was going on with him.

You are nothing to be ashamed of, she always told him. *You are special. You are loved. And no one will ever change that.*

He couldn't remember her face anymore. Or his dad's. It had been so long since they died, and most days, when

Owl tried to picture his parents, he saw only a blur where their features should have been.

They'd been right, in the end. Their songs had been what freed them from the terrarium.

Their songs—and Ary.

They would have loved this world. They would have loved Ary, Sootflank, Shrimp, and even cranky Briar. They would have loved the grass, and the sun, and the fact that there were more fairies in this world who had also been saved by the Gardener.

Owl's parents would have loved all of it. And he would have given it all up in a heartbeat, just to see them again.

He was so preoccupied that he didn't realize the whispers had led him on a familiar route until he was nearly there.

They'd taken him home.

Mrs. Dragonsnap lived farther down the trunk than a lot of the other fairies, in a quiet, small home overlooking the moss farms on the shaded lower branches of Siltshore's tree. Owl found he preferred being lower to the ground, anyway. A pale red door glinted near Mrs. Dragonsnap's. It was the only other home carved this far down. Mrs. Dragonsnap had said someone named Peony used to live there, but she said it with an uneasy smile that suggested she didn't want to talk about it further, and Owl hadn't pushed.

Unlike some of the airy, window-filled houses in the upper branches, Mrs. Dragonsnap's reminded him of Terra.

"Hello?" Owl called.

No answer.

Owl crept inside.

Mrs. Dragonsnap's home was dimly lit, with small, cozy rooms illuminated by glow-shroom lamps. Roots and strange plants hung from the ceiling to dry, and strange glass vials cluttered the shelves. The moss carpet was soft and dry to touch, and there was no shortage of acorn loaves and dandelion cookies. Shrimp had immediately rolled into a ball in the corner beneath the glow-shroom lamps with such a delighted trill Owl's heart broke a little, and even Briar had seemed comforted by the cool, gentle darkness.

But what Owl had noticed first were the books.

There were dozens upon dozens of them, many battered and far older than him, placed neatly in shelves carved directly into oak-tree walls. Owl had always loved books. It had pained him in Terra when they stopped restoring them, the resources stretched too thin to dedicate fairy dust to something as frivolous as stories. Books were their own kind of magic. They were like tiny bundles of hope you could carry around with you, packed with adventure and joy and danger. Owl had always thought the best *and* worst thing about a great book was that it always ended. That had always been a strange comfort to Owl. He might not know how his own story would end, but he knew that no matter how frightening or wonderful a book got, it would come to a close. In a book, there was always at least a reason bad things happened.

In life, they just . . . happened.

But the strange thing about some of Mrs. Dragonsnap's books was that they were sealed away.

Reach, the whispers hummed.

They were coming from the bookcase . . . or something beyond it.

Owl's heart thumped. He checked the kitchen and crept down the hallway, just to be sure. Mrs. Dragonsnap had made it very clear he was *not* to touch the books. The last thing he needed was to have to explain the whole random-whispers thing.

Her room was empty. So was Briar's. At Briar's room, Owl hesitated, remembering how frustrated she seemed with Ary. The day Mrs. Dragonsnap had shown them their rooms—cozy, clean, if not a little small—Owl had been grateful, but Briar had frozen solid. When she noticed Owl staring, she'd swiped at her eyes and cleared her throat.

"I've never . . . had my own, um, bed before. Or my own room," Briar had mumbled. "It's weird."

Owl didn't know much about Briar's life in the Underground, but from what he understood, it'd been pretty bad—especially in the last few years, after her family died and it was just her, living as the Ant Queen's prisoner. He'd had it pretty rough back in Terra, but at least he'd had a *bed*.

If Ary had been there, she'd have known how to put Briar at ease. She was good at that—being kind when someone was scared or upset. Making you feel like you weren't crazy for having big feelings even in the face of tiny things.

Owl had never been good at that stuff. So instead he said, "Well, if you get lonely, you're not cuddling with me. I kick."

Briar had rolled her eyes and gave his shoulder a half-hearted punch, and Owl had considered that a win.

He had a feeling that if Ary wasn't already in the process of ruining Briar's newfound normal life, he was about to get a head start. He drifted back toward the bookcase, his heart pounding.

It could be nothing. He could be reading too much into things again.

But why else would the whispers lead him here?

And why would someone seal a bookcase away to begin with?

He extended his hand toward the glass.

"Owl?"

"Ahhh!" yelped Owl.

"Ahhh!" yelped Shrimp.

"Shrimp!" Owl breathed. "You scared me—wait, why are you yelling?"

"Habit?" The pill bug hunched in the darkened hallway, his beady eyes taking in the odd sight in front of him. His antennae quirked hopefully. "Ary?"

"Uh, she's not here," said Owl. "I wasn't feeling good, so I left school early."

"Oh," said Shrimp, clearly not believing him, but also not really caring. Man, he loved that bug.

Shrimp crawled forward with a gentle patter of his many legs on the worn wooden floor. He looked comically big in Mrs. Dragonsnap's home, but he seemed to like the cramped, shadowy space.

Shrimp looked from Owl to the bookcase, a question in his eyes.

Owl's face burned. "This is going to sound ridiculous, but I swear something in Siltshore keeps . . . calling me. Like it did back in the terrarium. Like it's almost . . . alive. It keeps telling me to reach."

Shrimp approached the strange glass bookcase. The pill bug whirred thoughtfully and then looked at Owl. "Closer?"

Owl blinked. "Okay, sure. I'm already hearing whispers from a cursed bookcase. I might as well get closer." He drifted forward to stand beside Shrimp—and then the feeling returned, tenfold.

Owl had the sense he was floating outside himself. He looked at Shrimp and then back at the bookcase again. The pill bug stared forward determinedly.

"Shrimp," whispered Owl, "what do you know that I don't?"

The folk always loved to make fun of the pill bugs. They thought their endless wandering was a sign of foolishness, that their refrain of *we follow* meant they were weak. But Shrimp, and the other roly-polys, had seen far more of the terrarium than Owl ever had. Shrimp had known where the Underlake was, and it was Shrimp who had guided them through the Underground.

Creatures don't have magic, every teacher back in Terra had said. But newts had fire, which was its own kind of magic.

Who was to say others didn't have something, too?

Reach, the air seemed to sing. *Reach*.

Owl touched the bookcase—and he reached.

It was like back in the terrarium, but different. That pull of magic was still there, lying dormant all around him, but this magic felt older. It woke with ease at his touch, as if it had spent this entire time waiting for someone like him. It was as if the very walls of Mrs. Dragonsnap's home breathed, *finally*.

Everything began to glow.

The walls jumped. The floors trembled. With a thud and a shiver, the still-sealed bookcase slid *backward*. Cold, dusty air whooshed forward. The hair on Owl's arms stood on end as he stared into the endless, yawning dark.

Owl stood in place, frozen, his head buzzing and his hand trembling. He was afraid of the dark. He'd never told anyone, but Ary had figured it out, back in the Underground. The only thing that had gotten him through it was that he wasn't alone.

Shrimp nudged the back of his legs, gently.

"Owl," whispered Shrimp. "Together."

Owl wanted to say no. He wanted to back down, go back to school, and forget everything. Whatever was going on with Ary was a bunch of hero stuff that was none of his business.

But something was not right here.

And Owl Diggs had always been a little too good at paying attention to a mystery.

"Together," agreed Owl. "We follow."

Though it wasn't possible for a pill bug to smile, Owl could have sworn Shrimp grinned. The roly-poly ducked his head and slid Owl onto his back. The strange feeling whirled around them; the sense that something was watching, waiting for them, beckoning them.

Together, they descended into the dark.

EIGHTEEN

Another Creepy, Vague Prophecy

It was cool inside the tunnel. Only a faint rectangle of light glowed behind them where the bookcase still sat open. Owl would have liked to close it, but what if it never opened again? Owl's breath came in pants. His hands started to sweat. What if this was just an endless journey into nothingness, and they never got out? What if this was a trick and they were going to die down here? What if—

"Owl," whirred Shrimp. "Okay?"

Owl shook himself. "Yeah, Shrimp. I'm okay. Sorry. I, um, I might be a little afraid of the dark."

"No worries," whispered Shrimp, patting Owl's head affectionately with an antenna. "Shrimp's here."

The temperature dropped several degrees as Shrimp crawled; the sounds of the village faded away. There was only darkness, and the endless, spiraling tree trunk. Owl brushed his hands along the walls and was surprised to find them textured and rough, instead of the smooth rings of a tree. He wasn't certain how long they'd been down there—a minute or an hour—when Shrimp squeaked.

Ahead of them, pulsing faintly in the dark, was the gentle blue of glow-shrooms.

They hurried forward.

Owl touched the door, and it swung open.

It was a library.

Owl blinked. He wasn't certain what he had expected to find when they uncovered a tunnel behind Mrs. Dragonsnap's bookcase—a massive cavern, maybe? A path into the wilds?

But this felt a little . . . underwhelming?

Hundreds of old books were crammed into shelves that had been carved directly into the tree trunk. Glow-shroom lamps flickered overhead, lighting the room in gentle pastel blue, green, and pink hues. Owl stepped into the room, his heart thudding. That feeling was still there—the press of power, the urgency to reach—but it was far fainter now.

As if he and Shrimp had made a wrong turn somewhere.

A single desk occupied the center of the tiny study, covered in papers. Owl approached it and picked up the nearest book.

A History of Seedlings, it read. He flipped it open and froze. The very first image was a diagram of Siltshore.

But that wasn't right. Hadn't Mrs. Grumthrush said Oleander had founded their city? She hadn't made any mention of Seedlings at all, and this book and the map within it definitely seemed older than Oleander was.

Owl set the book down and began to thumb through the sheafs of paper. Most of them were weird sketches, or records of the seasons. One was just a list of dozens of names, going back years. His eyes skimmed to the newest page. Something strange was happening there. The first three names were written in a precise, neat hand like the earlier ones: *Dune, Bramble, Peony.* But the most recent three were written sloppily, as if in a panic, or by a child.

Marigold, Thistle, Mugwort.

"Owl," whispered Shrimp, nudging him. "Up."

Owl turned and, following Shrimp's gaze, craned his neck.

His heart sank.

"Oh, come on," groaned Owl. *"Again?"*

After a lifetime in Terra, he had grown used to the way the Seedlings loved to leave their cryptic warnings and messages scattered through his world. He'd hoped the Gardener's Warning carved in the bottom of the Underlake had been a weird fluke. But directly above him, etched so large that it occupied the entire ceiling of the library, was a new poem. Or pieces of one. Someone had been here long before Owl, and they had taken it upon themselves to try to destroy the final lines.

So much for Siltshore being normal.

Keep the balance,
Mind the wood,

And bid the green light grow.
Folk to summon,
Flyers to anchor,
And Divers to help it flow.
Beware the lies of Ghostwings freed
In hem the rot   mains
Seek he art within the reeds
F r the Bli ht shall rise again!

"Great. Another creepy, vague prophecy." Owl threw his hands up. "Why can't these people ever leave clear instructions? Like, *Dear person in the future, please do exactly this or your world will end, best wishes, your weird ancestors*. Is that so hard? I'm getting sick of these wannabe poets."

Shrimp whirred sympathetically. "Annoying."

"You're telling me." Owl glared at the words, careful to keep his voice casual so he didn't scare Shrimp. His stomach turned. Folk, flyer, and diver—Owl supposed he could be the folk, and a fairy with wings might be the flyer. But what did it mean by summoning, anchoring, and flowing?

Plus that last bit . . .

"A Ghostwing," whispered Owl. "That's what they called Ary."

And Oleander.

Owl's heart began to pound. If he was reading this right, being a Ghostwing might be a bad thing—a really bad thing. Was Ary in trouble?

"I knew something was weird about this place," Owl said darkly. He looked at the papers scattered across the table—mostly just a bunch of haphazard notes, but his eyes snagged on that list of names again.

Behind Owl, something creaked.

Owl whirled around. His heart pounded, and his hair stood on end. The press of that strange magic was all around him, but it didn't feel frantic like it had before.

"Hello?" called Owl. "Is someone there?"

"How did you get in here?" someone demanded from behind one of the stacks.

Owl locked eyes with Shrimp and gestured toward the bookcase. The pill bug twitched his antennae in understanding and scuttled forward, silent despite his size.

"It called me." Owl took an exaggerated step forward and thumped his foot on the floor as hard as he could.

"Don't come any closer!" the person behind the bookshelf squeaked.

He *knew* that voice.

"Okay, I'm not moving." Owl held his hands up. "But I need some answers. Because this place is freaking me out. What's with the poem on the ceiling? And the list of names?"

Ahead of him, Shrimp was only a bug-length away from the bookcase.

"You weren't supposed to find that," the person said, and as if to themselves, added, "You were never supposed to arrive. But *she* had to show up and ruin everything."

Owl had a feeling he knew who *she* was. "What's Ary done wrong?"

Silence.

"Ary's a good person," Owl prompted. "She saved all of us. It never should have been her job, but she did it. She's a hero."

"He started out as a hero, too," the person said bitterly. "It's not about what she's done. It's about what she *is*. And we're all going to pay the price."

Well, this sounded optimistic and totally great and like it wasn't about to cause Owl a ton of trouble at *all*.

Shrimp reached the bookcase. He looked back at Owl, and Owl held up a hand for him to wait.

"If you tell me what's going on, I can help you," said Owl gently. "And even if you don't want to believe me, Ary would help, too. If fairies are getting hurt, she'd want to stop it."

"It doesn't matter what she wants," the voice whispered. "Please, just leave. I don't even know how you got in here. But just—go back the way you came."

Owl hesitated. How had Ary felt the night before she fled for the Underlake or when she'd made her deal with Sootflank? Or later, with Chives, with Briar, and so many times after, when she had faced danger and uncertainty and plunged ahead anyways, not knowing what would happen to her, but knowing that *someone* had to try?

It had been so easy for him to tag along. To assume she would always say yes, that she would do the hard, right thing, and chase danger toward its uncertain end.

But now, standing in the library, a part of him hesitated.

This was his chance to turn around.

Something bad was obviously happening in Siltshore. Something that would make his life harder and put him in danger. And for the first time, Owl understood why Wren Mossheart glared at everyone from the parade line during that bad, awful year when so many had died.

Because it was easy to watch someone be brave and say *Well, I could do that, too.*

It was another thing to actually do it.

"Leave," the voice begged.

And honestly? A part of him wanted to. He wasn't a hero. He wasn't trained for this.

But Ary hadn't been, either. And sure, maybe Owl had told himself it was in her blood, that it came naturally to her, but he had *seen* how scared she'd been in the Underground. He'd watched her waffle, and backtrack, and make mistakes. Ary Mossheart had been terrified—and she'd plunged toward the truth anyway.

So Owl gathered the last scraps of his courage and said, "Get 'em, Shrimp."

Shrimp lunged. With a squeak, he tackled the bookshelf. The glow-shrooms flickered ominously; books went flying in every direction. There was a cry, and a thump, and the patter of feet trying to run—but Owl was already moving, sprinting toward the other end of toppled stacks. He flew around the corner, heart pounding, as Shrimp came from the other direction.

"Aghhh!" cried the voice. "Not you again! Get away from me!"

Of course. That was where he knew the voice from! The person who had been mean to Shrimp before—who had seemed almost afraid of him.

"Hi," whirred Shrimp.

"Don't eat me," the voice begged.

"What?" said Shrimp, clearly insulted. "Gross."

Owl turned the corner. "I *knew* it was you."

Sumac, Oleander's grandson, whirled to gawk at him, his expression quickly shifting to one of absolute thunder. "Oh, great. As if my day couldn't get any worse."

NINETEEN

Sumac's Secret

Of all the people Owl would have been thrilled to discover lurking in a secret library filled with cryptic secrets—and there were, surprisingly, a decent few—it was safe to say Sumac wouldn't have made the list.

"Um," said Owl. In a fit of awkwardness and desperately wanting to do something with his hands, he put one hand on his hip, and used the other to give Sumac a slow-motion salute. "Fancy meeting you here."

Sumac stared at him. "What . . . was that?"

"I don't know!" Owl threw his arms up. "I didn't know what to do with my hands! What am I supposed to say?!"

"Maybe something normal," Sumac shot back. "Like, *What is this place* or *What are you doing here* or *What's that weird, cryptic prophecy on the ceiling?*"

"Oh, good point." Owl licked his lips. "Hey, Sumac. What is this place, what are you doing here, and what's with the creepy prophecy on the ceiling?"

"I called it weird and cryptic, not creepy."

"I know. I changed that for dramatic effect."

Sumac groaned. Instead of answering Owl, he approached one of the still-standing bookcases and sat cross-legged in front of it, his face carefully blank. With great care, Sumac leaned forward and, very gently, began to hit his forehead on the bookcase, his words aligned with each precise bonk. "We. Are. So. Screwed."

"Hey." Owl grabbed his shoulder and pulled Sumac back as he was winding up for another bonk. "You're going to hurt yourself."

Sumac groaned and kept his forehead against the bookcase. An awkward silence stretched between them and finally he muttered, "Why are you here?"

"I think the library was . . . calling me? I'm not really sure. Why are *you* here? And what is *here*? And, seriously, what's with the prophecy? Because I'm about to start freaking out."

Sumac snorted, which Owl took as a win, but didn't remove his forehead from the bookcase. In a voice barely above a whisper, Sumac said, "You'll think I'm nuts."

All of Owl's humor faded. "Try me," he said quietly.

Sumac leaned back. There was a kind of hopeless light in his eyes that struck a familiar, painful chord in Owl. It was the look of someone who had tried everything, and had no one to talk to, and was so used to getting laughed at that they didn't want to bother anymore.

Sumac hesitated, scanning Owl's expression as if he was

looking for any kind of doubt, and then the words spilled out. "Something is wrong with this place. It's been wrong for a long time. I don't know what it is. But I think my mom was looking into it before she disappeared. I think . . ." Sumac gulped. "I think that's *why* she disappeared. Because she learned something she shouldn't have."

Chills crept over Owl. Here, in the cool shadow of the library, he could have been back in the terrarium. How often had his parents said those same words? How many times had Owl whispered them in the mirror, practicing for the day he finally got Wren Mossheart's attention, convinced if he could just make her listen, everything would be okay?

Owl pointed to the ceiling. "And you think that's the key?"

"I don't know," Sumac admitted. "Mom had gotten so panicky, always telling me to stay close, forbidding me from going near the woods or near my grandfather. Making me promise to remember the myths about the Keepers, for all the good that would do. One night she woke me up in the middle of the night and led me here, and she told me to trust no one. Then she disappeared. That was a year ago." He closed his eyes. "Her name was Marigold."

Owl recalled the list of names; the confident, neat handwriting that had suddenly shifted to an awkward panic.

"No one who disappears ever comes back." Sumac craned his neck to stare at the ceiling, a look of hopelessness on his face. "I thought I would have figured something out by now, but two more fairies went missing, and I'm just as lost as before. And I can't tell anyone, because I think . . . I think someone knew my mom was trying to figure this out, and they got rid of her."

Horror crept over Owl. If what Sumac was saying was true, they were in danger—and not just the danger of the terrarium, of a sickened world creeping in. Fairies were *missing.* This wasn't just magic gone awry, or a failed hero pushing the problem to the next generation.

Siltshore had a murderer among them. Someone who was picking off fairies one by one.

"Did your mom leave any clues about the cryptic ceiling warning?" Owl asked, careful to keep his voice light. What was the benefit of getting rid of fairies? And where were they even going?

"I don't know," Sumac said miserably. He pointed to a bookcase near them that was strangely empty. "She had all these notebooks and old books here. When she vanished, I came back, and they were gone."

Well, this was going from weird to downright eerie.

"Maybe we should tell someone," Owl said gently.

"No," Sumac said vehemently. "Whoever is getting rid of people got rid of my mom. We can't trust anyone."

It was a sobering thought. It felt like something too big for two kids to handle. But what were they supposed to do, when there was no one they could trust?

"We could tell Sootflank," said Owl. "And Ary—"

"Not her," Sumac said. He looked . . . terrified. "No, something is going on with her. And if she's in league with the newt, you can't tell them, either. Anyone close to my grandfather can't be trusted."

A chill crept over Owl. He had seen the way Sumac had glared at Ary, and he'd assumed it had been out of some weird jealousy of the girl who had appeared from nothing with wings that matched Oleander's own.

But the line in that cryptic message . . .

Something told Owl there was no way Sumac would trust him if he knew Ary was involved. Hero or not, she was a Ghostwing like Oleander, whatever that even meant. And it was clear Sumac had no love for his grandfather.

Maybe it was for a good reason.

"How about this?" Owl compromised. "We've got two weeks until the festival. If we haven't figured anything out by then, I'll bring in someone I trust. Until then, I'll come here every day, and I'll help you try to figure out whatever the heck is going on."

Sumac narrowed his eyes. "Why are you helping me?"

"I solved one world-ending prophecy." Owl shrugged. "How much harder could a second one be? Also, I don't want to like, die, and if that weird ceiling message is any indicator, it's not going to go well for any of us if we don't get this figured out."

"Yeah," Sumac said miserably. "Plus, this time, it's not

like there's a new world to escape to if this one gets screwed up."

The reality of his words filled the air. There would be no second chances here. No screwups.

It was, once again, up to a pair of underprepared kids.

Owl was really starting to understand why Wren Mossheart had been so cranky about the whole hero thing.

"Okay," Sumac breathed. He spat in his hand and held it out to Owl. "Until the festival."

"Um," said Owl, "I really don't want to touch your spit."

Sumac glared at him.

"Okay, fine," mumbled Owl. "This is how plagues happen, though. I'm just saying."

Reluctantly, Owl spit in his own hand and clapped his palm to Sumac's, suppressing a shudder. He was going to wash his hands until they hurt later. Since when was a good old pinkie promise not enough?

"Until the festival," said Sumac. "We try to find out who is getting rid of folk, and why."

"Until the festival," echoed Owl. "I promise."

TWENTY

Lesson Number One

It wasn't long before an unfortunate and undeniable truth emerged—the Siltshore fairies and the folk of Terra were terribly different.

As summer began the slow, lazy wind toward fall, the illusion that two villages of fairies could seamlessly knit themselves together as one frayed. It seemed every day some new, terrifying thing was unveiled for the Terrans that the folk of Siltshore had long taken for granted. It was charming the first week, and understandable the second. But as one month rolled into two, and the Terrans still struggled to adjust to their strange new world, the fairies of Siltshore found their patience thinning.

They began to roll their eyes and sneer at Terran folk who wobbled with fear on high branches or flinched at sudden gusts of wind. One day, when they were all working, the sky began to darken, and a breeze stirred up. A distant boom sounded—and then water began to fall from the sky. The folk of Terra bolted in panic, fearing that the world itself might collapse. The Siltshore fairies hadn't even blinked, laughing as drops of water fell on their heads and soaked them to the bone, adults calmly grabbing pails to collect the water while their children splashed in the puddles gathering in the crooks of the oak branches. The fairies of Siltshore saw the Terrans cowering beneath the trees, rolled their eyes, and grumbled at them to get back to work.

In turn, the folk of Terra began to complain about the Siltshore fairies. They complained that they ate better than the Terrans, that they were rude and stingy with clothes and supplies. There were more grumbles every day about leaving and starting their own village—but it seemed no one could ever agree on where they would go, or how they would survive.

Every time they looked to Nightingale, the former mayor informed them with tired eyes that they were not ready. Ary had almost begun to feel bad for her. She was completely at Siltshore's mercy but was still expected to answer to the Terrans, and blamed when the only solution she could offer them was to hang on a little longer.

Maybe it was just Ary's imagination, but sometimes it felt like the fairies of Terra blamed *her.* It was usually the older fairies who glowered at her as they worked, and not for the first time, Ary wondered if more people than Gran had known the truth and had just been content to die with the secret anyway.

No matter. They were here, now. They were safe. And Ary would keep it that way.

"We lost this section of the forest last spring," Oleander

was saying, his eyes tired. "I don't know if the festival will be enough to recover it."

They sat in Oleander's private office, high up in Siltshore's boughs. Golden light streamed through an open window. Ever since Oleander had found Ary in the wood, she had shadowed him as he went about his business—solving petty complaints, surveying the crop harvests, and giving comments on preparation for the festival. It was very involved, if not a little boring. She missed Owl and Briar more than she'd expected. But if they missed her, they didn't show it. She hadn't heard from them at all.

But today, when Ary set out toward the bakery where Oleander met her every morning, the old fairy surprised her.

"No chore tours today," he said. "Follow me."

With no explanation, Oleander turned, and led Ary up through the trees.

They ascended for what seemed like ages. They passed the school, and the platform for the Festival of the Gardener, and the acorn thickets. The homes thinned, and then vanished altogether. Soon, it was only Ary and Oleander, climbing rickety ladders and too-thin vine bridges. This high up, time seemed to stop; all of Siltshore sprawled below Ary in a massive, interconnected web. The vine bridge swayed, and Ary flinched.

Briar would have loved it up here. But Briar could fly.

For Ary, climbing higher just meant she had a longer fall.

"You get used to it," Oleander said with a sympathetic

lift of his eyebrow. He gestured to a simple wooden door.

Ary hesitated, and then she followed Oleander inside.

A small, cozy room stretched in front of her. Golden light filtered in through the window; a single desk and two chairs were tucked in the corner. Maps covered the walls. It was a surprisingly simple space for someone who was the leader of an entire city, a far cry from the mansion that Mayor Nightingale had lived in. Ary drifted around the room. Her eyes went to a small, pale vase. It was pretty and smooth, molded from some kind of opaque glass, with a lid in the shape of a flower. Ary reached out to touch it.

"Please don't," Oleander said tightly. "It's quite precious."

Ary's cheeks heated. "Sorry."

Oleander gestured for Ary to sit. "I know it's not much. It was built to be a guard post—so that a fairy is always up here, with an eye on the city below, and an eye on the sky. Luckily, Siltshore has never needed to fear invaders. After about a decade of realizing most of the guards we sent up here spent the time napping, I took the space over myself." His smile dimmed as he looked at the maps. "The privacy became an unfortunate necessity."

Ary's eyes drifted to the map. A chill swept over her.

It was a map of the Blight.

It took up the entire wall; dozens of painstakingly hand-drawn maps taped together to form one massive image of the devastation slowly creeping across the land. A fairy's-eye view of the wood loomed before her, broken into five different domains based on the creatures that ruled it—divers controlling the swamp to the east, flyers controlling the towering cedar trees to the west, the weavers in the center of the wood, the grazers guarding the grassy meadows to the far north, and of course the folk of Siltshore to the south. Black rings across the map showed where Oleander had found the Blight.

The entire northern section of the map was one dark ring.

"What happened there?" Ary asked uneasily, pointing to the territory where the grazers had their domain. "What lives there?"

"Lived," Oleander corrected softly. He shook his head. "No one knows. The north was the first to go—their Keeper was a fearsome creature called a stag, and they had always been the strongest of the domains. But they were also the first to fall. Many of the warm-blooded creatures that lived there have moved into the divers' or flyers' domains, but even those have started to suffer."

Ary shuddered, peering closer. There were other, smaller rings—dozens in the weavers' domains, and a few cropping up along the diver and flyer borders where they touched the weavers'. Only the folk domain was nearly untouched. Just a single dark ring, indicating the Blight Ary had discovered.

Had the Blight started in the north, then? Or was that just where the land was weakest? And if the divers, weavers, and flyers were all suffering—why hadn't Siltshore heard from them?

"And the festival will help?" Ary asked hopefully.

Oleander kept his gaze on the map, his expression pensive. How many rings had been added in recent years? How many more would, if Ary wasn't strong enough to help him fix this?

It was no wonder he took the festival so seriously. With the Blight getting worse, and a whole new village of fairies to care for, there was a lot riding on this going right. Her mind slipped, of all things, to the nightmares about the hollow. What if *that* was why she was having them? Because the wood itself was calling out, asking her to help?

What if Oleander had had them, too?

She ought to ask him. But when Ary opened her mouth, something else slipped out.

"Who died," she asked before she could stop herself, "to free your terrarium?"

Oleander looked at her, stricken. Horror crashed through Ary.

"I'm sorry," she blurted. "I don't know why—I should have never—that was so rude of me." She buried her face in her hands. "I'm sorry."

Oleander said nothing. Panic mounting, Ary scrambled to explain.

"Ours was my gran." Why was she telling him this? She didn't know, but suddenly she couldn't stop. The trees seemed to lean in to listen. "She was my world's last real hero. But she kept the secret of the terrarium and never told anyone—and it was on me to fix it. In the end, she helped me cast the spell. And now she's gone."

"A life most loved," Oleander said softly, his eyes holding a depth of grief Ary had thought no one else could ever understand. "Freely given."

It was as if he'd struck her. Ary swayed where she stood, every part of her aching. She had not heard those words since—well, since that day in the terrarium, when Atlas had towered over her, and Wren Mossheart had stepped forward to keep the Mossheart's promise at long last.

Ary hugged her arms around herself, her grief an aching, swelling thing growing bigger by the moment. And with it, that familiar anger that Gran had left Ary behind yet again.

An awkward silence filled Oleander's office. Shame burned in Ary's cheeks. She'd really done it now. She finally had a purpose here and she'd messed it all up because she couldn't keep her mouth shut about Gran.

How did everything always come back to Gran?

"It was my brother," Oleander said finally. Pain clouded his face. "His name was Hemlock."

A chill crept into the room. Ary held carefully still, giving Oleander the space to keep talking. Praying he would.

Oleander gave Ary a rueful smile. "This is where I make a confession, young Mossheart. It was never supposed to be me who escaped the terrarium. Hemlock was the golden hero. He received the training, the accolades, the support. We expected him to free us. When he asked myself and our friend Aspen to follow him, it was an honor—a chance to share in his golden light." His smile dimmed. "Then we reached Titan. And I learned, in the worst way possible, just how much my brother loved me."

Ary could hardly breathe. She could see it—two boys and their friend, wandering into a cavern so like her own, meeting another Atlas in a different life, and learning, just as she had, what it meant to give up a life most loved. The horror Oleander and his friend must have felt. It was one thing for Gran to sacrifice herself. At least she had been older; at least she had lived, and she had entered the Underground planning to give her life to spare Ary's.

But Oleander had been surprised. He'd gone in expecting to watch his brother become a hero. Somehow, he'd lost him instead.

"Hemlock never told us someone had to die," Oleander continued. "I realize, now, that's why he invited Aspen and me. He loved us both so dearly, I think he realized that if one of us couldn't complete the spell, the other would." He closed his eyes. "I am still so angry at him."

The world threatened to tilt out under Ary. Her eyes burned with the threat of tears. She was scared to believe what she was hearing—but, oh, how she wanted to.

"What happened to Aspen?"

Oleander flinched. "Who?"

"Aspen," said Ary. "The friend that went with you. What happened to her?" She didn't think she'd met an Aspen. She would have remembered.

Oleander blinked quickly, as if waking from a long dream, and then waved his hand. "She, ah, fell ill shortly after we escaped. It was a terrible shame." His tone suggested he didn't want to talk about it further.

Ary understood that. After everything she had suffered and lost, Oleander was *like her.* Not just in theory, not just from the wings on his back. But he carried the same scars as her, too.

He understood her. And with him, maybe she'd be safe.

Maybe Oleander could give her what Gran never could.

Wasn't this all she had ever wanted? Wasn't this what *Gran* would have wanted for her? Gran had been so miserable not only because of what she'd endured, but because she'd been alone. No one had understood; even the ones who'd tried couldn't bridge the gap between empathy and knowing what Gran had seen in the Underground.

But with Oleander, Ary wouldn't have to explain. He would just know.

Silence filled the office. Ary tried to think of something, anything, to say, to tell Oleander just how much she understood. But what would that change for him, really? His brother was long dead. He had a city to protect and a Blight to manage.

The best thing she could do for Oleander was be ready

to fill his shoes. She couldn't help him at the festival, and she couldn't fix the Blight. Not yet. But if trouble was coming, and Oleander would need her—well, she wanted to be ready.

She carried the thought long after she left Oleander's office. The Blight loomed in her mind, like a terrible stain, and Ary's feet knew where to take her before her mind did.

When she stepped through the storeroom door this time, it wasn't anxiety that burned through her. It was determination.

"Little Mossheart?" Sootflank asked, raising his head. "What is it?"

Ary met his eyes. "You were right. Something bad is coming." She took a step forward. "I was defenseless in the Underground, and again, when the spider attacked us. I'm tired of letting other people protect me."

Sootflank inclined his head to the side. "What are you saying?"

"I want you to train me," said Ary. "The next time a fight comes—I want to be able to fight back."

Sootflank watched her carefully. In the silence that followed, Ary's heart beat harder. He could tell her no. He could tell her she was just a kid, that she needed to move on, that this wasn't her place.

But instead, reluctantly, Sootflank nodded.

"Very well," he said. "We can start now."

"What? I'm not ready, I was just asking—"

Sootflank's tail lashed at her ankles, and Ary went sprawling. By the time she picked herself up, Sootflank had curled back into a ball.

"Lesson number one," yawned Sootflank. "Your enemies won't wait until you're ready. Now get up, Mossheart. And show me what you've got."

TWENTY-ONE

Someone Better

As the folk of Terra acclimated to their new life, Siltshore prepared for a party.

Okay, technically it was a *celebration of our reverent appreciation for the generosity of the Gardener and all the miracles She's performed*—but as far as Owl could tell, it was still a party.

On the main platform in the village's heart, a massive stage was being constructed, and workers set out dozens of tiny wooden chairs. One paused as Owl passed, scratching his head.

"I swear I put more chairs out yesterday!" he told his companion. "They keep disappearing!"

"Right," the other fairy responded. "What'd they do, get up and fly away?"

"How should I know? Rosemary was supposed to handle chairs, but no one knows where she's been."

Owl shuddered. Briar cast him a suspicious sideways glance. They were on their way to school, although Owl hadn't actually attended class in days. When Oakview loomed ahead, Briar turned to Owl and folded her arms.

"Okay," she said shortly. "What's going on?"

Owl blinked, distracted. "What do you mean?"

"You. Ary. *This*. Neither of you have been coming to school." Her eyes narrowed. "What are you two up to?"

Owl hunched his shoulders up defensively. "I have no idea what Ary's doing, or why she isn't in school."

That, at least, was the truth. He'd barely seen Ary. And though he didn't want to admit it, it stung. Owl had thought—well, he and Ary were friends now, right? Owl wasn't foolish. He knew that the relationship between him and Ary had always been unbalanced. But he'd thought the Underground had changed that.

Maybe he was wrong.

"You guys better not be doing something weird," said Briar. Briar shoved her hands into her pockets, refusing to meet his eye. "I like it here. The last thing we need is to get kicked out."

Owl looked at her, surprised. "Briar . . ."

"I know school isn't that big a deal to you or Ary," Briar continued. "But I never got to go, okay? I don't think you guys realize how good you had it. Even the worst of Terra was better than the Underground. And I'm *good* at school. I'm making friends. When you and Ary skip class, it's not just you who looks bad."

Guilt squeezed Owl. He hadn't thought about how everything might impact Briar.

If he was being honest, he hadn't thought about Briar at all.

"School means a lot to me, too," Owl said finally, his voice quiet. "I didn't really get to go in Terra, either. Once my parents died, I was kind of on my own. It's hard to sit in a classroom and memorize facts about plants when you're too hungry to focus." He hesitated. "I think it was the same for Ary, you know. I doubt either of us would skip, if it wasn't for a good reason."

The first time he'd stayed home had been a one-off. But then his parents had died, and the teasing insults of the other kids had felt like salt in the wound, and before he knew it, Owl's school clothes were gathering dust. He'd already been working the mushroom fields for a year before Ary Mossheart showed up, looking bedraggled, thin, and exhausted. She had been so weak in the beginning, and so slow, and it wasn't long before Owl started sneaking some of his ration tokens into her payment bag at their shift's end. After all, he was only working to feed one mouth; she was working to feed three.

He didn't know if Ary had ever found out about that. It didn't matter. If Owl was being honest, he hadn't just done it to be nice. He had done it hoping for a visit from Wren Mossheart.

Briar watched him with dark eyes. "So what's your reason? What's hers?"

Owl hesitated. Sumac had made him promise to keep the Keepers a secret . . . but would it be so bad, to let Briar in on what they were doing? Hadn't it *just* hurt his feelings to realize Ary was also up to something and hadn't involved him?

Owl swallowed.

"Briar," he said. "I don't think Siltshore is safe."

Briar took a step back, shaking her head in quick, panicked movements. She held up her hands. "No. *No.* Don't even start. We *just got here.*" A note of desperation crept into her voice. Her hands balled into fists. "We have food. A community. Why can't you and Ary ever leave well enough alone?"

"It's not me and Ary," Owl said, irritated. "I haven't even *talked* to Ary."

"Right."

"I mean it!" Owl said. "I have no idea where she's been, or what she's been doing. I don't even . . . what?"

Briar had the funniest look on her face. She stared at something behind Owl, her mouth twisted into a bitter frown.

Oleander, the leader of Siltshore, walked along a vine bridge not too far from him. Owl had seen little of him—something about the man made him uneasy. Oleander walked at an even pace, chatting with workers, checking on festival preparations.

At his side, trailing him like a tiny shadow, was Ary.

As Owl watched, Oleander bent down and whispered something to her. She nodded quickly, her expression tight, but her posture relaxed. It was clear they were used to being around each other.

Owl's heart did a painful squeeze.

Why hadn't Ary told Owl she was skipping school to, what, shadow the leader of Siltshore?

Why hadn't she bothered to talk to him at all?

Ary spotted Owl and Briar and froze midstep. Oleander kept walking, oblivious. Ary stared at Owl and Briar, guilt bright in her eyes. She looked tired. Dark circles ringed her eyes, and she was paler than usual, her cheekbones more pronounced. All the fairies of Terra had started to gain weight now that they had access to food, but Ary almost seemed to be shrinking.

"She looks terrible," Briar said flatly. "Like she hasn't slept in weeks."

Come say hi, Owl willed. *Tell us what you're doing. Tell us anything at all.*

Ary gave herself a little shake, tore her eyes away from them, and hurried after Oleander, her head low.

"I guess Ary's found someone better to spend her time with," said Briar.

Owl winced, trying to ignore the way his own heart was aching. "Briar—"

She held up her hands. "I don't want to hear it, Owl. I don't know what you guys are up to—but I don't want to be a part of it, okay? I like my life here. I'm *happy*." She scowled at him. "And if you can't be happy here, you can at least not ruin it for me."

Owl had never felt so alone.

"By the way," Briar said flatly, "you better come up with an excuse for why you're skipping class. I can only cover for you by telling Mrs. Grumthrush you're sick for so long."

She left before Owl could say anything, leaving him alone on the bridge. The school loomed before him. Owl had no desire to follow Briar—but she had a point. Him *and* Ary skipping class was too suspicious. And it wasn't like he and Sumac had made a lot of progress, anyway.

But it seemed he didn't belong with Ary, either.

TWENTY-TWO

Ghosts

Ary dreamed of the hollow every night.

It always started the same—she was alone in the cool darkness, and she was looking for someone. Someone who was afraid. Someone who needed her.

Sometimes, the hollow led her to Siltshore. Sometimes, it took her to a place she'd never been.

But this time, Ary dreamed of the Gardener's cottage.

She stood on the windowsill—but instead of looking out at the forest around her, Ary was looking in. And the cottage had changed: gone was the dust that had covered the table and blanketed the walls, the leaves that had cluttered in corners and the shattered holes in the window glass.

Bitter poison lingered in the air. Gleaming on the table, half-built, were three terrariums.

Ary's heart stuttered.

They were open at the top; three massive spheres of shining glass, carefully layered with soil, moss, and stone. Mushrooms, little bundles of plants, and bowls of soil lined the table. Her eyes blurred.

Here it was—the beginning of her world, before the days of mold, before the first fairy had set foot in Terra, before her ancestors smoothed away the ugly edges of history. Ary inched closer and felt a strange tug. Her feet lifted from the ground. She whirled, and the world ground to a halt.

She had *wings.*

Not a papery bundle, not the ghostly skeleton she'd carried since shattering the terrarium—real, full wings that caught the air with ease and held her aloft with little to no effort. Ary leaned forward, and her wings responded, carrying her toward the half-built terrariums on the table. She descended, relishing the control, the *freedom.* A kind of bittersweet sorrow washed through her. Ary didn't regret breaking the spell on her terrarium. If her wings were the price to pay, she'd have done it twice over to reach the world beyond.

But sometimes, she wished someone else could have paid it, instead.

A crackle came to her right.

Ary spun. Something darted away. In its wake, sheaves of bark paper fluttered to the ground.

"Hello?"

White flashed ahead. It wasn't possible. It couldn't be *her,* not in this time, in this life. But it shouldn't have been possible for Ary to be here, either.

Ary turned back to her reflection—and froze.

A different girl stared back at her.

She was young, like Ary, with a pinched, tired face, and pale hair that floated just below her chin. Despair lit up her eyes, and she pressed her fingers against the inside of the terrarium glass, saying something over and over again. But it was her wings that struck Ary. Ghostly and iridescent, twitching with every movement but catching no breeze.

Her wings matched Ary's.

The girl drummed her fists on the inside of the glass. Ary realized, finally, what she was saying. Just two phrases, over and over again.

Help me, she cried. *Free me. Find me in the wood.*

"I don't know how," Ary whispered. "Is this real? Who are you? What's your name? I don't—I don't know how to help you. I don't know how to find you!"

Despair carved the girl's face.

"I'm the thief," she said miserably. "And he was the liar."

"What?" Ary demanded. "What did you say? What does that mean?"

The girl didn't answer. Her gaze was locked on something behind Ary.

Dread burned through every part of Ary. She had a feeling she knew what it was.

Ary turned just as the spider bit down.

Ary couldn't remember the last time she'd slept normally.

The nightmares kept getting worse. Every night, she saw the girl. And every night, the girl begged for Ary to find her, but before Ary could question her, the spider killed her. Ary's days became a dull fog. It was getting harder to remember things. As the festival loomed closer, so too did her dread about the Blight and what it meant for everyone she loved. Every shadow felt like a monster; every little noise made her jump. She was constantly on edge, and always second-guessing herself. She needed to talk to someone. Anyone.

I'm the thief, and he was the liar.

The girl had not said those words again, but they haunted Ary all the same. Before, it had been easy to write off the dreams as the product of a scared mind. But those words . . . the way she'd said them . . .

What if she was real? What if she was out there, somewhere? Waiting for Ary to find her?

After Ary's awkward encounter with Owl and Briar the other day, she wasn't sure how to bring it up to them. She worried that if she told Sootflank, he might take action immediately and get himself hurt.

But there was one person she should have told a long time ago.

"Mama?"

Dust motes twisted in a sunbeam, filtering in through the cracked door. Ary looked around with a frown. Mama had been placed in a morning and evening work group, spending her time weaving cloth and making great loaves of acorn bread—midday, she'd told Ary, was typically when she was home.

So where was she?

Ary peeked into their shared bedroom. Something caught her eye—a package wrapped in cloth under the bed, tucked against the far wall. Ary lay flat and wriggled under, pulling it free. It was light, and the shape of it familiar.

Ary opened it.

A Seedling shovel clattered to the ground.

It wasn't one of the shovels she had carried in the Underground, but it could have been, winking dully in the late-morning light. Ary tested its weight in her hands, memory rushing through her. It seemed like only yesterday that she had plunged into the Gloom beyond Terra to save Mama, and ended their world instead.

What was the shovel doing here?

It was strange to hold this relic of her past, even as everything had changed. She hardly saw Owl or Briar anymore, and even Sootflank seemed to be keeping secrets from her. He disappeared every night, and when Ary asked where he was going, he'd just give her a look that said *not yet* and change the subject.

Ary clutched the shovel. She ought to put it back. Pretend she never saw it and carry on as normal. Maybe this was a sign she should keep her promise to Oleander and not meddle further.

Or maybe it was the opposite.

Ary hesitated—and a laugh split the air, ringing clear as a bell, followed by footsteps. Before she could think twice, Ary slid fully under the bed, the Seedling shovel clutched to her chest.

Footsteps thudded toward her.

"Thank you for all your help, truly," Mama said, her voice soft.

"Of course," said Alder. "I still can't believe what you two endured—it's a miracle you're here at all. Sumac and I have been lonely, since we lost Marigold. It's nice to have company. I know Sumac is glad for it, even if he can't show it."

"I'm sorry," Mama said quietly. "It never gets easier."

"It's hard, isn't it? Wanting to grieve, and knowing they're grieving, too."

Mama was quiet for a long while. Ary craned her neck, peering from under the bed. She could only see Mama's lower half as she drifted to the window, her posture tense.

"Sometimes I wonder if I did the right thing, never telling Ary how miserable I was. How miserable I still am, sometimes," Mama said. "How much I miss them both. But I look at her, and I see so much of them in Ary—and I know I owe her a better life."

What? Ary froze. *Miserable?*

"She's a wonderful girl. You're lucky. Sumac has been awful since Marigold left," Alder said. "It's like I can't get through to him. He won't talk to me."

"Ary never wanted to talk about it, either. And instead of acting out she just—I don't know. Shrank." The sadness in Mama's voice made Ary want to cry. "She holds everything in, and I can see in her eyes that she's suffering, but I can't get through to her. She carries so much on her shoulders. When I got sick, I knew she left school. I knew she was working to feed us. It killed me every time she brought home ration tokens instead of books." Mama sighed. "Sometimes it feels like she's the parent. And that's when I know I've failed her."

The room spun. A panic Ary didn't quite understand took hold. She barely remembered the days after Papa had died. Mama had been so sad, and Gran had been so cold, and everything had been a terrible, gray fog. And then, one day, Ary realized they were out of food.

She had shown up to the mushroom fields the next morning.

"I shouldn't have pushed her," Mama said softly. "But I worry about her. She's not said a word to me about her grandmother dying. And you saw her face when I brought her up. It was like I slapped her."

"Were they close?"

"Not in the typical ways." Mama hesitated. "But Ary looked up to her more than anyone. And were it not for Ary—well, I think my mother would have walked off into the Gloom a long time ago. She loved that little girl, more than she ever let herself love me. I was a risk, something to be taken away. But Ary . . . Ary was her hope."

Ary's vision blurred. The feeling was coming back—the heavy, twisting, drowning feeling that threatened to pull her under when she thought of Gran. With it came panic, and *anger*, and for the first time, Ary was angry at Mama.

Who was she to say Ary had been Gran's hope, when Gran herself had never bothered to say the same?

And why was she telling Alder any of this at all?

Alder and Mama said something too low for Ary to hear. They stepped closer to one another, their toes nearly touching.

"Have you thought about what I said?" asked Mama. "A new life. A new start."

Alder sighed and said something Ary could not hear. He took Mama's hand. "If it's what you want—well, we'll make it work."

The world slowed down. Ary inched forward, peering out from under the bed with a thumping heart. She probably could have done backflips in that moment and gone unnoticed. Mama was gazing at Alder with a funny look, a flush in her cheeks, her expression guarded but pleased as she held his hand. Gently, Alder kissed her. Their fingers twined together, and they looked like a painting, framed in golden light against the pale brown wood of their home. Ary couldn't remember the last time her mother had looked so . . . young. There had been such a weight to her after

Papa had died, and even more so later, when she got sick. Ary had started to think of her mother as someone who was only that—just her mom, just a widow, just someone to take care of. But the way Mama looked at Alder, eyes sparkling, with a blush in her cheeks, a new, painful truth began to unfold for Ary.

Her mother was falling in love.

A loneliness Ary hadn't known was possible opened a black, yawning pit in her heart. It had happened without Ary even noticing. Mama had begun to heal. She'd started to dream of a new life—had clearly started see Siltshore as her home and had something to hope for after the pain of losing Papa and Gran alike.

Which meant Ary could not tell her about the Blight. She could not tell her about the dreams, about her fear, or the way she missed Gran.

Wait, why was she thinking about Gran? She didn't miss Gran. She was fine. Gran had made her choice to leave Ary. She was *fine.*

Ary couldn't bring Mama this burden—not if Mama was finally going to be happy. Not after all they'd lost. Ary didn't move from her hiding spot as Mama and Alder slipped out the door with their hands still linked together.

When was the last time she'd seen her mother smile like that?

Welcome to being the chosen one, Gran's voice said bitterly. *It's a lonely place.*

Ary should have been happy here. But all she saw was a happiness she couldn't participate in. Not with the Blight. Not with the nightmares, and the constant tiredness that came from her being too afraid to sleep.

And not with the ever-growing, creeping terror that the girl from her dreams was out there, suffering, and Ary had no way to save her.

Ary had never felt more alone.

TWENTY-THREE

No One Is Safe Here

"You're late."

The cool light of the library enveloped Owl as he stepped inside and shut the door behind him. Sumac was already at the table, flipping through one of the hundreds of old, dusty books he'd pulled down from the shelf.

"Sorry," Owl said distractedly. "I had to walk with Briar to school. I think I'm going to have to start going again before someone tells Mrs. Dragonsnap I've skipped, uh, pretty much every single class."

Sumac waved his hand impatiently. "Who cares? We've got more important work to do."

"I care," Owl snapped. "Especially because we haven't *learned* anything yet."

They lapsed into an uneasy silence, returning to their separate tasks. They passed a lot of their time like this—Owl and Sumac in a comfortable silence, with only the rustle of pages between them. Shrimp came along, too, although since he couldn't read he wasn't the *most* helpful. Some days the pill bug slept in the corner; other days he wandered Siltshore's tunnels, crawling through the dark, searching for something, *anything*, that might give them a clue to what was happening.

Owl pored over the books, reading about Seedling magic and the strange ways they would connect their power to the wood and the creatures around them. Frustratingly, there was no mention of the faint call to *reach* that had pulled him into the Seedling tunnels—but the voices had quieted the day he found Sumac, as if that was all they had wanted from Owl. Or maybe they were just waiting for something.

Finally, Sumac closed his book with a thump. "Okay, what gives?"

"Nothing. I'm fine."

Sumac shook his head. "No, usually I'm the rude one. Seriously, Owl. What's wrong?"

Owl hesitated. His eyes darted around the library, from the books on the shelves to the prophecy gouged in the ceiling.

"Sumac," he said finally, "why do you hate your grandpa so much?"

Darkness crept across Sumac's face. "I don't hate him. I'm afraid of him."

Owl's heart sank, and before he could think better of it, he told Sumac what he had seen—Oleander, moving through the city with Ary as his shadow. Ary, looking at Owl and then breaking eye contact. As if she was ashamed to see him. Sumac's expression grew darker, and finally, he looked away.

"I have no proof," Sumac said quietly, "but I think my grandpa has something to do with the disappearances."

Owl's blood ran cold. "What do you mean?"

"He's careful about it," Sumac continued, "but a lot of the fairies who have gone missing have been fairies he didn't like. Folk who questioned him, or pushed back, or tried to raise concerns that someone went missing." Sumac raised his eyes to Owl. "About a year ago, my mom started acting all paranoid. Saying the wood had a problem none of us were created to fix. She wanted my dad to leave, I think. I heard them fighting. I remember her saying something about going to Oleander with proof, and Dad begging her not to. I don't know what she found out, but I have a feeling whatever it was, it was bad enough for my grandfather to get rid of her." He screwed up his face, plainly frustrated. "I've been trying to make sense of her notes, but I have no idea what they mean. There are all these references here—to the Keepers and some kind of blight and sleeping, to a liar and a thief, but it's all in pieces. And look—someone tore out a bunch of pages."

He turned the book around for Owl to see.

Owl looked closer. Sumac had pulled down a book about Seedling history. The pages, like so many others, were full of drawings of the Gardener's flower. The fat-petaled blossom was stamped into every corner of Siltshore's strange, secret underbelly, sometimes carved as small as Owl's hands, and other times so big it took up the whole ceiling.

"These were sacred, back in Terra," said Owl. "The Seedlings thought they symbolized the Gardener's power. The spell that let Ary shatter the terrarium with her gran had been stored in a flower that the Gardener gave to the Seedlings."

"Oh," said Sumac. "That's . . . cool."

"It made more sense at the time."

"Uh-huh."

Owl glared at him. There had to be a reason the Seedlings were so obsessed with the lilies—but they had enough mysteries to solve as is. He'd just have to add it to the list.

"Why do they look so . . . creepy?" Sumac asked.

Owl looked closer and frowned.

Back in Terra, the Gardener's flowers had always been depicted at full bloom, and then later, wilting—but these almost looked . . . violent. Their petals rotted, and thorns bloomed at the crest. Instead of looking like a symbol of hope, or a reminder of what had happened in the past, these looked almost like a warning.

Sumac was right; there had to be at least twenty pages ripped out of the book. The seam where they'd been was jagged and raw, as if the papers had been torn quickly. Owl thumbed through and paused.

One of the papers behind it was covered in a big, black blot.

Someone had smeared ink across an entire page of the book. In the top right corner, a note about *original Keepers* had been scrawled. A sea of black washed before them, and with a careful hand, someone had sketched the image of a spider; a bird; a weird, fat-looking newt; and some terrifying creature with horns on its head.

Standing before them, lily in hand, was a folk.

"What is this?" Owl whispered, looking up at Sumac.

He shook his head. "I don't know. There are so many books here, I never bothered with this one before."

"Why would someone draw over all the flowers?" Owl scratched at a corner of the ink, and it came up under his nail. "Sumac, the handwriting doesn't match your mom's."

The color drained from Sumac's face. "Then who would it belong to?"

"I might have an idea," a new voice said.

"Ahhh!" both boys yelped. They jumped, whirling, books raised ready to clobber whoever had intruded.

Mrs. Dragonsnap stood in the doorway, her spectacles glinting in the gloom. She raised an eyebrow at their makeshift weapons.

"Hello, Sumac. Hello, Owl. Took you long enough." She nodded in their direction. "I see you found my old notes. I'm ashamed to say I was hoping you would. I wouldn't mind some help."

Owl licked his lips. "Mrs. Dragonsnap? What going on?"

Mrs. Dragonsnap took one careful step forward and then another. Her eyes swept the room, but there was no surprise on her face—just a kind of weary acceptance. She adjusted her glasses and pulled her shawl tighter.

"Before I tell you what I know, I need you to understand something," Mrs. Dragonsnap said slowly. "While Oleander breathes, no one is safe. If you take up the work Marigold and I were doing, you will be in danger. I will not be able to protect you anymore."

Owl's blood chilled.

Oh, Ary, he thought. *What have you gotten yourself into?*

Mrs. Dragonsnap gave him a bitter smile. "I think I ought to start at the beginning."

TWENTY-FOUR

Wounds & Ghosts

"Your eyes need to be on your goal, *not* your feet," Sootflank sighed, watching as Ary face-planted for the hundredth time.

Ary groaned. Chairs fanned out in a ring around her, each ricketier than the last. Where Sootflank had procured them from, she had no clue. All she knew was that he somehow expected her to walk along the *backs* of them without the chairs tipping over, and Ary had never made it past the first two. It had seemed a fun challenge at first—but right now, the thought of getting up and trying again made her want to cry.

Ary was so tired. But she couldn't rest. Every time she closed her eyes, she saw the Blight. She saw the spiders that hunted her in her dreams, and the girl that cried out for help.

She needed to be ready. She needed to be able to defend herself if the spiders were real or if something else went wrong.

But right now, Ary's muscles felt like mud. And she honestly wasn't sure she could move.

"Taking a nap?" Sootflank asked sweetly.

"I thought I'd have learned something useful by now," Ary groaned into the floor.

"I'm sorry, did I get it confused?" Sootflank yawned and folded his forelegs beneath his chin. "Were *you* a prodigy newt general who mastered fire when you were still but a hatchling and spent the subsequent decades surviving alone in the Underground, battling hordes of earwigs and hungry worms with nothing but your wits to defend you?"

"Yesterday it was packs," Ary grumbled. "Now it's *hordes*."

"Tomorrow it will be an army or a swarm, depending on my mood. Now, back on the chair. Or do you have somewhere more important to be?"

"I thought you were supposed to teach me how to fight," Ary said miserably, her face still against the floor. It was a nice floor. Maybe she would spend the rest of her life on this floor.

"You cannot fight until you can defend," said Sootflank, and Ary rolled her eyes. Here he went again. "You cannot defend until you can drill. You cannot drill until you can run, and—"

"I can't run until I can walk, and how can I expect to walk when I can't even handle standing still," Ary finished. "Except I can run and walk and sprint just fine when I'm not *standing on a bunch of chairs*."

Sootflank padded closer. The tip of his tail slipped

under her chin, tilting Ary's face so she could meet his eyes.

"Young Mossheart," Sootflank asked, "what's going on?"

Ary stiffened. "What?"

"You look terrible," Sootflank said bluntly. "You're losing weight. I don't think I've seen you smile in days. You never talk about Owl or that annoying little Sunleaf anymore. And when is the last time you've checked on Shrimp?"

Guilt prickled through Ary. "I know, I know, I need to be better about—"

"I'm not saying you're not doing enough." Sootflank cut her off. "I'm saying I'm worried about you."

When Ary didn't answer, Sootflank lowered himself to the ground. Ary sat upright and pulled her knees to her chest. The newt was quiet for a long time.

"You know," Sootflank said, "what I said to you before, about your fear being right. That was irresponsible of me."

"But you were right," Ary said miserably. "Something *is* wrong here."

She had told Sootflank of the Blight—at least, what little she knew of it.

"Yes," Sootflank said gently. "But I forget, sometimes, how young you are. And it was wrong of me to encourage you to go hunting for new trouble. For that, I'm sorry." He looked at her closely. "How long have you been having nightmares?"

Ary's lip wobbled. "I'm not—"

"I may be old," said Sootflank, "but I'm no fool."

How was it that Sootflank was always making her cry?

In fits, Ary told Sootflank about the dreams she'd been having. About the terror that lingered long after she woke and the way it seemed to fill her days. She could not stop thinking of the spider that had attacked them—of the way it had felt angry *and* afraid of her.

Of what it had called her and Owl.

A thief and a liar.

"When I was young, I had nightmares after my first battles." Sootflank grew quiet. "The faces of the fairies I hurt and the newts we lost haunted my dreams. I jumped at every shadow, and I was so angry, and so scared. More than anything, I felt . . . terribly, horribly alone. I was not a kind creature, then. Not to my mate. Not to Quickspark. Though my physical wounds had long healed, it felt like I had wounds inside me, too, that kept getting worse. Wounds in my head. Wounds in my heart. And as new problems surfaced, they were made twice as terrifying by danger I'd long left behind."

Tears blurred Ary's eyes. "How did you get better?"

"Unfortunately, not on my own." Sootflank made an annoyed noise. "Didn't you ever wonder how I came to befriend that nattering old mole?"

Ary's heart lifted. "*Chives* helped you?"

"Who better?" Sootflank shrugged. "I was young. Desperate. I figured a Steward who knew all the stories of our world might know something about healing, too. I went to him hoping for a magic cure." He rolled his eyes. "Instead, all we did was *talk*. About *everything.* It was so annoying. The worst part was, it worked. Over time, the wounds on my insides turned to scar. They were still there—but they hurt less. And I realized that instead of all of me, they were just a part of me, like the color of my flesh or the flames I summon. No more, no less."

Ary hugged her knees to her chest. It sounded so maddeningly simple, and so hard, too.

"I don't think I can talk about her yet," Ary said in a tiny voice.

"I know," Sootflank said gently. "But when you're ready—I'm happy to talk about Wren, or anything else."

"I didn't mean Gran," Ary snapped. She winced. "I'm sorry. But that's—that's not what I meant."

Sootflank's silence said he didn't believe her.

Did Ary mean Gran? She wasn't sure. She mostly tried not to think about her. Which was pretty hard, because it seemed like everything reminded Ary of Gran.

I love you. I'm sorry, and I love you.

Gran wasn't perfect, but something told Ary she would have been good at this—helping her, after everything she'd done.

She should have been here. It wasn't fair.

"Here's what I know," Sootflank said gently. "You have wounds, Ary Mossheart. You will acquire more. That's life—hurting, getting hurt, and learning how to move past it. It's not our fault when we're wounded. But it *is* our job to heal. When pain festers, everyone suffers."

Ary closed her eyes.

"Like Gran," she whispered. "Her wounds never scarred over, did they?"

"I don't know," Sootflank said honestly. "Maybe she thought so. Maybe you felt different. Wren, like all of us, was just a person doing her best. But the good news is you always have the choice to be better."

Ary blinked slowly. Maybe it was foolish, but it was a hopeful thing—to know that maybe she didn't always have to feel this way, even if it seemed impossible now.

It fixed nothing about the Blight. It didn't take the nightmares away. But it did make her feel a tiny bit less trapped.

"You know," Sootflank said, "you are better at balancing than Wren was. Maybe there's hope for you yet."

Ary looked at him. "You trained her, too?"

"Not because I wanted to. She kept demanding it, and it's not like I had anything better to do."

Ary's heart ached. There was still so much about Gran she didn't know. So much she would never learn, now that she was gone. "Was she a . . . natural fighter?"

"A natural? Please! She was hopeless. I don't know what they teach their chosen ones back in Terra, but it wasn't anything useful. She was ill-balanced, earwig-brained, and *stubborn*, like someone else I know. She liked to fight dirty. And she would bite." Sootflank's tail twitched with ill-concealed pride. "Actually, I taught her to do that last bit. Better to fight dirty and win than fight nobly and die."

Ary's eyes blurred, and she turned her face away as she picked herself up.

"Ary," said Sootflank.

Ary froze.

Please don't ask if I miss her, Ary willed. *Don't ask me how I'm doing, because the answers are so obvious that the asking just feels cruel.*

That was the weird thing about someone you loved dying. People either didn't want to talk about it at all, which felt bad, because it made it seem like they wanted to pretend that person never existed, or they wanted to know *how you were doing,* but they only ever said it in a way that made it clear they didn't actually care, they just wanted to get the awkward stuff out of the way first.

Ary didn't know how to tell people she didn't want to talk about Gran, but she didn't want to *not* talk about her, either. She didn't want to talk about how she was doing after losing the only grandmother she'd ever known. She wanted to talk about what, exactly, she'd lost. She wanted to talk about Gran's laugh, or her stubbornness, or the way she always glowered at the statue in the fountain for getting her nose wrong.

Mostly, she just wanted to know that other people loved and missed Gran, too.

Sootflank watched her in the dark light of the storeroom.

He never spoke of his own family—but even before Quickspark, he'd had a mate, once, and parents of his own, maybe even siblings or friends that he'd loved. There was so little Ary knew about him. And what she did know always seemed to carry a story of loss.

"Yes, Sootflank?" Ary said finally.

"If you can't talk to me yet," Sootflank said gently, "it might help to talk to someone else. You'd be amazed how small our shadows grow when we invite the light of another in."

Ary gave him a wobbly smile. But his words lingered long after they finished training.

Instead of returning home, Ary went up.

Maybe Sootflank was right. She couldn't keep all this worry and fear in. It was still too hard to look at the newt and not remember Gran, and she didn't quite think she could talk to Mama, Briar, or Owl, either.

But there was one fairy in Siltshore who just might understand.

TWENTY-FIVE

Willow's Story

When the terrarium was freshly shattered, the dust still settling and the world blazing with light, a little fairy named Willow gazed into the sunlight of the new world—and knew she had made a terrible mistake.

The world they'd known before had not been well. When Oleander and Hemlock set out on a quest to save it, Willow was admittedly relieved. Her little sister, Aspen, had been helplessly in love with Oleander, who was always polished and smiling—but Willow had caught the glint of cruelty in his eye.

Privately, she'd prayed that both boys would disappear into the Underground and never return. She counted down the days to their departure, mentally planning ways to console Aspen when they died. Sure, she'd be heartbroken. But she'd also be free. They would move on, live their lives, and one day Aspen would forget Oleander entirely.

Then, on the morning of their departure, Aspen had woken Willow up before dawn and said the words that would doom them both forever:

"I'm going with them."

And what choice did Willow have, really? She may have loathed the brothers, but she loved her sister more than life itself. Aspen was her only sibling. The only person in the world who shared her blood, her memories, her life. She'd have followed her to the end of the world and back, if it meant she could keep Aspen safe.

They had been a simple enough fit: Oleander and his older brother had been the heroes, carrying the stories of their predecessors and the myth of Titan in their hearts, Aspen following merrily at their heels, thrilled to be a part of history in the making. Even Willow was susceptible to some excitement; they'd all grown up listening to the Seedling songs that proved to act as map and key at once, guiding them through the Underground's winding path in search of a great, tired snake named Titan. At first, Willow had pictured the lives that would follow like a dream wreathed in glittering light—Hemlock and Oleander would be heroes, and Aspen would be satisfied that she had been a part of something greater. Maybe, in the new world, she'd outgrow her childish love for the younger brother.

Maybe, in the new world, Aspen and Willow would be happy.

But the journey down to the Underground proved far more dangerous than expected. What had started as a fun adventure quickly lost its joy. Hemlock and Oleander fought constantly; Hemlock was selfish and impatient, constantly pushing the group forward. What Oleander lacked in size, he made up for in wickedness—sowing lies and mistrust in the group, turning them against each other, using Willow as a scapegoat at every turn. Together, the brothers were the perfect bullies; Hemlock the muscle, Oleander the sharp words. When Willow tried to talk to Aspen about Oleander's cruelty, her sister refused to hear it.

Willow had never felt more alone.

When they reached Titan's chamber, she was ready for it to be over. Her sister felt like a stranger, the wedge driven between them feeling more like an impassable canyon with every day. Any promise of a heroic journey had long lost its shine. As Oleander and Hemlock approached the chamber doors, Willow let her shoulders relax.

"You know what I hope?" Willow muttered to Aspen. "I hope whatever is in there swallows them whole."

"Willow," Aspen had hissed.

"What?" Willow had demanded. "They're *awful,* Aspen. I know you love Oleander, but he's cruel. As doomed as this world is—I think it'd be even more doomed with either of them in charge. I hope we never see them again."

She would always regret that—speaking so freely, thinking that in that final moment, she might get her sister back.

Aspen had shot her a furious look, her face pale and drawn. Willow could not be sorry. Those boys were bad news. Aspen would mourn them when they died, but in time she'd realize it was for the best.

The brothers approached the cavern. Willow could not get over just how cold it was—so cold it sank into her bones, so cold it would haunt her sixty years later. She'd watched, breath held, as Oleander and Hemlock bickered and fought over who got to put the Seedling shovel in the door. Hemlock won, of course. He was bigger than Oleander, and in those days, brawn still managed to outpace brains.

The giant stone door rolled to the side. Pale light leaked through, and beside Willow, Aspen sighed, a dreamy look on her face.

And Willow, traitor that she was, had dared to feel the tiniest thread of hope.

Maybe this just might work. Maybe they really could be free.

And then Oleander turned.

"Well," he said to Aspen with a wink, "what are you waiting for, then?"

The feeling drained out of Willow. "What?"

Something sharp pricked her leg. Willow gasped, collapsing sideways. Aspen caught her and lowered her to the ground, guilt bright in her eyes.

"I'm sorry," Aspen whispered. She kissed the top of Willow's head. "But Oleander said they need my help. He said he needs someone who loves him to help him cast the spell and he doesn't think Hemlock will be enough. I knew you'd try to stop me. But I'm going with them."

Willow tried to shout, but her voice was gone. She could only watch in horror as Aspen gently lowered her to the ground and approached Oleander, her chin lifted.

The Gardener's Warning spun through her, and she understood then what was happening.

A life most loved, freely given.

Willow had tried to cry out. She had tried to say anything at all. As the ant venom pulled her into darkness, the last thing she saw was Aspen disappearing through that door, Hemlock and Oleander flanking her like predators as she walked toward her own doom.

When Willow awoke, the sky was gone. Impossible light poured through. Her mouth was dry, and her body ached. When Willow finally dug herself out of the rubble, she learned she'd been unconscious for three days.

And Oleander's damage was done.

While Willow lay trapped in the ruins of their world, Oleander had spun a story she could not unweave—of Hemlock's bravery, sacrificing himself to free the terrarium at last. There was no mention of Aspen at all. If anyone noticed she was missing, they were too relieved to be free to say anything. Here was their savior in Oleander at last; here was their promised hero who had led them to the sun.

She asked him, once, what happened. They had been

free only a few weeks when Willow cornered Oleander, driven mad by not knowing.

"What happened to her?" she demanded. "If Hemlock was the life, why did you need Aspen? Where did she go?"

Oleander gave her a puzzled smile. "Who?"

"Aspen," Willow said furiously. "My sister. Your friend. Three fairies went into that cavern—one emerged. Where is she, Oleander? What did you do?"

"I have no idea who you're talking about," Oleander said evenly. "You must be imagining things."

"Don't start with me, Oleander. I know you did something to her—"

Oleander had looked Willow over, his eyes cold, and then he'd taken her by the arm, his fingernails sinking into the soft upper flesh of her forearm.

"Careful, Willow." His eyes were colder than the darkest part of the terrarium. "We can't afford troublemakers here. Look at this world we've found; look at our life. If you go around frightening people with some ridiculous rumors, someone might get upset. They might even hurt you." He squeezed until Willow's arm bled, his eyes cold. "Do you understand?"

And Willow, still just a child herself, and never as brave as Aspen had been, could only croak, "I understand."

Willow tried to move on. She really did. The ache of her sister's disappearance soured, like a bitter thorn turned to rot. As folk disappeared, and the Blight spread, Willow's dread only grew.

And when a new child appeared, ghostly wings flaring from her back and a Seedling at her side, this time, Willow was determined to see things end differently.

She knew better than anyone the worst villains could be born from a hero's story.

TWENTY-SIX

Illusions

Coming to Oleander had seemed like a good idea, as Ary headed up-tree, but now that she was here, standing in front of his office uninvited, she wasn't so sure. Sunlight blazed down on her. Her fingers sweated as she gripped the safety rail.

Would being up high ever make her feel less vulnerable?

The door loomed in front of her, but still, Ary couldn't make herself move. This was silly. Oleander would probably laugh at her. Or be annoyed.

Or . . . he might just understand.

Before she could second-guess herself, Ary pushed through the door.

"Hello?" Oleander's head snapped up. Yellow sheets of paper covered the desk in front of him, their edges ragged and torn as though they'd been ripped from a book. Oleander swept them into a pile with a tight smile. "Oh, Ary. It's you. What's wrong?"

Ary hesitated. Maybe it had been a mistake to come here. But the nightmares weren't going away—and who else but Oleander was likely to understand?

"I need to talk to you," Ary said.

Irritation flashed across Oleander's face, there and gone in only a moment. "It couldn't wait until tomorrow?"

It had been a mistake to come. But she was already here. She might as well try.

"I keep having these . . . dreams," Ary said slowly. "Nightmares."

Oleander relaxed. "About the terrarium? I used to get them, too. Completely normal, they'll go away eventually. If you like, I can have Alder give you some poppy syrup. Now, if you don't mind, I have a lot of work to do—"

"Not about the terrarium." Ary balled her hands into fists. "About here. Well, not quite here. Somewhere in the wood. In them, there's a girl I've never met before."

The color drained from Oleander's face.

"She just keeps saying *find me,*" said Ary. "And in the last dream . . . well, something strange happened our first day in the wood. I don't know if Alder told you, but a spider attacked us, and it called Owl and me a liar and a thief. In the dream, the girl said those same words." Ary's voice grew small, and for the first time, she found herself able to say what she'd been too scared to voice. "Oleander, I think she might be real."

And though it could have been a trick of the light, Ary could have sworn Oleander's hands were trembling.

"I don't know if it could be a Siltshore fairy," she continued, "or someone from your terr—"

"No," said Oleander. "It's just a nightmare, Ary."

"But it felt so real," said Ary. "And the words the spider—"

"You are a child," Oleander said through gritted teeth. "A traumatized child. Nightmares are understandable, but talking about them will only lend them credence—"

"If I could just go into the wood and look—"

"Enough!" Oleander shouted. Light flashed around him in a strange, dizzying blur. It happened so quickly that if Ary had blinked, she might have missed it. The silver-sweet scent of fairy dust filled the air.

To work a spell, Mrs. Grumthrush had said, *the caster must be calm and clear-headed. A burst of emotion could disrupt or even break the magic.*

And in the split second where Oleander had lost his temper—his wings had disappeared.

They were an illusion.

The feeling drained from Ary's body. She could not move, could not think. Her heart began to pound, harder, and then harder still. She needed to get out of here. She needed to get away from him right now.

Oleander gave Ary a polite smile. It made her stomach churn.

"Forgive me," Oleander said smoothly. "I have similar nightmares, and talking about them apparently still stresses me out more than I think. Truly, Ary, I am happy to have my men investigate the wood—but I promise, the only fairies here are the ones living in Siltshore."

Ary still hadn't moved. She was trying to understand what she had just seen. What shouldn't have been possible.

Oleander peered at her intently. "This dream. Did the girl say anything else in it?"

Ary hesitated.

Find Willow.

She had come here to tell him everything, hadn't she? But the way he was looking at her . . . what she had just seen . . .

Oleander was keeping secrets.

Maybe it was time she kept some, too.

"No," lied Ary, her voice small. "She didn't say anything else."

Oleander visibly relaxed. "Why don't I have Alder bring home some of that poppy syrup? I'm sure, after some time, the nightmares will ease."

"Okay," Ary said faintly, her mind a million worlds away. She needed to talk to Sootflank. "Sure. Um, I'm sorry for bothering you."

Ary took one step backward, and then another. It took everything in her not to bolt out the door. As she pushed it open, Oleander's voice stopped her in her tracks.

"Ary?"

She turned. He was still smiling, but his eyes were colder than the darkest depths of the terrarium. The hair on Ary's arms stood on end.

"Don't tell anyone else about these nightmares," he said levelly. "It would only cause trouble."

"I won't," Ary whispered.

She couldn't get out of there fast enough. Ary practically ran the whole way back to the storeroom, her mind spinning a million miles a minute, her heart fit to beat out of her chest. As she hurried, Siltshore seemed tilted on a terrible angle. She noticed, for the first time, just how *old* it was—the dents in the vine bridges, the stains of old mold on the tree trunks. They had been taught Oleander had founded this city, and she'd been so desperate to believe in it—to believe in him—that she'd looked away from the cracks in his lies.

When she saw the storeroom door, her legs nearly buckled. Ary burst right through, slamming it behind her with an audible thump.

"Ary?" Sootflank's head snapped up.

"He's faking it," Ary gasped. "Sootflank, Oleander's wings are *fake*. And if he lied about that, he could be lying about *everything*. Oleander isn't a Ghostwing. He's a fraud. He's been pretending this whole time. Whatever happened in his terrarium, if he really did face their Atlas—he didn't cast that spell. It's all a lie. We're not safe here. He's hiding something about the wood, about the Blight, and when I told him about my dream—Sootflank, I think the girl from my nightmares is *real*."

"Well," Sootflank said, a little miserably, "I had wanted

to do this a little differently. But I suppose we ought to get right to it now. What do you think, Iris?"

Ary's blood turned to ice.

She had been in such a frenzy, she hadn't realized he had a visitor.

Mayor Nightingale waved to Ary from where she leaned against the wall.

"I had my suspicions about Siltshore's leader, but this isn't quite how I wanted them confirmed," she said dryly. "Come take a seat, Mossheart. I think we have a lot of catching up to do."

TWENTY-SEVEN

Finally

The rest of Mrs. Dragonsnap's story came in bitter pieces. In the dull light of the library, she told Owl and Sumac the truth she'd spent sixty years guarding. Some of it they'd heard before—but much like Terra's history, it had been twisted at funny angles, the truth warped and turned upside down until it was no longer recognizable.

"I have no memory of the terrarium shattering," Mrs. Dragonsnap admitted. "They found me in the rubble after. I don't know how long I was out, but when I woke, the world had changed. Oleander had emerged a hero, the wings on his back carrying the proof of what he'd done. And I was a coward. Too scared to speak against him, and then, when we found Siltshore . . . I don't know. Our people were so tired, and so hungry. I hoped maybe leadership would soften Oleander. I hoped . . . well, I hoped the good of the new world could offset the bad he brought into it." She closed her eyes. "I was wrong."

Finally, Owl couldn't take it anymore. "Mrs. Dragon-snap, what happened to Aspen?"

The grief in her eyes turned Owl's blood to ice.

"I don't know," Mrs. Dragonsnap said faintly. "I never saw her or Hemlock again. Whatever happened in Titan's chamber . . . only Oleander knows the truth. When the first of the disappearances began, I did my best to convince myself it was just the natural dangers of this world. It had happened before—folk picked off by birds or spiders or other creatures hunting in the wood." Her gaze darkened. "It was a decade or two before I noticed the pattern. Only people who had become a problem for Oleander went missing."

"Like my mom," Sumac said quietly.

Hesitantly, she nodded.

"I had given up on justice ever coming to Oleander," Mrs. Dragonsnap said. "Then, one day, your mother showed up at my door, looking as though she hadn't slept in weeks. She was paranoid and on edge, and when I asked her what was wrong, she had the wildest tale: some girl was appearing in her dreams and calling for help. She seemed convinced the Keepers of old were still out there." She shook her head. "I don't even know how she found her way to the library through the tunnels. But I couldn't stop her. And when she disappeared . . ."

"You knew I was down here," Sumac said in a small voice.

"She asked me to keep an eye on you," said Mrs. Dragonsnap. "And I thought this was safest, since I knew exactly where you were. And—well, to be honest, child, I didn't think anything would ever come of it."

If Sumac was hurt, he didn't show it. He kind of reminded Owl of Ary in that way; always bracing himself for the next hit. Although Sumac was a lot more annoying than Ary, Owl supposed their anxieties were similar. It was a shame Sumac had picked her out as an enemy from the beginning.

"Mrs. Dragonsnap," asked Owl, "is Ary in danger?"

"Anyone near Oleander is in danger," Mrs. Dragonsnap said quietly. "But I worry his interest in her is no accident, especially with the festival drawing near."

The weight of this settled on them.

"We don't know enough," said Owl, frustrated. "So Oleander wants Ary around for the festival to . . . what? Keep an eye on her? Lend him credibility?"

Sumac's face was thoughtful as he thumbed through the books. "Maybe it has something to do with the Keepers? Or his Ghostwing magic failing?"

Mrs. Dragonsnap shook her head, frustrated. "What I wouldn't give to have Marigold here. Or Aspen—she always knew Oleander better than I. And even though he betrayed her, I think she could have gotten the truth out of him, in the end. She was always good at getting under his skin."

Sumac shook his head helplessly. "It still wouldn't be enough. My grandfather is too secretive. I know he's hiding something. But whatever it is, I don't think we're getting answers before the festival."

"Did Marigold say anything about that?" Owl asked, pointing at the weird, cryptic prophecy on the ceiling. "Or did she have any theories about the missing letters?"

Mrs. Dragonsnap looked troubled. "That message was here when we found Siltshore—but the damage is recent. I found the letters scratched out the day she went missing." She hesitated. "I think . . . Marigold did the damage."

"What?" Sumac demanded. "Why would she do that?"

Mrs. Dragonsnap looked helpless. "I don't know. To keep us from following her? She did a lot of things I'll never understand."

Owl watched the two of them go back and forth. It felt like he wasn't totally in his body. Like history was replaying on a loop, back on their way through the Underground, when they'd been desperately trying to puzzle through Dracaena's journals. His eyes drifted to the ceiling. The missing letters left him with an uneasy feeling. Marigold's notes had the tone of someone who was obsessed with her research, but Owl found it hard to believe she'd try to sabotage the work of whoever came next.

It was too much for them to figure out alone. He had promised Sumac not to tell Ary about anything—but that was before he knew Ary was in danger.

They were wasting time. And so what if Owl hadn't seen much of Ary lately? She was his friend. She was in trouble.

And Owl knew, if the situations were reversed, she'd stop at nothing to protect him.

"We've got to tell Ary," said Owl. "The festival is *tomorrow*. And if we think Oleander is going to hurt her—"

"She'd be in even more danger," said Mrs. Dragonsnap, her voice firm. "I'm sorry, Owl. But it isn't a good idea. The best thing we can do is try to find more information tonight. Once we're through the festival, there's a chance Oleander will lose interest in Ary. Then we'll pull her in."

Owl shrank. Sumac and Mrs. Dragonsnap weren't going to budge. They didn't know Ary the way he did. They didn't have any reason to trust her.

But what did that matter to him?

For most of his life, Owl Diggs had been ignored. He had been right—he had *always* been right. About Terra, about their world being sick, and later, about what had happened to Dracaena and Gran. Heat crept into his cheeks. Sumac was treating this whole thing like it was some kind of game. But there were fairies' lives at stake.

And one of them was his best friend.

Mrs. Dragonsnap and Sumac returned to their research. They were no better than the fairies back in Terra. How many times had Owl watched the Seedlings recite the old songs but never *do* anything? How many complaints had he heard about the rotting food, the murky water, yet no one wanted to venture beyond the fence? It was easy to keep doing the same thing. Comfortable.

And it was going to get them killed.

"I wasn't asking your permission," said Owl.

Mrs. Dragonsnap raised her brow. "I beg your pardon?"

Owl's heart began to pound. Ary had stood up to Sootflank. Surely he could stand up to an old lady and a boy who wasn't even his friend.

He put his hands on the table and did his best not to sound scared.

"I wasn't asking your permission," Owl repeated. "I'm going to go tell Ary. *And* Sootflank. The festival is tomorrow. This is ridiculous. For all we know, Oleander could be planning something, and we're just going to sit here and—what? Comb through books Mrs. Dragonsnap and Marigold have already read? Stare at some scratched-up prophecy that may not mean anything, and just hope?"

Sumac shook his head. "We agreed—"

"I don't care," Owl snapped. Heat crept to his cheeks. "You guys aren't listening to me. Ary Mossheart is my best friend. If she's in danger, I'm telling her. I'm stopping it. So you guys can either come with me or you can stay here, but I'm going."

"You're putting her at risk," Mrs. Dragonsnap began. "We can't possibly fix anything before tomorrow."

"Besides, it's not like she'd be of much use," Sumac muttered. "She keeps waking me up with her annoying nightmares. I'm pretty sure she's too sleep-deprived to understand any of this, let alone fix it."

"Plus the risks of Oleander finding out?" Mrs. Dragonsnap shook her head. "Be reasonable, Owl."

"What did you say?" Owl whispered.

"Oleander—"

"Not that. Sumac, did you say Ary's having nightmares?"

Sumac frowned and nodded. "I hear her yelling sometimes. Her mom and my dad were talking about it. I guess she has them every night now."

Briar's voice rang through his mind.

She looks terrible.

Like she hasn't slept in weeks.

Owl froze.

How could he have been so stupid? It was right in front of him. Ary had dreamed of Atlas back in the terrarium, and after every dream, she had been withdrawn, haunted by what she saw.

She hadn't been upset with him and Briar that day. She'd been having nightmares.

And Owl had a feeling he knew who was starring in them.

"Mrs. Dragonsnap," Owl said slowly. "Didn't you say Marigold came to you about a girl appearing in her dreams?"

She frowned. "Yes, but nightmares aren't that uncommon. We all had them when we left the terrarium."

Owl looked at Sumac. "Have you ever heard Ary say anything?"

Sumac shook his head. "I'm usually half asleep. I just know whatever she's dreaming about, it's bad."

"She had nightmares back in Terra," said Owl. "About

Atlas, right before we set out to find him. What if something else is calling her? What if whatever or whoever called Marigold is trying to get to Ary now, too?"

Owl's heart raced. It couldn't be a coincidence. Not with the disappearances, and not with Ary's strange wings and the way magic resisted her. Something weird was going on here.

And Owl would bet his hat Oleander was at the center of it. (He didn't actually have a hat, but it was something he'd heard old people say when they were really serious. And if he'd had one, he absolutely would have bet it now.)

"Ary is in trouble," Owl said. He looked at Sumac and Mrs. Dragonsnap. "She's my friend. She's a good person. I know you guys don't trust her—but if something happened to her, I'd spend the rest of my life wondering if I could have saved her." His voice cracked. "I already lost my first family. I can't lose my second one, too. So I'm sorry. But I'm going. I hope you come with me."

He got up before he could second-guess himself. It was silly, really. Why did he care so much about upsetting Sumac and Mrs. Dragonsnap? He hadn't known either of them long.

But he had started to feel like he'd belonged. And Mrs. Dragonsnap's home had started to feel like it was his, too.

"Wait," Mrs. Dragonsnap said. She rose and shook her head. "I still think this is a bad idea. But if you trust the girl—well, the festival begins in a few hours. It can't possibly make much of a difference either way."

Sumac shot her a look of betrayal and threw up his hands. "Well, since I'm outvoted. Fine. When my grandpa vanishes us all, I'm blaming you."

"Noted," said Owl. His heart pounded faster. He had the sense of the walls closing in, of time slipping away. He couldn't stop thinking about the dream. "We should go to Sootflank first. If Ary's mom is home, it's going to be hard to get her out of there."

"The newt? Perfect. There's a path to the storeroom through the tunnels." Mrs. Dragonsnap raised an eyebrow at their surprised expressions. "You think I built my home on top of a secret tunnel network and *didn't* use them to sneak around?"

"To do . . . what?" Sumac asked.

Her cheeks turned bright pink. "None of your business. Let's go."

She hurried out of the library before they could argue. Owl hurried to keep up, following Mrs. Dragonsnap down a dizzying series of paths in near-darkness. She turned a corner and squeaked as they all collided with something hard.

"Ow," said Shrimp.

Owl made a strangled noise. "Shrimp, you've got to stop *doing* that! What are you doing down here, anyway?"

"Bug stuff," said Shrimp. "Private."

Great, everyone had secrets. Owl glanced back at the library door. Shrimp said nothing, his dark eyes trained expectantly on Owl.

"Shrimp," Owl said, "we're going to talk to Ary. We think she's in danger. Do you want to come with?"

And though it wasn't possible for a pill bug to roll his eyes, Owl could have sworn Shrimp was doing his best.

"Finally," said Shrimp. "Get on."

TWENTY-EIGHT

The Enemy You Know

Ary's gaze darted frantically from Sootflank to Mayor Nightingale and back again.

"Um," said Ary. "Does someone want to tell me what's going on? And quickly, please?"

Sootflank and Nightingale shot each other brief, uncomfortable looks. Ary nearly laughed. It was absurd! Sootflank and Nightingale *together*, looking more uncomfortable about Ary intruding on them than the fact that they were working together at all.

"Iris came to me with concerns a while ago—" Sootflank began.

"You guys are on a *first-name basis*?" Ary blurted.

Sootflank gave her an irritated look. Nightingale snorted and cut in.

"I caught him skulking around and figured he was either planning to burn the city to the ground or do something to help it," she said dryly. "And if it was the latter, I wanted to be part of it. When he told me he was concerned about the time you were spending with Oleander, that sealed it."

Ary's face heated. She looked at Sootflank. "You never said anything."

"Would you have listened?" he asked evenly.

Ary looked away. She'd like to think so, but the truth was, she wasn't so sure. She cared about Sootflank. She trusted him. But Oleander had made her feel special. It had been so precious to think she'd finally found someone who understood.

Sootflank had clearly seen that. And Ary had never felt more embarrassed.

"That doesn't answer my question," she said. "What are you doing here?"

Nightingale looked at her. "Ary, are you aware fairies have been going missing?"

It was as if the wind had been knocked out of her. Ary shook her head, mind tripping to catch up. She'd been certain Nightingale was here to talk about the Blight, or her dislike of Oleander, or . . . or . . .

"The Frostlines," Mayor Nightingale said evenly. "I believe you are friends with their daughters, Tulip and Basil?"

Ary tensed. "We were friendly back in Terra, yes."

"Have you seen them recently?" Mayor Nightingale asked evenly.

"Yes, they go to the—"

"School you haven't been to in weeks? Yes, I know about that, too. Don't worry, you're not in trouble."

Ary's heart pounded. "What are you saying?"

Tulip and Basil were fine. Sure, it'd been weeks since she'd seen them, but as Nightingale clearly knew, Ary hadn't been going to school. She likely just hadn't crossed paths with them. That was it. Right?

"When we first arrived in Terra, I tasked their father, Yarrow Frostline, with keeping an eye on Oleander. I had a bad feeling about him, but no proof. He asked my permission to enter the wood. I gave it." Nightingale paused. "He didn't return."

The blood roared in Ary's ears.

"Accidents happen," Nightingale continued, "but Yarrow is smart. One of my best guards. I find it hard to believe something killed him in the wood, and that quickly. When he didn't return, Tulip and Basil's mother, Clover, asked my permission to look for him. I denied her. She kept asking. So finally I gave her my blessing."

"What are you saying?" Ary asked. "That Oleander . . . did something to them?"

"This morning," Nightingale continued, "I went to check on their daughters. If something happened to their parents—well, it would be on my shoulders." Her face was grave. "They weren't there, either. Just this."

From her pocket, Mayor Nightingale withdrew a handful of shining silver threads.

The last bit of feeling left Ary.

She had seen those threads before. By the swamp, on their first day in this world.

And later, in her dreams.

The same dreams that had angered Oleander.

"Ary," Sootflank said gravely, "I didn't want to bring this to you until I was certain. I don't mean to scare you, and you know the last thing I want is to ask you to take on another fight before you're ready. But I worry that you are in danger. That we are *all* in danger."

Ary shook her head. It was one thing if Oleander was a liar, if he was concealing something about the Blight. But getting rid of Tulip and Basil's parents? Of *children*?

Ary didn't like Mayor Nightingale. She didn't trust her, either. But what was it Gran had always said about the enemy she knew?

"Oleander's wings aren't real," Ary said quietly. "When I went to talk to him, I told him about these dreams I was having. He got so angry that his wings disappeared." She shook her head. "If he's lying about being a Ghostwing for sixty years, what else is he keeping secret?"

Nightingale leaned forward, her expression intent. "Did he say anything else? Anything that could tell us what he's planning, or what he plans to do for the festival?"

"No—wait, that's not true." Ary's brow furrowed. "His desk was covered in papers. They looked like they'd been ripped from a book or something. He hid them as soon as I walked in."

"A book like this?"

All three of them jumped. Mayor Nightingale whipped

a knife from her robes, and sparks flared around Sootflank. The door to the supply closet had swung open—and in the doorway was one of the strangest groups Ary had ever seen. Mrs. Dragonsnap, Owl, Shrimp, and *Sumac,* all of them with varying degrees of emotion on their faces. They looked surprised to see Nightingale, who looked equally surprised to see them.

In Owl's hands, pages fluttering, was an old, pale book that was missing a chunk of pages in the center.

"Owl?" said Ary. "What are you doing here?"

"And why are you . . . in a closet?" Sootflank asked.

"We don't have time to unpack that," said Owl. "Um, well, there's no fun way to say this. I'm pretty sure Oleander is a serial killer and we're all in terrible danger. So, yeah. Who wants to start?"

TWENTY-NINE

A Really Bad Plan

As dawn slipped over the wood, five fairies, a newt, and one very nervous pill bug huddled in an old, abandoned storeroom and came up with a really bad plan.

It was a chaotic catchup at first—everyone spoke over each other, piecing together what they knew, what they thought, what they feared. Through all of it, Owl watched Ary. She was quiet, like usual. It was something he'd noticed back in the Underground. Ary Mossheart tended to think first and speak second. Owl had watched people underestimate her because of it—they saw a small, timid fairy who was quick to apologize and faster to forgive, and they took her silence for acceptance. But in the Underground Owl had witnessed Ary's fire.

He saw it here now, too.

"So here is what we know," Nightingale said. After a lifetime of watching her from a distance, it felt odd to be so close to Terra's leader. She looked older, up close. More tired. Nightingale leaned forward and threaded her fingers together. "There is some type of Blight in the wood—we think it's influenced by magic, but we can't be sure. When

I sent two of my best guards to investigate, they vanished, and their daughters shortly after. Folk have been disappearing from Siltshore, one by one, and there seems to be a pattern of them being people who questioned or threatened Oleander's authority." Her eyes narrowed. "Is it possible the simplest answer is the correct one? That the Blight is his fault?"

Ary shook her head. "He was terrified of it. I don't think you can fake that."

"And if he caused the Blight, why?" asked Sootflank. "What does he get out of destroying his home? Why would picking his own people off one by one help that?"

"Is there a chance the leader of our newfound home—which happens to be the only city of fairies in this entire wood—isn't a murderer?" Owl asked hopefully.

"No," everyone chorused.

He figured. But, man, they really had the worst luck.

"So what does he get out of this?" Sumac asked in a small voice. "My mom. So many others. I don't think my grandpa is a good person, but I think he's more worried about power than hurting people."

"There's something we're missing." Mrs. Dragonsnap looked at Ary, who stiffened at the sudden eye contact, but the older woman's smile was gentle. "Ary, right? I've heard such good things about you from Owl and Briar."

Owl was pretty sure that was a lie—at least, the Briar part—but it was the thought that counted. Should they have been including Briar on this? She was pretty adamant she wanted to be left out. But if it was Owl, he'd be pretty hurt about being excluded from the secret . . . whatever this was. Rescue plan? Coup? It was kind of unclear.

"Do you remember anything else about the papers you saw in Oleander's office?" Mrs. Dragonsnap asked Ary. "Anything that can help us?"

Ary hesitated. Her gaze slid to the book, and Mrs. Dragonsnap, catching the glance, gently pushed it in her direction. Ary thumbed through it, her brow furrowed. "This whole book is about the Keepers?"

"It's an old myth," Mrs. Dragonsnap said. "A story we like to tell little folk, about old guardians of the wood."

Ary raised her eyes. "Oleander doesn't seem to think it's just a story."

Quietly, Ary told them of her conversation with Oleander. Of his private hope that this festival might catch their attention, and of the maps on the walls that tracked the areas of the Blight. As she spoke, Mrs. Dragonsnap's and Sumac's eyebrows climbed higher and higher.

If the festival was meant to connect them to real, living Keepers, they clearly had never been told. Owl had a feeling the rest of Siltshore would agree.

"I have a friend in the wood who might be able to help us," Mrs. Dragonsnap said thoughtfully. "He is . . . a nervous creature. But he knows the myths of the Keepers better than most. I could ask him for help, but it wouldn't be before the festival. And there's a chance that he won't know anything the library hasn't already told us."

Sumac had been quiet for some time. He'd been making a point not to look at Ary, which was kind of starting to irritate Owl. Now he looked at her directly and said, "Tell us about the dreams."

The color drained from Ary's face. "How do you know about those?"

And though Owl hadn't thought it possible—Sumac actually looked apologetic. "I've heard you yelling at night. And later, your mom and my dad were talking about it." He licked his lips. "I think my mom was having the same ones."

Ary seemed to shrink on herself. She looked so tired. It was worse than before. Her cheekbones jutted against her cheeks, and the skin beneath her eyes were so bruised it was nearly black. Had she been sleeping at all? In a quiet, tense voice, she told them about her nightmares—about the hollow, the spiders, the girl, and the strange words she used.

About the liar—and the thief.

A grim silence filled the room. The Blight and the disappearances were bad enough. Whatever Ary's cryptic dreams meant, they couldn't be good. But they had to take things one problem at a time.

"Whatever was in those pages is connected to the festival today," said Sumac. "It might be the proof we need."

"If not proof," said Sootflank, "at least it could point us in the right direction."

"I'll get them," Ary said quietly.

"Absolutely not," the adults said together.

Ary's expression was stubborn. "I know how to get there. Even if it's locked, there's a window big enough for me to get through."

"If he's not there, he'll definitely have guards," said Sumac.

"Not if we do it during the festival," Owl said. "Sumac, didn't you say *everyone* is involved?"

Sumac frowned. "Well, yeah. No one would miss it. I don't think we're allowed to. It's the one night of the year the entire city shuts down."

"I know my way through the tunnels," Mrs. Dragonsnap offered. "If Ary can make it to the storeroom, I can guide her to the library. No one will even see her."

"It's perfect." Owl licked his lips. Everyone was looking back at him with doubt—everyone but Ary, who had a thoughtful light in her eyes. He spoke faster. "This whole time we've been trying to beat Oleander's timeline, which is pointless because we don't know what he's doing. But we *do* know he'll be distracted. Ary, how much time do you think you'd need?"

"A half hour? Maybe less?" She frowned. "I could definitely get them, but if I'm gone, he might notice."

"Then we need to give him something else to pay

attention to," said Sootflank. "We need to cause chaos—multiple points of chaos, if we can. Give him other things to worry about, just long enough for Ary to get in and out safely."

Slowly, one by one, everyone looked at him.

Owl blinked. "What are you guys looking at me for?"

"Your specialty," said Shrimp.

Sootflank nodded. "I can think of an example where it was, quite literally, your specialty to cause chaos."

Owl threw his hands up. "I blow up the Ant Court *one time—*"

"I can think of two examples," corrected Sootflank.

Owl glared at him. But an idea had already started to take shape in his mind. A ridiculous, terrible idea, so much worse than any of the ones he'd had in the Underground. It was risky. It was the worst plan he'd ever come up with.

And it might just work.

"I know that face," said Ary, the slightest twinkle in her eyes. "That's your *I'm about to really stress out Sootflank* face."

Owl locked eyes with her, feeling the smallest thread of warmth.

Even with how dire everything was—it felt right, for them to be on the same side again.

"Okay, hear me out," said Owl. "I've got a really bad plan. Um, Mayor Nightingale, how do you feel about challenging Oleander to a duel?"

THIRTY

Not Quite a Hero

The festival rose with the sun.

The last of the preparations were finished at dawn. As Ary and her group snuck home, she watched as Siltshore's folk hung glow-shroom lights through the trees. There was a sense of promise in the air, of something building.

She just hoped it was building toward something good.

Ary crawled into bed, reciting the plan over and over, and slipped into sleep. When she woke, it was evening. The scent of sugary acorn loaves and honeydew candies floated through the window, and with it came the chatter of Siltshore's fairies as they prepared for the event they'd been waiting for all year.

Mama stood in the doorway, practically glowing in a pale goldenrod-weave dress that made her hair shine. Ary's heart softened a bit to see Mama smile so much despite her fear. For all the problems Siltshore had brought her, that, at least, was a gift.

"This came from Mrs. Dragonsnap," Mama said, her eyebrow raised in that *I feel like you have something to tell me* way of hers. It was a plain, soft package wrapped in twine.

Mama had already opened it. "I'd apologize for being nosy, but I'm your mom. That's kind of my job."

Ary took the package—and froze.

We need a way to upset Oleander from the beginning, Owl had said.

Let me take care of that, the spectacled old fairy had countered.

Mrs. Dragonsnap had given Ary armor.

It reminded her of guard armor, but far finer—flexible and soft, crafted from pale wood streaked through with gray. Ary knew this wood. She'd spent years protecting its source back in Terra. The armor had been crafted from the massive mushrooms her people relied on.

And this armor was not from this world.

It had been worn before—the arm guards were creased and battered at the edges, and there was a slash across one of the leg guards. It gave it character, and spoke of a history lived long before Ary had taken her first breath. A pale green dress, freshly spun and unworn, was folded neatly under the armor.

A small card with neat writing sat on top of the pile.

It simply said: *Wear it better.*

Ary tensed. An awkward silence filled the room. How was she meant to explain this to Mama? Ary and Mama had never had to walk lightly around each other before; that had always been the role they played with Gran. Their fight loomed between them.

Ary didn't know where to start. She didn't know how to explain, and she didn't want Mama to leave, either. She grasped for something, anything, and what finally came out was, "Will you do my hair?"

Something strange passed across Mama's face. She nodded.

When Ary was small, Mama would weave Ary's hair into twin plaits every morning, her fingers deft and quick. But when the sickness came, her hands shook too badly to do it anymore. Ary never learned how to braid; she'd tried one morning and tangled her hair so badly she cried and gave up.

Gently, Mama divided Ary's hair down the middle. There was strength to her touch as she combed her fingers through Ary's mousy brown hair, selected three strands at the top of her scalp, and began weaving.

"I always thought I was doing the right thing by protecting you from your grandmother's legacy," Mama said softly. "It was torture for me growing up. It got so much worse when I had you, and I saw the pedestal they intended to force you on. You were so, so small. You couldn't even walk, but they wanted you to hold a sword. You were just a baby. And they already expected so much." She blinked furiously, her eyes glassy and wet. "I tried to shield you from it all. But I think I shielded you from her, too. And I—well, I apologize."

Ary blinked. "You don't have to—"

"No, I do." Mama's fingers paused, already halfway through the first braid. "I wanted you to have a normal life. When you began questioning the terrarium, I panicked. I told you to ignore what was clearly wrong with our world. When you asked about your gran's adventures, I changed the subject, terrified any bit of information would only encourage you. It was wrong, Ary. I think at some point, it became more about protecting my own fear than keeping you safe. I should have been honest with you." Mama kept braiding. "No one gives you a manual on parenting. They don't tell you what to do if your kid asks about the things that scare you. I wanted to keep you safe, but I failed. And then I got sick. I wasn't there for you, and I'm sorry."

"There was nothing you could have done," Ary whispered.

"I don't know about that." Mama hummed. "I could have been more honest. I could have been brave with you. What's done is done, but I need *you* to know that that doesn't make it any more okay." She started on the second braid. "I know you don't feel like you fit in here. I know you haven't been happy. And I know you've been skipping school."

Ary froze. Mama finished her other braid, turned her around, and knelt so they were eye level.

"I am going to ask you to be honest with me. You're not in trouble, okay? But I want the truth." Mama swallowed once. The sounds of the festival faded away; there was only Mama, her hands on Ary's shoulders. "Ary, are you in danger?"

Ary froze. She could lie. She *should* lie. That was what Oleander had advised, right? He'd told her that her fate as a Ghostwing was something she had to bear alone. But Oleander had deceived her. And right now Ary didn't feel like a hero who had saved one world and was ready to save a second.

She was just a girl, alone with her mom. And she was scared.

So Ary met her mom's eyes and said, "Yes."

Mama flinched. She almost hid it—but Ary caught it, in the way her eyes flashed with panic, in tightness of her fingers on Ary's shoulders, as if Mama wanted to cling to her and never let her go. "Can you tell me about it?"

"I don't think I can," said Ary. Her lip wobbled. "I'm sorry."

"Are other adults helping you?" Mama's fingers tightened. "Is Sootflank?"

"Yes," whispered Ary.

"Are you going to have to—" Mama's voice caught. "Are you expected to do something dangerous again? Something only you can do?"

Ary nodded.

A heavy silence filled the room. Mama's breathing was heavy, and Ary could feel her hands sweating through the fabric of the dress. Ary wanted to crumble. She wanted to tell Mama to run far, far away from here, before the most important person in Ary's world got hurt.

"Ary," Mama said finally, her voice strained. "Can it be anyone else?"

Ary's eyes blurred. She tried to think of a name. She really did. Someone, *anyone*, who could step up and fill the role of hero expanding before her once again. She knew Mama wanted that, too.

But it was Ary who'd shattered the terrarium. It was her dreams the girl appeared in.

And it was Ary who carried ghost wings on her back.

What had Mama thought, when she'd woken to find Ary gone? Being Wren's granddaughter was bad enough. But how much worse had it been for Mama to be the failed daughter? To watch as an entire city expected her own child to step up and save them? Mama had tried to protect Ary. She had done everything she could to shield her—and then, one day, she'd woken up and learned Ary had chased after the very fate her mother had been so scared of.

What had Mama been more afraid of? What would have been worse? Ary returning and becoming Wren Mossheart—or never returning at all?

"There's no one else, Mama," Ary said quietly. "It has to be me."

Mama closed her eyes. She exhaled—and yanked Ary into a hug. It was not the gentle hug she'd given Ary before bed, or the quick ones she gave her before school. This was crushing, all-encompassing, the kind of hug that gave two heartbeats no choice but to become one. Ary was crying, and Mama was crying, too, and in that moment Ary never wanted to leave. She wanted to stitch herself to her mother so tightly the world could never pull them apart. And Ary knew, if she'd asked her, that Mama wanted that, too.

Mama had hugged Ary like this exactly once before, on the day Ary emerged from the Underground, their world shattered around them, and they'd collided to the ground, delirious with joy and relief they had not lost each other after all.

Mama pulled away. Slowly, she turned Ary so that she faced the mirror.

Ary's heart stopped.

Before, in just the green dress, Ary had looked younger. Girlish, even. None of that had gone away—but now, armor shining on her arms and chest, hair plaited fiercely away from her face, she looked like not quite a hero, not quite a girl. Like something caught in between.

Something more.

Oleander was not going to like this.

Mama stepped away and knelt before the bed, reached her arm under, and withdrew a familiar package. Ary's heart leaped. *Mama* had brought the Seedling shovel all this way?

But of course she had. Mama was, after all, a Mossheart. She knew better than anyone trouble was always around the corner.

"Sometimes, we need one person to be brave first, so others can follow," Mama said finally. "The problem with my mother—with all of them—was they tried to do the saving alone. And far too many people were content to let them do it." Mama held Ary's stare in the mirror. "You are not Wren Mossheart's legacy, or mine. You are Ary Mossheart. Brilliant, brave, and *kind*. It is the greatest joy of my life to be your mom. And if you feel like you have to do—well, whatever it is you're doing—I'm not going to stand in your way. But I can't just let you plunge into danger, either. I can't let you do the saving alone."

"But you could get hurt," Ary protested, panic rising in her. "You would be in danger—"

"That's my choice." Mama cut her off, her voice gentle but firm. "You're not responsible for my safety, my feelings, or my choices, Ary. You're not responsible for anyone's, but *especially* not mine. Do you understand?"

Ary blinked away tears. This entire time, Ary had tried to hide her feelings and her problems from everyone around her. She'd swallowed her fear to keep others strong, had hidden her terror about stepping up to save everyone to ensure they could follow. She'd shrunken herself down and twisted herself into knots of worry to protect the ones she loved—and where had it gotten her, in the end? She was still in trouble. They were still in danger.

Ary had tried doing things Gran's way. She'd played the role of isolated, lost hero, and suffered because of it.

But what if there was another way?

What if she didn't have to do the saving alone?

Mama held out the shovel. Slowly, Ary took it, her fingers curling around the familiar weight of the familiar handle, but Mama didn't let go. They held it together, Mama's face steady as she gripped Ary's shoulder with her free hand.

"Now, I'm going to ask you one more time," said Mama. "How can I help?"

Ary's heart pounded. She held Mama's stare and licked her lips.

"If something happens to me," Ary said quietly, "Find Sootflank and Owl. Tell them *Atlas awaits*. They'll know what it means."

Mama nodded. She didn't question Ary. It didn't matter that the phrase, to her, was gibberish. She was going to put all her faith in her daughter.

Maybe it was time Ary gave some of that trust back.

Ary told her everything.

THIRTY-ONE

The Festival of the Gardener

The festival was beautiful.

Owl walked along the branch path, trying to ignore the tangle of guilt twisting through him while he looked for his friend.

Hundreds of tiny baby glow-shrooms twinkled overhead, bopping gently from the vines they'd been strung across and illuminating everything in pulses of cool, pastel light. A platform had been raised, draped in petal garlands, and tables were packed with bowls of fairy wine and more food than Owl had seen in his lifetime. Ahead of them, Siltshore fairies danced on the stage, moving with strange, quick steps. All around them was an air of celebration, of shared joy and exuberance—but was it Owl's imagination, or was there an undercurrent of fear rippling through the crowd?

Dune, Bramble, Peony.

Marigold, Thistle, Mugwort.

Yarrow, Clover, Basil, Tulip.

How many others had gone missing? How many more would, if his plan didn't work?

The dancers cleared and Mrs. Grumthrush took the stage. She'd dressed neatly in a pale brown dress and left her hair loose, although it did nothing to make her severe face any less intense.

Owl let out a shaky breath.

Briar eyed him suspiciously. "What's wrong with you? You're all . . . sweaty."

"Nothing," said Owl. "Just, um, nervous about the spell. That's all."

Technically, it wasn't a lie. He *was* nervous about the spell. Just not in the way Briar would think.

The students were meant to cast some collective spell that would bloom flowers all over Siltshore. It was a simple enough display of magic; every student from Siltshore had been gifted a seed and a bag of fairy dust. Together, they were to coax the seeds to life, weaving a living tapestry of greenery.

Owl had different ideas.

"Oleander is obsessed with his image, right?" he'd asked the group. "And if he's really using an illusion on his wings, we might be able to make him drop it."

"How?" Nightingale had asked.

"Well," said Owl, "it sounds like we might need to stress him out. So I think during the festival, right before we cast some big, pretty spell, you should stand up and accuse him of being, you know, a murderer. And while he's distracted, Sumac can use his fairy dust to destroy Oleander's illusion.

His wings will disappear. And suddenly, Oleander's got a whole ton of things to worry about—and Ary isn't one of them. It won't fix anything, but it could buy us time. If everyone knows he's a liar, maybe they won't listen to him. Maybe we can lock him up or something until we figure out what's going on."

They'd all gawked at him. But they'd asked for chaos. Owl was determined to deliver.

"That is the most dangerous, ridiculous plan I've ever heard of," Sootflank had said slowly. "And I can't believe I'm about to say this—but it might just work."

By some miracle, the others had agreed. Owl had felt brilliant.

He was feeling less brilliant now.

"Welcome," Mrs. Grumthrush called. "It is such a joy to celebrate the festival once again—and this time, with a whole new class of students, and new neighbors!" She beamed. "Every year, students of Oakview Academy who have earned their wings perform a spell together to honor the Gardener and preserve the wood. Our students have been working incredibly hard, and I hope you'll be pleased by their efforts!"

One by one, the students of Mrs. Grumthrush's class filed obediently onto the stage. Briar was in line ahead of Owl, but instead of Sumac stepping up behind him, it was Violet. Owl's stomach dropped.

"Where's Sumac?" Owl whispered.

Violet shrugged. "Beats me. Hey, why are you so sweaty?"

Panic sang through Owl. Sumac needed to be here. That part was pretty much essential.

Had he betrayed them? Or, worse—had something terrible happened?

The students shuffled forward one by one, until they formed a neat line on the stage with Mrs. Grumthrush ahead of them. Delicately, she moved down the line and presented them each with a comically tiny bag of fairy dust—just enough to perform a single spell, but no more.

Owl clutched the tiny satchel of magic. Back in Terra, a wingless like him even *touching* fairy dust was unheard of. But here, beneath Siltshore's shadowy canopy, something about it felt wrong.

Reach, the leaves seemed to whisper, rustling among each other. *Reach*.

Except the pull he felt didn't come from the satchel of fairy dust; it came from all around him. It came from somewhere beyond, deep within the wood.

Where on earth was Sumac?

"Well," said a familiar voice, projected with fairy magic to be loud enough for every pointed ear to hear. "What a marvelous class we have this year."

Unlike his people, who were dressed in finery and draped in garlands of petals and leaves, Oleander had come wearing neat, plain clothing. His ghostly wings flared behind him, refracting the light as though they were made up of hundreds of tiny crystals. If they truly were an illusion, they were an impressive one. He scanned the students with a proud smile, his eyes lingering on Owl for a fraction of a second, just long enough to narrow, then moving on.

Oleander turned to address the crowd.

"Sixty years ago, I shattered my own terrarium and led my people to these trees. We have built a home here, a life we are incredibly proud of. Folk of Terra, you have seen firsthand the abundance we've cultivated; you have eaten our food, slept in our beds, and attended our schools."

Most of the folk of Terra nodded as Oleander spoke. Even though Owl found this place strange, it was impossible to deny it had been good for his people. Life had started to return to the Terrans' faces. The sharp gauntness of their cheeks had lessened to faint shadows; the furious bruises beneath their eyes reduced to a soft purple blush. The food was better, the air cleaner, and many of them were wearing new clothes for the first time in decades—if not their entire lives.

It was too bad Owl was about to ruin everything.

Oleander smiled out at the crowd. "It is my . . ."

He frowned, his words fading away.

Whispers rippled through the audience. Heads turned, and Owl's heart stopped.

Ary was here.

It was easy to get used to the way that poverty had withered the citizens of Terra; when Owl thought of Ary, he pictured thrice-patched clothes, the color long ago washed out and worn paper thin. It was out of the question to have something nice, something *new*, in a world where resources were already so scarce.

Ary looked like something out of a legend.

Instead of the dingy, faded brown clothes Ary had always worn, she'd come in a dress that glowed the delicate green of new leaves. Her hair was plaited away from her face, leaving her wide eyes exposed. But it was the armor that caught Owl's attention. While the other folk were dressed for a party, Ary looked like she was dressed for battle.

Every bit of color had left Oleander's face.

"What," Briar whispered furiously, "is she *thinking*?"

Ary shrank in on herself as eyes flew to her. Fairies whispered among themselves, some openly staring. Her mother put a protective arm around Ary's shoulder and leveled a cool look at anyone gawking. Together, they picked their way through the crowd.

Finally, Oleander recovered, his eyes never leaving Ary. His face remained deathly pale.

"It is my most sincere hope that Siltshore has started to feel like a home to you, too. We have been honored to welcome you," said Oleander, smiling again, though all the warmth was now gone. His next words came out clipped. "And now, we'll allow the students of Oakview to take the stage for their showcase."

Oleander turned away, and Mrs. Grumthrush started. Something told Owl there was supposed to be a lot more to Oleander's speech—but he was too busy staring at Ary, and Ary was too busy ensuring she didn't meet his gaze, her eyes directed straight ahead and clearly seeing nothing. Footsteps sounded behind him. An elbow dug into Owl's side as Sumac slid in line.

"Owl," hissed Sumac. "We have a problem."

"You're *late*," Owl hissed back. "Where have you been? Our whole plan—"

"Nightingale is missing." Sumac shoved his fist toward Owl. Panic lit up every part of his face.

Glittering in Sumac's hands were a fistful of shining, silver threads.

So much for their plan.

"What are you two whispering about?" Briar demanded furiously. "You better not be causing trouble."

"Yeah," said Violet. "But if you are, can I help?"

"Right!" Mrs. Grumthrush clapped her hands, shaking herself to regain her composure. "Class—please step forward."

Owl was about to pass out. Nightingale was gone. Taken by whatever had stolen Tulip, Basil, and their parents—and who knew how many others. What was it Sootflank had said? Causing chaos was Owl's job? He needed to think. And fast.

Owl spotted Ary in the audience. Her brow was furrowed. Her eyes scanned the crowd, searching for Nightingale.

Look at me, Owl willed.

Ary's eyes snapped to his. She gave Owl a tight nod. Her lips formed a single word, and though Owl couldn't hear her, he knew exactly what she was saying.

Reach.

The students stepped forward as one. Owl's mind spun a million miles a minute.

"Violet," Owl said quickly. "Are you down to cause some chaos?"

"I am chaos," Violet said seriously.

Quickly, Owl explained what he was thinking. He stepped forward, prayed Ary would catch the sign, and threw the plan to the wind.

Owl had practiced for the showcase so many times he thought he could have done it in his sleep. It was a simple enough work of magic. *Reach,* the wind seemed to whisper, but the voices came from far beyond, deep within the wood. *Reach.*

The students of Siltshore opened their bags.

Reach, the voices sang.

One by one, the students cast their spells. Magic swept through the air. Owl leaned into the feeling that had followed him ever since they'd emerged from Siltshore, of magic latent in the earth, in the trees, in the breeze. There was old power here, far stronger than anything he'd encountered in the Ant Court, and it had been ignored for a long, long time.

Flowers burst to life; vines danced. Greenery bloomed

from nowhere, moving down the line, racing closer to Owl and Briar. A strange smell of something burning filled the air.

Owl leaned into the magic all around him. There was a twinge and a shiver. A wrongness in the air—coming not from the wood, but from Siltshore itself.

Reach, every part of him seemed to beg.

Owl's grip on the fairy dust slackened. Who was he kidding? He was a wingless by blood, a Seedling by birthright. This magic was not for him.

But another kind was.

Owl braced himself, and he reached.

Nothing happened.

Owl frowned. Heat crept into his cheeks. He tried again, grasping for the magic, pulling as hard as he could, but it wouldn't respond. It was like the power was held back; as if the magic of the very wood was bound up in something he could feel, but not influence.

He had failed. Ary would have to figure out something better. And fast.

Behind him, someone shifted. Violet had somehow procured three bags of fairy dust. They glittered in her palms, electric with power, casting a pale pink glow over the planes of her face.

"Chaos," Violet whispered to herself, her face screwed up in fierce concentration.

"Violet," said Owl. "Wait—"

Violet cast the entire lot of dust over the stage and flung out her hands. *"Wake!"*

And the stage exploded.

Massive vines shot out from all directions. Thorns burst through the wood, sweeping in deadly rows through the crowd. Fairies scattered in every direction, crying out in panic as hundreds of swamp lilies burst to life around them and rotted before their eyes. The ground jumped and danced as the very fabric of Siltshore seemed to rebel against them, long-dead wood sprouting back to life, thorns bigger than folk appearing from nowhere. The students scattered with panicked cries. Fairies ran in every direction, crying out in alarm. For a moment, all Owl could do was stand there, mouth hanging open.

Well. He supposed that worked.

From across the stage, Violet gave him a toothy grin and a thumbs-up.

Behind her, in the distance, a coil of smoke writhed through the air.

Time slowed down. Owl watched as Ary stood and slipped away from the festival, her face tight with a worry he didn't quite understand. Briar's eyes narrowed, and she plunged off the stage after Ary, dark hair streaming behind her. Owl turned to make sure Oleander didn't spy them and frowned. He didn't see Oleander anywhere.

It didn't matter. Owl had to stop Briar. They only had a short window for Ary to collect the papers from Oleander's office, and she couldn't afford any distractions.

He took a step toward Briar, and something smooth and hard bumped against him. Owl turned.

"Shrimp, what are you doing here?"

Panic lit up the pill bug's eyes. He was breathing hard. He had clearly come a very long way as fast as he could.

"Library," squeaked Shrimp. "Burning."

THIRTY-TWO

A New Name

Ary ran.

Up the branch paths, over the vine bridge, hard pounding, blood roaring. They only had so long before Mrs. Grumthrush and the others got the situation back under control. The sounds of the festival faded behind them, and with them, the chaos Owl had caused.

Where was Mayor Nightingale? Why hadn't she shown up?

Siltshore darkened around her. Ary had never been uptree at night before. It was colder than she was used to, the breeze plucking at her hair, her clothes. Somewhere, far in the distance, a single bird let out a long, mournful hoot. Ary shivered. Even in the armor, she felt exposed. She passed one of the acorn-shelling stations and paused, lifting one of the caps and testing its weight in her hands.

It was no bucket. But it would work.

Ary popped the acorn cap on her head and kept climbing.

She wasn't sure what would be worse—if she found proof that Oleander was some kind of evil mastermind, or if she found no proof at all, and they were back at square one.

When his office finally appeared, Ary's pulse quickened.

Sumac was right. There were no guards here; no creatures that might stop her or get in her way. There were only the glow-shroom lamps, so familiar in their pale blue light despite the fact that they'd never known the world Ary had left behind.

Ary tried the handle. It didn't budge. No matter. Oleander was a liar, but he wasn't stupid—if he was hiding some kind of horrible plans in here, he was hardly going to leave the door open for her. She eyed the window high above. The walls were too smooth for her to climb, but far overhead, a thin, spindly branch stretched over the window.

She had a terrible idea.

Quickly, Ary backtracked. She scaled the tree and wiggled her way out on the branch. It bent precariously under her weight. It was too thin to crawl along.

Ary would have to stand. And she would have to run.

Heart pounding, Ary rose. She put her arms out for balance like Sootflank had taught her. The branch wasn't much thicker than the backs of those cursed chairs. Ary breathed the way Sootflank had taught her.

"Eyes on your goal," she whispered. "Not your feet."

Ary gripped the Seedling shovel.

She locked her eyes on the window.

And she ran.

The branch bent under her weight. Ary sprinted so fast she could have been flying. She felt it snap, and she leaped, hurling herself at the window. She hit it with a painful thud, jamming the tip of the shovel into the latch as she fell. The window creaked open.

Ary hauled herself up and flung herself through.

She hit the ground in a heap. Ary gasped, rolling, her elbow aching where she'd banged it on the floor. In the dark, Oleander's office looked grimmer. More sinister. The Blight leered at her from the maps on the walls. Ary drifted closer, studying the maps, staring at the giant inkblot that stretched across the northern domain where the warm-blooded creatures reigned. Something about it wasn't right. She just couldn't place what.

In the distance, shouts filled the air. Ary flinched. She could ponder about maps later. She needed to search—and quickly.

She started with Oleander's desk, rifling through papers, careful to leave them where she found them. The pages weren't there. Ary moved to the cabinets, the walls. As she searched, her hands began to sweat. There was nothing here. No papers. No clues.

This had been a massive waste of time.

Her eyes drifted to the vase. The one Oleander had said was precious to him.

Ary crept toward it.

She stretched her hand forward.

"What do you think you're doing?"

Ary froze.

Briar perched in the window, illuminated from behind

by the gentle pulses of glow-shroom lights. Someone had given her a pale blue dress, and her dark hair was brushed neatly, pinned away from her face by twin clips shaped like the Gardener's flower. Fury sparked in her eyes, and Ary remembered a different day, when Briar had perched above her just like this, looking at her with pure loathing.

Ary had been a prisoner of the Ant Court then. There had been so much she didn't know.

"Uhhhhh,"' said Ary. She'd never been a quick liar. That was Owl's job.

"Very convincing," Briar deadpanned. She slipped from the window and landed with a thud. "What are you doing here? And . . . why are you wearing an acorn cap on your head?"

"I couldn't find a bucket."

Ary reached for the vase—and Briar's fingers locked around her wrist.

"Briar," Ary said evenly. "Let go."

"No," said Briar. She shook her head, her face pure, cold fury. "I can't believe you, Ary. I really can't."

Ary's pulse quickened. "You don't understand."

"You know, my grandmother used to tell me stories about yours. About how easy it was to believe in Wren. To love her. 'Wren was so brave,' she said. 'Wren was so bold. I would have followed Wren to the end of the world and back.'" Her eyes blazed as she looked at Ary, words sixty years waiting spilling out of her. "'Those Mosshearts—they'll bring you ruin, if you let them.'"

Ary's skin prickled. After all the time she had spent away from Briar, *this* was not how she had expected their reunion to go. "Briar—"

"I like it here," Briar burst out. "Owl likes it here. Your *mom* likes it. Do you even care about that?"

"Of course I care," Ary protested, yanking on her wrist. "I—"

"Then *act like it*!" Briar shouted.

Ary had never seen Briar so angry before. The girl's chest heaved, and bright spots of color touched her cheeks. Ary had the sense of watching someone from a distance. Of knowing, before the flame even caught, that something precious was about to burn.

Briar's eyes flashed, and with her words, she lit the match.

"You act so tortured," Briar said bitterly. Her voice grew high and mocking. "Poor little Ary, the accidental hero, granddaughter of the chosen one. I'm Ary and I never wanted this, I just want to save my mom, and no one else will! I just want a normal life, but someone has to be brave!"

"Briar," Ary whispered, desperately trying to ignore the sting of her own hurt feelings. "Keep your voice down. Someone is going to hear us."

Briar rolled her eyes. "You had me buying it for a while.

You *really* did. But this—" Briar gestured at Ary, her face shadowed with disgust. "You skip school, break all the rules, and show up to the festival in *armor*. Do you know what they say about you? About Owl? About *me*?" Tears pooled in Briar's eyes. "I never had a home. I never got to go to school, or make friends, or be normal. We finally have that. We *all* finally have that. And you're—what? Breaking into Oleander's office? I know you had something to do with Violet blowing up the stage."

"She blew up the *stage*?"

"Don't play stupid with me," Briar snapped. "I'm done. I'm turning you guys in. I don't want to hear about danger and not understanding things and us not being safe, okay? I had that my entire life. I just want to be normal. Why can't you be *normal*?"

Ary drew back, her eyes stinging. She wondered why adults always loved to say things like *words can't hurt you*. Briar hadn't lifted a finger, and Ary had never felt more bruised.

Ary needed Briar to get out of here. They were going to get caught.

Ary could back down. Apologize. She could agree with Briar—she *was* messing things up. She was drawing bad attention to them all.

But where had that gotten her before?

"You know nothing about me," said Ary. "Or my family."

"I know plenty—"

"You know *stories,*" Ary snapped. "That's all any of us know. What you did know, you didn't act on. You knew about Atlas, the terrarium, and you did *nothing.*"

"It wasn't my problem to fix," said Briar.

"And it wasn't mine either!" Ary shouted. She wanted to shake Briar until some sense plopped into her head, to drag her by her wrist into the wood and shove her face into the Blight until she understood. "That's what you don't get! That's what none of you get! I didn't want any of this and I did it anyway because we all would have died otherwise. I'm not asking for gratitude. I'm not asking you to understand. But if you're not going to help me, then *get out of my way*!"

Ary had never yelled at Briar before. She had never yelled at anyone like this before.

No, that wasn't true.

In her entire life, there was one person she'd yelled at. Just one time.

"My gran wasn't perfect," said Ary. "I know that. She made mistakes. But she did what she could with what she had. She wasn't a hero, and neither am I. And *I am not her*!"

Ary twisted. Briar was bigger than her, but Sootflank's training had made Ary strong. They struggled against each other.

What was it Sootflank had said about fighting dirty?

Before she could think twice, Ary dragged Briar's arm up to her mouth—and bit down.

"Ow!" cried Briar. She let go instantly and staggered

back, bumping against the vase. It fell and shattered, pieces sliding over the floor in a sad twinkle. Briar cradled her arm in disbelief. "You *bit* me?"

"Like grandmother, like granddaughter," Ary spat. She took a step forward, jabbing a finger at the maps on the walls. "This world is sick. We're in *danger,* Briar. People are going missing one by one, and if I can't save this world, we're actually doomed this time. You think I didn't want to be normal? To go to school like everyone else and not worry about monsters in the world? Of course I did! But unlike you, I never had a *choice*!"

Ary had never been so angry before. She couldn't stop the words from coming. On the ground, Briar had picked something up from the shattered remains of the vase.

"Ary," Briar said, her voice small.

"No, it's my turn to talk. If you think you can do things better, or differently, be my guest! I'd love for someone else to step up! But something is *wrong* with this place, and we don't have a second world to escape to this time. So here I am, again. A kid, alone, trying to fix everything, because if I don't, we're all doomed." Ary shook with pure fury. "And if you want to be like everyone else, fine. Stick your head in the dirt and fill your ears with leaves. It makes no difference to me."

An uncomfortable silence stretched between them. Briar's hands were shaking. She clutched familiar, yellowed papers between them. Time slowed.

"Ary," Briar said, her voice small. "Why is my name on this list?"

Ary snatched the paper from her. It was a list of names—the same names Owl had shown her of the fairies who had disappeared.

Marigold, Thistle, Mugwort.

Yarrow, Clover, Basil, Tulip.

But a new name had been added.

Briar.

There were other papers here, too, covered in strange maps. They almost looked like—

"Well," a new voice said. "This wasn't how I planned to go about it, but you two being here is convenient enough."

Ary turned.

Standing in the doorway, hand glittering with fairy dust, was Oleander.

The smile he gave her was colder than the deepest depths of the Underground.

"Ary," he said coldly. "How disappointing you've proven to be. Ah, well. I suppose we might as well speed this up."

The magic hit them like a wall. Ary crumpled the papers into balls.

"Briar," she cried. *"Run!"*

Ary lunged sideways, crashing loudly against the wall. She flung the balls into the corner and whirled to face Oleander, her pitiful Seedling shovel held aloft.

Oleander raised an eyebrow. "And what, exactly, do

you think you're going to do with that?"

"You'd be surprised," Ary panted.

Beside her, Briar's eyes rolled back as she collapsed.

"You Ghostwings and your immunity," Oleander snapped. "Ah, well. I suppose we'll do this the old-fashioned way."

Oleander picked up a chair—and swung it at Ary's head.

Everything went dark.

THIRTY-THREE

Love, Shouting Louder

Smoke rose in the air in thick, dark swaths. Owl clung to Shrimp's back as they hurried down the branch paths. The closer they got to Mrs. Dragonsnap's home, the worse the burning scent grew. Owl's heart pounded. The magic of Siltshore vibrated all around him, frantic and electric, but every time he reached for it, it was like his mental fingers slammed against glass. Someone or something was blocking his ability to reach the magic of the wood.

He would have to fix this on his own.

As they hurried, Owl thought of Ary. He hoped she'd found what they needed.

He hoped she was okay.

"Hurry, Shrimp," urged Owl.

There was a chance Shrimp was wrong. Maybe it was a small fire. Maybe it wasn't the library at all. Was Mrs. Dragonsnap at the festival? He didn't remember seeing her in the crowd. But her plan had been to stay in the tunnels, right?

Shrimp scurried faster. They rounded the bend, and Owl's hope turned to ash in his mouth.

Mrs. Dragonsnap's home was burning.

Flames shot out the windows and licked through the gaps in the door. The very walls glowed, as though the tiny cottage that had become Owl and Briar's home was one giant ember lit from within. Heat blasted at him. Owl's heart stuttered.

Mrs. Dragonsnap couldn't be inside. He'd already lost his parents. He wouldn't lose anyone else.

"Shrimp," said Owl, "go get Sootflank. Tell him Mrs. Dragonsnap's home is burning. I'm going to see if she's inside."

"What?" squeaked Shrimp. "No!"

Owl slid off Shrimp's back. He turned and took the bug's face in his hands. Shrimp's eyes rolled with fear.

The folk of Terra had always made fun of pill bugs, making them out to be cowardly, stupid, and small. But Owl knew better. Pill bugs were loyal, and they loved fiercer than any other creature Owl had ever met.

And nothing made you braver than love.

"I need you to be brave," said Owl. "For me, and for Ary. Find Sootflank. Tell him Mrs. Dragonsnap's home is burning and we need his help."

"Scared," whimpered Shrimp.

"I know," said Owl. "But I need your love for us to be bigger than your fear. I need it to shout louder. Can you do that, Shrimp?"

Shrimp held his gaze. And though he still shivered with fear, his antennae flattened stubbornly.

"Yes," he repeated. "Be careful. Back soon."

And then he was gone. Shrimp hurried away, back up the way he'd come.

Owl turned to Mrs. Dragonsnap's home. This was either very brave—or very stupid. The classic Ary Mossheart special.

Maybe she was rubbing off on him a little too much.

Owl gathered his nerves and plunged into the flames.

"Mrs. Dragonsnap!" cried Owl. "Where are you?"

Smoke whirled around Owl. Heat pressed in at him from all sides. Mrs. Dragonsnap's home groaned as the fire sank into the walls and the very wood of the tree itself. A new panic stirred in him. If the fire got out of control, it might not just be the house that burned. It would be all of Siltshore.

Owl plunged deeper into the house. Mrs. Dragonsnap's kitchen table was snapped in half; dishes were scattered all over the kitchen and her chairs had been tossed to the side. There had been some kind of struggle here, and a bad one. The hallway toward his and Briar's bedroom was impassable with flame. Tendrils of red, orange, and blue snapped at Owl and he flinched.

If Mrs. Dragonsnap was down that hall, she was already gone.

No. Owl wasn't going to lose anyone else. He refused.

Owl approached the tunnel.

It loomed before him, yawning black and endless. He'd

gone this way a dozen times, but even still, it sent a skitter of fear through him. Owl had never gone in the tunnels alone. He'd made certain of it. The dark was too thick, too eternal. He always had Sumac or Shrimp with him. Owl hovered at the threshold. Smoke billowed out in choking waves.

"Come on, Owl," he whispered. "Move. Come *on*."

His legs wouldn't budge.

It was almost laughable. He could plunge into a *burning house* but he couldn't walk into the dark? He remembered back in the Underground, when he'd confessed to Ary how afraid he was. She had done him the courtesy of not asking why, and Owl had never had to tell her about the time he'd wandered into the Gloom alone, convinced he could find proof that Terra was sick. All that had happened was he'd gotten terribly lost in the endless black. He had wandered until he was so hungry and thirsty he'd curled up in a ball.

Then, somehow, he'd ended up back at the thorn fence. Someone had found him out there and moved him back home. And Owl had vowed he'd never wander into the dark again.

But this time, he wasn't wandering. Mrs. Dragonsnap needed him.

Ary's words came back to him.

We find the sun.

It had been their guiding light—literally. The hope they chased, the dream they followed. Well, Owl needed a new sun now. And he wasn't going to find one by waiting around all day. He was terrified, but he couldn't let that stop him. Everyone he loved was on the line.

And it was time for that love to shout louder.

He pictured the faces. The ones he'd let down, the new family he'd found, after so many years without.

"Ary," Owl whispered. "Briar. Mrs. Dragonsnap. Soot-flank. Shrimp. And, ugh, Sumac, I *guess*."

Owl bounced on his toes.

"We follow," he whispered. "Come on, Owl. *Go*."

Owl counted to three.

And he leaped into the dark.

THIRTY-FOUR

Monsters

The first thing Ary saw were stars.

They glittered overhead, fire-bright and eternal. Ary recalled the way Sumac had mocked her when she'd first come to Siltshore, when she'd believed stars were glowshrooms, gleaming from high, high up. A part of her still wanted to believe that—that for all she'd lost, all she'd suffered, she was never that far from home.

"Oh, good," Oleander drawled. "You're awake."

Memory rushed back in. The festival, Briar, and Oleander finding them in his office. Panic locked every part of Ary in place. She blinked twice, but the image remained—Oleander standing over her, a knife held loosely in his hand, his expression grim. Briar lay unconscious beside Ary. Magic glittered over her.

"How's your head?" Oleander drawled.

Ary jerked upright—or tried to. Her legs and arms were bound together with scratchy, heavy rope. She twisted, craning her neck.

"Relax," said Oleander. "I'm not going to kill you yet."

They were in a part of the wood Ary hadn't seen before.

Pale beech trees towered around them, silent and indifferent in the velvet blue of late night. Thorns bristled in the thicket, with no sign of a well-trod fairy path, no hint of a vine bridge or platform. Wherever they were, they were far from Siltshore.

"You know," Oleander said, "I had really hoped you could be the difference. All these years I've spent dealing with the Blight and those wretched crawlers, and when you showed up, I thought, *Here's my chance.*" Thunder crashed across his face. "And then you had to go and ruin it."

"What, so this is my fault?" Ary snapped. "You're disappearing people! I know about the spiders. I know you use them to get rid of fairies to stop the Blight."

Oleander gave her an incredulous expression. The old leader walked toward her until his feet were only a few inches from Ary's face. Oleander crouched down, his eyes glittering in the night.

"I know you won't believe me, but everything I've done has been necessary. Every choice I've made has kept Siltshore safe." Oleander's eyes narrowed. "I'm not the monster here, little girl. I'm the one keeping it at bay."

"You've been getting rid of fairies," Ary accused. "Picking them off, one by one—"

"Sure, I've been sacrificing the least essential of the lot." A weary grief clouded his face. "You think I don't mourn their lives? That they don't haunt me? Every child I've failed to protect. Every folk gone to meet their end and never knowing why. I have kept Siltshore strong, and I have kept it safe, but we are dying a death by a thousand cuts. And I would sooner disgrace the Gardener Herself than let some *child* speed up our eventual ruin."

From the wood came a rustle and a skitter.

Oleander flipped his knife, peering into the wood, his foot tapping impatiently. He was stalling. Or . . . waiting for someone?

Ary needed to keep him talking.

"Your wings are fake," she said. "You're not a Ghostwing at all."

"Wow," Oleander deadpanned. "We've got a real genius on our hands."

He was lucky her wrists were tied. Ary could have throttled him.

"Why?" Ary demanded. "Why do all of this? Why pretend to be a Ghostwing and pick fairies off one by one? Do you love power that much?"

"Love?" sneered Oleander. "You think I wanted this? Do you know how old I was when they sent me and my brother to die? *Thirteen*. A child." He leaped up, visibly agitated, pacing in the clearing. "They sent us off with flowers. They promised us greatness. The things I saw in the Underground—the things I did. I knew the myth of the Ghostwing. I didn't want this. I didn't want *any* of it. When the rubble cleared, I was alone. Terrified. But there was sunlight, and grass, and a new world. I told myself this was my chance to be normal.

To fit in." His eyes cut to her, vicious and black with fury. "Do you want to know what happened when we left the terrarium, little hero?"

In the distance, growing louder, came the strangest noise—a hum, and a scuttling almost like a whine.

"I watched a bird swoop down on one of my friends," snarled Oleander. "And *eat him*."

Horror swept over Ary in a dark, cold wave.

"We were targets. We knew nothing of this world, and we were convenient, easy prey, stumbling around in broad daylight like fools begging to be picked off. Creatures from every domain hunted us; Keepers refused to meet with us. What did a bunch of folk matter to them? We had no power to threaten them with. No authority. So I made my own. With some clever magic, and a single, tiny lie. What did it matter if I wasn't really a Ghostwing, so long as I looked the part? What did it matter that I sold them a false dream of prosperity and safety, so long as they believed?" Oleander's lip curled. "I led our people to Siltshore. We found it half-destroyed, overtaken by a bunch of tree rats and mice. And it was then I realized what the Underground had made me good at."

Oleander leaned down so that his nose was only an inch from Ary's, enunciating his next words carefully. "Eliminating problems."

A chill crept over Ary.

"But the wood is sick," Ary protested. "Picking people

off won't do anything to stop the Blight—"

"You stupid girl," Oleander groaned. "How have you not figured it out?"

Oleander knelt down and met Ary's eyes.

Something scratched in the leaves behind them.

"I never actually cared about saving the wood," Oleander sneered. "I *caused* the Blight."

THIRTY-FIVE

Broken Magic

Owl saw the flames of the library long before he reached it.

Smoke filled the tunnel. Owl plunged forward, his shirt pulled up over his mouth and nose the way Sootflank had taught him, eyes streaming as the gritty air stung his eyes. The roar of fire came from ahead, and with it, another blast of heat. But the tunnels themselves weren't burning. Which meant whoever had done this had set the library *and* Mrs. Dragonsnap's home on fire, but they'd done them separately.

It gave him a little more hope for Siltshore—and a lot less hope that their plans hadn't been totally and utterly ruined.

He hoped Ary was okay.

Heat came from ahead. Owl plunged into the library, shielding his eyes against the smoke. Bookshelves were toppled in every direction. It was a scene of utter chaos—the table cracked, books burning, all their work reduced to ash.

"Mrs. Dragonsnap!" Owl cried. He coughed violently. "Willow!"

The library groaned as flames licked up a far wall. Owl

fought his way deeper into the room, careful to avoid the gouts of flame consuming the table he and Sumac had spent so many weeks at.

"Mrs. Dragonsnap!"

"Here!"

Owl spun.

Mrs. Dragonsnap lay in the corner, her lower half pinned beneath a bookcase, her spectacles askew, sweat pouring down her face. Blood trickled down her temple where someone or something had hit her. Owl rushed to help her.

"Owl!" Mrs. Dragonsnap said. "What are you doing here? You have to go!"

"I'm not leaving without you," Owl said. He tried to move the bookcase off, but it was no use. It was too heavy.

Mrs. Dragonsnap was in pain, and scared, but her eyes were clear. "You can't help me. Listen to me very carefully, child. Oleander knows everything. You have to run."

Dread swirled through Owl. He had figured as much, but it was different, hearing it confirmed.

"No," he said stubbornly. "No, I'm not leaving you here to die."

Mrs. Dragonsnap gave him a wobbly smile. She reached out with one ash-streaked hand and cupped Owl's cheek.

"You are such a sweet boy," she said gently. "A proper Seedling, even if you don't see it. You can't be here, Owl. Sometimes, we can't save everyone."

Tears cut tracks down Owl's face. He knew that better

than anyone. He had learned it first when his parents, despite all their love and hope and dreams, were not stronger than the mold in the end. It hadn't mattered how much soup Owl fed them or that he spent the last of their money on cures that never worked. It hadn't mattered that he had prayed to, bargained with, and threatened the Gardener to save them.

Owl had been alone for so long. And then Ary had come into his life, and she had brought Shrimp, and Sootflank, and Briar. And then here, in Siltshore—he had started to belong. To think of Mrs. Dragonsnap's home as *his* home.

"I'm not leaving you," Owl said stubbornly. "I'm *not*."

"You have to," Mrs. Dragonsnap said. "There's nothing you can do."

"I'm sorry," said Owl. "I can't accept that. I spent my whole life believing there was nothing I could do when people got hurt. And I'm not doing it anymore."

Owl closed his eyes—and searched for power.

When he reached for magic in the Ant Court, his world had been wreathed in fire then, too. He had been scared—scared, and angry. Angry that Quickspark would betray them, that Briar wouldn't help them, that they had come all that way. Scared to fail, scared to die.

Whoever or whatever was blocking him had no right. Mrs. Dragonsnap was correct. He was a Seedling, a wingless. This magic had belonged to his parents, and their parents before them, passing through generations until it reached the very folk who had carved Siltshore out among the trees. It was his by right. And it was his to take.

Owl leaned into that magic. He felt the wall between him and the power in the wood; felt the shift and shiver. He could *taste* the magic living within the library walls, fed by years of folk who hadn't even known the impact they were having on it. The power in the Ant Court had been different; slippery like their carapaces, silent and waiting, but explosive when provoked.

This magic was wild. And it was scared.

Reach, whispered the wood.

Help me, Owl willed back.

This was the part he'd never really been able to explain to Ary. Seedling magic wasn't like the fairy dust the folk of Terra used. He couldn't exactly tell it what to do. He could only give it permission. The power in the library had been simmering for a long, long time. In it, he could taste fears of frustration, of grief.

It was time he gave it somewhere to go.

"Owl," begged Mrs. Dragonsnap. "Please, you have to leave before it's too late—"

Owl ignored her. He reached for that power. He bundled up all his anger and hope and fear and love—and Owl reached.

And nothing happened.

The floor did not heave; the walls did not cave. Just like before, the power would not come. Owl could feel the wood vibrating around him; he could *feel* every bit of life. But it was as if something was in the way, holding the magic back, like the magic was water that could no longer flow.

The magic wasn't just blocked. It was broken. It *wanted* to flow into Owl, to wake up after so many years dormant, but it was as if a string between him and the world had been cut.

The library groaned. The whole thing would cave in on itself soon. But Owl could not leave Mrs. Dragonsnap here. He refused.

A bookcase behind Owl groaned under the weight of flames licking up its shelves.

"Owl!" cried Mrs. Dragonsnap. "Watch out!"

The bookcase tipped toward him. Owl flinched back, shielding his face with his arms.

From in front of Owl came a different kind of groan.

Owl's eyes snapped open.

Sootflank was wreathed in flame.

The newt stood over Owl and Mrs. Dragonsnap, chest heaving as he held the bookcase up with his tail. His dark eyes blazed as he heaved backward and sent the burning wood flying in the other direction.

"I thought I told you and Ary," Sootflank panted. "You're not allowed to die."

In one quick, fluid movement, Sootflank shoved the rest of the debris off Mrs. Dragonsnap. He picked her up with ease and set her and Owl on his back.

"Hold on," Sootflank growled.

Owl didn't have to be told twice.

He flung his arms around Sootflank's neck and held tight as the newt carried him and Mrs. Dragonsnap out of the burning library.

THIRTY-SIX

Oleander's Choice

Oleander's words crashed over Ary in terrible waves.

"But why?" Ary whispered. "The wood, everyone who lives here—you've doomed us all."

"The *Keepers* doomed us all," Oleander snapped. "They forced my hand. The folk are an essential part of the web of power here, but the Keepers were all too happy to move into our domain after the ones who didn't make it to the terrarium died." His lip curled. "So we went to the heart of that power. We met with the Keeper of the weavers, who held the threads of power together, and we broke that web. We took power for ourselves. That's the part the Gardener never bothered to include—the power doesn't have to be passed down. It can be stolen, if you're willing." He gestured to the wood with a bored flick of his wrist. "The Blight sprang up a few weeks later, but it was in the far north. It took years to move into other domains. And suddenly, we were left alone. We'd solved two problems at once."

"But that day in the wood," sputtered Ary. "I don't understand. You were trying to fix the Blight, you were trying to—"

"Are all children this gullible? Or was your generation just particularly stunted by the lack of food?" Oleander rolled his eyes. "I gave up on stopping the Blight decades ago. I was just trying to keep you busy. Didn't you look at the maps? It moves so slow. By the time it reaches Siltshore, I'll be long dead, and it'll be someone else's problem. At least, that was the plan." Hatred bled into every line of his face. "Then *you* showed up. Some of the weavers started attacking instead of following our little arrangement. And suddenly the Blight sped up."

"You're blaming *me*?" Ary demanded.

"There was never Blight in folk territory before you entered my wood," Oleander said darkly. "I caused the Blight by pretending to be a Ghostwing. I don't think it's that far-fetched to believe it'd be hastened by the presence of a real one."

Horror crept over Ary. What was Oleander saying? That not only had he never intended to heal the wood—but that, somehow, its recent destruction was her fault just for existing?

Oleander had never truly believed they could heal the wood. All the time she had spent with him, all his lessons and speeches and promises. They had just been lies. Distractions, meant to delay her until she gave up—or he could get rid of her.

But the worst part was Oleander believed he was in the right.

He had been her age when he escaped the terrarium. Ary recalled how terrified she'd been when the spider had attacked. How might she have reacted if, every day, creatures ten times her size were picking off her loved ones? What might she have done, if the Keepers who were meant to protect her people condemned them to die, instead? Maybe Oleander had never been entirely good, but he hadn't started out wholly bad, either.

There is no good or evil, Sootflank had said. *Only creatures, making choices.*

Oleander had made his. And maybe, in the beginning, he'd tried to do the right thing. But the lines had blurred, and it had become too easy to pick folk off, to sacrifice them for some twisted greater good.

And why wouldn't he? Wasn't that what his people had done to him?

Wasn't it what the folk of Terra had done to Gran?

What choices might Gran have made, if she had emerged from one broken world into another?

Not this, every part of Ary cried out. *Never this.*

It terrified her that she wasn't so sure.

"Why get rid of fairies?" Ary asked.

Oleander gave her a bored look and gestured behind her. "They want folk. I want the fairy dust needed to keep Siltshore thriving. It's an easy trade, and it certainly doesn't hurt that they've made it terribly easy to get rid of anyone that gets in my way." His eyes sharpened. "You know, I'd started to get worried. After all these years, I was running out of folk I could stand to lose. Then you showed up and gave me the gift of an entire village whose lives mattered less to me than mold on a leaf. I should thank you for that, really. With your people, we'll be set for years."

Were it not for the ropes cutting into her ankles and wrists, Ary might have leaped at him. She hated Oleander in that moment—so fiercely and terribly that suddenly she understood why Oleander was willing to do terrible things to the Keepers. She understood why he'd twisted the story of them to the point where no folk would ever seek them out.

She understood, most of all, why he almost seemed to take pleasure in hurting them. Because right now, Ary wanted to do the same to him.

A scuttle came from behind her. It had haunted her in every nightmare, and it always ended in pain.

In the dark, a hundred blank eyes reflected the pale moon.

Spiders.

There were dozens of them; spiders of every shape and size, from small, scuttling yellow ones to giant brown ones even more horrifying than the wolf spider. They moved fluidly, in unison, drawing closer to Ary and Briar in a terrible wave. As Ary watched, one of the spiders approached Oleander and extended a long, spindly leg. Dangling from the end, glittering brighter than a thousand glow-shrooms or stars, was the pale pink shimmer of a fairy dust pouch.

"You're a monster," Ary spat.

Oleander ignored her. He nodded at the spiders. "Take them. I want more next time, since I'm giving you two."

Ary let out a furious scream. One of the spiders dragged her across the ground.

"I really am sorry," said Oleander, in a voice that said he was not very sorry at all. "But you got in my way."

"You won't get away with this," Ary cried. "I'm going to make it right for them. For Basil and her family, for Marigold, and everyone else you got rid of."

The spiders swarmed them. The last thing Ary saw was Oleander's expression when he heard Marigold's name. He didn't look annoyed or pleased.

He looked shocked.

As if he hadn't been the one to get rid of Marigold at all.

THIRTY-SEVEN

Maps

Sootflank ran for a long time.

Through the tunnels, back up into Siltshore's heart. Smoke filled the path around them but if it irritated his gills, the newt hid it. Owl held on tight, looking nervously at Mrs. Dragonsnap every now and then. Her head lolled and her temple was still bleeding. They needed to get her somewhere safe.

"Sootflank," Owl croaked. "We need to find Ary."

Hopefully, Ary had found the proof they needed. They could still do it—stop Oleander, prove to everyone else that he was a fraud. Mrs. Dragonsnap would be able to tell everyone he attacked her and set her house on fire. It didn't matter how charming Oleander was; you couldn't really come back from that. Owl hoped.

Sootflank clambered upright. The storeroom loomed ahead, and with it came voices. Owl tensed—and then he heard Sumac's voice, pitched with panic and babbling fast.

"They're gone," he was saying. "I—I followed her, because I was worried, and he caught them and took them."

Panic bubbled in Owl, but he refused to believe it. Ary was fine.

She had to be.

But when they entered the storeroom, she wasn't there.

Sumac stood in the center of the room, chest heaving, the very picture of distress. Shrimp was curled into an anxious ball beside him, his eyes barely visible as he whirred with concern.

Behind them, standing in a strange ring, were Sumac's dad and Ary's mom.

Dark circles ringed Robin's eyes, and her cuticles were ragged and bloody from constant, anxious picking. Alder gave her shoulder a reassuring squeeze.

"The night before the festival, Ary told me she thought she was in danger," she said. Her mouth wobbled. "I knew I couldn't stop her—so I asked her to let me help. She asked me to follow her to Oleander's at a distance but not intervene. To wait for her down the branch path in case she needed a quick escape." Robin hesitated—and then her eyes went to Owl's. "She told me that if anything went wrong, to come to you and Sootflank. To tell you: *a new Atlas awaits.*"

Owl and Sootflank exchanged quick glances. No one but Ary, Briar, Owl, Shrimp, and Sootflank knew the truth of Atlas. It was their secret. Ary must have known it would mean nothing to her mom, but everything to Owl. It would be a kind of passcode. A sign that said, *It's time to save the world. Again. But this time, we need a little help.*

It wouldn't matter that it was gibberish to Robin. She'd lost Ary once before; Owl knew Ary's mom would do anything to find her again.

Tears filled Robin's eyes.

"When she didn't come back, I went to Oleander's office myself. No one was there." From her pocket, Robin withdrew crumpled balls of paper. "But I did find these. And, well, Ary told me she'd gone looking for pages torn from a book. She told me you were the one who figured out everything in Dracaena's journal, Owl."

Owl's blood roared in his ears. His hands shook as Robin approached and placed the crumpled pages in Owl's hands. He undid them as gently as possible. They were entries from the books about the Keepers—a page for each of them, covered in handwritten notes. Everyone crowded around Owl, close enough to look, careful enough to give him space.

"They're maps," Sumac breathed. "Not just maps of the domains, but—"

"Maps," Mrs. Dragonsnap said grimly, "to the Keepers."

THIRTY-EIGHT

The Girl in the Hollow

Ary was in the hollow again.

In this dream, like all the others, her wings had returned to normal. The wind tugged at them, pulling Ary to the tips of her toes. A mixture of grief and joy washed through her. With her wings, the whole world felt possible. She stood under a great canopy of leaves, but no sunlight filtered through, only endless, cool shadow.

Someone was calling her.

This had happened before, back in the terrarium, with Atlas. Ary had wanted so desperately to believe in the dream Oleander offered her—that she could delay fate and trust someone else to take the world in their hands.

But Oleander was a fraud. He was a murderer and a liar. He had doomed this world long before Ary Mossheart had ever learned the meaning of the word *sun*.

Ary stepped deeper into the forest.

"I know you're there," Ary called, her heart pounding. "I didn't want to believe it before—that there could be a reason for you to call out. But I know now that something was wrong with Siltshore long before we arrived. I think you were trying to warn me—about the Blight, about Oleander, about all of it. I wanted you to be wrong. I wanted things to be okay."

A soft crack came from ahead, like a branch snapping under someone's foot.

"I wanted to ignore you," said Ary. "But I'm ready to listen now." Her hands trembled. "Come out and face me."

The girl from the hollow poked her head out from around a tree—and smiled.

"Finally," she breathed. "I was worried you'd never get out of that village!"

She was young, like Ary, maybe only a few years older, with a shock of pale hair that fell in straight locks just below her jaw. Her eyes were wide and dark, and she had the scrawny, underfed look to her of so many fairies from Terra.

The girl darted forward, arms thrown wide as if to hug her. At the last second, she jerked backward, limbs flailing like a puppet dancing on invisible strings. She scowled and looked up at Ary. "Well, it's about time. What took you so long?"

Ary's heart pounded. It was one thing to believe someone or something was calling out. It was another to be greeted so . . . casually? The wood was in crisis and Oleander was basically playing the ultimate game of sacrifice-a-fairy. And this girl wanted a *hug*?

"Who are you?" Ary demanded. "Why did you call me?"

The girl gave her a tired smile. "I think you already know."

Ary froze. And it clicked.

She'd known for a long time now. Maybe she'd known even before she'd heard the stories, had recognized a fellow fallen hero at first glance. What a fool she'd been, to believe Oleander was anything like her. There had been too many holes in his story. Too much pride in the wings he carried on his back.

Oleander hadn't shattered his terrarium.

But someone else had.

The girl twisted so Ary could see the ghostly wings protruding from her shoulders, her arms moving oddly, as though constrained by invisible strings. She twisted back around.

"I wish these were happier circumstances, but it's nice to finally meet another Ghostwing." The girl tilted her head to the side. "I'm Aspen. And I've been waiting for you, Ary Mossheart."

PART 3
GHOSTWING

THIRTY-NINE

Aspen's Plea

Ary blinked to clear her eyes, but the image didn't evaporate. The girl with the ghostly wings remained. That name—Ary had heard it before . . .

"You're Oleander's friend," said Ary. "From before. From his terrarium."

Aspen's expression darkened. "Oleander is no friend of mine."

Panic washed through Ary in cold, bright waves. She half expected a spider to leap out at her, but for now it was only her and Aspen. Ary needed to move quickly. She didn't know how much time she had.

But she also had no idea where to begin.

"I know it's a lot," Aspen said sympathetically. "I was hoping I could reach you sooner, but he found you so fast."

"How . . . when . . . why . . ." Ary shook her head. "I don't even know where to begin. You're *alive*?"

"You could say that." Aspen's eyes darted around. "Look, we don't have much time. I was hoping to get you out of the village sooner, but Oleander has so many protection spells it made it hard. I need your help, Ary." Her gaze returned to Ary. "I need you to find me. I need you to set me free."

The last thing Ary recalled was Oleander's betrayal—the spiders that had come in waves and traded fairy dust for Ary and Briar.

As though reading her mind, Aspen spoke quickly.

"You've been brought to the heart of the weavers' kingdom," she said. "I don't know what their plans are for you, but there's no time to waste. You must find me. I've been a prisoner here for a long, long time. I can't hold on much longer."

"How?" Ary asked desperately. "I don't know where to go or how to find you."

"Follow the weavers," Aspen said. "Find their nest and you'll find me."

"But I have no magic, I have no way to fight—"

A rustle came from behind Ary. Every hair on her body stood on end. She knew, without looking, that a spider was approaching.

"Please," begged Aspen. "You *have* to hurry. It's your only chance to stop the Blight. To stop all of this. You were made for this, Ary. You can do it. But you're running out of time."

Spindly legs wrapped around Ary from behind.

"Find me, Ary," cried Aspen. *"Hurry!"*

And the spider bit down.

Every part of Ary hurt. For a moment, she might have been back in bed, before the mold, before Papa was sick, when

Mama would wake her for school with a whisper and a kiss, and her biggest problem was the shadow Gran cast in every direction.

And it all came rushing back.

The terrarium. Gran. The fairies of Siltshore. Oleander and Briar and the spiders, trapping her.

And *Aspen*. She was real. All of Ary's nightmares, all of her worries, hadn't just been her panicked, addled mind.

The girl from the hollow was *real*. She was out there, somewhere.

And she was counting on Ary to rescue her.

Ary couldn't stop replaying what she had seen. Aspen, her arms jerking as if held by invisible restraints, smiling at Ary in the hollow. Talking to her as if she'd been waiting for her all along.

Begging for her help.

"She's awake," someone whispered. "Little Mossheart, are you okay?"

Ary's eyes cleared. She forced herself to breathe. They were in some kind of dim, damp cavern. High above, stars glittered. Briar slumped beside her, unconscious. Bruises bloomed on her legs and arms from being dragged, but she was otherwise unharmed. Ary tried to reach for her, but her wrists were still bound.

Exhausted forms slumped all around her—a few fairies, but creatures, too. Earwigs and pill bugs, and larger, strange creatures she'd never seen in the terrarium before, furred creatures with fluffy tails and bulbous-eyed amphibians that looked like newts with no tails at all. There were three other fairies here, too. Ary didn't recognize one of them, but the other . . .

"Mayor Nightingale?"

The mayor looked far worse for the wear. Ary had wondered why she hadn't shown up to accuse Oleander during the festival. Now she had her answer. Like Ary, her wrists and ankles were bound with rope, the skin around them swollen and purple.

"Where are we?" Ary whispered. "What *happened?*"

An earwig twitched with recognition when it saw Ary, and let out a furious hiss.

Chills crept over Ary. She squinted, eyes adjusting to the dim light. There were five earwigs in all—and unfortunately, if their hissing and snapping was any indicator, they remembered her.

One of the earwigs crawled toward her. "Ary Mossheart. It must be my lucky day."

The earwigs made a strange hiss-laughing noise among themselves and began to inch after their leader.

"I still haven't learned," the smallest among them snarled, "what a fairy tastes like."

Ary's heart beat frantically. She struggled against the ropes. After all she'd done, all she'd suffered, there was no way she was going to let a bunch of stinking *earwigs* end her story. She needed to distract them, buy time until she could figure out what to do. Her eyes darted around. They were in some kind of dark, circular room. The ground beneath her was spongy and wet; a murky, woody scent filled the air, like old mushrooms left to rot.

"Grab her legs," an earwig hissed. "Hold her down, and I'll bite."

"Now wait just one moment," Nightingale protested.

Ary writhed. She cast around for something—anything—but she was defenseless with her hands and ankles bound. Briar was still unconscious, and the other fairies imprisoned here stared ahead so dully, they likely weren't registering the scene before them at all.

"Please," whispered Ary.

The earwig opened its pincers.

"Wait," said a familiar, hair-raising voice. "She's mine."

Ary's blood ran cold.

She would have known that voice anywhere. It had haunted her ever since the Ant Court, since the day with Atlas when she had nearly lost everything. There was a pause, and a rustle in the dark, and then a terrible, familiar shape loped forward to tower over her.

"Well, well, well," Quickspark drawled. "Hello, Mossheart."

FORTY

A New Atlas

Owl stared at the crumpled papers in Robin's hands. The Keepers were real, and instead of being some evil, twisted hoarders of power, they could be the difference. They had to be. Otherwise, why would Oleander go to the trouble of hiding these? Why bother twisting the myths of them into a warning of terrible beasts lurking in the wood?

"Are there any tables in here?" Owl asked.

Something bumped against his hip. Shrimp crawled forward and stretched out so that his smooth, hard shell was nearly flat.

"Thanks, Shrimp," said Owl.

"Useful," whispered Shrimp.

Owl scratched behind his antennae. "The *most* useful."

With shaking hands, Owl smoothed out the maps Oleander had torn from the book. With all five laid out, the haphazard notes suddenly became much clearer—and much, much grimmer.

The map to the north had been colored in black. There was a drawing of some monstrous-looking creature with pointy horns. A winding path wove into the very heart of the Blighted territory, where something had been fiercely circled. Within it, Oleander had scrawled: *Problem eliminated.*

Next was the map of the swamp to the east, where the divers controlled the thick, soupy land. Oleander had written: *Hidden too well. No heirs, will die on its own. Not a concern for now.*

On the map to the west, where the flyers ruled the tall, towering cedars, he'd scrawled: *Successfully poisoned. Hatchling far too weak to take over; ought to fail on its own, and no heirs will remain.*

Dread rose in Owl. With each map, Oleander had written notes about the Keepers and how he'd apparently destroyed them as revenge for the way they'd neglected his people when they were at their most vulnerable. It was no wonder the Blight was burning through the wood. Oleander hadn't just upset the balance of power; he'd broken it completely.

"Owl," Sumac said, brow furrowed. "Look at this."

The last map was the center of the wood—the kingdom of the weavers, who ruled the crawlers and all other kinds of bugs. The heart of the web, which kept the rest of the power bound together. Instead of brief, cold notes about destroying a Keeper, Oleander's thoughts seemed scattered and panicked. Things like *weavers out of control* and *weavers demanding more* filled the page. The oddest line of all, though, was one written near the top, so faint it had clearly been written many, many years ago:

Did she fail?

Who was this *she*? Owl scanned the notes, but there was nothing else that could help them. Frustration boiled through him. There was still so much they didn't know, but they didn't have time to ponder and guess. Ary was out there. And she needed them.

"So Oleander emerges from the terrarium," Owl said slowly, raising his voice until the others looked at him. "He meets the Keepers and does something that upsets the balance."

Slowly, Owl put the pieces of paper together. A map of the wood stared back at them.

From his pocket, he withdrew the copy they'd made of the Seedings' ominous, broken warning.

Keep the balance,
Mind the wood,
And bid the green light grow.
Folk to summon,
Flyers to anchor,
And Divers to help it flow.
Beware the lies of Ghostwings freed
In hem the rot mains
Seek he art within the reeds
F r the Bli ht shall rise again!

"The Keepers must still be out there," Mrs. Dragonsnap mused. "Otherwise, Oleander wouldn't have been doing those ridiculous magic displays to get their attention. But why get rid of them, only to try to bring them back?"

"Chives used to tell me a story, one his father had passed down to him. Of magic inherited and made stronger." Sootflank had been silent this whole time. Now he moved forward, his dark eyes gleaming. "Oleander must have believed that whatever he did would bring the folk *into* the Keepers' web of power, not break it. Perhaps he tried to steal it or take more power than he meant to. It doesn't matter. What matters is that it spun out of control. And what matters is that we've been here before. It's obvious, isn't it?"

Everyone looked at him.

"The terrariums," Sootflank said gently. "The world was dying before. Maybe not because of the Blight, maybe not because of errant fairies, but the wood was in trouble once before. Yet it healed. The Keepers can heal it again. We just need to give them the tools to do so." Sootflank closed his eyes. "Ever since we've entered this world, I've not been able to summon flame. I can feel that the magic in this world is broken—held hostage, and held back."

"I feel it too," whispered Owl. Even now, the power of the wood swirled around him. It felt like water splashing up against a dam, unable to break through. They looked at him. "Back in Terra, I felt magic asking me to reach. When

I did, the very ground reacted. I've been hearing those whispers here—but I can't seem to get through to it. At the festival, and later in Mrs. Dragonsnap's library."

"Same," whispered Shrimp.

It wasn't just Owl's imagination, then. Something was blocked in the wood. Had been blocked for a long time.

Somehow, Oleander had broken the web of power that kept the wood thriving.

Maybe it was time they put it back together.

A horrible realization pricked Owl. He looked to see if anyone else had just realized what he had, but they were still focused intently on the maps Robin had salvaged.

Why did Owl always have to be the bearer of bad news?

"We can't go after Ary," he said.

Everyone looked up at him. Owl leaped into an explanation before they could protest.

"Whatever Oleander did to her—it's tied to the Keepers. Sumac, remember the silver threads you found in Nightingale's home? The spiders are involved, somehow. And everything in the Keeper myths says they're at the center of the power." Owl's mind spun furiously. "Our first day here, a spider attacked us. It said the strangest thing to Ary and me. It said we smelled like the liar and the thief, and begged that we let someone go." Owl paced. He picked up the maps and handed them out one by one, his heart pounding. "Whatever is happening here—the disappearances, the Blight, Oleander, the spiders. It's *all* tied back to the Keepers. If we find them, we find Ary. There's no point in rescuing her if we can't fix the reason she was taken in the first place."

Alder looked skeptical. "You don't actually all believe in these old myths . . . do you?" He gestured at the maps and the poem. "We have no reason to believe these mean anything. We could be chasing stories, for all we know."

"We've got no other leads," Owl said. He looked at Robin and Sootflank. "And honestly, the last time we listened to a bunch of vague myths, they ended up being the key to escaping our world. So, yeah. I believe in it."

Alder's skeptical expression hadn't budged—but Robin, Sootflank, and Mrs. Dragonsnap looked thoughtful. The Seedlings had written the myths that freed their terrariums. Was it really so wild to believe this one was the key to saving their world?

"We don't even know where Ary is," protested Alder. "There's an entire forest, and half of it is ruined by the Blight. What are we going to do, recruit all of Siltshore into a search party? If we breathe one word of this outside of these walls, Oleander will get rid of us as quickly as he's done to the others."

Owl was starting to see where Sumac got his sunshiny optimism from.

A grim silence filled the room. It was one thing to leave

Terra behind and plunge into the Underground, to ally with a newt they weren't certain they could trust, to have to escape ants and wander through darkness. The enemy in the terrarium had been time itself; it had been the mold growing stronger every year, and the magic that was running out.

But this?

If their interpretation was wrong, the wood would be doomed.

And Ary would die.

"So we split up," said Sootflank. His eyes swept the map. "I'll go to the domain of the divers. I can move faster through water than any of you and my word will hold more weight than a folk's. Is there a way for us to find the flyers?"

"My friend in the wood likely knows a way," Mrs. Dragonsnap said. "He'll vouch for us."

Sootflank nodded. "Take Owl and Sumac with you. You'll need to make a compelling case."

"What?" Alder demanded. "I'm not letting my son go on some adventure that's going to get him killed. We need to begin evacuating. Searching for somewhere else to live, far from whatever curse has taken hold here."

"But everything in the wood will die," Owl protested.

Alder's face was blank. Owl knew that look. It was the look the Terrans had when someone talked about other creatures starving or there not being enough to go around.

It was a look that said, *Sorry, I've got to save myself.*

A muscle in Alder's jaw twitched. "I won't risk the family I have over some myth I'm still not convinced the Blight is *real*—"

"Mom did."

Sumac stood with his arms wrapped around himself. Now he dropped them and lifted his chin, his expression stubborn as he looked up at his dad. Conflict warred on Alder's face as he looked down at his son. Sumac swallowed and took a step forward.

Alder was already shaking his head. "Sumac—"

"Mom knew something was wrong before any of us," Sumac said, his voice wobbly, but his eyes bright. "I heard you guys arguing. She knew for years. She would want us to fix this, Dad. Not run from it. This wood is our home. Leave if you want—but I'm not going with you. I'm staying. And I'm finishing what Mom started."

The two of them stared at each other. A thousand emotions washed across Alder's face. His jaw worked.

Robin put a hand on Alder's shoulder.

"We've got to let them go," she said, her voice soft. Her expression hardened. "And then, when this is all over, we make sure no child is ever asked to save the world again. And no parent will be forced to stand back and watch them do it."

Alder closed his eyes. Finally, he nodded.

Sumac leaped at his dad and wrapped his arms around his middle, burying his face in Alder's chest. Alder hugged him back so tightly his fingers were white, his eyes wet and shiny as he blinked. He whispered something into Sumac's hair that made Sumac hug him harder, and Owl had to look away.

A strange, knotty lump made it hard for Owl to swallow.

If his parents were still here, what would they say? Would they trust him with an adventure like this? Would they insist on helping, like Ary's mom had?

He'd never know. But Owl thought he knew how to make them proud.

"What about the north?" Sootflank asked, peering at the map.

"With their Keeper likely dead and the entire domain ruined, we can't afford to send someone out there just to return empty-handed." Mrs. Dragonsnap shook her head. "We can't safely walk across the land, and none of us are strong enough to fly such a distance. Even if we had a fairy to spare, I don't think they could make it if they tried."

"What happens if we're missing a Keeper?" asked Owl.

Mrs. Dragonsnap frowned. "I . . . I really don't know. The old myths make it sound like without every Keeper, the web of power will fail. That's already happened." She looked troubled. "None of us know exactly how the Keepers are tied to the wood to begin with. Maybe we need all of them. Maybe most of them is enough. There's no way to know."

"So there's a chance this could all be for nothing," Robin said quietly.

The grim reality settled on all of them. Without the northern Keeper, they might go through all this trouble and sacrifice and still fail. But they had no one to spare.

"Well, if we don't try at all, we're entirely doomed. If we try, there's still a slim chance this will work," said Sootflank. "Anyone have any better ideas? Because if not, I'd rather die trying to save our sorry hides than curl up and wait for death to come knocking."

It wasn't the happiest view of their situation, but any optimism would have just soured their moods further. Robin gave herself a shake and put her shoulders back.

"Sootflank is right," Robin said, her face worried but determined. "I failed Ary once. I let her save the world on her own, and I couldn't be there for her. I refuse to do that again. But I'm not an adventurer. I don't have special magic or knowledge of the old myths. But Alder was right about the need to evacuate. You should all continue with the plan; we'll stay behind to work against Oleander and prepare the citizens for evacuation."

Owl had only ever known Robin from a distance; she had seemed boring compared to Wren Mossheart, a footnote to the hero's story. She had always just been *Ary's mom.*

"You will be in danger," Mrs. Dragonsnap warned. "If Oleander finds out—"

"I am not afraid of Oleander," Robin said darkly. "I've dealt with washed-up, bitter heroes before. No one hurts my kid and gets away with it."

"It's settled, then," Sootflank said. "Owl, Sumac, and Willow will find the Keeper of the flyers. I will find the divers. Robin and Alder will evacuate Siltshore and meet us in the weavers' domain. And then we find Ary—and bring her home."

Sumac looked at them all like they'd lost their minds. "You all seem really calm about this."

Owl shrugged. "Once you've faced one apocalypse, they get a lot less impressive."

It was an easy lie. Owl had always been good at that—pretending he didn't care about things when he was scared. But he saw the way Mrs. Dragonsnap's hands were white-knuckled on her teacup, the sheen in Robin's eyes, and he knew it would not help to tell Sumac he had never felt so scared.

It was one thing to face the end of the world.

It was another to face the end of *their* world. And that was what Ary had become—the connecting point in all their strange, disjointed stories.

They could not fail her.

"And if the Keepers are all dead?" Sumac asked grimly. "If we're totally wrong and this is all for nothing?"

Owl glared at him. "Look, it's already Sootflank's role

to be negative and grumpy all the time, so if you're going to compete for the spot, you need to start doing some cool magic stuff to make up for it. Otherwise, I'm going to need you to shut up."

"I am not negative," protested Sootflank. "I am *realistic.* It's not my fault we're plagued by constant mortal peril and that it often feels like the very fabric of reality is bending to make our lives more difficult than necessary. Also, I'm old, and my bones hurt."

"See?" said Owl. "He's a real pro."

Sumac scowled and clicked his mouth shut.

Quietly, they made their plans. It seemed impossible—finding the Keepers, finding Ary, fixing the wood. But it was their best shot.

And they had done impossible things before.

Owl went to the far wall of the storeroom, where the fairies of Siltshore kept their old tools when they weren't using them in the off season. In the corner, glinting and a little rusted, was something familiar.

Owl picked up a bucket and put it on his head.

"I will not be wearing that," Mrs. Dragonsnap said politely.

Owl shrugged. Sumac accepted the bucket from Owl and gave it an experimental tap. "Huh. This thing is actually pretty sturdy."

"I know, right?"

What a funny, ragtag group they made—an orphaned wingless boy, the grandson of a fairy-sacrificing monster, and a weary old fairy who had never thought she'd live to make it to this world, let alone rescue it.

There was only one thing missing.

"Hey," said Owl. "Has anyone seen Shrimp?"

FORTY-ONE

We Follow

Shrimp had always been good at finding things.

This was nice, because he was not good at much else. Talking, mostly. Being brave, saving food, fighting. *Definitely* not fighting. But finding things—he had always liked that. Especially if it was something that mattered. That was why it hurt so badly when he couldn't find his pod. He'd spent years alone in the Gloom, wandering, looking for them. A part of Shrimp had known they were gone. He'd hoped he could find them anyway.

Shrimp trundled through the woods, his many little legs carrying him under the leaves and over the roots around the thicket. The sun had been too bright for him up in the trees, but he liked it down here, where the shadows were cool and the earth was damp.

As he skittered, Shrimp remembered what Mrs. Grumthrush had said about the north. About the Keeper that *might* be there, that had been the first to disappear.

Shrimp had listened intently as the others came up with their plan. They didn't ask him for his input or his help. Shrimp didn't mind. He had always been easy to forget.

Most creatures didn't think he was very smart, because he talked very little, which Shrimp had always found quite funny. He'd noticed long ago those who weren't very smart tended to talk an awful lot, and sometimes others would be listening so hard they didn't notice they weren't saying much to begin with. Shrimp didn't mind. It simply made it easier to do smart things quietly.

So as everyone discussed what to do, Shrimp left.

He could not make fire like Sootflank (And thank goodness! So scary!) nor could he fly like Briar (What a relief! He would stay on the ground, thank you very much!). He did not have Owl's magic, or his fast-silly words.

But Shrimp loved Ary. He had loved her before any of them (well, except her mom, but Shrimp didn't really think that counted). He had loved her from the moment she had tapped on his shell and offered him food, the first bit of kindness Shrimp had been shown after many long, dark years wandering through the Gloom alone. Yes, he loved Ary Mossheart very much. She needed him.

Shrimp descended the tree, straight down the trunk to the forest floor. And he found it—that whisper of new earth, of silver-sweet magic, and fresh leaves.

Ary.

Shrimp followed it through the woods, past the slashes, past the woods, and headed north.

As he crawled, other pill bugs joined in—some from the terrarium, but also strangers, pill bugs that had lived their entire lives on the forest floor. They did not ask Shrimp where he was going, or why. It was not the pill bug way. They simply followed. Other creatures made fun of them for this, but it was because they did not understand. There was safety in numbers, and if one pill bug cared about something enough to stop roly-ing and poly-ing and head in a straight line, it stood to reason that other pill bugs should join in. It reminded him of when he was freshly hatched—when his pod had been full of fifty bugs, and he had spent his days happily following them. But now Shrimp had a new pod—and one of them was missing.

Shrimp felt the Blight before he saw it. It felt like the mold in the Underground had—sick and twisted, always reaching for more. But even the mold hadn't been able to permeate the deepest depths of the terrarium.

And while Shrimp wasn't good at many things, he was good at two of them.

Finding things—and digging.

Shrimp paused. The other bugs paused, too. Fear shivered low in Shrimp's belly, through his legs, up his shell. But Ary needed him.

The pill bugs behind him grew restless. They would scatter soon, if he did not keep moving.

"Going?" one pill bug asked bluntly.

Shrimp twitched his antennae. If he was that cranky old newt, he might have told them why they needed to head into the terrible Blight. He would have given them a speech about Ary—about the years he had spent in the dark, wandering and lost, until a little fairy girl climbed on his shell and guided him toward the light. He'd have told them about the ants, and Atlas, and the way their woods was dying. But that was not the pill bug way of things, and Shrimp knew the pill bugs would not wait around to hear about it, anyway.

So Shrimp just said, "Pod member missing."

A buzz went through the pill bugs. They all knew what it meant to lose one of their own.

"Alive?" one called.

"Yes," said Shrimp. He hoped.

The pill bugs buzzed again. If they were other creatures, they might have told Shrimp about their own losses—about the pod members lost in the terrarium and outside of it, of the lonely nights and days spent wandering, looking, hoping. Many would have confessed they still didn't really have a pod, and that when they saw Shrimp skittering with purpose, with intent in his eyes, they knew they'd follow him until he stopped. Some would have confessed something extremely un-pill-bug-like—that they *knew* Shrimp, because he had been with the little fairy that set them free, and they had started to whisper among themselves that he was the one to follow.

But that was not the pill bug way of things, and if they had said all that, Shrimp would have been very concerned and probably would have asked them not to come.

So instead the pill bugs looked at Shrimp and said, "We follow."

Shrimp nodded. They would have to skitter nonstop to reach Ary. There would be very little chance for rest, and it would surely be dangerous. All he wanted was to curl into a ball and hide.

But Ary was family. Ary had brought Shrimp a new pod long after he thought he'd been destined to suffer the worst fate a pill bug can have—a life lived alone.

Shrimp had always been good at finding things, and for all his faults and fears, Shrimp was not the kind of bug that gave up on the ones he loved.

"We follow," said Shrimp, and he began to dig.

FORTY-TWO

A Life Debt

Ary's head spun. She blinked, but the impossible image did not evaporate. Looming over her was Sootflank's estranged daughter, Quickspark. Memories flashed behind Ary's eyes—of the fury on Quickspark's face as Ary taunted her in the Ant Court, of the flames that had reached for every living thing and wiped an entire insect kingdom from the terrarium. Of the hatred in Quickspark's eyes as she lay at the bottom of the pit Ary had tricked her into jumping in, as she vowed to find Ary again and burn everything to ash.

She'd certainly tried in Atlas' cavern. They'd hardly parted on the warmest terms.

"Quickspark," Ary said cautiously, still half-distracted by the last threads of her dream. "It's . . . nice to see you again."

"You," Quickspark deadpanned, "are a terrible liar."

Ary gulped. "What are you doing here?"

"Oh, you know, I was tired of living in freedom so I thought it would be nice to be imprisoned by a bunch of half-wit weavers." Quickspark rolled her eyes. "What do you *think* I'm doing here, you meddling little runt?"

She really was Sootflank's daughter.

Ary's heart thumped. "Quickspark—"

"I'm sorry, did I say you could speak?" Quickspark's tail lashed. "Give me one good reason I shouldn't feed you to the earwigs right now."

"I've got one for you," a new voice whispered. "Mold-lung."

Briar glared at Quickspark from where she slumped against the wall. She looked worse for the wear, but her eyes were fierce. "You owe my grandmother a life debt," said Briar. "And I'm calling it in. No one touches Ary."

Quickspark's eyes narrowed to angry slits. She was a terrifying sight, all fury and contempt—but Briar didn't flinch. She just glared right back, as if *she* was the one with a gang of earwigs behind her ready to pick a fight.

Finally, Quickspark growled, "That seems like a waste of a life debt, Sunleaf."

"I don't remember asking for your opinion," said Briar. "Call them off."

They stared each other down, and Ary wondered, not for the first time, just how tough Briar must have been to survive the Underground all alone for all those years.

Finally, Quickspark turned away with a disgusted huff. "*Fine*. Leave the Mossheart girl alone. If we're lucky, the spiders will take them first."

With a reluctant hiss, the earwigs retreated to the center of the room. Quickspark coiled among them, though her dark gaze remained fixed on Ary.

"Hey," whispered Briar. "You all right?"

"I think so. What, um—what was that all about?"

"Long story." Briar chewed on her lip. "She owes my grandma a favor. I was going to collect the day she came to the Ant Court for you, but *someone* ruined that plan."

"Oh," said Ary. "I would say I'm sorry, but I'm not. But, um, thanks for that."

Briar nodded. She hesitated, looking as though she wanted to say something more, and then turned away.

What had Ary expected? That she and Briar would suddenly be fine after the fight they'd had?

Still, Briar had saved her. That had to count for something, right?

Ary forced herself to breathe, counting up to ten and back again until finally her panicked heartbeat slowed. She flexed her toes, and then her fingers. She was uncomfortable, and she was still bound, but nothing was broken. Ary began to wriggle, trying to work her wrists free, and took stock of their surroundings. There was no food, no water, and no furniture. Just an endless, flat circle, and that opening high above with a glimpse of the stars.

"Where are we?" Ary asked again, louder this time.

The other imprisoned fairies twitched, turning to the sound of her voice. Their eyes were too wide, the pupils swallowing the irises from too long spent in the dark. Gloom eyes, the fairies of Terra had always called it. After a lifetime of adjusting to the soft-glowing mushrooms that had illuminated their world, many of the Terrans fared far better at night than the fairies of Siltshore, but even they were not equipped to handle the never-ending darkness of the Gloom. That was how this man looked now—eyes blown wide in the dark, his too-skinny arms wrapped around his legs. Recognition lit his face.

"You're the little Mossheart girl," he said.

Cold bolted through Ary. Tulip and Basil's dad had lost so much weight she barely recognized him. *"Mr. Frostline?"*

He nodded grimly. "Have you seen my wife? My daughters?"

Ary hesitated. If Clover, Basil, and Tulip weren't here, it definitely wasn't a good sign. "Um, no. They went missing not too long ago."

Yarrow's face did something strange. He breathed very heavily for a few seconds and then all the emotion vanished from his face. Ary had seen Gran do that before.

"Mr. Frostline," Ary asked, "what are you doing here?"

The other fairy who had been with Yarrow looked up, her hair hanging in oily, bedraggled strands over her face. "The real question is what did you do to anger Oleander?"

Cold bolted through Ary. "Oleander put you all here?"

They both nodded.

"We should have known," another fairy answered wearily. She was so weak that her voice was little more than a whisper. "Fairies were disappearing. But when life is good, and your belly is full, it's easy to look away. To keep your eyes down and just hope that whatever strange thing is going on doesn't come for you."

"There should be a lot more fairies here," Ary said quietly. She kept wriggling. She almost had her left arm free.

"The spiders come for us," Thistle rasped. "One by one. No one ever comes back."

"The spiders also brought Oleander fairy dust," Ary said slowly, mentally moving the pieces around in her head. To her left, she was aware of Briar listening intently. "It was like we . . . like we were almost some kind of trade."

"I should have never led us through those gates," Nightingale said bitterly. "I should have known. I should have kept our people far, far away from that man."

Ary's mind spun. The creatures imprisoned here seemed to think Oleander controlled the spiders—but he had seemed afraid of them. It was like the puzzle of Atlas all over again. The fairy dust, Oleander, the Blight, Aspen. They were all connected, she was certain. Ary just couldn't see the whole picture yet.

Were the spiders the ones holding them prisoner? And if so, why? What did they get out of kidnapping fairies? What did they gain from holding Aspen prisoner, too?

"Briar," Ary whispered. "I need to talk to you."

Briar gave Ary a miserable look. "I'm done listening to you. All you've ever brought me is trouble."

Frustration rose in Ary. "I know, and I'm sorry, but I

need you to trust me. I think there's something bigger going on here."

"I don't care," Briar said bitterly. "I told you. All I wanted was a normal life. You ruined that. Just—just leave me alone, okay?"

Briar turned away before Ary could say anything else.

Ary could have screamed. It was no wonder Gran had been so frustrated with the folk of Terra. How many times had she been in a situation like this—expected to carry all the blame when things went wrong, but forced into the role of savior when there was a chance that things might go right?

Ary had never understood her more than in that moment. It was so lonely, so *frustrating,* to have people stand around and wait for a miracle. People assumed that bravery was innate—that if you didn't have it at the start, you should just wait around for someone who did to come along.

Ary knew better. Being brave never got easier. It just became more familiar.

Her mind spun. She thought of Mama, of Sootflank, and Owl. None of them were safe while Oleander still led the town. Rescuing Aspen was the key to saving them all. It had to be. Ary had no idea how she'd do that, but first, she needed to get out of here.

Ary set her teeth to the ropes binding her hands and began to chew.

As the night stretched on, Ary thought of the ones she

loved, and that tiny spark of hope in her chest became a flame. She would not despair. She would not give in. She was a Mossheart. And somehow, some way, she was going to get out of here.

And then Oleander would pay for what he'd done.

FORTY-THREE

Pebble

The wood did not feel welcoming.

It should have been wonderful to be on the ground again. Owl had never quite gotten used to the sway of the vine bridges, the constant rustling of the leaves, or the cold—the way the wind always seemed to steal the warmth from his fingers and creep in under his door. The moment his feet touched earth, something in Owl clicked back together again—but it clicked back wrong.

"It's getting worse," Owl whispered.

The entire wood had a sense of being close to crumbling. The moon blazed overhead, illuminating the trees in an eerie silver glow. Owl, Sumac, and Mrs. Dragonsnap had hidden in the tunnels until nightfall, waiting for the other Siltshore fairies had put out the fire and Oleander was distracted enough that they could make their escape. Now, with their meager supplies secured in sacks thrown across their shoulders, Owl couldn't help but wonder if they were making a mistake. They looked awfully . . . well, *unprepared* was putting it nicely.

Owl knelt and dug his fingers into the soil. He should

have relished in the cool shadows of the forest floor, the scent of leaf decay and freshly sprouted things swirling around him. But all he could notice was how quiet the woods were. As if even the trees were holding their breath in fear.

"Follow me," Mrs. Dragonsnap whispered, shifting the giant sack of books on her shoulder.

She led them deep into the wood, heading west toward the flyers' domain. As they walked, the carpet across the forest floor changed, shifting from dead leaves to a layer of spongey orange pine needles. Silence enveloped them. Mrs. Dragonsnap walked with confidence, her face screwed in determination.

They rounded a bend, approaching the base of a tall pine tree. A tiny door crouched against the entrance. Mrs. Dragonsnap approached and did a strange series of knocks. They echoed loudly in the forest; the sound set Owl's skin crawling. If something hadn't known they were here before, it definitely would now.

After what seemed like an eternity, the door creaked open. A yellow eye set in a furry face peered out at them.

"Willow?" the creature squeaked. The door opened farther, revealing a squat mouse with a long, scaly tail. "What are you doing out here? Who is this? What's going on?"

"Can we come inside?" Mrs. Dragonsnap asked quickly. "It's a long story. And I'll be more comfortable when we're not out in the open."

Shadows blanketed the inside of the mouse's tiny home.

It was a cozy cottage that had been carved directly into the base of the pine tree, but three extra fairies made the space cramped. The mouse hovered before them anxiously, his round, furred ears flat against his head. His name was Pebble, and from the way he and Mrs. Dragonsnap interacted, they'd clearly known each other for quite some time.

The mouse held one of the books Mrs. Dragonsnap had brought up to the light, his whiskers vibrating in delight. "Oh, Willow. These are just marvelous, but you really didn't need to come all this way! I was due for a visit in a few weeks."

"Wait," said Sumac. "How do you two even know each other?"

"I'm a bit of a literary enthusiast," Pebble admitted. "Willow has always been generous with her books. It's hard to find them out here in the forest ever since that unpleasant Oleander fellow took charge. Folk and creatures used to share knowledge freely—not so much since he became their leader."

"I was quite the explorer when I was younger," Mrs. Dragonsnap explained. "And one day I got very, very lost. Pebble found me and I convinced him to lead me home in exchange for books. We've kept up that trade ever since."

Pebble's whiskers gave a mournful twitch. "It was my pleasure, truly. This forest used to bustle with life before the Blight returned. I had hoped the folk would repair what was broken—but it seems that was a fool's dream."

"Maybe not," Mrs. Dragonsnap said. "We're not actually here to bring you books, Pebble. I need a favor."

Pebble looked at her suspiciously. "The last time you asked me for a favor, it ended with us getting chased by a bunch of squirrels."

"This one will hopefully be more productive." Mrs. Dragonsnap took a breath. "I know you know the location of the flyers' Keeper. We need to find it."

"What?" Pebble squeaked. "Have you lost your mind? Do you know what birds do to folk and mice, Willow? They eat us!"

Sumac shot Owl an alarmed look. That hadn't been part of the earlier conversation.

"We think we may have a way to heal the wood for real this time," Mrs. Dragonsnap said gently. "But the forest is vast and even with a map, we have no hope of finding the flyer on our own. Please, Pebble. There's a new Ghostwing—a real one. She's a good girl, but she's in trouble. We need the Keeper of the flyers. We need all the help we can get. And maybe—just maybe—we can turn this forest around." Mrs. Dragonsnap put a hand on Owl's shoulder. "We've got a Seedling connected to the wood. A new Ghostwing who might just save it. It can't be an accident. What is the point of all the research we did and everything we learned, if not to put it in action?"

Pebble looked at them with pure loathing, but his nose gave a thoughtful twitch. "A Ghostwing, you say?"

He paused. "Small? Brown hair, constant look of anxiety, clearly in need of a long nap?"

"That's Ary!" cried Owl.

Pebble shook his head. "I was out hunting for nuts and she startled me and made me drop my books! And then . . . well, I actually found them stacked quite nicely later." He hesitated. "I will admit, I am loath to go near the flyers or put my faith in a Ghostwing again. If the world is going to end, I'd much rather curl up with some tea and a good book before it all goes down. You're certain about the girl?" His beady eyes flicked to Owl. "About him?"

Owl stiffened. What was Mrs. Dragonsnap not telling him?

"I'm certain," she said.

Still, Pebble hesitated. Impatience and worry flashed through Owl. They didn't have time to stand around waiting for some old mouse to decide whether or not he wanted to help them. There had to be something they could offer him. Something he'd want.

Oh.

Duh.

"If you help us," Owl said, "I can take you to a place that has all kinds of books. Ones you've never heard of, ones that have never been read."

Pebble's eyes narrowed with interest. "How?"

"Our terrarium had a ton of them. They're buried in glass and stuff, but I'm sure they're fine. If you help us, they're all yours." Owl didn't actually know how the citizens of Terra would feel about that, but he also didn't really care. He'd worry about that later.

Pebble flashed his squared teeth and rubbed his furred hands together. His eyes darted from Willow to Owl to Sumac and back again. "I don't know . . ."

"There's hundreds of books," Owl coaxed. "So many it would probably take you three lifetimes to read."

Pebble sighed. "Oh, very well then. If I die, bury me with my books." He looked at Owl and Sumac curiously. "What are your names, little fairies?"

"I'm Sumac," said Sumac. "And that's Owl."

Pebble rolled his eyes to the heavens. "This is going to be a disaster."

FORTY-FOUR

Not a Hero

It was difficult to tell how much time had passed. Ary's body ached, and there was a dizzy fog in her head that would not clear. The imprisoned fairies spoke very rarely, if at all. There was a sense of breath being held, of bracing for the inevitable, but only darkness rose to greet them.

"Briar," Ary whispered. "Please, just talk to me."

Briar didn't answer.

Ary wanted to shake her. After all that, she was just going to *give up*?

"Look," Ary whispered, "I know you wanted a normal life. I wanted that, too, okay? But that doesn't change that we're trapped here. Something is going on. There's someone trapped with us—a girl, who had reached out in my dreams. If we could just find her—"

"If she won't help," Nightingale said, "I will."

Ary looked up.

The mayor of Terra looked back at Ary evenly, her eyes glinting in the dark. Ary hesitated.

"I know you don't trust me," Nightingale said. "Wren and I had a . . . complicated relationship. But I want what's best for this world, same as you."

"Do you?" Ary couldn't help herself. She knew Sootflank seemed to trust Nightingale, but it didn't erase the hurt she'd caused. One right couldn't undo all those wrongs. "Is that why you hoarded food? Why you wanted to keep us in Terra, even after the terrarium shattered? Because you just *wanted what was best*?"

The color drained from Nightingale's face. The old Ary would have felt guilty. It had been easier, as the failed granddaughter of Wren Mossheart, to keep herself and her words small. Ary did not think she would ever be flippantly confident like Briar, or funny like Owl, but somewhere along the way she had gone from being a girl scared to use her words to a girl who chose to use them carefully.

She liked to think Gran would be proud.

To her credit, Nightingale held Ary's gaze.

"I have made mistakes," she admitted slowly. "But I was doing the best with what I had. Every year we had less food. Every year, the magic dwindled, and the choices got harder. Do you know what it's like to have to lead a people whose world is dying?" She shook her head. "I won't deny that I kept more for myself and those close to me. But I took no pleasure in it. Every hungry face—every child lost to mold. If you want to hear me say they were my fault, I'll say it. I bear it all. I cannot change the ways I failed you, your family, or any of the others." Her lips thinned. "But I want to help. Will your pride get in the way, like it did with your grandmother? Or will you be better than us both and put a stop to this—once and for all?"

Ary drew back, stung. She knew Gran was prideful. She *did*. And maybe it had been easy to hate Nightingale for the hungry pinch in her stomach and the despair that had hung over Terra like a cloud. If Ary was being honest, she didn't know what she would do in Nightingale's shoes or Oleander's. She didn't like Nightingale. She didn't trust her. But Nightingale was willing to take blame. That had to count for something, right?

"When did you suspect Oleander?" Ary asked. She looked at Yarrow. "When did you start investigating him?"

"From the beginning," said Nightingale. She inclined her head toward Ary. "It was your mother's idea. She asked me to put aside our differences for a common goal—to keep our people safe. I suspect she knows a thing or two about old heroes hiding things."

Mama had been suspicious of Oleander? Ary thought of all the days she'd come home to an empty house—the way Mama had seemed constantly distracted, occupied by other things. Ary had thought it was because Mama was falling in love.

But Mama had been trying to solve Siltshore's problem, too.

Yarrow jumped in to explain. "She said Alder felt the same. Your mother suggested we not get too settled here. Look for a way out, a chance to start out a new life, away from Siltshore, away from whatever problems were brewing beneath the surface. But she knew our people were desperate for stability. And she suspected Oleander would not let us leave so easily."

Ary stiffened. The words she'd overheard. The scene she'd witnessed between Mama and Alder.

A new life.

Mama hadn't been planning to keep Ary in Siltshore.

She'd been planning to *leave.*

"She was going to tell you the day of the festival," Nightingale said softly. "I warned her in advance what I planned to do. But I went to sleep the night before and woke up here." Nightingale shook her head. "Oleander must have known."

Ary didn't know what to say. She reeled, the weight of it settling on her. This whole time, she had felt so alone. But there had been others working in the background all along. Nothing had been wrong with her for feeling unsettled or unsafe.

They had felt it, too.

"I'm sorry, by the way," Nightingale said awkwardly. "About your grandmother. Wren and I had our differences, and we rarely agreed, but I respected her. She was a real hero."

What Ary would not have given for Gran to be here, with her bitter smile and fiery eyes.

Make me a new Mossheart's promise.

"She wasn't a hero," Ary whispered. Tears slipped down her cheeks. "She was just a person. She made mistakes, and she failed. She was selfish, and she could be cruel. She saved us. And I don't know if I can forgive her."

Silence blanketed the interior of the prison as every creature listened.

"I see her in my dreams," Ary confessed, not sure why she was telling Nightingale this, but unable to stop. "I'm chasing her, and I can't reach her. I'm so angry at her—but not for lying, or for hiding all her life. Not for being selfish, or cruel, or cowardly when I needed her most. I'm angry because she left."

She had been running from these feelings ever since they'd left the terrarium—maybe before. She had only just gotten Gran back, and then Gran had left, she *left* Ary, had decided to step up and keep the Mossheart's promise made sixty years ago after all. And Ary had never been angrier, because after a lifetime of selfishness, why couldn't Gran have been selfish a little bit longer?

Why couldn't she have given Ary more time?

This was all too much. This was not as simple as finding Atlas and unraveling a spell. Oleander, the Blight, and now Aspen—it was all too big for her. Ary was just one girl, and her grandmother *should have been here.*

She should have been here for all of it.

"I see my grandmother in mine, too," Briar whispered. Her voice was barely audible, just a scratch in the dark. "It's not her fault she died. I get that. But I wonder if she should have tried harder to find Wren again. It wasn't just herself she condemned to the Underground, after all. It was my mom, and me, and so many others, too."

Ary knew that all too well. How many times had Gran refused to play along with Nightingale, choosing her pride over her family's well-being? How many times had Ary looked at her and understood *why* Gran did the things she did, but she still wanted to shake her and remind Gran it wasn't just about her anymore?

Something still didn't sit right with Ary. There had to be something they were missing.

"Nightingale," Ary said. "You said it was spiders that took you? Not Oleander?"

Nightingale nodded. "I woke and found them in my room. They bit me before I could protest."

It didn't make sense. Oleander had traded fairies to the spiders for something, but why would they enter Siltshore and attack someone unprovoked?

Unless . . .

Ary didn't like Nightingale. She didn't trust her. But right now, they were on the same side.

"I need to tell you something," Ary said. "All of you. Oleander isn't the real Ghostwing, but there was one. Her name was Aspen. She shattered the old terrarium, and I think she's still out there somewhere. I think she's waiting for us to save her."

Nightingale paled. She opened her mouth to speak—and chaos erupted through the prison.

Spiders raced down the walls, scurrying across the earth to entangle Yarrow and Nightingale with webs that snapped their arms to their sides and their legs together. Nightingale howled, twisting to shout something to Ary, but webs twined over her mouth, her nose, her eyes, strangling her. The spiders paused for the briefest second and then snapped backward, retracting up the wall and taking Nightingale and Yarrow with them.

"No!" cried Ary. She lunged after them and threw herself after the mayor, digging her fingernails into the thick rope of web that bound her ankles. Nightingale shouted something, writhing, but Ary couldn't understand her.

The spiders shivered and began to haul them both up the wall.

"Ary!" cried Briar. "Let go!"

Nightingale kept shouting. The ground vanished, and air rushed by as they shot toward the sky. Ary caught the scent of something wet, and a strange, haunting song. Nightingale howled, twisting, fighting the spiders' webs. She was going to suffocate. A strange, skittering whine filled the air.

The spiders shivered and gave one final heave. They yanked Nightingale and Yarrow over the lip of the prison. The nearest spider hooked one of its legs through the front of Ary's shirt and hung her in the air. She dangled there, helpless, heart pounding, watching in horror as the spiders bundled Nightingale and Yarrow into a thick, silvery cocoon. The sound of rushing water swirled around her. Ary twisted, trying to get a sense of where they were, but all she saw was endless black. Below her, she could just barely make out Briar, the earwigs, and the pale orange blur of Quickspark.

Her stare met the spider's—and her heart dropped.

Its eyes were completely blank.

Ary had seen that kind of blankness before, in the glowmoths back in Terra.

And finally it clicked.

"You're enchanted," said Ary. "Someone's controlling you."

The spider shivered—and then it flung Ary away, and she was falling.

FORTY-FIVE

Webs

Shrimp had felt different ever since they'd escaped the terrarium.

Maybe it was freedom, but it felt like something more. Pill bugs could not work magic the way fairies could, but they could smell it. It could have been just his imagination, but if Shrimp was being honest with himself, he was not very prone to imagining most things. Besides food. Shrimp loved to imagine food.

Yes, something *had* been different ever since they left the terrarium—it was like there were tiny ropes binding Shrimp not just to Ary, but Briar, Sootflank, and Owl, too, and even that wicked newt, Quickspark. It probably had something to do with the spell Ary's grandmother had cast. Magic was a fickle, strange thing—which was why Shrimp left it alone. Spells never went exactly as planned.

Shrimp leaned into the tiny-tug feeling that tied him to Ary. Yet as he crawled, Shrimp felt . . . something else. A different pull, deep within the wood, that tasted of leaves in the fall and fresh earth in the spring. It made for a very dizzying crawling experience, because Ary was one way, and this thing was another. Shrimp did his best to ignore it.

The soil in front of Shrimp caved in, revealing a long, looping tunnel. He cautiously poked an antenna into it. If his sense of direction was correct, they should be in the weavers' kingdom by now. He needed to move faster if he wanted to reach the warm-bloods and their Keeper in time.

Of course, there was a chance the Keeper really *was* gone. But Shrimp refused to think that way. Worrying and negativity was Sootflank's job. Shrimp's was to find things.

And he was going to find that Keeper if it was the last thing he did.

Shrimp took off at a skitter through the spiders' tunnels. He was so much faster now that he wasn't digging! It felt nice to be underground again, like he was back in the terrarium. Then again, most of his time in the terrarium had gone pretty badly before he met Ary. So maybe it didn't feel so nice after all.

Shrimp was so busy leading the pill bugs, crawling as fast as possible, that he didn't hear one of the bugs next to him until it was too late.

"Web," said the pill bug.

"What?" said Shrimp. He did not know what a web was. He needed to find Ary.

"Web," repeated the bug.

"What?" said Shrimp again, annoyed now, and then he collided with something large and sticky and he could not crawl at all. Many of the pill bugs with him collided with the sticky barrier, too, crying out as they became tangled. Shrimp could not move!

"Web," the pill bug said again, crankier than before, which Shrimp found a tad unnecessary, given how he had just learned the hard way what a web was. Shrimp twisted, but he only grew more tangled. The tiny ropes binding him to Ary and Quickspark shivered.

A hum came from above him, like a string plucked on one of those tiny fairy instruments, and Shrimp looked up in horror as a massive, hulking spider crawled toward him.

FORTY-SIX

Sunrise

Ary fell.

Air rushed by her, biting cold and whistling as she plummeted toward the ground. She tucked herself into a ball. Maybe the ground would be soft—maybe she'd be okay—

The spiders were enchanted.

She had no proof. Nothing but a hunch. But it felt like something had *heard* her words—and punished her for it.

"Ary!" someone cried.

Ary twisted, flailing pitifully as she fell. Her wings flexed and twitched, but they were even more useless than they'd been back in the Ant Court. Air whistled right through them, filling the air with an eerie howl. She was going to die. Her bones would smash against the ground, and Mama would never know what had happened.

"Ary!" someone screamed again, closer. A dark shape was approaching—and fast. Ary flipped helplessly, and then she saw her.

Briar.

She flew straight toward Ary, dark hair streaming behind her in an endless ribbon. Her wings beat so fast they were a brilliant blur, a splash of blue against the endless shadow of their prison.

At the last moment, Briar swerved.

She'd missed.

Ary kept falling.

Briar was saving herself. With the spiders distracted, she could fly away from here. It was the smart thing to do. Why risk anything for Ary, when Briar could go back to warn the others?

The ground rushed closer.

Ary closed her eyes.

Something clamped around her wrist—and a horrible, ripping pain exploded through Ary's shoulder as she was yanked upright.

"Aaaaghh!" someone howled.

Ary hit the ground with a thud, fire blazing up her arm, her shoulder, her back. Briar collapsed on top of her, and together they tumbled to the ground, rolling in a tangle of limbs until they collided into the wall.

Ary wheezed, face down in the dirt, struggling to breathe. Her arm. She couldn't move her right arm. She tried to curl her fingers into a fist, but all she managed was a sad little wiggle. A horrible ache pounded through her shoulder and her upper back.

Someone touched Ary and rolled her over as gently as they could. Ary gasped, shuddering against the awful pain in her arm.

"Sorry!" said Briar. "Oh man, Ary, I'm so sorry. Are you okay? I didn't know what to do, you were falling so fast—"

"My arm," Ary whimpered. "It's my—my arm."

Briar reached for her, her hands trembling, her face wan and panicked. "I must have dislocated your shoulder. I'm so sorry—"

"It's okay," wheezed Ary. "Better hurting and . . . alive."

"Can you move it? Maybe I can—"

"Give me . . . a minute," Ary gritted out. "Please."

Briar's mouth snapped shut. She nodded, her face pale.

Waves of agony rolled through Ary. She kept waiting for the pain to pass, kept waiting for it to dull, but it was as though someone had sliced her open and lit a fire in the knot of muscle that wound around her shoulder. She lay there, room spinning, her mind consumed by the spiders, Aspen, the Blight, and everything that had gone so, so terribly wrong.

Dully, she was aware of a swishing noise. Of a large, orange shape, getting closer.

"Take her arm," a low voice instructed. "And do exactly as I say."

"But she's in pain—"

"She'll stay in pain if you don't listen to me. Don't argue."

Hands touched Ary's ruined shoulder.

"No," sobbed Ary. *"Please."*

"Mossheart." A familiar, angry face loomed over her. Quickspark. "Stop whining. Listen to me. I'm going to help Sunleaf reset your shoulder. It's going to hurt very, very badly, and then it will stop hurting."

"No," moaned Ary because, frankly, touching her arm sounded like the absolute worst thing someone could do to her right now.

"Sunleaf, take her arm—no, move your hand up." Something long and smooth wound under Ary—Quickspark's tail, she realized. "On my count. One."

Ary's breath came faster.

"Two."

Maybe Briar should have let her die.

"Three."

Ary screamed.

It was like the pain from before, but ten times worse. An endless, ripping agony, blazing through her shoulder, her arm, the side of her body. Ary saw white. The taste of blood flooded her mouth. Her entire world was pain; her very cells burned. She saw Alder, the Blight, the spiders—

—and her.

Aspen, no longer concealed by the wood, standing in a strange ring of silvery web. She cradled something small and glinting in her hand. As if feeling eyes on her, she whirled and looked right *at* Ary.

"You," she blurted. "You shouldn't be here. How are you here?"

And then she was gone, and Ary was back in her body, and the pain—

It was fading. It was still there, pulsing through her in waves, but growing duller with each pass. Ary panted. The room swam back into view. Briar hovered over her, her face pinched with worry; behind her, Quickspark loomed, looking as annoyed as usual.

"Ary?" Briar whispered tentatively.

Ary gave her a weak smile.

"Ow," she croaked.

A sob escaped Briar. She all but collapsed, her touch feather-light as she held the hand on Ary's good arm. Tears dripped down her face.

"I'm so sorry," she whispered. "I didn't want to hurt you, but Quickspark said it wasn't going to get better and—Ary. I'm sorry. I'm glad you're okay."

Ary closed her eyes. Now that her shoulder was reset, she could breathe again. The attention of the surrounding creatures was like a heavy weight. No one spoke in the silence that followed; no one breathed. She knew they were waiting on her.

"I couldn't see anything," Ary whispered, hating herself.

"Just—just stars. Everywhere. Above, below, in every direction. I'm sorry."

No one said anything. Briar settled beside her and threaded her fingers through Ary's. Nervousness fluttered through her. Ary tried to focus on something else.

"Quickspark," she croaked. "Thanks."

A long silence. And then, "Whatever. When I kill you, I want you in one piece."

Exhaustion settled over Ary in a heavy wave. She didn't have time to sleep—but after the pain, all she wanted was to sink into an endless nothing. She stirred, trying to sit up. She needed to figure out how to get out of here. She needed answers. She needed—

"Ary," Briar said gently. "You need to rest."

"I can't," Ary protested. "Nightingale and Yarrow, they're—"

"The brat is right," one of the earwigs hissed. "You cannot help them now. And after all your screaming, *we* would like some peace."

"Just try to lie down." Before Ary could protest, Briar shifted her so that Ary's head was in her lap. She touched Ary's hair hesitantly. "May I?"

Her heart in her throat, Ary nodded.

Gently, so softly that Ary could barely feel the weight of her fingers, Briar began to undo the braids Mama had made. Some of the tension in Ary's scalp eased as Briar combed her fingers through her hair, humming a low tune beneath her breath as she worked.

Tears swam in Ary's eyes. She knew that song.

It was the same one Mama hummed when she cleaned.

She opened her mouth to ask Briar where she'd learned it, but the words wouldn't come. There was only one person who could have taught her.

Framed in the early-morning light, Briar looked like a painting, her face rendered into soft edges by the pink dawn glow. Something was clearly wrong. If Owl were here, he might have poked and pressed at Briar to get her to talk, but Ary had long known that sometimes, the kindest thing you could do was sit with someone in their feelings. If Briar wanted to talk to Ary, she would. So Ary lay back on the platform and tilted her face to the sky, watching as it shifted into a brighter, impossible shade of pink. Bits of orange and yellow had started to creep across, coloring the clouds in impossible, beetle-bright hues. After a moment, Briar lay back with her, her arm brushing Ary's, their legs dangling off the platform as they watched the sky.

"Mrs. Grumthrush called it a sunrise," Briar said softly. "Pretty, isn't it?"

Ary kept her eyes on the clouds. Some of them were turning the color of fire.

Briar's eyelashes fluttered. "Before she died, Grandmother took me to meet this strange creature—he knew so much about this world. He'd spend hours telling me stories.

He did not know what the sun was, but he always told us we were special because we carried it in our name. He was very nice, and strange, and *hairy*."

"Chives," Ary whispered.

"You met him?"

Ary nodded. Quietly, she told Briar of Chives' anger toward Gran and how he had filtered what he told Ary about the key to Atlas. How even with the end of the world rushing toward them, it was Briar he wanted to protect.

"I always thought he was lying," Briar said in wonder. "It sounded ridiculous. He told me of sunrises and sunsets—of how the sky would change impossible colors, and it carried messages. But he got everything right—the impossible colors, how *big* it all is. I wish Grandmother could have seen it."

"Me too," Ary said quietly.

Finally, Briar turned to look at Ary. Her cheeks were wet with tears.

"It doesn't seem right," Briar said finally, her lip wobbling. "That I'm here, and she's not."

Ary swallowed. She recalled the vision Atlas had given her of the Underground where Briar had lived, the way the mold had eaten away at their homes before it had ever come to Terra. She remembered, too, the bright anger and pain in Briar's eyes when she'd found Ary. She still didn't know exactly how many years Briar had spent alone in the Underground, how long she'd been held prisoner in the Ant Court before Ary and Owl stumbled into her life. Ary had thought it was bad enough to lose Papa, and later, Gran—but she'd had Mama, and the rest of Terra.

Briar had been alone.

"I don't know what to say," Ary said finally, her voice barely above a whisper. "Other than I'm sorry. I know you must feel like this was your one chance at a normal life, Briar. I know you don't believe I want that for you, but I do. I really, really do."

A nervous energy buzzed through her. Before she could stop herself, Ary took Briar's hand, trying not to shiver against the strange rush it gave her. She half expected Briar to smack her hand away, but instead, Briar threaded her fingers through Ary's and squeezed tight.

"You know, I had given up before you came to the Ant Court," Briar said quietly. "I was so angry at the ants for keeping me alive."

"Did it ever occur to you to try to head for Terra?"

Briar shook her head. "After what Grandmother said . . ."

Ary understood. Dracaena had thought Wren Mossheart left her behind on purpose, returned a hero, and then turned the folk of Terra against their plan to free the terrarium. To a fairy like Briar, raised on stories fed by Dracaena's pain, Terra probably seemed worse than the worst terrors the Underground could offer.

"I wish it had been sooner," Ary said. "But I am glad we found you. I'm glad you're here."

"Me too," Briar whispered. "Thank you for finding me,

Ary. Thank you for—for not leaving me behind."

Ary nodded. Overhead, the first threads of blue worked their way through the sunrise. Light washed over the world as some of the brilliant fire of dawn faded. Ary's own vision started to blur. It was too painful, to step into that wash of memory, the expression on her face as the terrarium had shattered and the world went white and Gran had only looked at Ary, a fierce, desperate love in her eyes. She would have secretly loved this new world and would have complained about it every step of the way—the strange, swaying trees, the sunrises that painted the sky in fire. Ary missed her with a such a desperate ache, sometimes she thought she might just drown.

What she would not have given for Gran to be here.

"When I lost my mom, and then my grandmother," Briar said thoughtfully, "I'd tell myself they had turned into glow-shrooms."

Ary looked at her, too confused to be polite. "What?"

"Not *literally*. Man, Owl really is the brains of this whole thing." She sniffed. "No, I mean—Grandmother used to say, the people we love live on in every beautiful thing. Even when they're gone, they're in every glow-shroom, every pulse of a glow-moth's wings. The glow-shrooms were the only beautiful things for a long, long time. But this world . . ."

Ary's eyes blurred, and she understood.

"They are in every blade of grass," Ary said softly. "Every swaying tree, and every new breeze."

"Every sunrise, and every sunset," Briar agreed. "They're together again. And they're finally happy."

Ary and Briar did not speak for a long time. They still held each other's hands, both blinking back tears, watching as the last threads of pink and orange were swept away by morning blue. Behind them, the folk of Terra were stirring awake, murmuring to each other in the pale shadows of morning about what fate beheld them.

"Ary," Briar said. "I'm sorry about before. I wanted things to be okay so badly that I started to blame you when they weren't. But pretending wasn't going to fix it. It just meant that I left you alone. And please don't say it's okay, because it's not."

Briar returned to unbraiding Ary's hair, humming that gentle, familiar tune as she worked. The presence of their grandmothers loomed between them.

Briar had saved Ary instead of escaping. Quickspark had helped ease her pain, instead of leaving Ary to suffer.

It didn't fix everything between them. It didn't erase the bitter history.

But it had to mean something—right?

Ary wanted to tell Briar she would have been a good healer. She wanted to tell her she was sorry that Briar had grown up in a world where she was better off using sharp words and sharper weapons instead of a healer's touch.

And she wanted to tell her she understood why Briar had been so angry when she'd thought Ary was trying to shove her back into that life the moment she'd escaped it.

But instead, something Briar had said earlier crept back in. An idea itched at Ary.

"Hey," Briar said. "Are you still listening? I'm trying to apologize over here."

Ary's heart began to pound.

What if escaping wasn't the answer?

What if they needed to trigger the trap?

The spiders were taking the imprisoned creatures *somewhere,* right? She wasn't getting any more answers here. Ary looked around, taking in the gaunt, exhausted faces of the captured creatures.

Ary was on her own.

She needed to get out of here.

And that meant she needed to get the spiders'—or Aspen's—attention.

"I don't want your apology," Ary said. "I want your help."

Ary sat upright. She was so close to Briar she could see the dark flecks in the other girl's eyes. Briar's words about their grandmothers had been sweet.

But what if they were also the key?

An idea had started to take root.

This whole time, Ary had been trying to do things alone. She'd worried about sparing others' feelings, about protecting them, about doing things *right.*

Well, no more of that. Everyone she loved was on the line.

And Ary was tired of playing fair.

Briar's eyes narrowed. "What are you thinking?"

"Something dangerous," said Ary. "It'll either work or we'll die terrible, painful deaths."

Briar rolled her eyes. "Oh, great. Fine. Let me have it."

FORTY-SEVEN

Up We Go

Pebble led them deeper into the wood. It didn't take long to find the Blight.

At first, it was subtle—a blackened plant here, a shriveled root there. But the farther they ventured, the more it became clear that something had been wrong for quite some time. Even more concerning was the silence that pressed all around them. There should have been bugs humming in the distance and creatures picking their way through the undergrowth. Owl had been worried the woods would be full of danger, but now it was the *lack* of it that concerned him.

Where was everything?

The air grew damper as they ventured, the ground softer and shifting, sucking at their feet with a strange wetness. By the light of the moon, Pebble led their ragtag little group forward. They paused only to consult the map, taking shortcuts where he knew the forest to be thinner or thicker.

This had to work.

It *had* to.

The forest pressed in all around them. Owl could *feel*

the power vibrating in the land, churning behind the walls of its broken bonds.

Reach, called the wood.

Reach, sang the grass.

They had to be getting close.

"Last I heard, this is where the Keeper was thought to be," Pebble whispered, scrambling over a tree root.

They'd come to the base of a great tree.

It towered over them, eternal in its height, bark worn smooth by years of time and weather. Even from here, Owl could see that it towered over the other pines in the forest. Blight crept up its trunk; the trees around it were withered, their branches twisted and gnarled with pain.

"I didn't realize the Blight had crept this far," Pebble said miserably.

Hopelessness threatened to drown Owl. He stared up at the tree. "If something this ancient is susceptible—how are we meant to save the wood? How can any of it be okay?"

"The others made it sick," Mrs. Dragonsnap said quietly. They turned to her. The old fairy peered up at the pine, her face distant. "That's the funny thing about trees. People think they're so powerful, so infinite. But they rely on each other to survive. Every one of these trees has tangled their roots with another. If one gets sick, the rest do. If one thrives, so do the trees tied to them. They've got family, and friends, and alliances. They know they're stronger together—and that whatever power they have, it grows when it is shared."

It was a nice dream. And maybe Mrs. Dragonsnap was just saying it to be kind—but Owl had to admit it helped.

"So if we can cure one," Owl said quietly, "maybe it can cure the rest?"

"Hope is free," Mrs. Dragonsnap said with a soft nod. "There's no reason to believe otherwise."

The idea of it settled on them. Maybe they didn't have to fix the entire wood. They could find the root of the sickness—and if they could stop it, the network of the wood could heal itself.

Sumac peered around, his face troubled. "Uh, where is the Keeper of the flyers, anyway?"

Pebble pointed up. "When the last Keeper died, the flyers took his hatchling up there—to a nest at the very top of the pine, where nothing could reach it."

Sumac and Mrs. Dragonsnap scrambled up beside Owl.

"How on earth are we going to get up there?" asked Sumac.

"I don't know!" Pebble threw his paws up. "I'm just a mouse! I don't even want to be here. You asked me to lead you to the flyer. This is as far as I can get you."

Owl craned his neck to look up the tree. Just like in Siltshore, he could feel the power of the wood. It lay dormant all around him—but there was something different here. Something new.

Something . . . alive.

"We'll climb," said Owl.

"You can't be serious," said Sumac.

"The Keeper is up there." Owl looked at the others, determination rising in him. "So up we go."

"Is this a bad time to say I'm afraid of heights?" asked Sumac.

"You spent your entire life in a treetop village."

"Worth a shot."

Owl ran his hands over the rough bark of the pine. Unlike the oak tree that cradled Siltshore, this pine was textured and hard. The climb would be exhausting, but he had done impossible things before.

Owl pulled himself up. It took everything in him not to look at the impossible height overhead.

One hand at a time. That's all that mattered.

For Ary, Owl told himself. *For all of them*.

Owl gathered his courage and began to climb.

FORTY-EIGHT

Into the Web

It was go time.

As the sun rose over the wood, Ary stayed awake, her plan forming in her head. She caught Briar's eye from across their prison and leaped to her feet.

The captured creatures stared dully back at her.

There was no sound save for the strange gurgling outside and the rustle of the spiders overhead. The earwigs remained coiled inward, as if they could save themselves from the fate of Briar, Alder, and the other earwigs by being as small and passive as possible. The other captured fairies huddled against the wall, their faces turned away. No one moved or spoke.

Ary paced the room. The creatures flinched at her restlessness, but she didn't care. Heat flushed through her. Her pulse sped up, and her fingers curled into fists.

She was getting so *sick* of everyone sitting back and waiting to be saved by a little girl.

"Look at you," Ary said. "We're getting picked off one by one, and you're just going to . . . what? Lie down and die? Hope that someone comes and saves you?"

No one answered her.

"Well, guess what," Ary said, her voice growing louder. "No one is coming. No one even knows we're here!"

Ary whirled, addressing Quickspark directly. "And what about you?"

"What about me?" Quickspark answered dully. "What do you want me to say? We're doomed. Give it up, little folk. Some webs are wound too tightly even for the smallest midge's escape."

Ary shook her head. "No, that's not good enough. I'm not dying like this."

Quickspark turned away, curling into herself so tightly she looked frozen, like a statue carved from pale orange stone. Ary stared, stunned.

"We've tried everything," one of the earwigs rasped. "There is no escaping here."

Ary was beginning to understand why Gran was so fed up with everyone all the time. It was one thing to step up and be heroic because others couldn't. It was another to have to do it because others *wouldn't.*

The worst part was that Ary kind of understood. Back in Terra, it was easy to accept the mold and the rot as inevitable. Life was hard enough. No point in drawing attention to herself. Briar, Alder, the captured earwigs—maybe they'd just been unlucky. They'd drawn attention to themselves. If the others remained small and quiet, they'd be okay. Maybe they'd even survive.

Ary wanted to shake them and shout that they were playing a losing game. She knew better than anyone how it felt to see something terrible and turn away, hoping someone better and brighter and braver would come to save them.

A faint rustle came from overhead. The captives twitched in fear but made no other move.

Ary made eye contact with Briar. Then threw her head back and screamed.

"Ahhhhhhhh!"

Her fellow prisoners jumped. Ary ignored them. She began to stomp around as hard as she could, banging on the walls, shouting and kicking up a scuffle in every way possible.

"I know you're out there!" Ary shouted. "I know you can hear me!"

"What," Quickspark said scathingly, "are you doing?"

"Come out!" Ary yelled. She drummed her fists against the damp, woody wall of the prison. When that didn't make enough noise, she put her fingers to her lips and let loose an ear-splitting whistle. "Come get me! I'm ready!"

"Great," muttered an earwig. "It's gone crazy."

Ary picked up a nearby twig and stalked toward Quickspark.

The newt eyed her cautiously. "What do you think you're doing?"

"Hey," said Ary. "I'm really sorry."

"Sorry about what?"

"This," said Ary.

Ary raised her arm—and bonked Quickspark on the head.

The newt leaped up with a snarl. "Have you lost your mind?"

"Probably," said Ary. She took another swipe at Quickspark, and the newt lunged sideways with a hiss.

"Stop it!" Quickspark snarled. She twisted, looking at the earwigs. "Stop her!"

The remaining earwigs exchanged glances. "Do we have to?"

"Yes."

Reluctantly, they rose. Ary's heart hammered harder. Her hands shook. But instead of backing down, she lunged for Quickspark again.

"Enough!" Quickspark roared. In one fluid moment, she picked up Ary with her tail and flung her backward. Ary hit the ground with a wheeze and sprawled there while the newt stalked toward her. "We are trapped here. I am tired. I am scared. I am sorry about your friend, I am sorry for what I did in the Ant Court, I am sorry I wasn't good enough for my father—but I can't fix any of that now, and if I'm going to die in a miserable, wet hole at the legs of a bunch of nattering spiders, *I'd like some peace before it happens*!"

Quickspark towered over her, eyes sparking with fury. This close, with her chest heaving and tail lashing, she'd never looked more like Sootflank. They were twins not only in their anger, but in their constant weight of grief.

"It wasn't about being good enough," Ary said softly to Quickspark. "Sootflank abandoning you wasn't your fault. It was his. He should have protected you. That has everything to do with him—and nothing to do with you."

Quickspark flinched as if she'd been slapped. She opened her mouth to respond—and then a rustle came from overhead.

Ary looked up, and her stomach bottomed out.

Her "plan" had worked.

Dangling from the ceiling, slipping down the walls, were a dozen of the largest spiders Ary had ever seen. They rustled, legs twitching, abdomens writhing—and then they lunged for Quickspark.

Quickspark howled, whirling to fight them off. Silvery webs shot over her, and the spiders snatched them up, weaving with an incredible speed. The newt howled with fury as they dragged her to the ground. Ary braced herself.

And Ary leaped.

As she leaped, so did Briar. They hurled themselves into Quickspark's side.

"Mossheart, what are you—"

"Quiet," Ary hissed. She wound her arms around Quickspark's neck, pressing herself as close to the newt as she could manage. Briar wriggled closer alongside her. The spiders kept spinning, wrapping her into a suffocating, silvery pod with Quickspark, their eyes blank of feeling, entirely unaware someone else was tagging along.

"What are you doing?" Quickspark demanded, real panic creeping into her voice. "If you come with me, you'll die."

The spiders wove over the last gap, plunging them both into a tight, uncomfortable darkness. Ary did her best to hold still, focusing on the hum of the spiders, the pulse of Quickspark's frantic heartbeat. Her body shifted as they rose.

"Ary," Briar whispered, "I hope you're right about this."

"Me too," Ary whispered.

The webs closed over their heads as the spiders dragged them away.

FORTY-NINE

A Debt, Owed

Shrimp was not sure of many things, but he was fairly certain of this: he was about to be eaten.

He had rolled into a ball the moment the weavers approached—and then they had begun to roll *him*, binding him tighter and tighter in their sticky ropes until Shrimp was stuck. He twisted, twitched, and writhed, but it was no use. From the muffled cries around him, he could tell that the other pill bugs were suffering the same fate. This was a disaster! Shrimp thought of Ary, of how she had been so brave for him, and now she was in danger. And these bugs were being so *rude*—they had not even bothered to ask where he was going, or why. They had no respect for the pill bug way of things!

So Shrimp did something very strange and un-pill-bug-like.

Shrimp got mad.

It sparked in him like fizzy mushroom spores, snapping through his fourteen legs, his multi-segmented body, and his antennae. These bugs were *not* going to keep him from Ary. They were *not* going to stop him from finding his friend.

And if they were not going to follow him, they needed to get out of his way.

"Let," squeaked Shrimp. "Shrimp. *Go!*"

Shrimp gathered all his strength and unrolled—and he felt it. A tug on one of the many ropes that had been tied to him in Atlas' cavern, spiraling away, back through the wood, connecting him to Ary, Owl, Briar, and Sootflank. He felt a buzz, and a zap, and everything went green as magic surged through the world. Suddenly Shrimp was not in that web. He was somewhere else entirely—still in the wood, but in a dark, cool place, where roots tangled in the earth and the light did not reach. He saw Ary, curled in the dark, and knew she was afraid. But as soon as she was there, she was gone.

In the heart of the forest, Shrimp saw a mountain that moved.

It was so old that many creatures had forgotten about it. It curled in the loam, indistinguishable but for the gentle rise and fall of its flanks. The rot destroying the forest pressed in on all sides, but a circle of green enveloped the resting mountain. No matter how the Blight strained, it could not reach it. Not yet. Fairies who Shrimp had never met before approached; they begged, pleaded, threatened, and cajoled. All were ignored. All returned without whatever they had come to the mountain for. Shrimp pressed closer, trying to understand exactly what he was looking at.

The mountain shivered—and a massive eye blinked open.

Shrimp snapped back inside his body just in time to watch the webs crumble.

He unrolled with such force, he flew from the web and landed several bug-lengths away. The entire web withered, and every pill bug dropped free, plinking to the ground with startled squeaks. The spiders let out a collective cry. They gave a terrible shudder and began to twitch; legs dancing, bodies heaving, shiny black eyes wheeling. Shrimp and the pill bugs shrank back.

And then, one by one, the eyes of the spiders began to clear.

They looked at each other, and then at Shrimp. A strange hum moved through them. Shrimp had never learned to speak spider well, but he understood words like *Keeper* and *free*. The spiders flexed their legs, reveling in their newfound freedom. They drew closer to Shrimp. All he wanted to do was curl into a ball, but Shrimp forced himself to stay still. Ary wouldn't back down in this moment, and neither would he.

Movement came from the woods. Another spider scuttled forward, this one bigger and uglier than the others, covered in bristling brown hairs. It looked an awful lot like the one that had tried to attack Owl and Ary. It approached the spiders tentatively, legs tensed as if prepared to flee, and let out the softest, most pathetic hum Shrimp had ever heard.

The other spiders hummed back, and then—well,

Shrimp didn't know how else to describe it. It was ridiculous, really. But the spiders leaped on top of each other, and Shrimp could have sworn that the way they tangled their legs was something like a hug, and the high-pitched squeaks coming from them were sobs.

How awkward. He would have liked to leave, but that seemed awfully rude. Then again, it might be wise to crawl into the underbrush now while the spiders were busy hugging and crying, or whatever it was they were doing. As usual, Shrimp's indecision made the decision. He was still deliberating when the spiders quieted and turned to face him as one.

Shrimp tensed.

The ugly, hairy spider that had been hiding in the woods picked its way forward. It towered over Shrimp, mandibles twitching, dark eyes revealing nothing. Delicately, the spider extended a leg and rested it on Shrimp's shell. This time, when it hummed, words rippled through Shrimp.

We owe the crawler, said the biggest and ugliest of the spiders, *a debt.*

This was ridiculous. Shrimp had no idea what had just happened, but he was pretty sure it was because of whatever Owl was off doing. He thought about telling them that, and then took a closer look at the spider's sharp, hungry mandibles, and decided against it.

Tell us what you desire.

Shrimp hesitated. A part of him wanted to send the spiders away. Even if they'd temporarily decided not to eat him, they were still quite frightening! Shrimp thought of the mountain in the wood, and the way it had called him. He thought of Ary, alone in that terrible place.

Shrimp had never been very good at saving people—but he was good at finding things. An idea bubbled up in him. It was the scariest, most un-pill-bug-like idea Shrimp had ever had.

But it felt right.

And if this could help Ary—well, he had to try.

Shrimp inched closer to the ugly spider. He whispered his request. The spider drew back, dark eyes glittering. If spiders could sigh, it probably would have heaved the longest one ever uttered in the wood. Instead, it rubbed its legs together and tapped them on the ground.

Very well, the ugly spider whispered. *Consider it done.*

The spider left without a backward glance. The other spiders waited there, still staring at Shrimp. The pill bugs waited as well. The whole thing made Shrimp very uncomfortable. If they were hoping for some kind of speech, they'd have to keep waiting. Shrimp had better things to do.

He turned. He gathered his courage. (There wasn't very much of it, but there was a little, and when he thought of Ary, and what she meant to him, it made it easier.)

Shrimp leaned into the feeling and started scuttling in a

new direction. There was a scurry behind him, and above, too. The pill bugs resumed following him—but now several spiders followed him, too.

Oh well. Ary would know what to do with them.

FIFTY

Keeper of the Flyers

Every muscle in Owl's body burned.

He didn't know how long he'd been climbing. Sweat soaked every part of his body and dripped into his eyes. Below him, Pebble, Sumac, and Mrs. Dragonsnap wheezed as they climbed. Owl had not asked them to come with him, but they had all the same. A new burst of energy washed through him.

Was this how Ary had felt in the Underground? He recalled that day in Chives' cavern, when Ary had told them they didn't have to go with her. It had never been a question in Ary's mind that Owl would follow her to the end of their world.

It was a lot scarier to be on the receiving end.

As they climbed, the air grew cold. A sharp, biting breeze whistled through the trees and stole the heat from Owl's bones. Slowly, the forest drew into view. From this high up, he could see the patches of rotted Blight that had overtaken the wood. Owl's heart sank.

It was so much worse than they'd thought.

There was at least double the Blight than what had been

visible on Oleander's maps. It crept into every territory, an eternal, dark scar.

If they failed—if they were wrong about this—they were doomed.

The trunk of the pine grew slimmer, the branches that jutted out slender and almost spindle-like.

Owl climbed higher. He reached his hand up to grab another section of bark, and something sharp pricked his fingers instead. Owl craned his neck. Thousands of sticks formed a massive wall overhead. Owl wrapped his fingers around the nearest and hauled himself up.

And then he made the mistake of looking down.

The forest floor was so far away it was nothing but a blur. It was an impossible distance. Far, far higher than he'd ever been in Siltshore, higher than they'd been above the Ant Court pit. The concerned faces of Sumac, Mrs. Dragonsnap, and Pebble peered up at him. Owl swayed. His hands sweated; his heart pounded. His legs felt like jelly.

If he fell now, he would die.

"Owl," hissed Sumac. "Don't look at the ground. Look at me."

Owl forced his gaze to Sumac.

"You've come this far," Sumac encouraged. He trembled where he clung to the tree, exhaustion lining every part of his face. "No backing down now, right? For Ary. For all of us."

"I can't," Owl croaked. He was frozen. Were his hands

slipping, or was it just his imagination? "I can't move."

"You *can*," Sumac said fiercely. "You're a Seedling, Owl. The magic called out to you—you said so yourself."

Owl trembled.

And he thought, of all things, about his parents.

Of the way they had always believed so fiercely in the Gardener and the old myths, and later, in *him*. His mom had always said that children carried their parents' hopes and fears for the world in each hand, and it was the parents' job to ensure the hope wasn't what they set down when life got too heavy. They had believed in Owl, long before he'd thought himself capable of anything, back in the days when he'd loathed himself for being wingless and having nothing in common with the kids at school.

They would want him to do this. To be brave—and build a better world.

Owl blinked away tears. He gathered the last scraps of his strength and hauled himself over the ledge.

He tumbled, rolling down the side of the wall of prickly sticks until he bumped up against something soft. A scrambling noise came from behind as Mrs. Dragonsnap, Pebble, and Sumac cleared the ledge. Owl turned and his heart dropped. It wasn't a ledge. It was a *nest*. Bigger than he'd ever imagined, bigger than he'd ever dreamed.

Mrs. Dragonsnap, Sumac, and Pebble froze on the lip of the nest, their eyes wide with shock.

"Owl," Sumac whispered. "Behind you."

Owl turned.

Behind him, wings folded against itself, eyes closed, was the biggest bird Owl had ever seen.

It was like Atlas, but so much worse. The bird was terrifying, with a massive, razor-sharp yellow beak and tawny brown feathers that gleamed under the night sky. Owl froze, but the bird hadn't moved. It was fast asleep.

He took a cautious step forward and something crunched underfoot.

He'd stepped right on a flower. One so old, it had long dried to a husk under the sun. It was a swamp lily, like the ones the Seedlings had carved all over Terra. The inside had been whittled out; seeds, cracked open, were scattered around the nest.

A terrible suspicion pricked Owl.

Oleander had gotten rid of the Keepers, but they were clearly still alive. Maybe he had killed some, but not all of them.

Reach, murmured the wind.

Reach, murmured the trees.

Owl took a cautious step forward. The bird was so close he could nearly touch it. He recalled that day in the Ant Court, as Ary had held his hand.

"I'm going to try something weird," Owl warned. "And it might work, or it might do nothing, or it might make everything a lot worse."

"Great," deadpanned Sumac.

"If you die," said Pebble, "I still want my books."

Owl leaned into the call of power.

The taste of sunlight flooded his mouth; the world flashed white. A dozen images whirled behind Owl's eyes, just like they had back in the Ant Court. He had never told Ary about what he had seen that day—a girl, eyes blazing with power as she confronted the Ant Queen. He'd known instantly it was Wren.

He saw a different fairy this time.

He was young, like Wren, with dark hair and faded, hand-me-down clothes. He approached a great bird with his head bowed and his hands behind his back. In one hand, he held a fistful of seeds.

In the other, he held a knife.

It was Oleander. Owl knew it in his bones. This was the moment he'd found the Keeper. But if Oleander had met with the Keeper of the flyers, then who had betrayed the weavers?

Who had spun everything else into chaos?

Owl leaned into that power. In his ears he felt the whistle of the wind; in his blood he felt the thrill of what it meant to soar. He could feel . . . something waiting, sleeping, that had been hiding in these trees all this time. Pebble had it wrong. Oleander hadn't killed the other Keepers. He'd merely subdued them. Owl felt them, from the top of this tree to the deepest waters of the swamp where Sootflank now swam—and there, in the north, nestled beneath the crown of a great willow tree.

It was time to wake them up.

Power swirled around him, spiraling from the bird in front of him to the others. They were like one great, tangled knot, the whole power of the wood coursing through them, trapped for the last sixty years while the Blight wreaked havoc on their home.

Owl didn't know what would happen if he pulled on that knot.

But he was about to find out.

Owl reached—and *yanked*.

And the bird's eyes flew open.

FIFTY-ONE

The Wolf Spider

The spiders carried Ary, Briar, and Quickspark for a long time. Trapped in the darkness, crushed against Quickspark's lithe form, it was impossible to tell where they were traveling or how far. Ary's neck ached from the odd angle she was trapped at. She wriggled, trying to turn over, searching for any scrap of light, any hint as to what fate she'd signed both her and Quickspark up for.

"Um," muttered Quickspark, "can you stop puncturing my organs with your elbow, please?"

"Sorry."

The newt had been uncharacteristically quiet. Maybe she trusted that Ary had a plan, or maybe she'd returned to her earlier, grim resignation toward their inevitable deaths. Either way, the silence gave Ary an opportunity to think.

She had been suspicious before, when the spiders had come for them in the woods, and later again, when they took Nightingale prisoner. But now that she had been up close and personal, Ary knew for certain.

She recognized that blank look in their eyes. The way the spiders moved in unison, as if they were caught in a strange dream. Ary had spent her entire life watching the glow-moths float about Terra without any awareness of where they were or what they were doing, lost in the thrall of Mayor Nightingale's enchantments.

Someone was controlling the spiders.

The spiders dropped them with a *thud*. Whatever they'd been thrown onto was a lot harder than the spongy, wet floor of the strange prison. Ary strained, listening intently. A faint scuttling sounded all around them—but it was growing fainter by the second. The spiders were leaving.

What Ary wouldn't have given for some kind of light, just a glimpse of what was going on in the world beyond. Ary tried to twist again, and then a hiss filled the air. The scuttling resumed, but now it was frantic. Scared. A shrill whine like a scream began and then cut off abruptly.

A single, scratching scuttle moved toward them.

Ary held her breath. A *rip* came to her left, then another to her right. Someone was untying them! Her heart beat harder.

The webs fell away. Ary, Briar, Quickspark flopped apart. Ary rolled onto her back, looked up, and froze.

Eight large, black eyes blinked down at her.

Standing over Ary was the largest spider she'd ever seen.

"It's you," she gasped.

The wolf spider from that very first day. The weaver whose territory they had violated, and who the folk of

Siltshore had "rescued" them from. Saving the wolf spider had been the first strike against Ary in the eyes of the folk of Siltshore. Ary had not understood, then, why the wolf spider had hated the folk so vehemently.

She was starting to suspect it had its reasons.

The spider loomed over her.

Behind it, curled inward and twitching pathetically, lay the five spiders that had captured Ary and Quickspark.

The spider's mandibles twitched. Delicately, it extended a hairy leg and braced it against Ary's throat. It hummed—but now, its vibrations rippled through her bones to form words.

She waits at the heart of the web. Find her, Ghostwing, and weave a better one.

"How? Where do I find her?" Ary asked, her heart pounding so hard it hurt. "Why—why are you helping us?"

The spider's hairs bristled. It extended one of its many legs beyond Ary, pointing down the mouth of the long, dark tunnel.

It didn't make sense. Alder had said wolf spiders *hunted* folk. And hadn't this very one tried to kill her and her friends their first day in the new world? Ary had spared it, yes, but honestly, it still had every reason to hurt her. She had the sense that wolf spiders hated the folk with a type of detached acceptance; it wasn't like the personal grudges fostered by the newts, but the cool dismissal with which a hawk hates a mouse. Because it is prey. Because it is weak.

Because in the eyes of the hunter, it was born to die.

So why, now, was this one helping her?

"Mossheart," Quickspark said, her eyes darting between them. She took a long drag of air and her gills flared with alarm. "More weavers are coming. And fast."

The spider shivered. It scooped Ary up effortlessly and set her on her feet, turning her in the direction of the tunnel. With the impatience of a weary grandparent, it poked her in the back.

"Wait," said Ary. She spun. Swallowing her revulsion, Ary laid a shaking hand on the spider's hairy leg. "Thank you."

Tell the crawler, hummed the spider, *my debt is paid.*

It turned before Ary could ask what it meant and scuttled straight up the wall. Ary watched it go, turning the strange words over in her mind. She had no idea what a crawler was, or why helping her would repay the spider's debt. But if the spider was helping the wrong fairy, she was hardly going to correct it.

"Briar," said Ary. "You have to go."

Briar's eyes widened. *"What?"*

Ary clutched her hands. "You can fly. No one else can—find Owl and tell him where we are. Tell him about Aspen."

"I'm not leaving you," Briar protested, shaking her head.

"Ary, you can't do this on your own. You'll die."

"You can't help me here," Ary said. "The best thing you can do is find the others—fast."

"She's right."

Quickspark loomed behind them, her good eye blazing furiously. She gave Ary a look of pure loathing. "There are only two paths here, and considering one is full of weavers, I'll travel with you until I see a chance of escape. And then I'm going to hope I never see your pinched little face again."

Briar looked between them with an expression of absolute agony.

"Briar," Ary said gently. "You wanted a chance to live a normal life, right? Well, this is how we fight for that. Find our friends. Tell them what happened—and help me put a stop to this once and for all."

A million arguments flashed across Briar's face, and Ary wondered if she was thinking of a different fairy, in a different life, she'd been forced to leave behind. Tears blurred her eyes. Briar shook her head.

She stepped forward, and before Ary knew what was happening, Briar kissed her.

Nerves rushed through Ary. She felt wobbly and off balance, as if the world had been tilted on its axis. And suddenly, she understood why Dracaena had been willing to follow Wren Mossheart to the end of the earth.

Briar squeezed Ary's hands.

"You better not die," Briar whispered. "I just stopped being mad at you."

Ary gave her an unsteady smile. "I'll do my best."

"If you're done being disgusting," Quickspark said, "the weavers are coming back. We need to leave before that happens."

"Right," Ary said dizzily.

Briar blushed, her fingers still linked with Ary's. Reluctantly, she let go. When she met Ary's eyes, her gaze was bright with determination. "I'll find them, Ary. I promise."

"I know," Ary whispered.

Briar leaped up, and then she was flying—zipping up through the tunnel, wings beating as she disappeared back the way they'd come. Ary watched her, the frantic pounding of her heart driven by something other than fear.

"Sometime today," Quickspark said.

"You know," Ary said, struggling to keep a straight face, "back in the Underground, it was a lot faster when Sootflank let us ride on—"

"If you want to live," Quickspark said scathingly, "do not finish that sentence."

"Worth a shot," Ary muttered. She turned to the tunnel and tried to quell the sense of foreboding rising in her. It was honestly kind of fitting—unlike in the Underground, which had been a maze of tunnels and looping paths, there was only one way to go.

She was going to find Nightingale and the others. She'd set them free.

And then Ary would rescue Aspen and put a stop to this once and for all.

FIFTY-TWO

Carl

Owl could feel the whole of the wood.

In the moment the Keeper of the flyers woke, he felt the others: a great, shelled beast deep within the swamp, and a fierce horned one resting in the north. He felt their attention snap on like glow-shroom lamps flaring to life at night. But where the Keeper at the center of the wood should have been there was a fierce, dark rot. Owl leaned closer.

The first threads of memory began to wind around them, and in flashes, he saw the strangest thing—a girl he'd never seen before, not much older than Ary, with pale hair and tired eyes, kneeling before a great, black spider. Owl didn't have to hear her to know the word her lips formed.

Keeper.

"Owl!" someone shrieked. "Watch out!"

A pair of hands yanked Owl backward. The magic slipped away, and with it, the memory. Two massive, taloned feet landed with a *thump* on the earth where Owl had been.

A bird with a terrible hooked beak, wicked talons, and gleaming amber eyes towered over them and spread its pale wings wide.

"Whooo are you?" the bird hooted, leaning over them, wicked beak glinting in the moonlight. "And *what* are you doing in my nest?"

Sumac and Mrs. Dragonsnap staggered back, but Owl stayed put.

The massive bird glared down at them.

"I am no friend of the folk. You must be very foolish to come here. Or perhaps you're merely tired of living."

They were off to a great start.

"Hi, mister, um, terrifying giant bird thing." Owl held his hands up in what he hoped was a peaceful gesture. "We're not here to cause any trouble."

"Right. And I was hatched yesterday." The bird's eyes narrowed. "I am not in the mood to listen to more lies from meddling folk. I think I will eat you now."

Owl cast around frantically for any sense of magic, but whatever he'd found earlier was gone. So much for his super impressive and powerful Seedling abilities.

The bird reared back his neck as if to strike—and then a familiar voice sputtered, "You will do *no such thing*!"

Owl watched, mouth hanging open, as Mrs. Dragonsnap picked herself up, fixed her glasses, and jabbed a vicious finger in the bird's direction.

"Now you listen to me, you feather-brained menace," Mrs. Dragonsnap said. She took one step forward, and then another, wagging her finger imperiously at the bird. "We will have *none* of that. I don't know why you've got your tail feathers in a twist, but I promised I would take care of these two boys. We climbed that awful tree to wake you up and save this wood, and I'd sooner be turned into a toadstool than let all our hard work come to nothing because we were eaten by some dim-witted, ear-grating, self-important turkey!"

"Turkey?" roared the bird. "I am not a *turkey*! Do you think the Keeper of the flyers would be a *turkey*?!"

Mrs. Dragonsnap adjusted her glasses imperiously. "I don't know. I met a turkey once. You act an awful lot like that one."

"Owl," whispered Sumac. "What is she doing?"

"I don't know," Owl whispered back. "But we're definitely going to die."

Pebble covered his eyes with his paws and shrank into a tiny, furry ball.

"I was a coward years ago when my little sister set off on her adventure," Mrs. Dragonsnap said fiercely. "I said nothing, and I've spent my life regretting it. I refuse to make that mistake again. We're not here to hurt anyone—we're here to save the wood and put it back to rights. Now, I don't know exactly *what* this nice boy did a moment ago, but considering the way you woke up in a fury, my bones tell me you're the one we're looking for! So be a good turkey, put those talons away, and do something useful."

The bird made a strange hooting noise that Owl was pretty sure was the possibly-not-a-turkey equivalent of sputtering with rage.

"I am *not*," the bird boomed, "a *turkey*!"

"Then what," Mrs. Dragonsnap asked slowly, in the tone of an adult speaking to a particularly annoying child, "are you?"

"I," seethed the not-turkey, "am the Keeper of the flyers, protector of the western wood. I am the knowledge of the trees, the memory of the leaves, guardian of all wisdom sacred to the forest and those who dwell beneath its boughs. I remember, and recall, and record."

It paused, chest puffing out proudly. "I . . . am an owl."

They all stared at him.

"Um," said Owl, "no, I'm Owl."

"Oh dear," sighed Pebble. "Here we go."

The bird blinked. "Excuse me?"

"I'm Owl," said Owl.

"You are not an owl," said the bird. "I am an owl."

Sumac stepped in to explain. "You're *an* owl, he's *our* Owl." He frowned. "Oh, man."

"Enough!" cried Mrs. Dragonsnap. She looked at the owl, not to be confused with Owl, the boy. "What's your name?"

"Owl," said the owl.

"Your name is Owl the owl?"

"Yes," said the owl. "Owl the owl. The third."

Pebble buried his face in his paws. "We're going to die here."

Owl tried a different tactic. "Do you have any other

names? A nickname? Something you'd want to be called? Do you even like being called Owl the owl?"

The giant bird—otherwise known as Owl the owl, otherwise known as the creature still considering whether or not it ought to eat them, a creature that was decidedly *not* a turkey—inclined his head to the side. He blinked several times, as if contemplating, and said, "Carl."

They stared at him.

"Carl," the owl formerly known as Owl the owl repeated. "I have always wanted to be a Carl."

Mrs. Dragonsnap, amazingly, had nothing to say to that.

Owl held up his hands.

"Carl," he said slowly, "this is going to sound absolutely wild, but you've been asleep for sixty years. The forest is in trouble. We need your help."

"I know I've been asleep," Carl said crossly. "The last thing I remember is that awful fairy boy coming here with some nonsense about replacing the Keeper of the weavers. Then he shoved a bunch of seeds down my throat! I gave him a good whack and sent him flying." He blinked. "And then I woke up and—did you say *sixty years*?"

As quickly as he could, Owl explained.

The great Keeper listened thoughtfully as Owl spoke, his yellow eyes narrowing. "How do I know this isn't a trick?"

Owl gestured at the wood around them. "See for yourself. Take a look at what's happened to your home while you slept and then try and tell me something isn't seriously wrong here. If we're wrong, you can eat us."

Pebble squeaked in protest. "He may not eat *me*."

Someone shushed him. Owl kept his attention on Carl.

"The wood is dying," Owl said urgently. "It's been dying. We have a chance to save it—but we need you and every other Keeper to do it."

Carl's eyes narrowed. "You've found the Keeper of the north?"

"Well, um, no." Owl's face reddened. "But we have someone going to the divers right now and we were kind of hoping. . . ."

"That we would be enough," Carl finished grimly.

He didn't say what they already knew; that without the northern Keeper, there was no guarantee they could succeed. But with the land impassable, there had been no other choice.

"Please," Owl said quietly. "I already watched one world die. I can't lose this one, too. We have to try."

Carl eyed him a moment longer. Then he spread his wings and leaped.

The force of his takeoff was so great it sent Owl, Mrs. Dragonsnap, Sumac, and Pebble flying. They crashed against the side of the nest, forced to watch as Carl glided overhead, wings spread wide. What a marvel it must have been to be able to fly so high and so fast. Even a fairy with wings could never rival a bird like that. Carl flew higher, and higher still, until he was only a smudge against the dark sky. In the silence that followed, only the wind stirred. The trees around them groaned painfully. On the breeze, growing stronger, was that scent of chemical rot.

They were running out of time. *Ary* was running out of time.

"For the record," Pebble muttered, "I very much resent being volunteered as owl food."

Owl ignored him. He craned his neck, watching as Carl flew in tight spirals, his great wings spread wide. He seemed to hesitate in midair.

Then Carl folded his wings and dropped like a stone.

He slammed back into the nest with such force the tree trembled and jumped. It knocked them all backward again, and Owl didn't dare to rise. The great bird paced back and forth, his beak clacking with agitation, eyes rolling.

"My wood," he said finally, his voice equal parts mournful and furious. "My beautiful wood. Where are the robins? Where are the crows, the jays, the hawks?"

Scared as he was, Owl's heart ached for Carl. He knew what it meant to see your home brought to ruin. He just had to hope Carl would want to save this one before it was too late.

"Carl," Owl said carefully, his heart beating, "there's still a chance to fix this. But we need your help—and we need it now."

The great bird eyed him skeptically. He looked from

Owl to the forest beyond, a million emotions flashing behind his eyes. Owl didn't dare breathe. Without Carl, they were doomed.

The Keeper ruffled his feathers and fixed one yellow eye on Owl. "You can fix this, Seedling?"

"I can," said Owl, even though the words made him cold with terror. "If you help us, I'll find a way. I promise."

Carl gave his beak a decisive click. "Tell me what you need me to do."

Owl's heart soared. "Do you know how to get to the weavers' domain from here?"

FIFTY-THREE

Choices

Ary and Quickspark traveled down.

A tense silence bloomed between them. With every step, Ary half expected Quickspark to turn and attack her. She could practically feel the intense dislike vibrating off the newt. And could Ary really blame her? So far, none of their interactions had been very pleasant.

"Quickspark," Ary said, sidestepping a puddle filled with black liquid. "About the Ant Court—"

"Please," Quickspark sighed. "Don't waste your breath."

"I'm sorry."

Quickspark stumbled, and Ary didn't know what it said about her that it was a little satisfying to see the mean newt almost face-plant into a bunch of old spiderwebs.

"Not for tricking you," Ary clarified, her voice firm. "But I'm sorry about your eye. I was just trying to protect my friends. I know that doesn't fix anything—but I wish I'd done something different. And I wish I hadn't hurt you."

The newt peered at her suspiciously with her good eye. Again, a twinge of guilt washed through Ary. The loss of her wings had been devastating to her. Quickspark had lost her fire *and* half her vision.

The newt made a disgusted noise and lashed her tail. "You are *insufferable*, you know that?"

Ary stiffened. "I'm trying to apologize!"

"I don't want your apology!" Quickspark snapped. "I don't want your self-serving sorrow. You cost me an eye. You destroyed my home. You think a simple *sorry* fixes that?"

"Well, no, but—"

"You're as bad as he is," Quickspark spat. "No wonder he likes you so much. My father always knew how to say the right thing, but he somehow forgot to follow through. Well, you know what, Mossheart? I'm tired of empty words. I'm interested in *action*."

She stalked ahead before Ary could respond. Ary followed her, cheeks burning. Her first instinct was to brush Quickspark off for being rude with her usual bad temper—but something like unease prickled at her.

Because . . . Quickspark kind of had a point.

"You know what's funny?" Ary said. Quickspark didn't turn to look at her. "Terra was always really good about telling Gran how much they appreciated her."

Quickspark kept walking.

"They put up a statue," continued Ary. "Threw parades. Everyone called her a hero and made it a point to say how *grateful* they were to Wren Mossheart. But it didn't fix the holes in our walls. It didn't fill our cupboard or help my papa when he got sick. Gran always liked to say you couldn't feed a family on *thank you*." Ary hesitated. "And I guess—well, you can't fix an eye with sorry, either."

Quickspark didn't turn around—but from the tenseness of her shoulders, Ary knew she was listening.

"I want to believe it matters that I feel bad about the things I had to do in the Underground," said Ary. "Even when those things felt necessary. Even when they came down to my life or yours. But that doesn't bring any of the ants back. And it certainly doesn't fix your eye." Her voice wavered. "I always thought—good and bad was always an easy line, you know? If I said the right thing, and usually did the right thing, things would be fine, and the few times I slipped up, an apology was enough."

All that fire. All those ants. They had been her enemies, but they had had lives of their own, long before the mold came for them.

"The worst part is," Ary whispered, "when I go back, I can't think of another way to get us out of there. If I hadn't started that fire or hurt you—my friends and I would have died. And that's what scares me." Her voice grew smaller. "Because honestly? It was so easy."

That was the worst part of it all. Because now there was forever a part of Ary that understood creatures that made terrible choices—even when it wasn't to protect someone they loved. The hardest thing about her actions that day in the Ant Court hadn't been wrestling with right and wrong. It had been setting herself in motion.

Once she'd thrown that crystal—once the fires had started—instinct had kicked in.

And what did it say about her, that her instincts lent themselves so easily to causing so much destruction?

"My father has this annoying saying," Quickspark said finally. "There is no good or evil. Only creatures—"

"Making choices," Ary finished.

Quickspark remained facing away from her.

"You made your choices," Quickspark said finally, her voice barely audible. "And I made mine. No amount of hand-wringing will undo what has already been done. What matters is what you do next." Her eyes flashed in the dark, and she had never looked more like Sootflank. "I meant what I said. I'm tired of empty words. You want to make things up to me, Mossheart? Fix whatever is going on in these woods so for the first time in my life, I can live in *peace*."

Ary nodded. It was as good as she would get from Quickspark—and honestly, more than she deserved. They continued on in silence, sidestepping old spiderwebs. A light glowed ahead, signaling the end of the tunnel. Ary tensed. The wolf spider had taken care of the spiders behind them—but there was no telling what might lie ahead.

"Quickspark," Ary whispered into the dark. "When we met that day—it felt like you hated me from the moment you saw me."

"Is that a question?"

"It can be. If it's one you want to answer."

Quickspark was silent for a long moment, staring at something Ary could not see. Ary braced herself for some snide remark, but instead, when Quickspark spoke, her voice was barely audible.

"Did he tell you my mother was already gone when he decided to try to help Wren Mossheart?" Quickspark asked. "It was just me and him. And he helped her and lost everything, and I lost *him*. I was glad he spent most of his life alone. It felt fair that, after he abandoned me, he was cursed to solitude. And then you show up, and suddenly he's a hero again. Suddenly, he cares. I didn't even know he was still alive until the earwigs said a newt general had threatened them with fire to protect two fairy pups. And I just *knew*. He'd been out there that whole time. And he'd never even looked for me."

Ary hugged herself close, recalling how Sootflank had been so bitter and lost when they had found him. He had barely been able to speak of Quickspark at all. Had he truly not looked for her? Or had he assumed she was better off without him?

Still, what a terrible thing, to be a child—or whatever a young newt could be considered—out there alone. She thought of Owl, Briar, Mama, and Sootflank. She missed them so desperately. It had been foolish to keep secrets from them—to think she could handle this all on her own.

Even now, after the terrarium had shattered, she was still trying to fold herself into the shadow Gran had cast.

"He wasn't going to help us at first," said Ary. "If that makes you feel better. He didn't care about me or my gran at all. When I tried to reason with him he actually threatened to eat me."

"That sounds like him," Quickspark said dryly.

"And someone else I know."

"Careful, little folk. Our alliance is a very temporary one."

Ary fought a smile. They kept walking, always at an incline. Softly, Ary told Quickspark about the first time she had met Sootflank—of how terrifying he had seemed, of his bitter anger toward Gran, and the way it had been Ary's story of the glow-moth, not anything Ary herself had done or said, that had changed his mind.

"When we were on the journey to Atlas, Sootflank made it sound as though he didn't expect to live long enough to leave the terrarium," Ary said softly. "But he was still so determined that we would break the spell. I wondered, then, who it was for. I think maybe some of it was for you."

"It doesn't excuse what he did."

"You're right," Ary agreed. She had a dizzy sense of being caught in a memory, on the opposite end of a conversation she'd had in a different time, with a different girl. "But I hope it matters that the people who loved us tried, even if they failed. Even if they hurt us. That at the end of the day, Sootflank just wanted you to inherit a better world. That doesn't mean you have to let go of your anger or forgive him. You don't even have to *like* him." Ary hesitated. "But it does mean you're allowed to stop blaming yourself, if that's what you want. It's like you said—creatures, making choices, right? And it doesn't sound like your dad left you with very good ones."

Quickspark was quiet. Ary wondered, for the first time, how her life might have turned out if Gran had been all she had. She had been so lucky to have Mama growing up, even as Gran's coldness and the weight of her expectations threatened to crush her.

What a terribly lonely thing, to have the person who is your entire world all too willing to sacrifice themselves to save it.

Fatigue crept over Ary. The strange, pale light ahead was brighter now, shining from around the corner. Quickspark drew to a halt. Every line of her body was tense, and her eyes wide. A sense of foreboding rose in Ary.

"What was that we said," Quickspark said slowly, "about no good or evil?"

Ary turned the corner, and her heart stopped as her mind scrambled to understand what she was seeing.

A cavern stretched before them. Spiderwebs glittered throughout, sagging under the weight of dozens upon dozens of pods of tightly wrapped spider silk. Some of the pods twitched and jumped; some hung terribly still. A few spiders scuttled about, their eyes blank. As Quickspark and Ary watched, they ran their legs over the pods, as if . . . testing them for something. A spider plucked down a shriveled pod and began to unwind it. Even from a distance, Ary could see a few stray glimmers of fairy dust lining the silvery threads. The spider trundled away, carrying the fairy dust off with it as the shreds of the pod floated to the floor.

Ary had wondered where Oleander was getting his fairy dust.

Now she knew.

Horror crept through every part of Ary—but with it came the burn of something new.

Fury.

Everyone who had gone missing, everyone who had been stolen. They'd been in those pods. Turned into fairy dust, just like the wings of the folk had been back in Terra, but this time they'd paid with their whole lives. And for what? A bit of power? A little more comfort in the lives of those that remained?

Beyond the cavern, a single tunnel sloped down. Ary had a feeling she knew who was trapped at the end of it.

Ary curled her fingers around the handle of the Seedling shovel.

"Quickspark," she murmured, "do you think you can get those pods open?"

The newt's eyes narrowed. "Not with the spiders here."

Ary's heart began to pound. "What if they were gone?"

Quickspark grew still. "What are you thinking?"

Ary's eyes drifted from the pods to the tunnels.

I was worried I'd never get you out of that village.

How had Ary not seen before? Ary was the one Aspen wanted. All the fairies that had gone missing; all the dreams and the call she had felt from the beginning. Even that very first wolf spider that had been under her thrall.

Aspen had been calling to Ary from the beginning.

She was finally ready to listen.

"You wanted action, right? Not words?" Ary asked. "I'm about to give it to you."

FIFTY-FOUR

The Mountain

Shrimp crawled faster.

If he was keeping track of time right (and, like finding things, that was something Shrimp was actually quite good at) he ought to be near the warm-bloods' territory soon. The insects and spiders that had chosen to follow scuttled after him in an eternal, writhing wave. It was starting to get a little stressful, honestly. The whole *we follow* thing was a lot more fun when Shrimp was doing the following.

Crawler, one of the spiders hummed, extending a spindly leg toward a tunnel. *This way.*

Shrimp felt the land shift around them. The soil grew bitter and dry; stones replaced the roots that had tangled through the tunnels, and even the bugs that followed him began to drop off one by one, too scared to move forward.

Shrimp crawled ahead without them.

If this was before Ary, he might have stopped. It had been scary to crawl through the Underground alone. But Shrimp had watched Ary lead even when she was afraid.

He had watched her plunge ahead, hoping the ones she loved would follow, and knowing she'd have to try to stop Atlas even if they didn't. He crawled, and skittered, and scampered, and when the tunnel ended, he dug. Shrimp could feel the Blight high above them, a wicked, dark poison spreading across the earth.

The others had been right—no fairy would have been able to fly this far, and no creature like Sootflank would have been able to walk.

Shrimp dug until all fourteen of his legs ached, until his antennae felt rubbed raw. He could sense something ahead of him. Something ancient and waking up. He dug and thought of Ary, and Owl, and all the others who had become his new pod.

He was so tired. But Shrimp was not going to stop.

Shrimp gave one final heave, and the earth collapsed.

Moonlight washed over him. Shrimp had popped out of the earth beneath a great, towering tree whose tendrils of leaves hung like locks of hair in a great, green ring. A massive beast curled at the base of the tree, covered in years of leaves that had blown through the window. Moss grew on its antlers; grime covered its fur. The beast was so large, it was practically a mountain. It craned its neck toward Shrimp, watching with interest as bug after bug emerged from the tunnel behind him.

"It has been many years since I've seen a crawler," the

mountain-like beast boomed. Its dark brown eyes threatened to swallow Shrimp whole. "Tell me, little bug. What do you seek?"

Shrimp froze. He was used to Ary and Owl doing the talking. It was so much to explain.

"Help," Shrimp whispered. "Shrimp seeks your help."

FIFTY-FIVE

Be Better

As the spiders wove, Ary and Quickspark lay in wait.

The plan was a simple one—so simple, something was certain to go terribly wrong.

It was also the only one Ary had.

Here, in the heart of the weavers' webs, it was difficult to keep track of time. Ary had grown accustomed to the sharp contrasts of light in Siltshore—the golden brightness of a new day, the velvet black of night. The gloom of this place reminded her of Terra, where there was never full brightness, only a lessening of the darkness that had persisted her entire life.

"Mossheart," Quickspark whispered, "are you certain about this?"

"Nope," whispered Ary.

Even as she said it, a thrill went through her. She didn't know when the change had happened. She had been scared her whole life—even in the terrarium, when she'd faced Atlas, she had been scared. She had been ready to die, had held her grandmother's hands, and fear had burned through every part of her. From the way her heart pounded and her hands sweated, Ary knew that fear was still there.

The anger was new. Fury was a gift, and Ary held it close, let it fill her lungs like smoke.

They waited as a new spider entered the room. Ary and Quickspark had lain there for the better part of an hour, keeping count as spiders entered one by one to check the pods, spin the webs. A new spider came every few minutes. They'd have to act fast.

The spider scuttled out of the cavern—and Ary and Quickspark exploded into action.

Ary scaled the nearest string of web ropes, hands flying over hands. She reached the nearest pod, drove her Seedling shovel into it, and sliced. A gasp came from within. Ary's heart soared as a fairy tumbled out and Quickspark caught them below. Ary leaped to the next, and the next, hands flying as fast as possible, slicing open pod after pod. One by one, fairies and creatures alike tumbled out. She sliced open the next and saw the familiar face of Mayor Nightingale.

"Mossheart!" Nightingale gasped.

"Do you have something sharp?" Ary demanded. "Help me."

Nightingale nodded.

Ary counted down. She didn't have much time.

With shaking hands, Nightingale crawled from her pod and began to cut others free. To their left, Quickspark ripped pods open with her teeth. Earwigs poured out, hissing and snapping their pincers, but when Quickspark barked orders at them, they turned and began ripping open the other pods in quick succession. Tulip and Basil stumbled out, sobbing and clutching each other, and ran to Yarrow in tears.

"Mossheart!" Quickspark called. "We've got company!"

Four spiders loomed ahead of them. Fear rose in Ary. There were still so many pods to cut free—but she'd saved who she could for now. Ary scrambled back down, her feet hitting the ground with a thud, and pointed frantically up the tunnel.

"Go while you can!" she cried. "Run!"

The freed fairies and creatures needed no convincing. They began a pathetic, shambling run toward freedom.

All of them except the earwigs—and Mayor Nightingale.

Mayor Nightingale knelt on the cavern floor, a bright, determined light in her eyes. Pink fairy dust glittered along her hands and arms, harvested from the very bodies of the fairies she'd been sworn to protect. The mayor was pale, but her eyes were bright.

"What are you doing?" Ary demanded. "We've got to go!"

Nightingale ignored her. More spiders approached them, but at the sight of the fairy dust glittering over Nightingale, they hesitated.

"I have made many mistakes," Nightingale said quietly. "I failed my people. I stole, and lied, and cheated, and I told myself it was acceptable, because I could have been worse. But I was a coward. I missed my chance before, to right my wrongs and be better. I'll not miss it again."

Her eyes flashed. "Tell me, newt. Would you rather live a coward—or die fighting as someone worthy of their fire?"

"What?" Ary protested. "No!"

They ignored her.

Quickspark's eyes narrowed. Before she could speak, the earwigs drew closer to her, their pincers flashing. Their stance was clear; if Quickspark fought, they would, too.

"You give me fire," Quickspark said quietly. "And I promise, no weaver will make it past me."

"Quickspark, *no,*" protested Ary. "You were supposed to come with me. What about Sootflank? What about everything you said?"

The newt gave her head a stubborn shake. "Do it."

Mayor Nightingale took a breath. She raised her hands, fingers glittering with the power of the fallen, and breathed a single, familiar word: "*Ignite.*"

Heat and light blasted out from her hands. For a beat, Ary could see nothing. The light cleared, and in its absence, a single glow illuminated them all.

Fire wreathed Quickspark in a dozen brilliant ribbons—pink, orange, and yellow. She looked like the beginning of a sunrise.

"Oh," breathed the newt. "Oh, I have missed this."

With each breath, her fire rose. It painted the cave in hues of red, blue, and orange, burning brighter and hotter than any flame Ary had seen before. The spiders leaned back with a whine.

"Go," Nightingale ordered, her face sweating in the heat. "We'll hold them off."

Before Ary could protest, the mayor flung a hand in Ary's direction. The rocks under Ary's feet buckled and hurled her backward into the tunnel. Before Ary could protest, a glittering wall of magic slammed between Ary and the way back into the cavern. Ary cried out and hurled herself against the wall, but it was no use. She might have been immune to magic being worked *on* her, but didn't hold true for the world around her.

Tears cut tracks down Ary's cheeks. It wasn't fair, but when had any of this been fair? And wasn't this what she had wanted—for the adults to finally step up and act as though they had something at stake here, too? And if that was the case, if this was what Ary had wanted, why did she feel nothing but grief?

The nearest spider lunged; an earwig leaped to meet it, and the two creatures collided, pincers and fangs snapping in the air as each fought for victory. Quickspark sent a streaming blast of fire toward another pack of spiders. They squealed as they burned. More appeared, their eyes blank with enchantment.

Spiders poured from the tunnels overhead and crawled down the walls. Quickspark, Mayor Nightingale, and the earwigs turned to face them. How many earwigs had killed folk back in Terra? How many newts had Nightingale ordered executed? All those decades of bloody history, of theft and pain and betrayal, vanished in a blink, in hopes they might build something better.

"Mossheart," Quickspark bellowed, her tail lashing. She looked back at Ary, a wild, thrilled light in her eyes. "Make it worth it. And be better."

Ary blinked furiously. Before she could respond, Quickspark turned away. She let loose a roar and an inferno swept through the cavern. Nightingale raised her hands and used magic to bring down the remaining pods, bellowing for the captured creatures to flee.

Ary wiped her eyes. She had gotten too used to doing everything alone. She didn't know how to handle this part—letting someone else do the sacrificing and saving.

"I will," Ary vowed in a whisper. "I'm going to put a stop to it, once and for all."

She clutched her shovel to her chest and adjusted her acorn cap. The tunnel loomed ahead of her, dark, endless, and cold.

Ary plunged in.

And behind her, Quickspark burned.

Ary ran.

The smell of smoke filled the tunnel behind her. In the distance, she could hear Quickspark's roars and the earwigs' hisses as they fought. They wouldn't be able to hold off the spiders forever, but they were going to give her a good chance.

Down the tunnel, arms pumping, legs flying. It was as

if there was a string tied around Ary's middle drawing her forward. As she ran, the landscape became familiar. She was aware of the ground sloping upward, and a cool breeze, carrying with it the scent of things dead and dying.

Ary burst around the corner and entered the hollow from her dreams.

Spiderwebs formed a massive cocoon, closing the area in. Nothing grew here; nothing thrived. Overhead, the moon was a great silver disc in the sky, reflecting silver light off the eerie hollow.

A massive spider curled inward—dried and unmoving. It was bigger than any spider Ary had ever seen. It had to be the Keeper of the weavers. But it was long dead. An old, dried lily flower, the seeds picked free, lay off to the side. The hilt of a knife glinted in the spider's carapace.

The Keeper had been murdered.

Ary blinked. Aspen hadn't said anything about a murdered Keeper. A sense of foreboding rose in her. This was probably more of Oleander's work. And sixty years later, his people were still paying the price.

Ary took one cautious step forward. There was no sound in the hollow; no breeze, despite the open sky overhead. Her Seedling shovel trembled in her hands.

"Hello?" Ary whispered.

"You shouldn't be here."

Ary flinched and turned. Oleander hung suspended in the web, his wrists and ankles bound, looking far worse for wear. Purple bruises shadowed the undersides of his eyes; blood was crusted along his temple.

Ary expected to feel rage at the sight of him, but instead, terror lanced through her. "*Oleander?* What are you doing here? How—"

"Run," Oleander said urgently. "Run, before she realizes you're here."

From the center of the spider's webs a pair of eyes blinked open.

An old woman, long withered by time, turned her face toward Ary and smiled. She lay perpetually trapped in the embrace of the long-dead spider.

"Ary Mossheart," she croaked. "At last."

Recognition cracked through Ary. Of course. The woman's face was lined, her hair wispy and white, but her eyes were the same as they'd been in Ary's dreams.

"Aspen?" Ary breathed.

Aspen's eyes fluttered. "The one and only."

Ary's hand trembled. Her eyes darted from the flower to the knife buried in the spider's heart. She expected to feel—she didn't know. Relief at the sight of Aspen? Joy? But the hollow had the sense of walls closing in around her. Ary took one uncertain step forward. Oleander had lapsed into an unusual, strained silence, the last bit of color drained from his face.

Ary's skin prickled. She'd expected Oleander to be angry to see her.

Instead he looked . . . scared.

Ary turned her attention back to Aspen. Oleander was probably just uneasy because he knew Aspen was going to tell everyone the truth once she was free. Ary could still salvage this. She could still save them all.

"You made it," Aspen breathed, the relief in her face easing some of Ary's tension. "I was worried you wouldn't, but you made it."

Ary tried to quiet her nerves. "I came to rescue you."

Oleander closed his eyes. "You stupid girl."

The hair on Ary's arms stood on end. She clenched her shovel tighter. "That's why I'm here, right?" She looked at Aspen. "You wanted me to save you. To set you free."

Aspen gave her a funny smile.

Behind Ary, a pair of spiders wove webs over the tunnel she'd entered through. Ary's blood ran cold. She had known the spiders were enchanted. That they were being controlled.

But she hadn't wondered about who was controlling them.

Aspen cocked her head to the side.

"You're not here to rescue me," Aspen said. "You're here to *become* me."

FIFTY-SIX

Hurry

Carl soared.

Owl clutched Carl's feathers as they flew over the woods at an incredible speed. On Carl's back, the wood passed in a blur. Owl could see the extent of the damage the Blight had caused, snaking through the wood in an eternal, dark scar.

"The weavers are close," warned Carl. "But something . . . feels wrong."

A dot appeared ahead of them. It was approaching, and fast, growing bigger by the minute. Carl let out a hiss. Owl's heart leaped. Was something coming to attack them?

"It's a fairy," said Carl.

"Wait," said Owl. "That's not just any fairy—that's Briar! *Briar, up here!*"

The tiny dot that was Briar jerked in midair and then zipped toward them. She was flying so fast she collided with Owl. He tumbled backward, and for a terrifying moment, the feeling of Carl's feathers beneath him disappeared, and Owl felt only empty air.

Then a hand locked around his wrist.

Sumac looked down at Owl with wild eyes. "You're not

allowed to come up with the worst plan ever and then *die*!" he shouted. Mrs. Dragonsnap lunged forward and grabbed Owl's other hand, and together they hauled him up.

Briar collapsed on Carl's back, her whole body covered in sweat, her chest heaving. She'd been flying for a long time, and hard.

"Briar," said Owl. "Where's Ary? What's going on?"

Briar looked at Owl with wide, terrified eyes. "Owl, we have to hurry. She's going after the Keeper of the weavers alone."

Carl flew faster.

The wood changed as they flew, the trees thinning as they neared the forest's heart, taking them to the weavers' domain. They crossed over the swamp, and Owl could see his panicked face reflected in the endless dark water.

There was a ripple in the swamp below.

Something was swimming—no, hundreds of somethings. At their lead was a creature Owl had never seen before; a massive, shelled beast that cut through the water. Bulbous, newt-like creatures without tails swam around it.

Leading it, orange tail flashing, was a creature Owl would have known anywhere.

"Sootflank!" he cried, pointing. "Carl, down there!"

Carl dove, flying so low his talons nearly skimmed the water. As they flew closer, Sootflank and the creatures that followed him drew into shape. Owl's heart soared. The massive-shelled beast that swam with them could only be the Keeper of the divers. They dipped closer.

"Sootflank!" Owl shouted. The newt jerked and did a double take. What a sight Owl must have been, soaring along on the back of a giant bird with Mrs. Dragonsnap, Sumac, and a mouse. Owl's heart leaped at the sight of the giant, shelled Keeper.

They really might be able to pull this off.

"We must hurry," Carl said softly. "I can feel a shift ahead. The Keeper of the weavers—it's waking up."

"Anything from the north?" Sumac asked hopefully.

Carl's grim silence was all they needed. Owl tried to scrape together his last bits of hope. This would simply have to work without the final Keeper. It had to.

"I know the way," the great shelled Keeper intoned. "She lurks in the heart of the swamp, in a long-hollowed tree filled with webs." The beast seemed to hesitate, as if debating something, and then blinked its wide, yellow eyes, and turned back toward the swamp. "This way."

The Keeper plunged ahead, with Sootflank and Carl in its wake. Owl clutched Carl's feathers and tried not to think about the terror in Briar's face.

Hold on, Ary, Owl willed. *We're coming.*

FIFTY-SEVEN

The Next Ghostwing

Every part of Ary was cold.

It didn't make sense. Aspen had been a victim, just like Ary. Forced to shatter the terrarium, to become a Ghostwing. Manipulated by Oleander, asked to take on too much, too soon. Right?

Why else call out to Ary? Why bring her here, if not so Ary could stop the Blight and set her free at last?

"Don't you see?" Aspen said eagerly. "It's perfect. You're—you're like me, truly. Not a pretender, like Oleander. A real Ghostwing. Special. You are the only one who can take my place." She let out a happy sigh. "And I can finally be free."

Horror crept over Ary in a dark, freezing wave.

Aspen moved as if she wanted to reach for Ary and frowned down at where her hands used to be. She turned, those wide, desperate eyes drinking her in. Impatience flickered across her face. "Well, what are you waiting for?"

"I can't . . ." Ary stammered. "I'm not . . ."

She had come here on a rescue mission. Not to become . . . whatever Aspen was.

Ary's eyes darted around. Spiders surrounded her on all sides. Oleander was strangely silent in his prison, his face drawn, pale, and hopeless. Horror crept through Ary.

She was trapped.

Think, Ary, she willed. *Think like your life depends on it.*

"How?" Ary whispered.

"Ary," Oleander said urgently. "Don't."

"You don't get to speak," Aspen said viciously. Oleander flinched. Icy terror washed through Ary. Suddenly, Oleander was no longer the looming villain; he was as scared as she was. Aspen exhaled impatiently and looked back at Ary. "It's simple, really. The Keepers pass down their magic. Feed me one of those seeds over there—" She nodded toward the dried husk of the flower. "And then you can use the fairy dust to take my magic. Unlike the weaver, I'll give it up without a fight. I'll finally be free." Her beady eyes cut viciously toward Oleander. "And then I'll have all the time in the world to repay you the kindness you did me."

Oleander turned a very interesting shade of gray. "Aspen, I couldn't have known—"

"I couldn't have known," Aspen mocked. Her face twisted. "You knew, Oleander. You were all too happy to let me die for you, because *you* were supposed to end up with the wings. But when it came down to it, it wasn't you that Hemlock loved, was it?"

Oleander stared back at her, his face bright with hatred. Horror crept through Ary.

Every part of Oleander was an imposter. He had never cast the spell at all; Aspen and Hemlock had.

It was all a lie. Every single word.

"Sixty years I've watched you from the wood," Aspen whispered viciously. "Sixty years I replayed what you told me, when you sent me to the weavers. You lied to me. You created this prison. And once my hands are my own again, the first thing I'll do is wrap them around your throat."

Ary couldn't breathe. She took a step back and collided with the leg of a massive black-and-yellow spider.

Think, she willed. *Stall.* Aspen was unstable, and Ary could use that to buy time.

"Why hurt the Keepers?" she asked carefully. "Why kill the weaver at all?"

Aspen's expression darkened. "When we entered the world, we found it occupied. The Keepers would not meet with us. They claimed Oleander and I were unclean, *unworthy* of entering their web." Aspen frowned. "Oleander had an idea, though. He said—well, he said we could just take their power. He promised me that he'd take on the flyer and the diver, and suggested I go to the weaver." Her lip curled. "She let me right in. But then everything went wrong. When I killed her I got . . . stuck."

The myth of the Keepers. There had been a folk among them, once. A Ghostwing capable of carrying incredible power. Oleander had sent Aspen here to make her a Keeper of the folk—but they had gotten greedy. They had tried to steal the power of the Keeper of the weavers, too, and thrown everything out of balance.

The Blight. The spiders. All that death.

It wasn't just Oleander.

It was Aspen, too.

"Oleander lied to me," Aspen said, her voice low and furious. "He didn't kill the other Keepers. He just put them to sleep. He returned a hero while I was stuck here. Trapped, in pain, the wood eating away at me." She shuddered. "I can hear her, sometimes. The Keeper. Scratching at me from inside."

Ary was going to throw up.

Aspen smiled at Ary. "I thought I'd be like this forever, until you showed up."

Ary's eyes darted from the flower seeds to the knife, the same one Aspen had used to kill the Keeper of the weavers all those years ago. Had she wanted to weep, as Ary did now? Had she felt angry regret as she stole magic from the rest of the wood and started the Blight?

Or had she felt only hunger?

"Hurry," Aspen said eagerly. "Oh, I'm so *glad* there's finally another Ghostwing. I tried with that other fairy, and it didn't work."

Ice splintered through Ary. "The other fairy?"

"The one from the village," Aspen said, her voice taking on a vicious bend. She wasn't strong enough in the end. The magic burned her up. She was too weak."

The color drained from Oleander's face. Ary recalled the way he'd looked startled when she'd accused him of hurting Marigold.

"It was you," Oleander rasped. "All these years. The spiders, the threats. You couldn't hurt me yourself. So you found another way."

"You deserved all of it," Aspen snarled, her voice low. "And you were all too happy to grow strong on the fairy dust I made from them. Don't get all holy on me now, Oleander. We both know you've never cared for anyone but yourself."

Oleander stared back at her, his face bright with hatred, but he didn't deny it.

Ary was going to be sick.

Maybe, at some point, one of them had been more in the wrong. But it didn't matter anymore. As far as Ary was concerned, Aspen and Oleander were two faces of the same monster.

Ary took a cautious step toward Aspen. Her heart pounded so hard her hands trembled. She felt like she was floating outside of her body. Like she was back in those dreams, watching from afar as they turned into the worst kind of nightmare.

"What happens after?" Ary asked carefully. "When—when I don't want to be"—she gestured in Aspen's direction—"this anymore?"

"You *cannot*—" Oleander shouted. A spider shot toward

him, weaving silk over his mouth. He shouted and writhed, but whatever else he wanted to tell Ary was lost.

Aspen rolled her eyes. "I should have done that from the beginning." She cocked her head to the side, her gaze focusing in on Ary. "Someone else will come take your place eventually."

"And the Blight?" Ary asked.

"It should go away for a while," said Aspen, although she didn't seem convinced. "I was better at controlling it in the beginning. But I'm so tired now. Hurry up, would you?"

Ary's skin crawled. Aspen spoke as if the lives of others were dolls; things to be moved and bent in any shape she desired. But of course she would think that way. She had spent sixty years tormenting Oleander. She had taken Marigold, and when the woman had not bent to the right shape, Aspen had broken Marigold and thrown her away.

Aspen scowled. "Someone is coming."

Ary's hands trembled. If she did this, maybe she could hold back the Blight. Buy everyone else more time. Free the spiders from their enchantment, at least, so they no longer terrorized the other inhabitants of the wood.

But it wouldn't actually fix the problem.

Be better, Quickspark had demanded.

Someday, Ary would become like Aspen. The Blight would return. And a new child would have to take her place. She would turn into the worst version of Gran, bitter and resentful of all who failed her and everything she lost, causing the ones she loved to suffer most. She would become like Oleander, willing to cast away lives that were less important for some false greater good. Ary could see it so clearly—an entire line of young heroes, the burden passed down through generations, an endless cycle of Blight, torment, and pain.

It would never end.

Weave a better web, the wolf spider had said.

"It has to stop," Ary whispered. "Forever. For good."

Oleander had told Ary she was alone. He'd said only a select few were chosen or made great, and Ary had believed him. She had pushed Owl away, ignored her mother, and hurt Briar, because she had believed this was her burden only.

But she hadn't found Atlas by herself. And Ary hadn't cast that spell alone, either.

Maybe being brave didn't have to be a solitary act.

Maybe the most heroic thing Ary could do was leap—and trust someone to catch her.

Ary scooped up a palmful of seeds. Her fingers trembled.

Aspen's eyes closed, a dreamy smile spreading across her face as she stuck out her tongue. She looked like a child waiting to catch dewdrops from a nearby leaf.

How much pain must she have been in these last sixty years?

How much would Ary feel if she took her place?

She could do it. Become Aspen. Buy them time. It was

the kind of noble, self-sacrificing nonsense a girl like her was primed for. Maybe she was the exception. Maybe somewhere, along the way, Ary had become remarkable enough that this could work.

But if Ary was being honest? She wasn't that special. Aspen had been a good, kind little fairy, too. Six decades of torment would make anyone a monster.

Ary wanted better. For herself, for her friends, for all the folk to come whose names she'd never know, but whose futures she was determined to protect.

And she did not want any other child to be forced to take up the mantle of hero.

Not now.

Never again.

They realized what she was doing a moment too late. Oleander shouted from behind his gag; Aspen screamed for her spiders.

Owl, thought Ary. *Catch me.*

Ary palmed the seeds—and swallowed them down.

FIFTY-EIGHT

The Mountain

Quickly, Shrimp told the mountain what he'd come for. Of the girl in the weavers' kingdom, and the Blight that ravaged the land. The mountain paused. It looked at Shrimp.

And then it said:

"No."

No?

Shrimp could not believe his ears! (Shrimp did not actually have ears. But he had heard Owl and Ary use this expression before, and he thought it had a better ring than *vibration receptors.*)

"A fairy came here many years ago," said the mountainous Keeper, "spinning promises of great power—but he brought deception instead. I watched what happened to the flyer, the diver, and the weaver who listened to the thief and liar they welcomed into their domain. The web may be failing, but I will not accelerate its destruction by welcoming *folk* in. She is not worthy." The mountain yawned, clearly intending to return to sleep. "Now go away."

Shrimp looked back at his bugs. There were so many of them now—pill bugs and centipedes, ants and grasshoppers, and of course the spiders. They waited expectantly, watching as the strange pill bug who vibrated with power rubbed his antennae anxiously together. It was ridiculous. They believed in him, and for what? Shrimp hadn't done anything special. He had no clue what he was doing! The bugs didn't even know it, but they weren't even here for him. Not really. They were here for Ary.

He had promised to follow her, and in turn, they had promised to follow him.

Anger vibrated through Shrimp. Who was this creature to deny him? Who could be worthy, if not Ary Mossheart, a girl who had found a lonely bug in the dark and offered him the light of kindness when no one else would?

Shrimp had spent most of his life struggling with how to use his words. It had been easier, always, to speak quickly, simply, and softly. He had been mocked for it, ignored, and shut out—so it had been a relief when he had met Ary Mossheart and she had not asked more of him. She'd made an effort to meet Shrimp exactly where he was, and maybe Shrimp had grown a little too comfortable relying on Ary and Owl and the others to fill in the gaps.

"Worthy?" Shrimp blurted. "*Worthy*? Ary is dying, and you want Shrimp to talk about her being *worthy*?!"

The pill bugs behind him shivered; if pill bugs had jaws, they would have dropped. Even the weavers froze.

But not Shrimp.

The words just kept coming.

His voice grew louder, and louder, rising like startled birds, and before he could stop himself, before he could think twice, or puzzle over the consequences, or consider every possible way that things could go wrong—Shrimp began to yell.

With fury and love and fear bubbling through every cell of his exoskeleton, Shrimp told the mountain about the day he had met Ary Mossheart. He told it of the years he had spent lost in the dark, before a tired, brave little girl had offered him kindness and the only food she'd had. He told the beast of the grandmother she'd lost, the friends she'd made, and the burdens she'd shouldered—some of which, *need he remind him*, the mountain should have figured out a long time ago, thank you very much! It wasn't Ary Mossheart's fault this world was sick. It wasn't her problem to fix. But she had stepped up, just like she had back in the terrarium, because no one else would. Because it was the right thing to do.

"So," Shrimp squeaked, nothing but pure, vibrating fury, "if the mountain will not help Shrimp, then the mountain needs to GET. OUT. OF. SHRIMP'S. WAY!"

Finally, the words ran out, and then it was only Shrimp again, shaking, his little body whittled out and exhausted. He'd said more words in the last minute than in the last decade of his very long life!

A crushing silence filled the clearing.

Shrimp was certain he had just violated some very

important rule. He didn't really have it in him to care. The rules of folk and the warm-blooded were always so needlessly complex. The other bugs might cast him out after this; it was clear Shrimp had no regard for the pill bug way of things, and that was fine. Sometimes, there needed to be a new way of doing things. And if Shrimp was being honest, he didn't have time for this. He could feel Ary's pain and fear rippling through him—but worse, he felt it fading, which meant Ary was fading, too.

At last, the mountain whispered, "Why? You are a bug and she is a folk. Why come all this way to save her? Why not flee? Why do any of this at all?"

Such a silly question. Shrimp could have spent an entire lifetime answering. Instead, he gathered the last shreds of his patience and said, "Because Shrimp loves her."

The mountain waited.

"Ary is the family Shrimp chose," continued Shrimp. "She is good, and she is kind. She's the forest's best chance, and even if she wasn't, Ary is a part of Shrimp's pod now. Without her, the pod breaks. And we follow pod members until the end." Shrimp paused, and asked crossly, "Are you going to help? Or does Shrimp have to start yelling again?"

The bugs behind him whispered among themselves in shock. This was the most un-pill-bug-like conversation they'd ever heard! Surely Shrimp had just messed everything up. Surely the wood and this Ary he spoke of were now equally doomed.

What the pill bugs wouldn't admit to each other was that they hoped this was not the case. They'd all had moments where they wished they'd been braver.

"Oh, fine," grumbled the mountain. "Get on."

And the mountain rose.

FIFTY-NINE

Reach

The forest was screaming.

It started in the wind. A keening between the trees, and a rumble in the earth. It was as if the very wood was crying out in pain.

No, not pain—anger.

Carl staggered in midair. He groaned, straining, and righted himself.

The weavers' domain came into view. Spiderwebs glittered in every direction. Carl dove and landed with a *slam*, dust flying in every direction. It took a moment for Owl to understand what he was seeing.

The biggest spider he'd ever seen curled in the center of a hollow tree stump, dried and long dead. Clutched in the center of its legs was a furious old woman. She had one hand wrapped around Ary's wrist, and Owl could *feel* the magic pulsing off her. It was violent and twisted and wrong.

And Ary wasn't moving.

Ary slumped on the ground as though she was asleep, one hand splayed open. A single seed gleamed in her palm.

Horror washed through Owl. Ary had swallowed the

lily seeds—the ones that had been powerful enough to put the Keepers to sleep.

Sumac and Mrs. Dragonsnap slid down off Carl's back. The great bird looked at the scene before them with dismay. Owl staggered forward, mind spinning, trying to understand how he'd get Ary away from that creepy old woman—

"Willow?"

The woman trapped in the spider looked up, her face slack with shock. In that instant, she seemed younger. More vulnerable.

"Aspen?" Mrs. Dragonsnap looked as though she'd seen a ghost. "You're alive?"

"She was supposed to take my place," Aspen said bitterly, giving Ary a cruel shake. "I planned to make the spiders force her, if she couldn't do it. Instead, she swallowed the seeds like a coward."

Horror crept through Owl. The girl in Ary's dreams had been Mrs. Dragonsnap's *sister*?

"You were alive?" Mrs. Dragonsnap repeated, stricken. "All these years?"

"You call this living?" Aspen snapped. "Oleander got to live. Oleander got everything. He couldn't even give me a proper replacement."

Mrs. Dragonsnap trembled. She looked at Aspen as though she was seeing her for the first time. "What do you mean . . . a replacement?"

"The girl," Aspen said impatiently. "His girl! I thought a normal fairy would work, but she wasn't strong enough."

Owl was going to be sick. He looked quickly at Sumac, but Sumac didn't seem to understand what Aspen meant.

She had killed Marigold. And now she would kill Ary, too.

A rustle came from behind them. Sootflank slipped into the hollow, water dripping from his flanks, his eyes wide. A massive shelled creature crawled after him.

"Owl," he gasped. "I found the— Oh, no."

Ary didn't move. Owl wanted to lunge at Aspen; he wanted to peel her awful fingers off his friend.

Aspen's eyes snapped to Owl, and her face grew mocking. "Oh, they brought a Seedling. Did you really think you'd be able to fix this? You're too late, little boy. And even if you could—the Keeper of the north will not come. They were always the strongest among us. Without them, your efforts will fail. You'll lack the power needed to undo any of the damage I've done."

Was this how it ended, then? Oleander had been exposed, and Aspen with him. They'd still have time until the Blight destroyed *every* kingdom. They could move beyond the wood, seek better and brighter lands. The forest would be doomed—but Owl, at least, would be safe.

And Ary would die.

Owl trembled. This couldn't all be for nothing. But

Aspen was right. They didn't have all the Keepers, and they needed all of them here to work magic powerful enough to repair what was broken in the wood. Owl had no training, and he was just a boy, and this was all too much. He didn't know how to do this. It wasn't enough to just *be* wingless. It didn't matter that he carried the history of the Seedlings in his blood, his breath, his bones. His own history had been lost; his practices erased. He was just an echo, a straggler left over from the once-powerful folk that had guarded this world.

"Why?" Sootflank croaked, blinking furiously. "Why would Ary . . . ?"

"She didn't want anyone to take her place," Owl whispered.

It couldn't end this way. He refused.

They just needed a little more help.

A *boom* came from behind them. The very forest seemed to jump. Owl twisted, and his jaw dropped as he took in one of the strangest sights he'd ever seen.

A massive horned beast crashed toward them. Blight swarmed up its legs, but the beast paid it no heed. Owl could feel the magic crackling off it even from here. But stranger still was the beast's fur. It was . . . moving? It drew closer. Owl's heart soared.

Covering the beast from horn to hoof were hundreds upon hundreds of bugs.

Pill bugs and ants, spiders and beetles, earwigs and worms. They writhed, danced, and crawled, clinging stubbornly to the great, warm-blooded Keeper.

And perched on its nose, eyes shining, was the bravest pill bug Owl had ever seen.

"Weeee!" cried Shrimp. *"Follooooow!"*

SIXTY

Terra

Ary dreamed of Terra.

The press of darkness hit her at once. The cloying stench of mold was in her throat, in her lungs, in her *eyes*. She had thought she'd freed them, but she had been wrong. They had never left the terrarium—it had all been a lie. It was as if she and Gran had never cast the spell; the homes of Terra squatted together, free of that strange, silvery dust that had exploded from Atlas, their doors shut neatly and windows shuttered. Glow-shroom lamps bobbed overhead, casting the world in a faint, blue glow.

"Hello?" called Ary. She turned and was met with a familiar crackle. Her hand flew to her back. Her wings! Her wings were there, wrapped in the itchy papery cocoon that had plagued Ary all her life. Ary stood in the potato field where she'd gone with Tulip and Basil. The soil was undisturbed, its pale brown surface pocked with rocks instead of scorch marks and signs of ruin.

A sense of foreboding rose in Ary.

"This is cruel, Aspen," Ary whispered. "Even for you."

It was one thing to kill her. But first Aspen would taunt

her with memories of the last world she'd failed before Ary left this one, too.

Ary began to run.

She knew where Aspen would be.

Faster than ever before, legs pumping, bound wings crackling, Ary sprinted up the well-worn road from the fields to the cottage she'd spent her entire life in, anger filling her up, piloting her legs. Aspen could take her mind. She could take her life. But she would *not* let her have this, in Ary's final moments.

Ary burst through the door. "Enough, Aspen! This ends here!"

"Oh, Canary." A familiar, tired face turned toward her. "What have you gotten yourself into now?"

Ary's eyes filled with tears. Her voice emerged in a whisper.

"Gran?"

SIXTY-ONE

Reach

A silence fell over the wood.

Time slowed down. The Keepers crowded forward—flyer, diver, and grazer, with Owl at the center. He drifted forward, faintly aware that some other fairy had been here before. More creatures were coming: mice and frogs and squirrels and spiders. Folk, too, led by Robin and Alder from Siltshore. They crowded around and in, whispering about the little fairy girl who lay stretched in the center of the web.

Owl knelt beside his friend.

She was so small. He had thought that before, when she faced Atlas, and he thought it now, as he took her hand. Her eyes were closed, and there was a look of peace on her face. As though there had been no fear in her when she had made that terrible decision to swallow the lily seeds.

Because that was the thing about Ary. She would sacrifice, and save, and suffer, but she drew the line at asking it of others.

It wasn't fair. It wasn't right. It had been wrong to ask Ary to give her life for them in the Underground—and Owl almost let her. It had haunted him ever since.

Ary knew what it meant to live the life of a hero doomed. And she had refused to make it so that someone else had to take her place.

Magic crackled around them. Aspen hissed furiously, and Owl could *feel* the power rolling off her in waves. She was trying to force it into Ary, but it wouldn't take.

For the first time, Owl knew how Wren Mossheart could turn her back on Atlas and the rest of the world to save one person. He'd always wondered how she'd weighed a single life against so many others.

Now, Owl understood.

Because what was his life without the ones he loved?

Maybe it was ridiculous and selfish to think someone like him could fix this, to risk the fate of the entire world for one person. But Owl didn't want to be the kind of person who let someone suffer for the greater good, because once that line started to move, where it did stop? When would it go from letting one person suffer to hundreds? Wren Mossheart had been set up to fail. Hemlock and Oleander, too. They were just kids. They'd been handed the world, and was it such a shock that, when it grew too heavy, they dropped the weight and let it shatter?

Owl didn't want to pass the problems to someone else.

And he didn't want to live in a world that let girls like Ary Mossheart die.

Owl knelt and took Ary's hand in his. He could *feel* Aspen's power burning through Ary, and beyond it, the power of the entire wood. In Aspen's rage was the wind of the flyers; in her grief was the water of the divers. She'd held her power for far too long, and it had whittled her out, turning her into a hollow, bitter shell of the girl she'd once been. Her magic was keeping Ary here for now, but it was too much for even Ary Mossheart to hold.

I have to bear it, Ary had said once, about the terrible fate she'd been handed. Owl hadn't known what to say to her. He certainly couldn't take Ary's burden from her. He wasn't a Mossheart. He didn't even have wings.

But he did love her. Maybe sometimes, love wasn't about lifting the world from someone's shoulders. Maybe it was just crawling under that weight with them, so they didn't have to carry it alone.

He was still missing one piece—the message scratched in the ceiling. It was a warning of the Blight, but why Marigold had scratched out those letters, he might never know.

It didn't matter. He still had to try.

"Ary," Owl whispered. "Hold on."

Reach, whispered the wood.

Owl let the voices rise.

And Owl reached.

SIXTY-TWO

The One in Every Sunrise

Gran crouched over the water bucket, her fingers slick with algae. It was such a familiar sight: Gran in the midst of some unpleasant, menial chore, one that would have her complaining later about her tired bones and aching back. It was the most beautiful thing Ary had ever seen.

"Canary," Gran sighed. "How many times have I told you not to slam the door?"

Ary choked on a sob and threw herself into her grandmother's arms.

Gran grunted—and then her arms were around Ary. She was bonier than Ary remembered, her papery skin smelling of musk and mold and dust. Ary breathed her in and thought if she never had clean air again, at least she had this: her grandmother's arms around her, the scent of home filling her lungs, the certainty that she had not, in fact, lost someone whose preciousness she'd only now started to understand.

Maybe it all *had* been a dream. It seemed so ridiculous. Sootflank, Shrimp, Briar, Owl, and Mama—she could see them in her mind, vivid as a newly sprouted glow-shroom, but even now they faded. Ary let herself relax.

Gran was alive. She was here, she was *real*, and everything was okay.

"Canary," said Gran. "You know that's not true."

Cold descended.

Nothing had changed in the cottage, but for the first time, Ary noticed Mama was gone. She hadn't seen anyone in the village. And when she looked at Gran, at the tired bags beneath her eyes and the sad-sorry crease to her mouth, her relief crumbled to ash.

"You died," whispered Ary. "You're dead, because of the terrarium. Because you kept your promise."

"Yes," said Gran.

"You're not sorry."

"I'll never be sorry that it was me, instead of you." Gran paused. "You're angry with me."

"No," said Ary, and then she began to cry. "Yes."

She *was* angry. Gran had given so much. She had lost the love of her life in the Underground when she was only a little older than Ary and had spent a lifetime suffering in silence. She had shouldered the hatred of her friends and loved ones as her world grew sick and brittle, and when she finally was ready to do something, it had been too late. Then along came Ary—finding the Underlake and Sootflank, heeding the call of Atlas as it pulled her deeper into the Underground to pay a terrible price and set them all free.

And Gran had paid it instead.

"I miss you," whispered Ary. "I spent my whole life wanting you to be proud of me, and you finally were, and you *left*. You left me, Gran, and I don't know how to do this without you—how to carry these scars, or shoulder their hope, or survive the nightmares. You were supposed to help me through it. You were supposed to be there. And I was supposed to finally make you proud."

Gran sighed into Ary's hair and hugged her tighter. "I was always proud of you. I didn't show it. And for *that*, I will always be sorry."

Ary blinked furiously. When they had left the terrarium and found the fairies of Siltshore, some part of her had hoped for a miracle. For Gran to emerge from the trees, healthy and smiling, ready to make up for the years she had lost with Ary. But she understood, now, that Gran was not coming back.

So why was she here?

Behind Ary, the door creaked open.

A cold wind blew in, bringing with it things that did not belong in Terra—the scent of leaves, of metallic soil and swamp water, and something rotten. Something new. She had sensed it when they had first left the terrarium, an irregular wrongness that did not belong in their world. A byproduct of magic unbalanced.

A Blight.

"I feel lost," Ary admitted. "I didn't want to be a hero, because I didn't want to suffer. But it found me anyway."

Gran swept a hand through Ary's hair. "There is always suffering. No matter where you go, what you do, or who you are—no matter if you answer the call of a prophecy or spend sixty years hiding from it. Pain will find you. It always does."

Gran cradled Ary's face with her hands.

"There is no love without loss. Without the ache of sorrow, we'd never know the warmth of joy. Grief is just love that got a little lost, in need of somewhere new to go."

Tears filled Ary's eyes.

"I may be gone—but my love for you isn't." Her leathery fingers tapped Ary's chest, warm despite the cold of the terrarium, real despite the impossibility of this final dream. "It lives in here, and all around you, too. It is the earth beneath your feet, and the moss thriving in the darkest corner. It is the strength in your limbs, the sweetness of new water, the warmth in the smile of your friends. In every little miracle, in every little joy, my love for you is there, Canary Mossheart. And so long as you breathe, and laugh, and love, I am with you."

Tears slipped down Ary's cheeks.

"You are in every sunrise," Ary whispered. "And every sunset."

Gran gave her a funny little smile. "I don't know what those are."

The floor shifted beneath their feet, and then came a terrible *groan*.

"You have to go now." Gran hugged her tightly. "I don't think we'll see each other again."

"What?" Ary protested. "No, I want to stay with you. There is so much I still need to tell you. So much I need to ask. We didn't have enough time, Gran."

Pain blistered through Ary. She gasped, her knees buckling. She was growing solid again. Green light raced through her veins, filling her up, and Ary could hardly speak, so burning and all-encompassing was the pain that lit up her world.

"I love you," cried Ary. "I forgive you."

"Oh, Ary," said Gran. "It was never about that. You don't owe me forgiveness. You never owed me anything at all."

Ary couldn't speak. There were people shouting; she tasted earth and felt something burning in her skin. She did not want to leave. Not yet, not when she had only just gotten Gran back. The cottage crumbled around Ary as she clutched her grandmother's hands.

She knew, in her bones, she would not see her again.

"I'm scared," gasped Ary.

"I know. But you'll be okay. Whatever comes next, you can handle it." She winked. "After all, you *are* a Mossheart."

And then Gran braced her hands on Ary's shoulders—and *shoved*.

SIXTY-THREE

A Better Web

In the heart of the wood, as the Blight raged, the Keepers crowded around Owl—and felt him call for power.

Owl leaned into the magic that had always been there. It was the same power that lived in his blood, his breath, his very bones. He may not have done this before, but he was a Seedling, and the muscle memory of the miracles they'd worked lived in him and in the soil at his feet long after his ancestors had passed.

Owl had reached. Power had rushed in.

Now he had to know what to do with it.

Oh, it *hurt.* It burned. It was too much magic for one creature to bear. It was no wonder it had driven the last Ghostwing mad; no wonder the Keepers had considered it a burden. The power threatened to eat him alive. It would have been easy to abandon it, to let go of his friend's hand and let her slide away from life. But some stubborn, self-punishing part of him held on.

Some part of him truly believed he could do this.

Reach, the voices had instructed. But they were gone now. It was just Owl, his friend's limp hand clutched in his own as an entire wood crashed through them.

Power lit up his world. He could see every life in the wood—every insect in the earth, every hawk in the sky. Every creature a seed of their own. They had believed they had lost their magic when Aspen stole it, but they were wrong. There had aways been a shred there, dormant, waiting for someone to wake it up.

Or connect it.

That's the funny thing about trees, Mrs. Dragonsnap had said. *People think they're so powerful, so infinite. But they rely on each other to survive. Every one of these trees has tangled their roots with another. They've got family, and friends, and alliances.*

They know they're stronger together—and that whatever power they have, it grows when it is shared.

And then it clicked.

The message Marigold had been trying to leave them. It wasn't a spell, not like back in Terra. She hadn't scratched out the letters to hide something. She'd made them a key on how to fix everything. It wasn't a path to some hidden message. It was the message.

The missing letters spelled the word *together.*

The problem from the beginning was that a handful of Keepers held too much power, while far too many others held none—but what if things could be different? What if instead of one creature hoarding an entire garden of magic, they all got to carry a seed?

It was ridiculous. It was absurd. It was dangerous, terrifying, and almost certainly guaranteed to fail.

But the things most worth doing were never easy or comfortable. And Owl had promised himself he would be brave.

Owl held his best friend's hand.

He reached.

And he wove a better web.

SIXTY-FOUR

I've Got You

Ary's wings burned something fierce.

Ary remembered Gran, and the blistering pain that had rushed through her. She remembered Aspen, the wood, and every terrible thing she had learned.

Ary was so, so tired.

She was ready to let go. She didn't want to; it wasn't fair. But if this was what it took to ensure no more children had to step up and take her place, then she was ready. The world dimmed. Ary relaxed.

But then—the world brightened.

Ary had the sense of hurtling downward into herself as every nerve in her body lit up, crackling with *power*. She braced herself for the pain that had blasted through her in the terrarium, but it didn't come. A different kind of magic settled in her; gentle and warm, rooting in her heart and unfurling slowly, like water lilies stretching their blooms toward the summer sun. The magic settled, and waited, just a flicker of the power she'd had before—but power all the same. It was like sunlight, but inside her.

Tears slipped down her cheeks.

The power settled, and Ary's eyes opened.

The first thing she saw was Owl.

He knelt over her, chest heaving, his eyes lit up green as the magic moved through him. The oddest scene surrounded him. A massive, terrifying bird towered over him; a huge, shelled creature crouched to the right; and a giant horned animal loomed beyond. And . . . was Shrimp balanced on its nose?

"Ary?" Owl whispered, his voice shaking.

"That," Ary croaked, "hurt."

Owl's eyes widened—and he burst into tears.

He wrapped his arms around her, and then there were more. Briar, threading her arm through Ary's, Shrimp pressed against her front, Sootflank pressed against her back. A cry came up from the crowd, and then Mama was there, running, *sprinting* toward Ary, tears of relief streaming down her cheeks. She threw herself onto the heap of family Ary had found in the Underground and forged in the new world, and then they were all crying, and Ary could not believe how lucky she was to have found the kind of love that would pull her from one world to another.

A groan came from around them. One by one, the spiderwebs began to snap. Sootflank scooped Ary up and scrambled backward.

"This whole place is going to collapse," he boomed. "Everyone out, *now*."

"No," a voice behind them rasped. "No, no, *no*."

Aspen's prison was crumbling—and it was going to take her and Oleander with it.

"Help me," Oleander cried.

"No," Aspen demanded. "Help *me*!"

Spiderwebs snapped all around them. The great bird that had come with Owl screeched and scooped Ary and her friends up in his claws. He flew upward, wings beating, and Ary twisted, peering between the talons.

"Wait!" cried Ary. "They'll die!"

Sootflank snapped, "So will we, if Carl doesn't get us out of here."

Ary turned, reaching her fingers desperately through the gap in Carl's talon. "Take my hand!"

Time slowed as both Aspen and Oleander reached for Ary's hand. They seemed to realize the same thing at once—only one of them could be saved. After all their betrayals, and all their games, only one of them was going to get to win.

The hollow groaned. Oleander and Aspen looked at each other, hatred and terror sharing equal space on their faces. Maybe Oleander would want Aspen to have a new chance at life; maybe Aspen would believe Oleander could be better.

Then instead of lunging for Ary's hand, they lunged for each other.

The web snapped. For a moment, they hung there, suspended.

And Aspen and Oleander plummeted together.

Ary cried out. Someone seized her waist and pulled her back into the safe cocoon of Carl's claws. *Mama*. She folded Ary against her and hugged her so tightly Ary could hardly breathe, and she was grateful, then, that the wingbeats of Carl rising through the air drowned out the sounds of the hollow collapsing.

"You're okay," Mama whispered, over and over again, long after they were high in the air and only the whistle of the wind remained. "You're okay, Ary. I've got you. It's over."

SIXTY-FIVE

The Statue

Two weeks later

Owl told Ary what had happened in pieces—describing in a tight voice the way the folk of Terra and Siltshore and the creatures of the wood had linked their magic together to bring Ary back. In their attempt to save her, they had broken the system of the Keepers entirely; no more would there be any one creature or folk whose magic wildly outweighed another's. They each carried their own little seed of it.

They didn't speak of Aspen and Oleander again. Though no one had returned to the hollow, anyone who had been there knew no one could have survived that kind of fall.

Some things, Ary decided, were best left buried.

There was much debate between the folk of Terra and Siltshore over what was to be done about their new home. Many of the Siltshore fairies wanted to return to the trees, to the canopy that had separated them from the forest floor for most of their lives; many of the folk of Terra wanted to return to the Gardener's cottage, missing the familiar darkness they'd once taken for granted.

Eventually, it was decided: they would do neither.

Instead, with the help of the creatures of the wood, they would build something new.

There was debate, too, about where they should live—what was most suitable. At one point, the bickering got so bad Ary had to walk away. It was Sootflank who solved their problem.

"The swamp we found when we first came here," he suggested. "So that the newts and frogs may live nearby as allies—and the birds in the canopy above."

Every eye turned to Mrs. Dragonsnap. After the dust had settled and it was clear neither Terra nor Siltshore's leaders were coming back, Robin proposed she and Mrs. Dragonsnap work together to build the new city, until someone else could fill the role. The folk of Siltshore trusted Mrs. Dragonsnap; the folk of Terra liked her because she remembered her own terrarium with fondness and understood their fears about this strange new world.

Mrs. Dragonsnap had paled. *"Me?"* She hesitated, a million emotions flashing across her face. If she'd turned them down, Ary wouldn't have blamed her. She'd only just begun to mourn the Aspen she thought she knew. Surely, every day leading Siltshore would just remind her of the ones she'd loved who had spent decades terrorizing it.

And maybe she would have—if it weren't for a certain mouse, who looked very seriously at Mrs. Dragonsnap and said, "This is your chance, Willow. To make it right."

Mrs. Dragonsnap had stiffened. Then she nodded.

"Very well," she said quietly. "This time, we do it right."

Everyone agreed.

Ary walked along the site of the new village now, watching as folk worked in tandem to weave vine bridges and sprout mushroom platforms from the bark of the tree. Other folk worked on shelters that would be built into the tree roots, or clustered near the water. The new village was like a strange marriage of the best parts of Terra and Siltshore. Homes were built on the ground for fairies who could not fly and in the lower branches of the trees for folk happier in the air. Shelters were built for other creatures, too, to make it clear from the beginning: as long as they meant no harm, anyone was welcome here.

It had been a kind of chaotic miracle to watch everyone learn to use their magic once Owl had pulled Ary back. It seemed the key to working spells was to work them together, as the Seedlings had once done. The more fairies and creatures that linked together and willed the same thing, the grander the spell could be.

It was early morning, still dark and cool from the night prior, but the very first threads of pale color had begun to appear on the horizon. Ary was never going to get over that—the blue sky, so eternal and endless.

"Ary?" a familiar voice asked.

Ary turned.

Sootflank stood alone, his eyes tired but calm.

"It's time," Sootflank said gently. "The others are ready."

Ary nodded and followed Sootflank to the water.

They said goodbye at dawn.

At first, there had been debate over how to handle the ones they had lost—there were bodies for a few, but none for far more. Some proposed they do nothing; others wanted a memorial. A few fairies even suggested a statue of Ary, which she immediately shut down.

"No more heroes," Ary said firmly. "It's up to all of us now."

In the end, Owl came up with their solution.

They built a flower.

In the years that followed, there would be some debate about what it meant. It looked awfully similar to the Gardener's flower remembered by the folk of Terra, but it also looked like the flower the Seedlings had carved all over the old ruins of Siltshore. Still, different folk argued, it was clearly the water lilies that blossomed across their swamp. Some insisted it was a symbol; others suggested it wasn't supposed to mean much at all, that the last heroes chose the flower simply because it was beautiful. The heroes hadn't bothered to leave them with any inscription to tell them who the flower memorialized or why it mattered. Everyone knew the story of Newlily—but the players were murky, the details exaggerated, changed, and omitted depending on the teller. Over time, it blurred into myth until most agreed on one thing, and one thing alone: the strange tale of a brave little fairy and her companions who escaped one dying world and saved another had never been anything but a story.

But the ones who were there that morning knew better.

They saw the little Mossheart girl with her ghostly wings standing in a protective ring of love as the flower statue was raised. They were certainly an odd sight: four fairies, a pill bug, a newt, an owl, and a mouse, clustered together in the early-morning light. One by one, they each approached, clutching something in hand or paw or claw to bury in the soil. Ahead of them, rising over the swamp in a fiery ball, painting the sky in a watercolor of red, orange, and yellow, was one of the most brilliant sunrises the folk of Newlily had ever seen.

Tears blurred Ary's eyes as she stepped back to survey her work.

"I like it," said Briar, her fingers damp with soil. "I think they would have liked it, too."

"It's sufficient," said Sootflank, but the bite was gone from his voice, and he was looking not at the statue, but at the tiny patch where he'd planted his own flower.

"Pretty," agreed Shrimp, although it was clear he still didn't really understand what a statue even was, and hardly cared. He was just happy they were all together again.

"I still kind of think we should have let them build statues to honor us," said Owl.

They all glared at him.

"What?" he protested. "It would have been cool! Ary technically died. And we saved the world. *Twice.*"

"You know," Sootflank said thoughtfully, "I would look pretty good as a statue."

"See!" said Owl.

"But only of me," said Sootflank. "Owl doesn't get one."

Ary laughed and leaned her head against Mama's shoulder. Behind her, the rest of Newlily was waking up, preparing for another day of rebuilding, resetting, and securing their future. Ary would have to go help them soon. Not because she was chosen, not because she'd saved them, but because every fairy and creature alike needed to step in and keep the web of magic strong. Ary closed her eyes, relishing the dawn light on her face. The ache she felt for Gran was still there. It always would be. But there was so much other love living alongside it.

And for the first time in her twelve years, Ary Mossheart knew one thing to be true. She was going to be just fine. More problems would come. Peace was never simple, never lasted. But the web they'd woven was strong—she could feel it, even now, tying her to the ones she loved, to the creatures in the wood, the wolf spider in his den, and the earwigs scuttling beneath the earth. And Ary? Ary was just a blip, no brighter or more important or more chosen than the others. She was just a girl, a tiny sliver of a larger story that would keep spinning long after she was gone.

She was not alone. With family like this—with a love like this—no matter what came, Ary Mossheart would be okay.

And she was.

Acknowledgments

As an author, you hear a lot about how second books are terrible and hard. I thought I escaped that curse when *The Mossheart's Promise* poured out of me. Then *The Ghostwing's Lie* showed up and said, *ha, good joke, prepare for PAIN!* Consider me humbled.

First and foremost, to my wonderful editor Kristin Rens—*thank you*. Thank you for believing in Ary and helping me wrangle this beast of a sequel into something actually book-shaped. Thank you for your patience, kindness, encouragement, and for pointing out I probably can't have a middle grade heroine impale herself through the heart. Most of all, thank you for believing in this book when I couldn't. Please give Shirley a treat for me.

Another huge thanks to my powerhouse agent, Jim McCarthy. You always have my back, and I am forever grateful for your humor, kindness, and for never blinking when I send you another unhinged book idea. You are the best. Please never retire.

Thank you to the team at Harper for championing my

books. Special shout-out to my copy editors, Jessica Berg and Christina MacDonald, for once again catching the typos of my nightmares and remembering more about my books than I do (seriously, your brains are marvels); and everyone on the Harper team, including Emily Mannon and Robby Imfeld in marketing; Taylan Salvati in publicity, Patty Rosati and team in school and library marketing; proofreader Samantha Hoback; editorial assistant Christian Vega; Vanessa Nuttry in production, and Kerry Moynagh, Kathy Faber, and the rest of the sales team. Thank you also to Molly Fehr and Amy Ryan for designing yet another gorgeous book, and to Cathleen McAllister for giving me two absolutely stunning covers.

Publishing is a weird industry, and when you find good people, you've gotta hold on tight. Andrea, Kristin, Ayana, and Meriam—this is a middle grade novel, so I can't swear, but imagine a lot of bad words in the phrase "I love you!" Thanks for being the very best kind of publishing-friends-turned-normal-friends-turned-family. All the love and thanks also to Kay Smith, Aimee Carter, Amelie Wen Zhao, Katie Zhao, Grace Li, and Andrea Tang, who have always helped this industry feel a little kinder. Special thanks to Abby Foster-Mills and Alyssa Eatherly, who read early versions of this book when it made—and I cannot stress this enough—*absolutely zero sense*, and who still managed to be encouraging and enthusiastic even while agreeing it was a mess in there.

Mom, Dad, Hannah, my grandparents, and the Lorias—I love you guys. Thank you for all the support and for not getting too annoyed when I send your calls to voicemail because I'm writing. (Except Hannah. I am well aware that you find it annoying. I'm going to keep doing it anyways.) Aunt Diane and Uncle Dusty, for reading and believing in my books from the beginning. Meagan, Melissa, Natalie, Jackie, Sarah, and Katie, thank you for loving my books and me, especially when I can't stop talking about publishing. And of course, David. I love you so much. I can't wait to marry you.

Thank you to the readers, booksellers, parents, and librarians who have championed *The Mossheart's Promise* and pushed them into young readers' hands. Every letter, tag, shelf-talker, and message means the world. Special thanks to Sidetrack Bookshop for supporting my books with so much enthusiasm, particularly Jen, Jenny, Alyssa, and Megan. You guys rock.

I have a tradition of including people and things in my acknowledgments that have no idea I exist, but brought me joy during writing all the same. It's my book and I can do what I want, okay? So, special thanks, in no particular order, to: the Detroit Lions, the maker-of-puzzles for *New York Times* Connections, Wyna Liu (depending on the day . . . sometimes you take it too far . . .), Taylor Swift, and the sausage burrito I'm currently splitting with Meriam at Atomic Coffee. (It's really good.) And, of course, to my cats, who were literally no help at all.

And lastly, to my grandmother Carol Wilson. Every time I type *the end*, I think of you. I'll keep looking for you in every Florida-worthy sunset. Love you always.